PRAISE FOR ASH BISHOP

"This book is so much fun it ought to be illegal in all known galaxies. Ash Bishop has written a wildly imagined, deeply felt, swashbuckling page turner. I loved it."
—Jesse Kellerman, *New York Times* bestselling author of *The Burning*, on *Intergalactic Exterminators, Inc*

"Bishop's sci-fi debut is recommended for readers who think Larry Correia's "Monster Hunter International" series should go intergalactic, those who enjoy stories featuring the people who get the dirty jobs done, and especially anyone who wishes that Martha Wells's Murderbot would become a superhero."
—*Library Journal*, on *Intergalactic Exterminators, Inc*

"With gruesome alien battles, layered conflict, and a sprinkling of humor, this is sure to find an audience."
—*Publishers Weekly*, on *Intergalactic Exterminators, Inc*

"For those who like space adventures with mystery, intrigue, and some scary beasties, this will be an engaging read."
—*Booklist*, on *Intergalactic Exterminators, Inc*

"Well-drawn characters, an action-packed plot, and Bobby's complicated love life keep the pages turning. Readers will be eager to see what Bishop does next."
—Publishers Weekly*, on *The Horoscope Writer

"Ash Bishop immerses the story with grisly detective investigations and their powerful outcomes from the start . . . filled with realistic scenarios and satisfying twists."
—Midwest Book Review*, on *The Horoscope Writer

"With this unique mystery, Bishop offers a fun, if murderous way to explore fate, free will, divine intervention, and science."
—Library Journal*, on *The Horoscope Writer

"[A] fast-paced, high-tension, steamy murder mystery."
—Booklist*, on *The Horoscope Writer

INTERGALACTIC
WASTE MANAGEMENT, LLC

ASH BISHOP

INTERGALACTIC WASTE MANAGEMENT, LLC

CamCat Books
2810 Coliseum Centre Drive, Suite 300
Charlotte, NC 28217-4574

Hardcover ISBN 9780744312157
Paperback ISBN 9780744312164
eBook ISBN 9780744312188

Library of Congress Control Number: 2025940385

Book and cover design by Maryann Appel

5 3 1 2 4

To the Irish Magnifico,

Mr. Edward O'Connor

PROLOGUE

CLARK WESLEY

"TREVVY, CAN YOU HEAR ME?" Clark Wesley whispered into the comm. "This is the part where you tell me if anybody's watching the hallway." Clark waited for a response. "Trevvy? C'mon, man . . ."

Clark's stomach twinged with worry. He absently munched a nerve-stabilizing pill from his pocket. He knew he only had a few moments before his pleasure technician returned. He waited, tapping on his collar where he'd hidden his comm.

The massage table in room 479 of the Hotel Narcellena, on Romcube Pleasure Satellite #91, in the ZunVia cluster, was lumpy. Clark was happy to lower himself off it. As his feet hit the floor, his hand drifted through his equipment pack, his fingers squirming under the thieves' kit to fall on the reassuring length of a portable, destructible Waypoint. The device wasn't legal, but not much of what Clark did was these days.

He put the Waypoint together deftly and slid it under the table, stopping only to cough. He pushed his mouth against his bicep doing his best to muffle the sound. Fully assembled, the portable Waypoint was just big enough for him to crawl through on his hands and knees. For a moment he considered what coordinates to set. He and Trevvy were supposed to rendezvous on Satellite UAlphaZ, but Trevvy's silence had him reconsidering that decision. He settled on a different destination entirely.

Clark checked his watch before setting the self-destruct sequence for twenty-eight minutes. He would have to be back by then, or the Waypoint would heat itself into a puddle of metal and wax, and he'd be taking the interstellar bus home with all the rest of the perverts. Or worse.

He heard the doorknob jiggle and knew it was his pleasure technician returning with clean towels, heated rocks, and oil in each of her four arms. "Trevvy, I'm going for it," he whispered into the comm.

The technician had only taken a few steps through the door when her eyes moved to the empty table. "Hello?" she asked, just as Clark brought his clenched fist across the back of her neck. She fell forward into the crook of his right arm. With his left he snatched the massage oil from the air before it clattered noisily to the ground. His blood churned from a mixture of nerve stabilizers, mild uppers, and pain pills.

He held her steady, moving to affix a metal transformer into her upper ear. It would cast an illusion over her appearance, changing it entirely. As he pushed aside the wavy ringlets of her hair, he discovered a transformer was already there. He removed it and the pleasure technician immediately shifted from an exotic, beguiling, four-armed Romgulang into an aged, ordinary, slope-armed Toer. Toers usually had smooth skin that changed colors with their mood. Hers was calloused, and stuck a permanent dull brown, likely the result of years of hard living. She must have been in her mid-sixties, no more than ten years younger than Clark himself.

"They never match the picture," Clark mumbled, swapping her transformer with one of his own. In an instant, the visage of the old Toer disappeared, replaced by someone who appeared in every possible way to be Clark himself. Clark picked up other Clark and lowered her down onto the massage table. "You only have to be me for another twenty minutes or so," he promised the unconscious pleasure technician.

He affixed her transformer into his ear, pocketed her key card, and helped himself out the door and down the corridor. He only paused a moment at the floor-to-ceiling mirrors to admire the beautiful Romgulang grinning back at him.

The designers of Hotel Narcellena had made it impossible to take the elevators past the seventh floor, but a good "friend" had sold Clark information about a secret staircase in the back of one of the closets in the staff changing quarters. Clark used the pleasure technician's keycard to let himself into the changing quarters, flitting quickly past the other girls—all identical Romgulangs—and straight up the staircase.

He entered the main corridor of the eighth floor cautiously. It was bedecked with expensive-looking paintings. Most were hung recklessly, while others were simply propped against the wall. Someone was sleeping face down on the floor between rooms 834 and 835. As Clark moved closer, he realized the person wasn't sleeping, but dead.

A quick look at their face told him it wasn't Trevvy and that the corpse had been there a long time. It held an empty money purse clenched in its rigid hands. Clark wasn't sure if the body had been left there as a warning, or simply out of carelessness. He shook the money purse to make sure it was empty, then moved toward room 899.

When he reached the door, he unpacked the thieves' tools and set a sonic ambulizer to work on the lock. He swallowed a fresh nerve stabilizer to keep his hands from shaking. The ambulizer began to hum softly in an ever-shifting pitch. It was trying to identify the door's encrypted frequency patterns so it could mimic the unlocking command. At a normal hotel, this sort of brute-force hack would alert the front desk, who would either shut down the door remotely or send guards.

Clark was counting on the Hotel Narcellena having a different system. Thieves never trusted anyone, especially not each other, and it was likely that the door's lock was not linked to any central server.

Either that or Clark would be dead in the next few minutes.

The ambulizer vibrated slightly, a sign that it had identified the first of three musical frequencies in the locking combination. Clark glanced nervously down the hall, but it was just him and the corpse. "Trevvy, where are you? I'm almost in," he whispered into his collar-mounted comm.

The tool vibrated again. Clark mopped at the sweat forming on his forehead. Only one more frequency to find. In the time it took him to say a little prayer, the tool vibrated, the lock clicked, and the door swung open.

"Wes, is that you buddy?" Trevvy said, from inside the darkened room.

"Trevvy? If you were already inside, why didn't you let me—" Clark Wesley's mouth often moved faster than his mind, but not this time. This time he answered his own question moments before he finished asking it. He stepped backward, just as a barrage of bullets burned into the hallway wall behind him. He crouched there a moment as silence once more descended onto the eighth floor.

"That was just a warning. For fun!" a gravelly voice said.

"The whole thing was a setup," Trevvy said, his voice quivering with fear. "They caught me right after I disembarked. It's Grnder and Bunda. There's nothin' valuable in room 899. Just two really ugly mercs."

"I thought it was a little too good to be true," Clark mumbled.

"We just want to know where you took the device," the second voice said. It was Grnder, a hulking species called a Bryn-Tyr, his skin made entirely of rock. "Tell us where it's hidden, and we promise not to kill your friend."

"Yeah, of course you won't," Clark said. He stayed crouched beside the damaged door frame.

"We just want the Liafen device back," Grnder said, his voice low and menacing.

"Tell them where you put their Liafen thingie," Trevvy pleaded. "I mean, it belongs to their client, right? Originally?"

Clark stood up and peeked around the damaged door frame to look into the room. The lights were on now, and he could see Trevvy, his hands bound, the hulking Grnder standing beside him. Another mercenary, a Lixil named Bunda, loomed to his left.

Bunda frowned. "It's been a long day, and this wasn't easy to set up. Planting the information, waiting for you to buy the information, waiting for you to arrive in this nasty hotel room. You'd think a rock creature like Grnder would smell okay." Bunda pointed a slim thumb at his partner. "Like earth or something? He doesn't. Despite all the trouble, if you give us the coordinates to the device, you and your friend can walk right out of here, safe and sound. I promise." The Lixil idly stroked the pistons on his short-range scattergun.

"I get it. I understand." Clark paused a moment as a series of coughs racked his chest. When the coughing stopped, he raised a hand in a gesture of peace. He took off the transformer and morphed back into his own visage. "Before this goes any further, I do have one question." He spoke to Trevvy. "Did you hire these two mercenary thugs, or did they hire you?"

Trevvy's eyes widened in shock. "What? Look at me!" Trevvy shook the bindings around his wrists. "Wes, I'm on your side. I came here in good faith, same as you. I was just as surprised as you that—that . . ."

Grnder looked at Trevvy, his heavy stone eyelids hanging half-mast across his eyes. "Give it up. He knows."

"Well, now he does," Trevvy said, letting the rope binding fall from his wrists. "Sorry, Wes. I have a number of outstanding debts to settle, and the reward on your head is so enticing. We're criminals, right? Isn't this what criminals do?"

"Trevvy, there's a reason I always insist on making the decisions. It's because you're an idiot. Once I tell them where I hid the machine, we're both dead. Men like this don't split things three ways when they can split things in half instead. Hell, it's a miracle they haven't killed each other."

Trevvy looked at Grnder nervously. "No. I don't think so. I mean—sorry Clark, but I approached them with the plan—I couldn't resist!"

"You are going to kill him, aren't you, Grnder? Probably before you leave the hotel?"

"Of course not," Grnder said. He tried to sound sincere, but the lie was evident in his voice.

"Bryn-Tyr aren't masters at faking sincerity," Clark said. "It's ironic that so many of them are criminals."

"We're just a couple of ugly mercs?" Bunda asked Trevvy.

"I just said that to be convincing!" Trevvy exclaimed. He lunged at Grnder's gun just as Clark dove the opposite direction, back out of sight line.

A fraction of a second later, blaster fire rang out from multiple weapons. Bullets struck the wall where Clark had been standing. He raced at a dead sprint toward the staircase.

"Rest in peace, Trevvy, you dummy," Clark said as he ran. He cleared the corner, then scrambled to open the door to the changing quarters. One of the two thugs was firing in his direction, kinetic bullets leaving the weapon with a lethal-sounding *thump*.

Clark's breath felt ragged in his chest, and he fought back a racking cough as he stumbled down the stairs and back out the door to the changing room.

He was huffing mightily as he weaved through the hallways, barely catching himself on the massage room doorknob. His worn-out lungs fought him for every ounce of oxygen. In his periphery, he saw shadows round the corner at the end of the hall, and a second later a bullet tore through his upper hip, spinning him off his feet. He managed to fall forward into the room, a trail of his own blood decorating the door frame behind him.

On his hands and knees, he pulled himself over to the pleasure technician who was still unconscious on the massage table. His own blood was soaking through his pants and gliding the length of his thigh down to the floor. He gathered as much as he could on his open palm and smeared it all along the hip of the technician. Then he slithered all the way to the far side of the table, realizing as he did that he was already losing sensation in his left arm. The timer on the Waypoint read six minutes left. Too much time. Propped on his elbows, he drew in ragged breaths.

Clark used his remaining good hand to roll the Waypoint timer forward. Four minutes, three minutes . . . the dial jammed at 1:49. *Sonofabitch*, Clark thought in a panic. He pounded on the device, watching the timer tick down at an impossibly slow pace. Heavy footsteps filled the hall outside.

Grnder and Bunda burst through the door. Clark was hidden on the far side of the table, so they didn't see him when they dragged the pleasure technician's body onto the floor. "How's he going to lead us to the device if he bleeds to death?" Grnder demanded.

"I was just trying to slow him down. He's a fast old bastard."

"We gotta make sure he lives long enough for us to torture him to death," Grnder said.

"In the hallway, I shot him in the ass; I'm sure of it. I can't find the wound." Bunda cautioned, lifting the disguised masseuse body. "Ahh shit. This ain't even him—"

Despite taking pain-blocking pills and nerve stabilizers, Clark's knees were shaking as he lurched forward. The Waypoint display clicked **:03**, beckoning him with its white-hot light. If he timed it just right . . .

. . . Clark welcomed the warm vibration of intergalactic teleportation. Relief flooded over him as his molecules shifted and blurred, then slowly rearranged into the correct shape. All those mistakes of judgment, and he'd just blinked straight out of the trap, his escape hatch melting into a puddle behind him.

Clark started to look around, once again filled with dread. His coordinates were supposed to find the closest Waypoint to his old hometown, not drop him directly into the storage closet of his wife's bookstore. *Why is there a Waypoint here?* Clark was not an easy man to shock, but this did the trick.

Equally surprised was the young man on the other side of the room, wide-eyed and holding a stack of bills, gaping back at Clark in the shadow of a powerful Tech 12 SAS unit.

"Russ?" Clark's voice boomed. "Is that you, grandson?"

Russ's mouth hung open; his jaw nearly planted on the floor. "Grandpop?"

Clark scanned the floor for an Obinz stone that he'd left in the very spot he was currently standing. He'd stashed it in the bottom of a box, covered in books. The books were gone. So was the box. So was the stone. "I'm sure you have some questions . . ." Clark began, as his eyes searched the rest of the room.

Blood pumped out of his gunshot wound onto the floor of his beloved bookstore, and his head felt lighter and lighter. He lost his footing, falling forward. Even with the ground rapidly approaching, he was still thinking clearly enough to resolve that he shouldn't tell Russ the truth about all the crazy things that had happened since Clark had officially died.

RUSS

Five Months Later

RUSS WAS PLUNGING TO HIS DEATH.

It felt like that, at least. The egg-shaped EFlyer pitched recklessly downward, its nose trembling against the gathering forces of gravity, inertia, and friction.

Far below, the ocean waters churned, dragged to-and-fro by Planet Xodli's three moons. Through the porthole on his left, Russ could see Nina's concerned face staring back at him. She was in a separate EFlyer, side by side with Kendren. Kendren had his hand on her shoulder, holding her steady against the maniacal wobbling of the other craft.

"This doesn't feel right. Why are these EFlyers so much s-s-s-shakier than usual?" Russ asked, his teeth clattering together.

"B-b-bah'ren got a deal on refurbished models. R-r-returned because of glitches in their stabilizing systems," Atara told him.

Russ looked down as the ground rushed up. The deep, endless ocean wasn't blue. It was clear, like water flowing out of a kitchen sink—albeit choppy, violent, and rising toward them very quickly. Disposable

EFlyers tended to crack open when they landed on sand. He wondered what they did when they landed in liquid. "S-s-stabilizers seem like something important to have," Russ said.

"T-t-they mostly make the trip smoother." Atara glanced out the porthole grimly; her short brown hair bounced with each vibration. "They also make sure the ships fall on a s-s-straight trajectory . . ."

Russ looked back at Nina again. Her EFlyer was now only a few feet away.

He was astonished to be looking directly into her beautiful brown eyes. She was mouthing words, urgently. A fraction of a second later, they came blasting through the comm system: "Look out!"

The portable, disposable, egg-shaped ships made contact midair with a terrible cracking sound.

"Not good!" Atara shouted as hairline fractures opened between her feet.

Russ glanced through the porthole again, quickly enough to see Nina and Kendren's EFlyer speeding away, the collision tossing them in opposite directions. Nina was still staring out the porthole, back at Russ, as her EFlyer dipped into a cluster of clouds. Cracks traveled up the curved walls on either side of her ship and he could see shavings fluttering behind like the tail of a comet. And then she disappeared into the clouds completely.

Hopefully she's not dead, Russ thought as the deep translucent sea rushed up from below. *Hopefully I won't be dead either.*

Twenty seconds later, Russ discovered what EFlyers did when they hit water. First, they burst beneath the surface like a stone dropped into a pond. Once the water had eaten most of their momentum, their automated jets engaged, sending the ship careening back upward.

The EFlyer popped out of the water, ejecting itself into the air before crashing down again and coming to rest on its side, only to bob up and down violently in the surf. At impact, Russ had been holding the handrails with all his might, but they came off in his hands, and he thumped hard against the wall of the flier, his elbow punching a hole through its shell-like fabric.

"Was it really worth the few dollars you saved getting EFlyers without stabilizers? Or chest restraints?" Atara barked into her comm.

"They're disposable," Bah'ren replied from the deck of her new ship, the *Aldersochi,* far above. "You want to pay top dollar for something we leave behind every mission?"

"Yeah," Russ groaned, lying on his side, still clutching the broken handrails. "That would be okay." Water was pouring in through the hole his elbow had made.

"Then you must not know how much mixed-species baby formula costs for seven newborns." Bah'ren's voice was clipped and no-nonsense. After months of trying, Bah'ren and her partner Starland had just welcomed a clutch of genetically grafted newborns. Though she was now running on zero sleep, motherhood hadn't changed Bah'ren one bit. She was just as grouchy and results-driven as she'd ever been.

Russ scrambled to his feet while Atara strapped on her rebreather. She pulled a device about the size of a snowboard off the split wall of the EFlyer, her feet kicking up water that was now six inches deep and rising. During the briefing, Bah'ren had called the device a Helder-Tech Underwater Boost Rocket, or HBR. She'd showed them how to grip it in both hands and use its miniature twin engines to power-dive through the water. It was fast, effective, and very maneuverable, but aside from a limited weapons system, it provided little protection from the elements—or the creatures beneath the surface. "Xodli's water contains dramatically high levels of salt, and about five times as much hydrogen as the ocean water on Ren'Div, and Earth, for that matter," Bah'ren had said.

"Do not get the water in your eyes; it will sting," Kendren had cautioned them.

"Extended exposure will also put you in an advanced form of nitrogen narcosis. We're going to give you a DOM shot that will dissolve excess nitrogen in your bloodstream for a while, but if you stay under too long, you'll feel as drunk as a Blurian sailor."

Russ pulled the other HBR down and its wall mount came with it, tearing another hole in the damaged EFlyer. More water poured in, splashing against Russ's chest. He ticked the screen on his wrist-mounted transponder. It read: *Nitrogen levels in balance.*

"Let's gooooooo!" Atara cheered as she kicked her way through the damaged wall. Water engulfed the inside of the ship. She tucked her knees against her chest and rolled herself into the deep, salty sea.

Russ followed. Behind him, the EFlyer sank, leaving a trail of bubbles in its wake. He floated for a moment, taking in the bizarre sights of the underwater world. They must have landed in a kelp bed because there were enormous stalks of green seaweed churning in the current on every side. He gasped for air, and it made him realize he had been holding his breath. He tried to relax enough to breathe normally, trusting the rebreather to do its job. Though the water was clear, the seaweed was thick enough that he was worried he'd lose sight of Atara.

She thrust forward on her HRB, a stream of liquid fire belching out of both handgrips. As it moved, the HBR's exhaust left a trail of greasy, rainbow-colored debris. Atara glided through a huge wall of kelp and out of sight.

Russ turned to follow, but a large eel zipped through the kelp on his other side, snapping its teeth toward his shoulder. He rolled quickly away, then kicked hard at the eel. As he groped for the HBR's weapons systems, he accidently clutched the accelerator instead. The device fired him smoothly forward. The eel gave chase, but it was distracted by the oily rainbow left in the HBR's wake. Russ glided through another huge wall of kelp. The water felt both there and not, like wind. The kelp, on the other hand, felt like diving through the beard of an unwashed lumberjack.

Russ dove down, then up, trying to get Atara back in his line of sight. The kelp shifted dramatically. It had been in constant swirling motion but suddenly all of it—the kelp on his right, his left, above him and below him—began to move as if it was attached to the back of a giant creature.

It *was* attached to the back of a giant creature.

The thing swam forward, its massive fluke kicking the water. The sixty-foot stalks of kelp covering its entire body moved with it. It was an ecosystem unto itself. Long spear-shaped fish and fanged eels followed it, feeding on parasites buried within its outer shell.

With the creature moving away, Russ suddenly had a direct line of sight to Atara. He heard a crackling in his ears and realized it was the comm going active.

"Lev-i-a-than," Atara whispered.

Russ nodded. The creature had been ten times the size of a whale. So big he hadn't even realized he was motoring around on its back.

"Everybody alive?" Bah'ren snapped in their ears.

"We are," Atara said. "Me and Russ, at least. Kendren? Nina? You out there?"

There was no response.

"We lost contact with them on impact," Bah'ren said. "I'll bring the *Aldersochi* down on their last position. You two take care of the Zypper."

The Zypper was their target. It was a B-class, a mission with "limited danger." But, Bah'ren explained, it had plenty of financial danger. The Zypper was a protected species. If they harmed it in any way, they would face significant fines. They were to pacify it with nonlethal force and prep it for relocation.

During the briefing, Bah'ren theorized that someone had tried to domesticate the amphibious creature. An infant Zypper was roughly two feet long, tip to tail. It was shaped like a crocodile, but with spiky canines that extended from its bottom jaw all the way to the edge of its large nostrils. Though it walked on feet and swam with its tail, it had the smooth, gray skin of a dolphin. The archival photo was sort of cute, which was probably why someone had tried to adopt it. Unfortunately, in adolescence, they reached six to ten feet long. Once the creature had grown large enough to not fit in a bathtub, and puberty had turned it frisky—extending those cute teeth into fully formed ten-inch canines—the owners had probably decided it was time to set their beloved "pet" free. It had only been on Planet Xodli a few hours but had already caused enough havoc to set off the UAIB scanners and issue an automated municipal relocation order.

Floating just beside Russ, Atara unrolled the parts of a portable Waypoint from her own pack. Atara put it together with expert, deft motions. She powered it on, and neon blue light spread through the clear water. A current flowed toward the activated Waypoint, spinning in a vortex as it disappeared between the bars of the handheld teleportation device.

"You're getting water onboard the ship," Bah'ren informed them from far above.

Atara spun the hoop in her hands and shut it back down, sliding it over her own shoulders for safekeeping.

Russ threw a leg over his HBR so he was straddling it and withdrew the tube of Spindex from his pack. The side of the tube read "Creature attractant: one hundred percent guaranteed!"

"Ready with the chum," Russ told Atara.

When she nodded, he pulled a small ripcord attached to the tube. Attractant globbed over his gloved hand, spreading into the water, diffusing bloody mucus in all directions.

Both exterminators slid backward, away from the spreading Spindex. Then they waited. Russ checked his transponder and his HBR weapon systems. The weapons registered "active." He waited and watched as the Spindex spread into a reddish, chunky cloud.

The only creature that seemed interested in the Spindex was thin and stick-shaped, roughly four feet in length. It was brown and woodsy, about the diameter of a quarter. It seemed better suited for a forest than an ocean. It had a slimy, pink propeller, roughly an inch wide, about where its mouth must be. When it reached the Spindex, the propeller started to spin, sucking the chum directly into the stick creature's mouth. It only took moments before the stick creature had sucked down all the Spindex. It filtered the food into its body and purged out the excess liquid, leaving the water once again clear as plastic.

"Well, shit," Atara said.

"Just the opposite," Russ observed. "It's eating up the shit and pooping out clear water. It's a living filter. We could really use a few of these on Earth. That was my only tube of Spindex, though. You bring one?"

Before Atara could respond, the stick creature stabbed itself toward the waste from their HBRs. One moment there were cloudy puddles of rainbow-colored grease, and the next moment the grease had disappeared down the creature's thin gullet.

"We're going to need to kill the stick thing before we bother to add more chum," Atara pointed out.

"Don't touch the stick thing," Bah'ren said over the comm. "It's called a Woos. That's the type of creature we're here to protect. They keep the water filtered clean."

"But it ate our chum," Atara said.

"Spindex doesn't always work by attracting the predator directly. Many higher-end evolutions are too smart to fall for something so simple. This Spindex works by attracting the creatures that the Zypper *eats*."

Just as she finished speaking, a huge gray crocodile-like creature swam into their range of vision, headed directly toward the stick creature. The Woos, sensing danger, fired its propeller in quick bursts.

Russ dodged his HBR forward, trying to position himself between the Woos and the Zypper, but the Zypper was too agile. It slipped around Russ without a moment lost.

Atara fired a low-impact plasma pulse from the HBR's weapons systems. The shock slowed the Zypper for a millisecond, but a moment after that it was tearing into the Woos. It ripped the Woos's woodsy flesh into small bites, like it was eating a four-foot churro. Within seconds, the Woos's remains were floating between Russ and Atara, scattered through the not-quite-as-clear water.

"Switching to high-impact-non-lethal," Atara said.

"Firing my net," Russ countered.

Atara pivoted her HBR in an arc, hitting the creature with another burst of its weapon system. The impact sent shock waves through the Zypper's body. It lashed around in agony, beating at the water with its legs and tail. From the other side, Russ launched a long thin net from the bridge of the HBR. It was a good shot. Russ rarely missed a shot. The heavy net wrapped around the Zypper, cinching against its body.

"These HBRs might be undercalibrated. I'm going to hit it once more so we can wrap this shit up." Atara switched back to low-impact and zapped the Zypper a final time.

The result was the opposite of what either of them expected. Instead of permanently crippling the monster, the plasma bolt seemed to power it back to life. It tore through the polymer net with its long foreclaws and lunged at Atara, crunching her HBR between its jaws. It held the device in its mouth and rolled its body in a powerful spiral.

Atara kicked her feet and paddled desperately in the other direction, but now she was moving at a snail's pace compared to the amphibious predator. The Zypper stopped its death roll, bit all the way through her HBR, and snaked in her direction, its fanged jaws wide.

Russ piloted his HBR toward them. "Dive!" he shouted.

Atara swam downward, dolphin-kicking hard. She managed to clear just beneath Russ, who met the Zypper head on. The impact almost shook the HBR free from his hands. Seconds before the creature chomped down, Russ trigged the weapon system, pouring as much plasma as he could straight down its gullet.

The Zypper didn't like the taste or the sensation. It fired mucus from a blowhole at the top of its head, then turned tail and fled. Russ tried to follow, but the huge blast had drained the HBR of its battery. The device lumbered forward in a short burst, then went dead.

Atara drew a long knife from where she had it sheathed across her back. Probably working against her own instincts for self-preservation, she reached out and grabbed the creature's tail as it swam, the knife ready in her free hand.

"Don't kill the creature," Bah'ren reminded them over the comm. Their radio chatter, or perhaps the heartbeat sensors on their transponders, had clued her in to the shift in combat.

The creature swam for about ten yards, then snapped its tail free of Atara's grip with a powerful thrust. It curled into a semicircle, pointing its jagged fangs directly at her.

"You're just a fraction too slow," Atara told the creature as its wide jaws opened in front of her.

The Zypper couldn't have anticipated how quick Atara was. She put her hand on its lower jaw and used the leverage to slip just beneath its bite. Then she punched the wicked knife upward into its relatively unprotected belly.

The Zypper spasmed, trying to dislodge Atara. The knife was buried deep, and she hung fast, the creature's body flipping and twisting with each frenzied convulsion. The Waypoint, which Atara had hung around her neck and shoulder, shook loose, gliding through the water toward Russ.

He grabbed at it as he swam toward the fight, barely registering the yellow warning light flashing on his transponder.

Even through her rebreather, he could see a look of fear on Atara's face. Ignoring the fact that he had no net and no HBR, he swam toward where she grappled with the Zypper.

The Zypper tossed its body back and forth, snapping at Atara's feet. As long as she hung on, she would remain out of its reach. Russ knew she was strong, but it was still only a matter of time. "I'm going to get it to come after me. When you're close, jump into the Waypoint."

"You think . . ." Atara huffed, ". . . I can slide through that three-foot circle . . . with this thing going . . . nuts?"

"Just like diving through an inner tube," Russ promised. He kicked hard, getting within ten feet of the thrashing Zypper, then waved the Waypoint wildly.

The Zypper's eyes tracked it like a red cape. The creature reoriented in his direction.

"Get ready!" he shouted. As the Zypper launched toward him, Russ powered on the Waypoint. It sucked at the water all around him, creating another whirlwind vortex. He had to brace his feet against its ring to keep from being pulled inside. One of the sleeves of his compression suit rolled off and blinked away into the quantum pattern. He watched it go, holding the ring with all his might.

"Hey," Bah'ren's voice barked over the comms, "you're getting a ton of water onboard the ship!"

Maybe it was the movement of the current, or some shadow thrown across his own cheek, but Russ swiveled back just in time to see the huge creature was already on him, Atara flapping beneath it like a human loincloth.

Russ tried to somersault, thinking he could move the ring that way to give Atara a chance to glide through. Unfortunately, the current was strong and he'd positioned the Waypoint about two feet higher than he should have.

The Zypper smashed into the device. It wiggled and thrashed, wedging its bottom jaw and one long gray arm through the teleportation device.

"Water is getting everywhere, turn off the—what the fuuu—" Bah'ren's voice blasted through the comms as the crocodile-like monster started to appear on the ship far above, clawing its way across the intergalactic gate.

The whole creature twisted wildly, trying to shake Atara free while simultaneously swiping at Russ's chest. Only its top jaw and one foreleg were through the teleporter. Its right front claw ripped a hole in Russ's thick compression suit. Its razor-sharp bottom jaw had sliced a quarter of the way through the graphene piping, when Russ finally managed to turn the Waypoint off. The teleportation device shut down with a *pop*.

The Zypper's head, its front left leg, and some of its torso made it to the *Aldersochi*. Its back half, however, remained on Xodli, floating in a bloody pool of disemboweled crocodile guts.

Atara swam beside Russ, her knife sheathed. She hugged him in relief as they floated together in the clear water. "Thank you," she said, still breathless. After a moment, she waved her hand through the guts and said, "Weren't we supposed to pacify it with nonlethal force and relocate it?"

"I did relocate it," Russ pointed out. "The top portion."

Russ disengaged from Atara and restarted the Waypoint. For a moment, the quantum pattern returned, blinking a faint blue, but light trailed out of the puncture the Zypper had put in the metal, and then faded away.

Attracted by the gory remains of the gray crocodile, a large pack of eels began to form near the perimeter of Russ's vision. He could see their sharp, white teeth gleaming through the clear water.

It was only then that Russ noticed his transponder blinking red. The readout said: *Nitrogen levels critical. Return to the ship's Medbay immediately.*

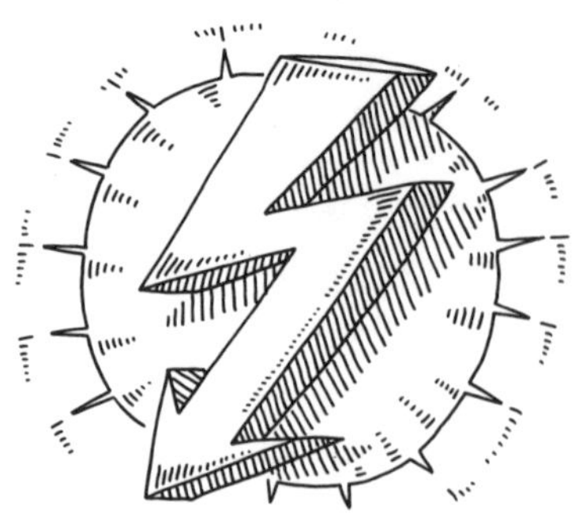

2

NINA

KENDREN'S CAN OF SPINDEX UNSPOOLED beneath the churning waters, and a cloud of gory mucus swirled all around Nina. Even though her rebreather protected her from it, she instinctually held her breath as she kicked backward.

She waited there, floating just outside the cluster of creature attractant, her eyes scanning the underwater world. They landed on Kendren, who was staring back at her. The big man shrugged and tapped a finger on his transponder to indicate it wasn't working. Nina shook her head. Her own transponder had spiderweb cracks down the screen. She could see the edges of a circuit sticking out the side. She ran her finger against the circuit and felt it wiggle loose.

Eight feet above them, the left half of their egg-shaped EFlyer was all that remained. The HBRs had come loose and spun off into the clouds about ten seconds before impact. Nina tried to ignore the helpless feeling welling up inside her. She tread in place as the thinning Spindex expanded across more of the surface of the water. Far below, creatures swam among the depths, but nothing came for the Spindex. The creature attractant wasn't attracting. Nina waited impatiently, then paddled to the surface.

She hoisted herself back into what was left of the EFlyer and rebooted what was left of her transponder.

"Russ?" she asked into the device. "Can you read me? Are you there? Are you okay?" Over the sound of churning water, she could hear a gentle hiss from the device, but nothing else. "Your Geo-Link better still be working," she told the device. She looked over the horizon. The ocean stretched on for miles. "Or we're in for a very long swim."

She was encouraged to see that the screen was still mostly reacting to her commands. When they'd passed the probational training period, Bah'ren had unlocked the full potential of Nina and Russ's transponders. Now she could use it to access her Universal Banc Account, transfer money, send and receive documents, and surf endless databases of information. To test for functionality, she opened her bank account and looked at the flashing red zero under "balance." She was used to that.

She tried the other functions, and many of them seemed to be working. The transponders functioned a lot like a cell phone but people in intergalactic space had never taken to texting. They usually used the linked comms or made direct calls, which Nina found ironically old-fashioned.

Most of the transponders' functions were written with an open-source programming language called SUKTIS. SUKTIS was intuitive, and the more Nina tinkered with it, the more it made sense, so she'd written her own texting protocol and had even been able to "push" the program to her friend Jaq'li's transponder. Every day or so they'd send each other messages, usually accompanied by old-fashioned letter-based emoji. The texting program was the only communication application still functioning, so Nina sent a message to Jaq'li:

crash landed on Xodli. if you don't hear from me, it's because im in the middle of the fricken ocean. send help. (^o^)

She stared at her transponder for a moment, but there was no response. She looked through the clear water at where Kendren swam below, kicking his powerful legs toward a school of eels. The Zypper was nowhere in sight.

Nina doomscrolled through the functions of her transponder, closing the texting app and flicking open her other custom-made application. Just the previous night, she had been tinkering with SUKTIS and written the bones of an adaptive program to get the transponder to surf Earth's internet. She'd fallen asleep before being able to give it a proper test run.

The alien browser opened, and she directed it to Instagram. The screen said: **405 Method Not Allowed**. *Seems to be working though*, she thought, satisfied. She was so focused on the small digital screen on her wrist, she nearly jumped out of her skin when Kendren surfaced from the water grabbing the edge of the craft with his meaty hands.

He vaulted back onboard, spraying salt water. "Nothing out there," he grunted. "Except a shit ton of fish. The Spindex is gone and nobody showed up to munch on it." He unzipped his waterlogged orange jumpsuit and rolled it down to his waist. His arm was bleeding from two wounds that Nina realized were teeth punctures. She disconnected the sleeve of Kendren's compression suit, wrung the water from it, and wrapped it around his bicep, cinching it tightly to close the wound.

"Nobody except a few hungry eels," Kendren corrected. "Thanks for the patch up."

Nina nodded. A drop of blood squeezed out from beneath the fabric, and she wiped it from his bicep with her thumb. When she looked up at him, she saw an unexpected softness in his eyes. It was intimate enough to send her, casually, to the other side of the craft.

Nina tried the comms on the transponder again. "Russ?" she said into it.

Droplets of water struck her face, and she glanced across the small craft to see Kendren was stripping off the rest of his jumpsuit. He lay down across the small craft in only skintight skivvies. Kendren was exotic and beautiful, human-shaped but at least seven feet tall with a hairy chest, a mane of wavy brown hair, and rippling muscles. His face resembled a comic book character's, with long eyelashes and high cheekbones complementing a hero's chin. Everything about him reminded her of the larger-than-life male models from the covers of all her favorite romance novels. More right now than ever.

"Anything from your transponder?" Nina asked.

"It's fucked." Kendren said. He took off his transponder and tossed it to her. It was almost the only thing he had still been wearing.

"If the Geo-Link isn't working . . ." Nina began, tapping ineffectively at the screen of his device.

"Bah'ren will find us," Kendren assured her. "She always does. Consider it a half day off while we wait." Kendren gathered his discarded suit behind his head for a pillow. He draped his forearm over his eyes.

Nina took the opportunity to guiltily run her eyes the length of his well-muscled body. "Any reason you took off your jumpsuit?" she asked.

"Many reasons. We're only two planets from this galaxy's sun, and I have an interview tonight on Divian Frontline Actual. I can't be on camera with a bricklayer's tan."

"That would be terrible," Nina said with a small smile.

"And," Kendren said, adjusting the scant material of his bungies, "the jumpsuit has so many badges on it, it becomes heavy and uncomfortable when it's soaking wet."

Nina's eyes traveled to his suit, folded up beneath his head. It had close to fifty badges affixed to every available inch of the fabric. One of the badges, visible beneath his right ear, was the image of a ferocious feline. Beneath the image read: "TigilMart—A one-stop shop for the wanderer inside each of us."

"Maybe you shouldn't have accepted so many sponsorships?" Nina suggested.

"I grew up with almost no money. My parents were both miners and they scrimped and saved every credit just to put me through CERT school."

"We're not exactly overpaid even *with* our CERTification," Nina said, opening her banc app again.

"Yep. That's why I'm not going to miss any chance to make more money."

Nina thought about the irony of Kendren's commercial sponsorships. Somehow, he had emerged as the central beneficiary in the viral success of the Intergalactic Exterminators' heroic rescue onboard the *Flashaway*. He had appeared in a number of news broadcasts, received endless sponsorships, been appointed to the junior board of a security forces startup and had even done a cycle as the star bachelor on an interspecies dating show. Nina had suggested to Russ and Atara that they take some credit for the victory over the Triwin, but Russ had just shrugged it off.

"I definitely don't want to be a celebrity of any kind," Atara had said.

Nina wasn't sure what Kendren's bank account looked like these days, but it had been a while since she'd caught him stealing precious resources from exotic planets. He mostly spent his time working on his hair, muscles, and tan, all of which were currently on display and, admittedly, very impressive.

Nina caught the glow of her transponder and dragged her eyes from Kendren back to the screen. To her surprise, it was a message from Jaq'li.

Jaq'li: *Need to talk to 99999ou. Iiiiiiiimmportan7.*

Nina shielded her eyes and glanced at the sky. As far as she could tell, the transponders relayed data via antennae deployed all over UAIB space. Sometimes her tiny text program struggled when it was attempting to broadcast across a lot of galactic interference, like a particularly powerful sun, or a passing meteor storm of certain metallic compounds.

Nina: *UR message is unclear. i might need a rescue from Xodli. do you understand?*

Jaq'li: *Pleas. Qu++ick++ly. No jo. I told him e$e$th0n@. I'l so so$$y*

Nina stared at Jaq'li's text, growing concerned.

Nina: *comms are smashed whats happening? u ok? who needs to rescue who?*

Jaq'li: *Cal;;""*

Nina: *Jaq? what's going on?*

There was no response. Nina cocked her head at the broken device on her wrist. She sent another message to Jaq'li and again got no response.

Nina felt Kendren's hand on her right boot. "Comms are down," he reminded her. "Nothing we can do about it. You should take off your jumpsuit and tan beside me." He was lying on his back, but he still managed to shrug. "The sun feels nice and females in many, many galaxies would literally kill to change places with you."

"Uhh—" Nina started to say. Kendren had a habit of mild flirting without ever making a real effort. She was looking at her transponder again, hoping to get something, anything, from Jaq'li, when the *Aldersochi* suddenly cratered through the atmosphere with a thunderclap. The ship's arrival created enough displacement to scatter the clouds in its wake.

The noise caused Kendren to open his eyes and squint upward. "Never mind," he said. He climbed to his feet and slowly pulled on his jumpsuit. "Looks like we're rescued already."

"Please call. I don't know where you are. Your last message has me worried and the text program is spotty." Nina finished her second call to Jaq'li's voice mail. She hung up reluctantly.

She was in the Medbay, having just used its clean room to replace the screen and comm link on her transponder. The door slid open with a hiss and Starland trudged in, soaking wet. Starland's eyes were heavy, her mouth held closed in a tight line. She had a speckled baby in her arms.

"Can you hand me the DOM shots?" she asked Nina. She bounced the baby on her shoulder, and it cooed happily. "I feel like I just bailed your boyfriend out of danger for the one hundredth time."

"Boyfriend? You mean Russ?"

"Who else?"

Nina ignored the incorrect categorization. "It was a nifty piece of flying you did, dropping the ship into the water." They'd found Russ and Atara deep in the water, surrounded by ill-tempered predators. Starland had dropped the twenty-ton ship beneath the waves, then flipped on the *Aldersochi's* backup thrusters at the exact right moment to suck the eels into a bloody vortex of whirling, heated metal. Then she'd turned them off at the exact moment necessary to prevent Russ and Atara from being sliced to pieces themselves. She'd piloted the ship back to the surface, pieced together a portable Waypoint, and then dove gracefully from the open pilot's canopy into the clear water below. It had been one of the coolest things Nina had ever seen, and after working in deep space for the last five months, she'd seen a lot of cool things. Still, Starland didn't seem to be in the mood to be complimented about it. She seemed tired, grumpy even.

"I'm sure Russ appreciates everything that you do for him. I know I do," Nina told her.

"He's going to have to appreciate it from Earth for a little while," Bah'ren said, appearing at the door of the Medbay.

"What do you mean?" Nina said.

"I'm suspending him," Bah'ren told them.

"Really?" Starland said.

"Why?" Nina asked.

Bah'ren grunted. "Where do you want me to start? He killed the Zypper, a protected species. Last mission he jumped on the back of a Pero-ru, while it was headed into a fragmentary dust storm at full gallop, just to—and I'm quoting here—'keep it safe,'" Bah'ren counted off on her stubby fingers. "In case you forgot, we were there to neutralize the Pero-ru. They were invasive."

"That one seemed nice," Nina said.

"Two missions ago he went completely off script to—I'm still quoting—'follow his gut' about where to find the Wendiwamu we were tracking."

"He found it."

"Alone. Without the rest of the team. If we'd arrived a few seconds later—" Bah'ren took a deep breath. "You're lucky it's just a suspension. I think I'd be doing him a favor if I fired him. Maybe ten cycles without a paycheck will remind him to be more careful. Especially on no-kill missions that carry extremely"—Bah'ren took in a shaky breath—"extremely . . . large fines."

Nina knew what it was like to go without a paycheck. In fact, she was on her fifth month working for free on an eighteen-month contract, the result of a deal she made with Bah'ren in order to save her father's life.

She had no regrets. "After what he did on the *Flashaway*, Russ deserves at least another chance, if not your endless gratitude. Maybe you've forgotten that he saved the Intergalactic Exterminators, as an entity?"

"I haven't forgotten. But it won't do him any good if I let him die while freestyling on a mission," Bah'ren pointed out. "He's reckless, immature . . ."

Nina didn't actually disagree with Bah'ren. Russ's carelessness had her in a constant state of worry. He took spectacular risks and rarely followed orders. "It's not fair to call him immatur—" Nina began, but the rest of her sentence was drowned out by Russ's singing voice. He and Atara stumbled through the door caterwauling off-key to an old Irish drinking song:

My lady love is there when I wake . . .
She's as pretty as a thick slice of cake . . .
And for a fine pint of ale . . .

Russ had his arm around Atara's back and they swayed together drunkenly. Atara sang along with Russ, but she didn't know the words, so she just echoed what Russ sang, a fraction of a second later. She was dragging the corpse of a deep-sea eel, which was leaving a trail of red guts on the corridor behind them. It looked like she wanted to hold the eel's snout up to her nose to use as a microphone, but it was too heavy to lift one-handed.

"What's happened to them?" Nina asked.

"Severe nitrogen narcosis," Starland said. She turned to Russ and Atara. "Come on, drunkies, let's get you your DOM shots."

Bah'ren held her hand up to stop Starland. "Only Atara gets the shot. Russ is suspended."

Starland nodded, neither approving nor disapproving. Those who knew Bah'ren understood it was impossible to get her to change her mind, and her mate Starland knew her better than most.

Russ frowned as Starland pulled away his singing partner and gave her a shot.

Immediately, clarity descended down Atara's face. She looked at the eel in her hand and then set it carefully aside.

"He's welcome back aboard in ten cycles," Bah'ren told Nina. She took the baby from Starland and nuzzled it affectionately. The baby cooed, its huge eyes blinking back at one of its moms. Bah'ren checked the date on her transponder. "Services, and his paycheck, stop until Rensway the 19th. That's the exact day our babies are set to be baptized, so we'll lift the suspension then."

"Whas-going-on?" Russ asked.

"At least give him the DOM shot," Nina said, but Bah'ren just shook her head stubbornly. Nina was about to point out how unreasonable Bah'ren was being, but Russ launched into the rest of the verse:

And for a fine pint of ale . . .
She'll let you drink from the grail . . .
And slide down the hooker's bent sail . . .

He began a modified Irish jig, kicking his feet forward clumsily. His stumble-dance brought him dangerously close to Bah'ren, but Nina intercepted him before they collided.

Atara put her hand on Nina's shoulder and whispered, "Get him home to sober up. I'll talk to her."

Nina nodded hastily. "Excuse us," she said to Bah'ren and Starland. On her way to helping Russ through the door, she stopped and waved to the baby. "Let's get you back to Evanstown," she told Russ, propping him against her body. They stumbled together down the corridor in the direction of the Waypoint home.

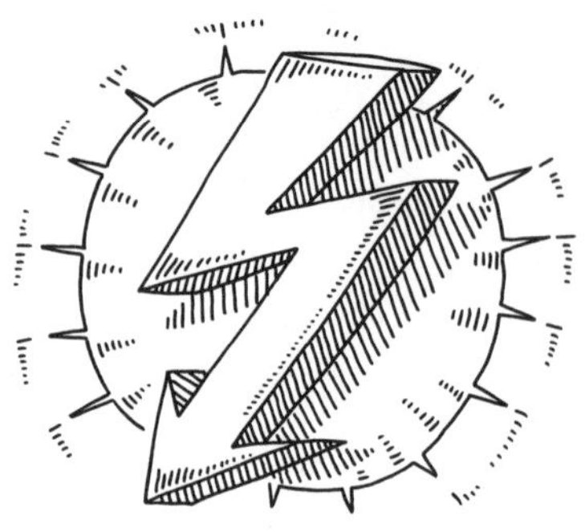

3
NINA

"WHAT DO YOU MEAN, HE'S SUSPENDED?" Clark asked, incredulous. "How are we supposed to afford this motel room without his paycheck?"

"You don't strike me as the type of guy who has trouble making a buck," Nina told him. "Or spending one . . ." Clark's motel room was a mess. Various room service trays were stacked on the floor and the desk near the window. She had to step around the clutter as she half dragged Russ to the empty queen bed and lowered him there gently.

"I'm broke," Clark told her. "And injured." He gestured to the bullet wound on his backside. They hadn't been able to get him to a CRC machine and had been treating the injury with Earth tech—meaning a lot of gauze and hydrogen peroxide. But that had been months ago, and the wound was now just a jagged burn on both sides of his hip.

Nina moved to the window and pulled aside the drapes. "We won't be paying the rent with my paycheck because I don't have one." She glanced outside. The Riverview Motel was on the outskirts of Evanstown, Wyoming, nestled against rolling hills on its south side and the roaring Bear River to its west. The nearby road, State Route 105, was virtually untraveled. Despite that, Nina could see a car meandering away from the motel. It looked, alarmingly, like an old, beat-up Mercury Tracer, the car Russ's grandmother Norma drove.

"We need an income. If we lose the room, we lose the Waypoint," Clark reminded her. He yawned and lay back on the bed.

"Or we could just move it again," Nina pointed out. Over her shoulder, the Waypoint stood tall in the back of the motel closet. It was still swirling a blue quantic pattern, painting the bathroom hallway in an eerie light. Nina grimaced at Clark. She'd found him endearing when he'd been dying in the hospital in Banville so many months ago, but then he'd faked his death and escaped his wife Norma and their "normal" life in exchange for adventuring in outer space. Despite reviving himself with advanced alien technology, he still didn't seem entirely healthy.

As she watched, Clark coughed into his bicep. Then he belched, rubbing a hand on his own belly. Then he yawned again. He seemed to have exaggerated versions of all of Russ's worst qualities: wanderlust, recklessness, and a strong aversion to responsibility. Fortunately, he wasn't staying in the hotel room completely alone.

"What happened to Russ?" Applebum asked. The robot moved his large metallic body from where he'd been reading a book in the corner. Applebum stared at Russ as he collected the room service trays and stacked them. "Sorry, I meant to clean these before you got home, but I got wrapped up in another mystery." He waved a copy of Raymond Chandler's *The Lady in the Lake* in front of Nina's face. "Reader to reader, who do you like best? Hammet, Chandler, Christie, Cain, Crumley, MacDonald, or McDonald?"

"All are great," Nina said. Then: "MacDonald. No contest. Can you take a look at Russ?"

"I'ms fine," Russ told Applebum from the bed. He had his forearm draped over his head as if he were attempting to apply enough pressure to make the world stop spinning.

"He's got nitrogen narcosis. Any idea how long it lasts?" Nina asked Applebum.

"Usually just a few minutes," the robot told her. Applebum was now, basically, an endless repository of knowledge, having consumed every book in a fifty-mile radius. "Give me a moment with him."

Nina took off her jumpsuit and went outside. She stared down the visible length of State Route 105 again, but the car had moved out of sight. Clark had never told his wife that he was still alive, so there was no way she would be out on State Route 105 visiting him.

Nina removed her transponder from her wrist and held it up to her ear, creating a fairly decent imitation of a cell phone. She called Jaq'li. "Jaq, call me back. Your last message—your silence—I'm starting to get nervous . . ."

4

RUSS

RUSS SAT ON THE MOTEL room bed and used his free hand to rub his forehead. It was two days later, and he was still feeling faint nausea but determined not to show it. "I could take the transponder off, if it would help," he suggested.

Nina was holding his other hand in her lap, loading her texting program onto his transponder. Despite working side by side for the past five months, this was the first time in a while they had actually touched.

Atara was always grabbing his hand and hugging him, touching his arm at any excuse. Nina was almost the exact opposite, keeping herself at a constant, respectable distance.

Russ looked into Nina's eyes. Soft light was spilling through the off-kilter drapes, and he was close enough to see its reflection and refraction in her iris. His eyes traveled to her mouth. Normally her lips parted naturally, giving her the faint impression of smiling, like she knew a secret about you but was trustable enough never to share it.

But today her mouth was held in a tight line, her ever-present smile nowhere to be found.

"You and I are the only ones to have this texting application," Nina told him. "And Jaq'li, but . . ."

"You still haven't heard from her?" Russ asked.

Nina shook her head. She got up and moved across the room to look out the window. Knowing Nina was a private person, he let her stand quietly in her worry for a moment.

Applebum glanced up from the desk where he was reading another detective novel and patted Nina on the arm. Russ could hear Clark in the shower singing, ". . . *and for a fine pint of ale, she'll let you drink from the grail* . . ."

Nina moved away from the window and dressed for work.

"Feels weird driving here just to be stuck in the room doing nothing. I wish I was going with you," he told Nina, suddenly.

"To work?"

Russ nodded. "It's not as fun hanging around here with Applebum as I expected. No offense, Applebum."

"None taken," the robot said. "I also feel restless."

"Can you feel?" Nina asked Applebum.

"I'm working on it," he told her.

"I've been working on the exact opposite," she told Applebum. Nina looked worried for a moment, but Russ couldn't tell if it was concern for Jaq'li or because of what Applebum had said.

"How about I go to Jaq'li's apartment and do a welfare check?" Russ offered. "I don't have much else to do."

Nina finally smiled. "I'd love that. I asked Bah'ren to track down Jaq'li's address through the MERC/CERT council. She said she'd get it to me as soon as she can. If she has it at work today, I'll text it to you."

"And I'll go right there," Russ promised.

Nina's transponder beeped with an incoming call, and she answered it with a hasty, "Hello?"

Russ watched her as she listened. Her forehead creased and she said, "One second." She took the transformer off her wrist and handed it to Russ. "It's for you," she said.

Russ put the transponder to his ear.

"How's the hero of the *Flashaway*?" Lanie said playfully from the other end.

"Lanie?" Russ opened the door of the motel and stepped outside. He had an odd habit of not wanting anyone to listen when he talked on the phone.

"Good to hear your voice again, Russ," Lanie said.

A pale man by the vending machine glanced in Russ's direction. Russ realized that to people without nanotranspods, Lanie's voice would have sounded fully alien. Vending machine guy would have been even more surprised to see the speaker, an eight-foot praying mantis with jet-black eyes and fully articulating antennae. Russ walked nonchalantly around the corner, toward the back of the motel.

"What can I do for you, Lanie?" Russ said, holding the transponder like a cell phone.

"I've been trying to reach you for two days. Bah'ren said she couldn't share your contact information because you were suspended. She is a superbitch, isn't she?"

"She just likes to be in control of things, including battle planning, weapon allocation, budgets . . . people. And she has six babies, so I'm not sure how much she's sleeping."

"She's unappreciative," Lanie spat. "You've done so much for her. Anyway, I finally figured out to ask for Nina's number because I knew you two wouldn't be very far apart."

"What do you need?" Russ said again.

"We're a man down with our new business. And we've stumbled onto a nasty infestation."

"I thought you and your sister had gotten out of the exterminator racket?" Russ said.

"We did. That's part of the reason we need help. We can handle the work, but it's an F-class threat. UAIB bylaws state we've got to bring at least one person along with an active Ecosystem Preservation CERTification. What do you think? Want to make a quick buck shaking out a bunch of nasty, hungry Mortumzees? We've been on a union-mandated break but deploy back to the Darkzone tomorrow. We could even pay your girlfriend per diem if she wanted to come along."

"Not my girlfriend," Russ said. "And I'm already dying to get out of this hotel room. What time should we show up?"

"Open of business, galactic time. It will be wonderful seeing you again, Russ." Just before hanging up, Lanie added, "One more thing. Mortumzees feed on flesh, so make sure to wear long sleeves."

5
RUSS

LANIE HAD SENT EXACT COORDINATES, so Russ and Nina were able to step through the Waypoint directly onto Lanie and Linnie's ship. While Russ had always thought that Bah'ren's old ship, the *Flashaway*, looked like a garbage truck, Lanie and Linnie's ship really was a garbage truck.

"Welcome aboard the *Nightfire*!" Lanie said, hugging Russ.

Nina was speaking into her transponder. She threw a quick wave in Lanie's direction. "I don't understand why it's taking so long. It's just her registered address. Russ had time to go yesterday. I have the day off today. Yes, I know you make the schedule, Bah'ren. Please send Jaq'li's address as soon as you get it." Nina stared at her transponder frowning, then gave Lanie a distracted, delayed hug.

"Impressive place you've got," Russ said, gesturing to the wide walls of the ship.

"Wait until you see the rest." Lanie led them down a long, poly-tungsten corridor toward the ship's bridge. "It's at least three times the size of the *Flashaway* and the *Aldersochi* combined," she explained while they walked. "We've got a crew of ten! Can you believe that?"

"How are you affording all this?" Nina asked.

They passed a large recreation room. It held a bar along the far wall, a wide table for playing cards, and a popular alien tabletop game carved from rock called *Menace of Mondania*. Beside the board game, a tiny hairy man of indeterminate species was shaking one of the play pieces and yelling at a male and a female Klung. The Klung looked back at him, appalled.

"After the collapse of Gas 'em and Trash 'em, Linnie and I got reCERTified as Refuse Disposal technicians. We took out a shit ton of loans, but we wanted to do it right."

"You register a new IP? What's the new name?" Russ asked.

Lanie grinned. "Intergalactic Waste Management, LLC."

"Wow, that's . . . familiar," Russ said.

"We may be capitalizing a little bit on the Intergalactic Exterminators' viral success. Hey! Do you think you could get Kendren to record a commercial for us?"

When he didn't answer, Lanie pulled Russ and Nina farther down the corridor until they stopped together at a starscreen that looked out over the length of the ship.

She pointed to a heavy metal arm affixed to the top. "The *Nightfire*'s equipped with two laser-guided fifty-foot-diameter saws for cutting up space refuse, and two more thirty-by-thirty-foot vise grips for pulling it back to the compactor. Each tool is discretely controlled by onboard workstations with a crew of two. The onboard compactor can shred and compress metal at a 10,000 to 1 ratio. We're fully equipped to slice up to 4,000 metric tons of space salvage into manageable pieces," she said proudly. "And then put those pieces right in the trash. We're leveraged hard, and we invested pretty much everything we had just to lease her for the year, but this is as first class as a garbage truck can get."

"Sounds nice," Nina said wistfully. Russ could tell she was remembering their shaky trip through the sky in Bah'ren's discount EFlyers.

"It's even better when we get old friends onboard," Lanie's fraternal twin Linnie called out, appearing at the end of the corridor.

Russ jogged down the corridor and hugged Linnie. He had to reach high to get his arms around her powerful exoskeleton. Lanie and Linnie didn't look exactly alike, but you had to know them a while before you started to notice the differences, such as Lanie's longer antenna, and Linnie's more powerful thorax.

"Welcome aboard," Linnie told him.

"Thanks for having me—for having us," Russ corrected himself.

"What do you know about Mortumzees?" Linnie asked.

Russ nodded sagely and said, "Nina, what do we know about Mortumzees?"

Nina was still a way down the corridor. She was looking out the starscreen, examining the huge vise grips that were curled, inactive, on the roof of the ship. "We've never fought them before. I don't know if they're animal, mineral, mammalian, or ophidian . . ."

"Mortumzees are insects. Unique insects. They're carnivorous necrovores," Linnie explained, "meaning they prefer to eat dead flesh. Because of that, they're considered generally nonthreatening to organic life."

"You mean I wore long sleeves for nothing?" Russ joked.

Lanie shrugged. "They prefer dead flesh. That doesn't mean they eat it exclusively. Can't be too safe," she said.

Linnie continued, "Mortumzee bodies are soft and they fly with four fixed wings that run the span of their backs. It's the reason they're known by their more common nickname, Death Angel. They tend to move in swarms of fifty to one hundred."

"Sound like Triwin," Russ said.

"That's part of what made us think of you."

"Why are we in the Darkzone?" Nina asked. "We can't be working a municipal contract out here, can we? I thought there were no services this far out."

"With an expensive ship like this, we can't take any chances with government work," Lanie explained.

"We have an exclusive contract with a company called Providence Travel Solutions," Linnie piped in. "We can tell you more once everyone is suited up."

The two Kruxfasians walked them to the *Nightfire*'s weapons closet. Like the rest of the ship, it was top of the line. The weapons were indexed, with purchase, cleaning, repair, and refurbish dates listed electronically onboard their casings. There also weren't many to choose from. Russ grabbed an S10 NoxFire energy pistol and hung it from his belt. He also grabbed a stunstick for the harness on the back of his jumpsuit.

"This is the smallest weapons closet I've ever seen," Nina whispered. "Refuse control might be peaceful work."

"I wouldn't count on it," he whispered back.

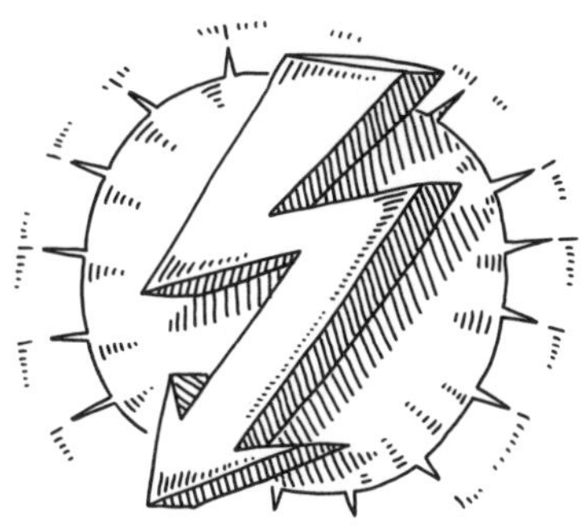

6

NINA

NINA STILL GOT OCCASIONAL PHANTOM pain from their final trip onboard the *Flashaway*, small bursts of dull ache in the spots where the Triwin had attacked. In an effort to cripple her, they had dug channels into her flesh with their sharp beaks. Bah'ren's CRC machine had cured her body but hadn't done anything to take away the memories.

"Why not just flush the Death Angels?" Nina asked, into her comm. They had pushed through the membranous wall protecting the *Nightfire* and were standing on an inflatable space bridge just beyond the edge of the known universe.

Lanie's voice piped back: "They're Astrogroms, meaning if they can find a cloud of essential gases, they can survive in the vacuum of space. It's probably how they got onboard in the first place."

"Astrogroms. Necrovores. These things are a marvel of modern evolution," Russ said.

"Right up until we zap them," Nina added. The salvage ship on the other side of the bridge looked like a mining vessel, its long jagged metal body coming to a point at the end of a gigantic drill. "But what does it matter if they survive out here in the Darkzone? UAIB law doesn't apply, right? No government, no municipal services, no Dexa-drive lanes, no friendly civilizations. Plenty of pirates. Isn't this already one of the most dangerous places in existence?"

No one answered. Nina took her first step across the bridge. She'd felt weightless the moment she'd pushed through the membrane, but it was still an adjustment to cross the long distance between the crafts, supported by nothing but a fragile, disposable length of polymer.

"It should be, but it's not," Lanie finally said, her throaty voice carrying across the vacuum of space. "'All of Providence's higher-end cruise ships finish with a thrilling trip into the dangerous wilderness of the Darkzone,'—those are the exact words of the brochure. But they're stuck on a prearranged, carefully patrolled loop. The bourgeoisie onboard think they're in danger from space pirates and what have you, but really there are multiple private security teams at the ready. And us. We run the path before each ship arrives, cleaning up the unsightly space trash and anything that might be truly dangerous while leaving just enough flotsam and jetsam to make the rich types feel at risk."

"That's ridiculous," Russ said.

"It's sort of ridiculous. But sort of not," Linnie admitted. "Providence analytics show that more business deals are finalized, more babies are conceived, and more return trips are booked while in the Darkzone than all the other stages of the cruise combined. This part of the journey is their biggest attraction."

"If a handful of these Mortumzees make it back to the cruise liner and mistake someone's rhinoplasty for dead flesh, a five-star review becomes a one-star, just like that," Lanie added.

To Nina, the Darkzone looked like every other expanse of deep space she'd encountered, meaning it was the most beautiful thing she'd ever seen.

Ten thousand miles to her left, a new star was being born, firing off a trail of cosmic dust and gas that lit the darkness with bright fluorescent light. The mask on her rebreather was refracting the light, causing brilliant blue and purple lens flares across her entire range of vision.

She finished the crossing reluctantly, stepping off the bridge and leaving the shining, purple-blue sunburst pattern behind her.

She disengaged from the bridge and stood to the side to let the others fit on the small docking platform. "The wealthy elite pay Providence to put them at risk. Providence pays us to make sure they're not," she said. "Makes perfect sense to me. Let's get to work."

The salvage ship was as sparse on the inside as on the outside. It was a functional demolition vehicle, but that was all. The walls were rough, burnished chrome, and there was no furniture. Just a handful of crates and a few scattered, rusted tools. The owners must have abandoned the craft in the same way someone would leave a beat-up car on the side of the road.

What bothered Nina was that they were in the Darkzone. The Darkzone had no Dexadrive lanes, and it wasn't supposed to have any work vessels either.

She adjusted her rebreather to make it easier to speak. "Do we have any idea how this ship got stranded out here?" she asked.

"Most likely abandoned," Lanie said.

"But it's a working craft. I mean, a vehicle for laborers. Why would it be in the Darkzone? There are no jobs out here."

"That's a very good question," Russ said as the first Mortumzee buzzed past his face.

"It is not our job to ask questions," Linnie said. "It is our job to stomp bugs and to crush scrap."

The insect stopped a moment to investigate Nina, hovering at eye level. It had dark red eyes and fishhook teeth extending from the end of a three-centimeter beak. Nina felt her heart start to race. Her eyes locked on the fishhook teeth. *What good is an exterminator who's afraid of insects?* she chastised herself.

"Hold still," Russ told her. He unholstered his stunstick, powered it up, and swatted the bug, watching with casual indifference as it dropped to the floor, burning. In the relative absence of oxygen, the flame snuffed out with a popping sound.

There seemed to be more Mortumzees farther down the corridor. The four of them traveled swiftly, zapping the bugs out of the air as they moved, Nina lingering just a half step behind.

The ship's tube shape left them with few directional choices to make. They were funneled south, toward the stern. The main corridor opened into a small equipment room, then a kitchen, then crew quarters, then a Medbay.

There weren't any humanoids, or any sign of humanoids having occupied the space. The Medbay was unstocked, and there were no sheets on the beds or gear in the storage boxes.

Lanie and Linnie moved through the rooms with military precision, checking every closet and cupboard big enough to hide a Death Angel.

Nina triggered the heat index on her transponder. The scanning pulse fired out in a flash of light. It shocked Russ enough that his hand went to the gun on his belt.

They all watched the pulse zip through the remaining rooms of the ship, sending back information as it traveled. Nina saw Russ's, Lanie's, and Linnie's heat signatures appear, but nothing from the insects.

"The Death Angels aren't showing on the heat index," she said.

"They're warm-blooded, but they don't have a signature," Lanie admitted. "Nobody knows why. Try not to think about it too much."

"These little fuckers are terrifying—" Nina started to say, but before she could finish her sentence, a fifth heat signature appeared on the screen. It was in the farthest corner of the last room on the ship. "Someone else is onboard," Nina realized. "Alive!" Before the others could respond, Russ barreled forward, headed in that direction.

"Russ, wait!" Nina said.

"He still rushes headlong into danger?" Linnie asked.

"Every. Dang. Day," Nina said.

She trailed Russ to the last, enormous room of the ship. It housed the non-business-end of the ship's engines, huge, round, sixty-foot cylinders in various states of decay. The Mortumzees were thick, and Russ had stopped short of the cloud.

Nina didn't blame him. The onboard lights cast only a faint glow from the base of each wall, lit by an emergency generator to show the way to the exit hatch. The light was reflecting the red of the Mortumzees' eyes, flashing beams of menacing color as the insects moved in a collective swarm.

"I'm worried about the owner of the heat signature," Nina said when she had caught her breath. "If they're alive, but somehow crippled, it's possible they're in the middle of that mess."

"Can you get a better bead on their location?" Russ asked.

Nina pulsed the transponder again. It lit the room in bright light. She tried to look down at the screen without taking her eyes off the cloud of insects. Again, the screen showed Russ, Lanie, Linnie, and herself. The fifth heat signature finally registered, late and faint.

Linnie looked distastefully at the large swarm. "C09 won't work on Astrogroms. Grab a Smokepop from my pack, please. We'll just suffocate them."

Russ removed a canister from Linnie's backpack and popped it open.

"Make sure your masks are sealed tight," Linnie said as Russ rolled the canister into the cloud of Death Angels.

As the thick smoke spread, the insects began to fall from the air, covering the floor of the engine room in a gruesome organic carpet. Nina watched them die with a troublesome thrill.

For a tick of a second, a section of the smoke near the floor swirled, just in front of the main engine. Something was displacing it, even in the still air of the derelict ship. Through the swirling smoke, Nina caught a glimpse of a body, prone, its limbs twisted painfully. She checked her mask, then marched resolutely toward the body.

Her heart was now pounding in her chest. The dead insects crunched under her boots, but she still looked warily toward the darkened ceiling, where a cluster of Mortumzees had retreated to avoid the swirling reach of the Smokepop. "The heat signature is so faint," she told the others. "Whoever is in here is either dying . . ."

". . . or they're masking their signal. Which makes them very dangerous," Lanie cautioned.

"I saw a shape . . . someone prone . . ." Nina said. "I think it might have been a—" Nina was groping around blindly when her fingers found the soft flesh of someone's arm. There was a body here, cold, and blanketed in the gooey remains of Mortumzees. The insects had been feeding on it, their tiny mouths affixed to its flesh like so many leeches.

Nina locked her grip on the corpse's elbow and dragged the body back, moving quickly to escape the circumference of the suffocating smoke. Even with her vision completely obscured, she tried hard to wipe away the dead insects with her free hand. They held firm against her efforts, their fishhook teeth digging deep into the body's flesh. The body was light and no more than five feet tall. Nina worried it might belong to a child.

"I've got someone," she told the others.

"I have a first aid kit in my pack. Come to the northwest corner," Linnie instructed her. "If they still have a heat signature, they still have a chance."

"The body doesn't feel warm at all," she said. "And it's covered in Mortumzees. You said they only eat decaying fleshhhh . . ." Nina didn't finish her sentence. She had reached the perimeter of the cloud of smoke and looked down to see the mangled corpse of her friend Jaq'li staring back at her, the Gnurian's eyes glossy with death. Nina screamed.

A second later something heavy struck the back of her neck and knocked her to the ground.

7

RUSS

RUSS HAD WATCHED NINA DRAG a body out of the cloud of smoke, her hands brushing at the flesh on the corpse's arms. Her scream caused a chill to run through him, but the abrupt way it ended was even more frightening.

Russ was rushing to Nina's side when he heard a faint cough that stopped him in his tracks. He drew his pistol and listened. There was another faint cough and then a squelching sound. Then another. *Squelch. Squelch. Squelch.* Russ squinted through the smoke.

"What happened to Nina?" Lanie shouted into the comm.

"Shh—" Russ said tersely.

Squelch. Squelch.

Russ followed the squelching sounds, his eyes drawn to the tiny insect corpses that littered the floor. He saw them flatten in a boot pattern. More boot prints appeared in a line. His eyes followed their movement until he realized they were headed toward Lanie and Linnie in long strides, impressing on the bodies of the dead bugs with each step. Russ opened another Smokepop and rolled it right between the twins.

"Russ what are you doing?" Linnie cried as thick gray smoke billowed from the canister, enveloping the Kruxfasians. *Now nobody can see anything,* Russ thought, *including the invisible dude.*

"Someone else is here," Russ quickly explained. "Invisible. He clubbed Nina and now he's in the cloud with us. Listen."

In the silence, they heard a cough. Then another cough. Russ pulsed his transformer, but only four heat signatures appeared.

Russ couldn't see the knockout blow as it arced toward him, but he could hear the weapon whistling through the air. He rolled left and something metal clanged hard against the ground. He scrambled back to his feet in time to see a person-shape lurching toward him, displacing enough smoke to give him a generally good guess of its location. He raised his pistol, but the butt end of a knife came down hard on his wrist and there was a sharp popping sound. Russ felt the gun slip from a hand that was no longer capable of gripping it.

He kept a small roll of pain pills hanging on a string around his neck. He drew in a deep breath then removed his rebreather long enough to pop one into his mouth. The person-shape dodged forward again, and he felt a knife's blade tear open the edge of his compression suit, just above his ribs. The blade had missed his skin, but he cried out in surprise. Fortunately, the sound brought Lanie and Linnie. The two women crashed into the middle of the fight, sending both Russ and his attacker sprawling; mantis arms flailed everywhere. Russ landed on a scrap of cloth on the ground and tied it hastily around his injured wrist. He could still move his fingers, and he knew if he could stabilize the break, he could finish the fight in a single shot. He found his gun on the ground, just as the original cloud on the far side of the room finally dissipated. Russ stumbled in that direction, and he wasn't the only one. He could see his invisible opponent's footsteps once more leaving impressions in the bodies of the fallen Mortumzees.

"He's left the cloud!" Russ told the others. "Watch the floor, you can see his footprints."

Russ raised his pistol tracking the invisible creature. "Warning shot," he shouted. Then he fired once, aiming just above where he imagined the attacker's head was located. "Next one doesn't miss," he called out.

"Don't shoot!" a female voice responded. It was the attacker. Russ could see *her* footprints had stopped moving. He imagined she had her hands in the air. "You've got me. Don't shoot."

"Give me a good reason why not," Russ said.

"It's safer to shoot her," Lanie said.

"Definitely," Linnie added.

"She was trying to kill you just a second ago," Lanie reminded him.

"I was not trying to kill you," the voice said matter-of-factly.

Russ didn't shoot.

Instead, the five of them waited, silently. Nina climbed, woozy, to her feet.

"Who are you?" Russ called out, but there was no answer. "Are you the murderer?" Russ nodded toward the dead body.

"No," the voice said.

"I don't believe you," Russ said.

"She might be telling the truth," Lanie said. "For a Mortumzee larva to hatch on the body, then lay enough eggs for this large a swarm . . . the corpse has to have been here at least a day or two, if not longer."

"And I didn't kill your teammate either, when I had the chance," the voice said.

"Make yourself visible," Russ said. "And I promise I won't shoot."

There was no answer, but the room suddenly blazed with light. It looked like the light of a Waypoint, but it was white instead of blue, and it came from a ring, floating seven feet off the ground.

"Waypoint ring!" Lanie called out. Before she had finished identifying it, the Waypoint clattered to the ground, and the invisible opponent was gone.

Linnie reached the device first. “Portable jump-gate,” she said, looking at the ring, which still hummed with electricity.

“Can we get a read on the destination?” Russ asked.

Linnie shook her head, pointing to a small countdown timer around the ridge of the device. It said **:13**. “Looks like it’s rigged to self-destruct. This is either illegal or emergent technology. Or both. It’s impossible to know where this thing leads.”

:06 . . . **:05** . . . **:04** . . .

“Not completely impossible,” Russ pointed out.

“Don’t . . .” Nina yelled.

But without another thought, he jumped through.

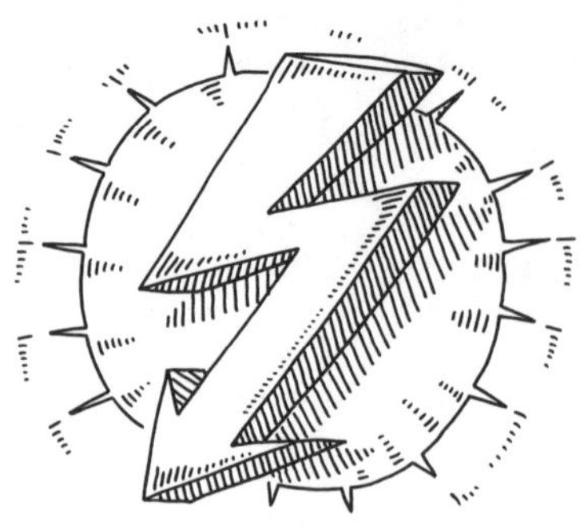

8

NINA

NINA STUMBLED TO HER FEET and rushed to the Waypoint ring, but it had melted into the floor, leaving only a circle of bubbling metal and wax. "Russ!" she said, louder than she wanted to. "He keeps doing that," she told Lanie and Linnie. "He keeps taking bigger and bigger risks. Like he wants to die!"

"Kruxfasian men are known for their wisdom and accountability," Lanie said sagely. "And they still do a whole bunch of stupid shit too."

Nina's eyes fell on Jaq'li's body, and she moved back to make sure it hadn't been her imagination—some expression of her worst fears playing out in real time. When she saw it really was her friend, body twisted wrongly, Nina blinked her eyes, trying not to cry. Jaq'li had been by her side during the infestation on the *Flashaway*, and they had grown very close over the last few months. Nina was flooded with the memory of celebrating together with one too many drinks the night Jaq'li had resigned from SOL Pest Control. Nina had called it an "ethical resignation." Jaq'li had called it "getting away from a bunch of assholes."

Nina felt like she was violating her friend's memory as she ran her hands over the body, turning Jaq'li's pockets inside out and examining her friend's arms, torso, and legs to look for clues about her death. Nina found a twelve-inch burn mark on her upper chest and another on her shoulders near her neck. She unzipped Jaq'li's jumpsuit slightly to follow a particularly long, angry burn to the center of her back. Nina's stomach clinched tight as she felt the chewed-up flesh on Jaq'li's biceps, where clusters of dead Mortumzees still hung. She had to sit for a moment while her stomach settled. She finished her search, but Jaq'li wasn't carrying anything. No weapons. No identification. No transponder. Nina rose unsteadily back to her feet as Linnie hurried over.

"Are you all right?" Linnie asked. "Maybe you should sit down a little bit longer. That was quite a hit you took." As she spoke, Linnie gathered Jaq'li's body up and hefted it over her shoulder.

Nina flinched. She felt a strong impulse to protect her friend's dead body. "What are you doing?"

"Biowaste, especially the biowaste of a registered UAIB species, requires special treatment," Linnie told her. "We've got to store it in the *Nightfire*'s freezer until we can remand it to a spaceclerk to investigate for next of kin."

"Shouldn't we call the police?" Nina said.

"In the Darkzone? No police out here. No police will come out here either. Providence Travel Solutions has private security, but we do not want their help. They're monsters. Some of them are literal monsters. Huge aliens, hopped up on all sorts of pills, looking for a reason to enforce made-up regulations and cause violence."

"But—" Nina finally found her voice. "This is my friend. This *was* my friend."

"The dead body?" Linnie said. The Kruxfasian's jet-black eyes curved downward in sadness. "Oh, Nina. I'm so sorry."

Lanie approached. She held Nina's arm to stabilize her. "We will make sure the body is treated with dignity. CERTified work is so dangerous. I've run into a few dead friends over the years. Linnie, do you remember that mission to Jafbog? With Tyrano?"

Nina dropped back into a sitting position. She felt like she might throw up.

Lanie rubbed her shoulders. "You're welcome to rest on the ship. Please stay as long as you'd like. I'm sure Russ will be back soon, no doubt in one piece."

"Your per diem check will also be available in your account at the end of this pay cycle," Linnie added.

Nina opened her mouth to ask if she could stay with Jaq'li's body at least until they could identify a next of kin. She felt a flush of shame that she still didn't even know her friend's address. A moment later, the screen of her transponder lit up with a voice mail. Bah'ren's voice filled the room, tiredly announcing, "Jaq'li's address came through. Thank God you can stop bothering me for this, finally. It's 31534571 West Bollvel Avenue. Apartment 390.11K. Star's Crescent Nebula, Y Alpha Vixen Cluster. You owe me. Again."

Nina logged the address into her contact list. "Guess it's not time to rest just yet," she told the twins. "Would you mind if I used your Waypoint?"

The streets leading to West Bollvel Avenue were empty, fronted on either side with a line of commercial buildings that had been retrofitted into dense residential units. The faded shop signs still hung from the windows, a nostalgic relic of when Star's Crescent used a traditional marketplace economy. Jaq'li had once complained to Nina that everyone on her adopted planet did their shopping through a purchase-and-delivery system and, consequently, almost never left their homes. Nina hadn't understood what that meant until she glanced down the silent street, seeing nothing but carefully cinched blinds blocking out everything except the faintest flickering of screens on the other side.

Nina took a left onto Jaq'li's street and was shocked by the sudden noise of three sentient deliverymen carrying boxes past her at high speed, their boots clomping heavily with each hurried step. They were just as surprised to see her. Another two deliverymen trailed behind, moving only a fraction slower on smallish battery-powered craft. The craft were dragging pallets loaded with more brown boxes of various size. *They look like Santa Claus*, Nina thought. *Except these guys bring stuff every day of the year*. She waited for another deliveryman to move past, watching as his partners on foot scouted ahead, searching for specific addresses.

She passed two more blocks and another two delivery crews—but no actual inhabitants —before reaching Jaq'li's sprawling apartment complex. She followed the numbers on the doors in the direction of 390.11K. Turned out that the *K* represented the subterranean basement section. Down below, the plumbing was mounted externally. It was dark, and Nina could hear water whooshing through pipes that stretched the length of every hallway. Jaq'li had been to Earth twice but had never invited Nina to visit her own apartment, and Nina suddenly understood why.

The door of apartment 390.11K was locked, so Nina tried the neighbors' doors. Two didn't answer her knock. One yelled, "Leave it on the doorstep, like the contract says." The fourth slid aside a small viewing window and studied Nina's face.

"I'm a friend of Jaq'li K'l'w'qi'," Nina explained. "I need to get inside her apartment. Do you know anyone who might have a key? Maybe there's a floor manager somewhere?"

The woman behind the door was a gaunt Romgulang. She had likely been pretty when she was younger, but the years hadn't been kind to her skin, hair, or teeth. She shook her head. "Floor manager? Have you looked around? Does this place seem managed to you?"

"Not effectively," Nina admitted.

"You don't want to go inside that apartment anyway."

"Why not?"

"There's been a lot of traffic through there. Dangerous people—and things. Best you can do is head on back to whatever alien planet you came from."

"Well . . . how did those people get keys?" Nina asked.

The Romgulang shrugged.

"Did you see their faces?"

The Romgulang shrugged again.

"Do you know what Jaq'li was involved in? Why would dangerous people be searching her apartment?"

"Why do you want to know?" the Romgulang asked.

"Jaq'li was my friend. She's dead. I'm going to find out what happened to her."

The Romgulang grimaced. "Shame. I liked Jaq'li. She had a gruff exterior, but she always treated me kindly, even when others on the floor judged me for my past work choices."

"These dangerous people in her apartment, did you talk to them?"

After a faint hesitation, the Romgulang shook her head no. "But, I heard them moving shit around. Heavy shit. It sounded like they were tearing through the place."

"They're looking for something," Nina realized.

"I am certain you are right."

"But what? Do you have any idea?"

The Romgulang sighed, then closed the viewing panel abruptly.

"Hello?" Nina said, knocking again. On her third knock the entire door swung open. The Romgulang stood on the other side. Her clothes were dirty, and she had an angry red rash on her wrist peeking out from the tattered end of her sleeve.

"They're looking for this," she said, holding a dense silver cube about the size of a bath bomb. "Jaq'li asked me to keep it safe before she left, but I didn't think a bunch of pill-popping corpo gun-thugs would be outside my door sniffing around for it. I don't want any part in whatever is going on." The Romgulang held the cube out and dropped it into Nina's hand. Then she shut the door firmly.

9

RUSS

THE LAST TIME RUSS HAD jumped willy-nilly through a Waypoint, he'd nearly died on an unincorporated alien planet. This time he found himself . . . in the middle of someone's office?

The office was large, roughly four hundred square feet wide. There was a long executive's desk along one wall and ornate table in the center, surrounded by five executives' chairs. The Waypoint behind him was smooth and woven seamlessly into the architectural design—a series of pale, rolling arches lining the length of one of the walls. The room was free of dirt, dust, and personality. It had a hygienic staleness to it that he always associated with white-collar work.

Only one thing was out of place. On the floor, not three inches from the toe of his boot, was a dense, silver cube about the size of a superball. He bent down and picked it up.

When he stood again, he looked through the enormous picture window on the farthest wall. On the other side of the window, he could see aliens sitting around a large conference table in full business attire.

An older female Divian stood in front of a glowing whiteboard, holding a laser pointer in her hands. Russ's arrival had caught her attention and her neon eyes blinked, the light from her laser pointer dancing on the window between them.

The others around the table followed the laser's movements, turning to stare at Russ. Those with eyes squinted in confusion.

On the far side of their room, more gigantic picture windows looked out over a green grass park. In the distance, an ocean churned with rough blue waters. They were so many floors up, and there were so many windows, Russ almost felt like he was flying. He also felt awkward for interrupting. He waved at the businesspeople. Not sure if they could hear him through the glass he said, "I come in peace."

The Divian at the head of the table spoke a voice command and the windows went from translucent to opaque. The folks in business suits were suddenly obscured behind foggy glass.

An instant later, a knife blade appeared right at the base of Russ's neck. He held his hands in the air, cupping his fingers closed to hide the small cube.

"Who are you?" a woman said. It was the same soft purring voice from the derelict ship. "And why did you follow me here?"

"Who wants to know?" Russ said back. He knew his chances of taking away the knife were minimal with his wrist broken.

The woman shoved him hard, and it took all his balance to not flop on the floor. He caught himself on one of the large windows and turned slowly to be as unthreatening as possible.

The woman became visible, her body materializing a few feet in front of Russ. She was also Divian, with similar features to the one with the laser pointer, though much younger. She was tall, like most of her race, almost eye-to-eye with Russ, who himself stood at a swarthy six foot two. She had a mop of wavy, purple hair pinned atop her head in something like a loose Samurai topknot. It made her seem even taller. Her skin was also purple—a dynamic, breathtaking purple, like the swirling electric colors Russ had seen light up distant galaxies. She wore a simple business suit, with a gray sling stretched across her chest.

She held the knife in her right hand, but it was balanced, tip down on her slender index finger. "Are you going to speak, or just stare at me like you've never seen a Divian before?" she asked.

Intergalactic television was loaded with Divian newscasters and Divian celebrities, but Russ had only seen one up close like this, a bastard named PT Kling. With her long, muscular body, she seemed an entirely different species from the square, froggy Kling. She looked like she belonged on television—there to remind the masses that, in contrast, their lives were uninteresting and physically plain and imperfect and monocolored.

Russ was absorbed in the color of her eyes. He broke his gaze long enough to glance around the large office. With the businesspeople gone, they were suddenly alone. "Did I just fight you?" he asked.

"No," she said, but her denial was punctuated by a familiar cough.

Russ cocked his head to the side. "Yeah, I think I did." He wanted to say it with more confidence, but she hadn't moved her mouth. The coughing sound was coming from somewhere else in the room.

"It wasn't really fighting," she said. "You were just in the way." Her lips pulled over her gums, revealing rows of strong white enamel attached to purple gums.

"I definitely could have shot you. Just before you teleported."

She raised the knife still balanced point-down on her finger. "And I *could* kill you right now," she said calmly. "You're trespassing."

"Where?" Russ asked. "I'm trespassing where? And who are you?"

"You're in Ren'Div, the crown-jewel capital of UAIB space. This is my mother's office at Waymore Industries. And I'm Nurcia Fragnar, currently the director of public relations for Waymore's tourism subsidiary, Providence Travel Solutions. Does that answer all of your questions?"

"It raises a few more."

"Who are you?"

"I'm Russ Wesley. Of the Intergalactic Exterm"—Russ caught himself—"of Intergalactic Waste Management, LLC." He glanced around one more time. "Are you sure we're alone in this room?" he asked.

Nurcia was punching away at her transponder as he spoke. She was silent a moment, and Russ thought he saw a strange emotion flicker across her face. She said, "It seems you're an employee of Providence Travel Solutions as well. You signed a single-day work pass with one of our subcontractors just a few hours ago?"

"Yes," Russ said. "What's your screen say about me?"

The Divian reached out and grabbed Russ's wrist. He couldn't feel any pain because of the pills, but his right hand hung limply in her own. It was the second time today a beautiful woman had been holding his arm like this. "As a subcontractor, you're not even allowed to be in this building, much less this office. But if you'd like, I can take you to the nearest medical station. You're welcome to use Waymore's state-of-the-art CRC machines—for a nominal co-pay and under my supervision. For the record, we take no official responsibility for the damage."

"But off the record . . ." Russ prompted her.

Nurcia laughed, a soft, lyrical sound. "Off the record, I broke the shit out of your wrist. It was a clean hit."

"Why did you attack us?"

"On the record or off?" Nurcia asked.

"I'm not a reporter or anything."

Nurcia nodded. "When our subcontractors—you—reported the infestation of Mortumzees, it triggered an automatic MUP scan. This happens with any subclass of necrovore. The scan found . . ." Nurcia paused looking for the right word, ". . . *concerning* aspects to the ship."

"It belonged to Providence Travel Solutions—your company," Russ told her.

Nurcia smiled at him slightly. "Why would you say that?"

He held up his broken wrist showing her the ribbon he'd used to stabilize it. It was an eight-inch red banner with the phrase "Providence Cruise Lines—What a way to go" emblazoned across the fabric. It was partially crusted in blood. "There was a body onboard," Russ reminded her.

"No one of consequence," Nurcia said. "According to our records, the deceased was not rich, had no political power, no social influence, wasn't related to anyone of import, and was, in fact, between jobs. A drifter."

"Then why attack us? One of your own subcontractors?"

Nurcia flipped the knife so the handle was in her hand and then placed it on the long, ornate wooden table in the center of the room. "I discovered a dead body onboard a company ship. I'm the director of public relations. When something like that happens, it's my job to control the flow of information, regardless of the identity of the deceased. What do you think people in public relations do?"

"Write eblasts." Russ tried to withdraw his wrist from her grip, but she held firm. He still held the cylinder, curled tight in the other hand.

"I was establishing dominance over the situation until I'd learned enough to determine the proper course of action. At Waymore, we call it the doctrine of forceful control. I'm still doing that now." She tugged at his arm, refusing to let go.

"This is a nicer version," Russ said. He watched her cheeks darken slightly.

Nurcia dutifully untied the ribbon from his wrist and folded it. She withdrew a plastic bag from her backpack and dropped the ribbon inside. She put her hand on Russ's chest, her slender fingers nearly reaching his Adam's apple. He'd thought her eyes were blue, but as she took a step closer Russ saw a mixture of many other neon colors: bright green, orange, red, and electric yellow.

"Just to confirm, you're officially refusing medical treatment?" she asked.

"I doubt I can afford the co-pay. Whether it's nominal or not," Russ told her. Then he heard the cough again. He realized it was coming from inside the sling she wore across her chest. "I've got to know," he said. "What the hell is that?"

Nurcia smiled and moved even closer. Russ felt his heart beat faster. She still had her hand on his chest, and he hoped she couldn't feel the uptick, just beneath her palm.

"Pleasure meeting you, Russ Wesley," she said. "Maybe we'll see each other again."

She shoved him backward, and the Waypoint swallowed him whole.

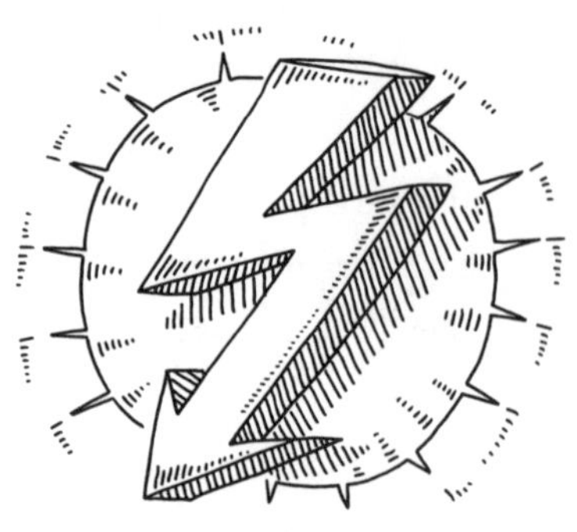

10
NINA

WHEN NINA JUMPED THE WAYPOINT back to Earth, she found Clark half asleep on one of the motel room beds.

"Where's Russ?" he asked, rolling on his side and turning down the TV.

"He jumped through an illegal Waypoint that self-destructed immediately afterward," Nina said.

"Never heard of such a thing," Clark responded.

"He won't stop doing that kind of stuff," Nina said. "He's trying to kill me with worry."

"His transponder is reporting normal vitals," Applebum said, putting down his book. Then he added, "There was a small hormonal spike about half an hour ago, but no sign of any danger."

"Hormonal spike?" Nina asked. "What could he be up to?"

"Something more fun than we're doing," Clark answered, changing the channel.

Nina texted: *where are you? are you SAFE?*

She stared at the screen, but Russ didn't respond. Nina turned to Applebum. "Can you help me? We found a dead body on the salvage ship. It was Jaq'li, a friend of mine."

Nina was once again checking for a text from Russ, so she was caught completely off guard by what happened next. Applebum hugged her. "I'm very sorry," he said.

"Thank you?" Nina said. Her cheek resting against the chrome of his chest, she stared up at Applebum. He looked back down at her, and she caught something in his eyes she'd never seen before—the faintest glimmer of authentic emotion. The corners of his eyes and the edges of his mouth curved downward. It could have been the pretense of sadness, a face he'd learned to show when someone needed comfort. Applebum had been mimicking human emotion since the first day he had discovered and read a book. *Hopefully that's all this is*, Nina said to herself. Still, she couldn't shake the fact that for just a moment, the depth of his expression had hinted at genuine empathy and sorrow. Alarmed, she continued to study his manufactured face.

Clark remained splayed on the bed.

The Waypoint flashed, and Russ appeared from the closet. "Why are you hugging the robot?" he asked.

"He's hugging me," Nina said. She carefully disengaged from Applebum's strong chrome arms, taking one last look at his face. Then she rounded on Russ. "What's it going to take to get you to stop disappearing? To stop taking chances?" Nina waved her arms in front of Russ. "Every single day you do something that could get you killed. Do you know what happens to creatures in nature when they behave like that?"

"They get the early worm?" Russ hazarded a guess.

"They get removed from the gene pool," Nina said. She was quiet a moment, letting herself breathe. "You can't die! You, specifically, can't die."

"Are you okay?" Russ asked. "You seem very frazzled."

Nina glanced again at Applebum. “The dead body was Jaq’li—” she said. Her friend’s name caught in her throat, even though she was doing her best to keep the emotion out of her voice.

Russ crossed the room and hugged her too. Then Applebum wrapped his arms around them both. She was encased in a Russ/Applebum sandwich, human and robot holding her tightly. She let herself feel the emotion, *but what emotion was it? Worried? Thankful? Protected? Loved?*

She pulled him as close as she dared. “This job is too dangerous,” she whispered. “There’s no safety precautions, nothing to protect us.”

“We protect each other,” Russ said. He rested his cheek against the top of her head. Nina felt her skin tingling. “I’m sorry about your friend.”

“His hug is better than mine, somehow,” Applebum observed.

Clark changed the channel.

“The least I can do is figure out what happened to Jaq’li,” Nina said. “She called me for help three days ago, and now she’s dead. And I only have one clue.” Nina reluctantly freed herself from Russ and Applebum and showed them the silver cube.

“That’s a pretty big coincidence,” Russ said, absently.

“What is?”

He reached into his pocket and held out the cube he’d found at Waymore Industries. It was identical to the one in Nina’s hand.

“What could these be?” Nina asked, holding both cubes side by side. They gleamed in the light of the lamp. Nina rubbed her fingers over their slightly rounded edges.

“This device is not something I can identify,” Applebum admitted. His eyes lit up. He moved quickly to the corner of the room and retrieved his copy of Raymond Chandler’s *The Lady in the Lake*. “Oh my,” he said. “This is exciting! I just realized we’re in the middle of a murder mystery. Are we sure the body was Jaq’li? These sorts of things usually involve elaborate disguises, overlapping crimes, double-crosses, and a femme fatale.”

"This isn't a book," Russ said gently. "A friend really is dead. On a derelict ship in unincorporated space."

"I'd like to get both devices back to my lab and take one carefully apart," Nina said.

For the first time since she had ported to the hotel room, Clark rolled himself off the bed, yawning. He ambled over to take a closer look.

"No need to do that," he said. "I know exactly what those are, and I know how to get them open."

11
STEVEN APPLEBUM

"SEVENTY-FIVE CENTS SAYS MINE'S MORE important than yours," Russ told Nina as the two of them unzipped and stepped out of their borrowed yellow waste management jumpsuits and back into Earthling clothes.

Applebum lay on the bed watching them.

"Mine was being secretly held by the neighbor of a murdered friend. Yours was on the floor of an otherwise innocuous office building," Nina said.

Russ was quiet for a moment as he buckled his belt. He opened the motel room door, waved goodbye to Applebum, then turned back to Nina. "Okay, it's a bad bet," he said.

"But one you already made. Sucker!" Nina pushed him out the door, her hands on his hips. Applebum wondered why Nina was always so happy when she was with Russ. When he'd learned of Jaq'li's death, Applebum had hugged Nina, just like Russ. Why hadn't Applebum's hug had the same effect on her mood that Russ's did?

Clark was on the other bed, turning the mysterious cubes over in his hands. He had a faraway look in his eye. When he finally focused his gaze on Applebum, he said, “Do you think he can see how happy he makes her?”

“I was just considering that,” Applebum admitted. “I don’t believe so because he’s never exposed to her melancholy. When he’s around, she’s always happy. Even now, he has her laughing, and her friend has just died. He must think being cheerful is her normal stasis.”

Clark turned and looked at Applebum. “You don’t usually lie on the bed.”

“I thought I’d try. Since everybody else does it.”

“Everybody else isn’t a robot,” Clark pointed out. “Is it any more comfortable to lie there than it is to stand?”

“It feels . . .” Applebum paused a moment, computing,“. . . exactly the same as standing. And sitting.”

Clark held the second cube under the light of the motel lamp, studying it.

“You can unlock those devices?” Applebum asked.

“I have a friend who can.”

“Is he coming here? I’d like to see how he does it.”

Clark smirked. He hadn’t showered in a few days, and his hair was unkempt and oily. He stroked his beard as he spoke, “Didn’t you work briefly in immigration? You should know how much effort it took to shield this place from detection. The Waypoint is completely off network. It registers different departing and arrival locations every time anyone uses it, and it’s never, ever Earth. I also jailbroke and scrambled Nina and Russ’s transponders to keep them from pinging this location. Anonymity is not simple in this day and age. But it’s worth it.”

“Your friend is not coming here.”

Clark pursed his lips and scrunched his eyebrows together. Then rolled onto his other side, facing the wall.

Applebum felt . . . something. He tried to classify it. Irritated? Excluded? A few weeks prior, he had created an emotional database in his memory banks. Each day since, he'd been attempting to manually assign his own responses to the appropriate location in the database. He decided to put the response Clark had just elicited in both "sad" and "frustrated." But then Clark rolled over again.

"You're very lucky, you know?" Clark said. "There are so many things you don't have to worry about. That includes the big one."

"The big one?"

"Death. You don't have to worry about death."

"I can be erased, reformatted," Applebum assured him. "I can be destroyed."

"But do you fear it?" Clark swung his legs over the side of the bed and sat up. He rubbed the thick hair that sprang untamed from the top of his head. It gave him the appearance of youth, even though he had to be nearing the end of the human life cycle.

Clark rolled out of bed and approached the window. He watched Nina's truck exit the parking lot, then he put on his coat and pulled on his hat. "Death by reformatting sounds okay to me. You know what's a lot worse? Getting so old that the grim reaper is creeping up on every inch of your body: your heart, your kidneys, your liver. And those are just the organs that get all the press. My ligaments ache all day, every day." Clark stopped a minute and coughed into his bicep. During his time in Norma's bookstore, Applebum had read a series of medical journals. He decided the cough sounded powerful and dry, just short of paroxysmal.

"I've noticed you're on a self-prescribed regimen of illegal pharmaceuticals," Applebum said.

Clark nodded. Then to punctuate the point, he drew three pills from his jacket pocket and swallowed them dry. "It's not enough. My skin is so thin that when I bump my ankle on the bed frame climbing into bed, it bleeds for fifteen minutes." He grinned. "You talk about being destroyed? Try fighting back when the things killing you are gravity and cellular degradation and time. You, sir, are special. And not in just the ways everyone thinks."

"Thank you," Applebum said, sorting his emotional response into "happy." Upon further review, he also added it to "curious."

Clark walked over to the Waypoint and activated it. He had been leaving, almost nightly, since the first day he arrived. Clark had sworn Applebum to secrecy about this, but Applebum was still sorting through his feelings about concepts like swearing or making and keeping promises.

With the loud humming of the Waypoint, Applebum almost couldn't make out what Clark said next. "If I ever don't come back from one of these trips, stay near Russ. Never leave his side. He's special too. In a different way. But still special. You two fit together well. Promise me you'll stay close to Russ."

"Okay."

Applebum watched Clark disappear into the Waypoint, leaving him alone in the hotel. He filed the emotion he felt under "envy." Then he pulled open the nightstand drawer. Every evening when she finished work, Nina would always change out of her gear. She would fold her jumpsuit, then take off her transponder and leave it in the top drawer next to one of the queen beds.

Applebum rested the transformer on his powerful chrome-colored chest and began to scroll through a video sharing protocol called YouStar.

He usually started watching it when Clark left and stopped just before Clark returned, which was always thirty or so minutes before Russ and Nina arrived for work the next morning. The people on YouStar made Applebum laugh, and he felt he was learning a lot about other alien cultures aside from just Earth's. Russ had had many, many talks with Applebum about staying away from cloud-based information collectives known locally as the Internet, but Applebum didn't feel

YouStar counted. The people whose videos he watched were amiable and extremely enthusiastic.

The first video loaded up. He realized, with some concern, that his relationship with YouStar shared many qualities with the Complete Medical Encyclopedia's definition of addiction. That realization disappeared from his mind the instant the video began. He watched happily as a young, attractive Southern Blurn couple rebuilt a derelict transport ship, speaking loudly into the camera. He felt like they were speaking directly to him, welcoming him into their happy world without judgment. When the sixth video in the series ended, he forced himself to take a break.

He spent a few minutes examining Nina's self-made texting protocol, nodding in appreciation for how she'd built it. On a whim, he downloaded it into his own system. Then he spotted a new program that he hadn't seen on Nina's transponder before. She had labeled it www. WWW didn't sound like the Internet, so he gave it a look.

Six hours later, his head was buzzing. He'd visited a site called Reddit and another called Facebook. His system had rebooted twice, including a full, forced reboot when he'd happened upon a site called Twitter. Or was it X? Even the name was inconclusive.

Apparently, the United States of America, which had previously seemed so idyllic, was, in fact, on the cusp of social and political annihilation. Applebum had been trying to treat the information he found on www like he had the books in Norma's bookstore, absorbing the facts and sorting them into useful databases. But the facts he found kept contradicting other facts even when they were from the same source. Maybe "fact" wasn't even the right designation. A single politician was somehow a dedicated public servant with a spotless record, and simultaneously a deranged maniac intent on murdering Christians and drinking the blood of virgins. Automatic weapons were killing children, and automatic weapons were keeping children safe. *The Winds of Winter*, a book Applebum had been greatly anticipating, was coming out in Earth year 2014! But wait . . . that was more than a decade ago.

Because of the planet's miserable ecological rating, Applebum had always assumed that Earth itself was at dire environmental risk, but he found endless information indicating that it was perfectly healthy . . . that the polar ice caps weren't melting . . . that the ozone layer wasn't real and certainly not damaged . . . that science itself was a lie, and the planet Earth was flat and resting on the back of a giant turtle.

Applebum purposely rebooted his own systems, but his head still ached. He knew that this was the Internet Russ had warned him to avoid, and he wished desperately that he'd kept his promise. Earthlings acted fundamentally different on this Internet than they did in books. They were far crueler to one another, and they seemed dangerously obsessed with status and attention in ways he had previously attributed only to vain cultures like the RreRriaNnians. He'd been trying to assign the emotions he was feeling into different categories in order to not be overwhelmed: "disgust," "disbelief," "uncertainty," "fear," "envy," "exclusion," but every new site he visited reset the standard for each of those feelings.

He forced himself to look a little bit further. *Humans had to be better than this*. He'd fallen in love with a culture whose books rewarded acts of great humility, servitude, valor, and sacrifice. Why would this internet be predicated on such a different system of values?

In a moment of inspiration, he searched for the most popular websites on Earth. He was discouraged to learn that most of the places he'd already visited were on the list, Instagram, Twitter (X?), Facebook, Reddit; all except the top site had shown up on his initial searches. He would check there. *Maybe this last site was where they stored all their dignity and compassion? Surely this Pornhub.com would be able to reaffirm his faith in all mankind . . .*

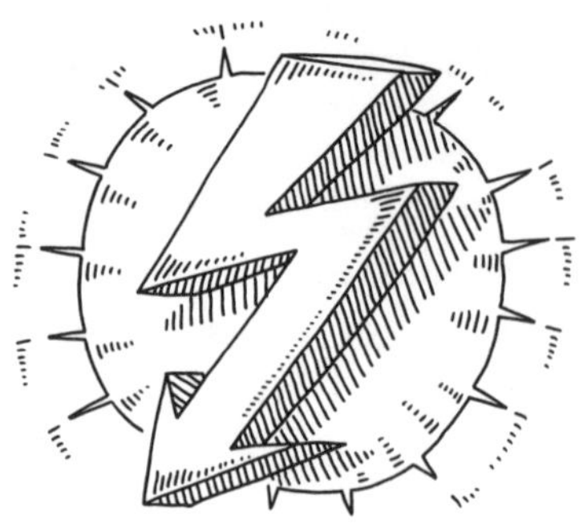

12
NINA

THE NEXT WEEK, FALL DESCENDED early on Evanstown, Wyoming, and the Bear River began to swell with rain. On that crisp morning in late August, Nina could hear river water rushing past the collection of trees that lined Russ's grandmother's house.

Russ's car had stopped working months ago, so Nina gave him a ride to the motel every day. Even though he was suspended, they decided to keep up the practice to stop Russ's grandmother Norma from asking too many questions. She was under the impression that they worked for a farm co-op in Banville. Nina liked Norma a great deal. In fact, Nina always got to her house early enough to enjoy the older woman's company for a while before the day of work started.

"I hope you like pregnant princesses in distress," Norma said, dropping two books into Nina's hand as she walked through the door. "Because these are loaded with them."

Nina looked down at the book titles, *The Sheikh's Pregnant Prisoner* and *One Night with Consequences: An Innocent, a Seduction, a Secret.*

She held the books to her chest, happily.

Norma's boyfriend Rufus Ensine was sitting in the small living room watching TV. He waved to Nina and smiled. "Russ is still sleeping. I'm worried about his wrist. He told me he'd sprained it, but it gets more swollen every day. Do you think you could talk him into seeing a doctor?"

"We'll get him fixed up," Nina promised.

"How's your father doing?" Ensine asked. "I haven't seen him at the bookstore lately."

"Good," Nina said. "Too good. My parents keep asking when I'll be restarting my graduate program in Laramie. Since my dad recovered from his illness, they've been uhm . . ." Nina didn't know how to talk about her parents' restarted—and seemingly endless—sex drive. "They've been like two newlyweds. I sneak out to the barn every night to read my books and give them privacy. But it's been getting colder and colder out there."

"I'm so happy for your parents," Norma said, her eyes twinkling. "Maybe sleeping with someone else would help you stay warm too?"

"We know a little something about that," Ensine said. "Norma's a firecracker!" He clapped his hands together.

Norma jumped at the sound, but then she laughed, putting her hand over her face in demure embarrassment. Russ had been spending a lot of time at the Riverview Motel, and Nina suddenly knew why. At least his refuge had a wall heater.

She moved into the room where Ensine sat, hovering close enough to whisper, "Is there any chance Norma was out on State Route 105 last week? By the Riverview Motel?" The more she thought about it, the more Nina was convinced that she had seen Norma's old Mercury Tracer from the window of the hotel room the day before. It wasn't exactly a common car. Mercury had stopped making the Tracer in 1999, and then Mercury had shuttered its doors as an automaker twelve years later.

"Why haven't you gotten Russ to a CRC machine?" Ensine whispered back, completely ignoring her question. "His wrist is shattered."

"He's unemployed. What CRC machine are we supposed to use?" Nina stared at Ensine, wondering if he had dodged the question about the car on purpose. He looked back at her, his eyebrows scrunched together. Of course, he didn't actually have eyebrows. Ensine was a Southern Blurn, an amphibious species covered in sparkling albacore-colored scales. He wore a transformer to hide his true identity from Norma.

His was a rare and illegal "hard-light" transformer, one that bent and hardened the illusion into a touchable shape, but standard transformers were fairly common in UAIB space. They could be very useful to make you look younger, or thinner, or in the case of Ensine, a completely different species.

To the credit of UAIB lawmakers, transformers had to be manufactured to attach to the top of the ear, limiting potential shenanigans and making it fairly obvious when someone was wearing one. To Norma, it must have looked like a fancy earring, a holdover from a very long midlife crisis.

Nina sat down at the table while Norma uncovered breakfast, spooning eggs and sausage onto Nina's plate.

"You haven't borrowed any of my dresses, have you dear?" Norma asked. "A few of my favorites have gone missing. I can't imagine they'd fit you . . ."

"Nope. Maybe they're at the dry cleaner?"

"I suppose that's possible. I must be getting older because it seems like I'm losing stuff every day." Norma looked at Nina. She studied her face. Self-consciously, Nina looked down and away from Norma's gaze.

"Is everything all right?" Norma asked.

Nina chewed, using the time to keep careful control of her expression. She nodded.

"You seem less bubbly than usual." The old woman smiled a crooked smile that reminded Nina a great deal of her grandson. "Can I be honest?"

"Always."

"You seem exceptionally sad."

"What do you mean?" Nina asked, pretending Norma's observation was totally off base.

Uninvited, Norma added a dash of salt to Nina's eggs. "You know the best way to free yourself from negative emotions is to talk about them? I happen to be a pretty good listener," she said.

Nina sighed. *Where to start? Dead friend, lingering stress and trauma, super dangerous job, afraid of bugs, parents constantly boning.* She flipped through the pages of *One Night with Consequences* without looking at them. "I've been having trouble at work," she admitted. "The job in Banville? A friend of mine got . . . hurt. It's hit me pretty hard."

"Someone from Evanstown?"

"No. A little farther out." Nina and Ensine glanced at each other. It was safer for Norma if she didn't know about their jobs in outer space. Or that her boyfriend was a fish. Or that her dead husband was just a few miles away, in bed watching TV. They'd protected the information with a different set of lies that Nina felt increasingly guilty about. "I've been a little down for a while. Even before my friend got hurt. I'm not sure why."

Norma met Nina's gaze without judgment. "I noticed it. I figured you'd talk about it when you were ready."

Nina must have been ready, because now that she'd started talking, she couldn't seem to stop. "I lived with so much stress the past year, with my dad's illness and everything. Even though he made his miraculous recovery, I still feel the stress. Randomly. And pretty often. It's like these bad feelings moved in and even when they weren't appropriate, or even logical, they stuck around. In a twisted way, it's a good thing my friend got hurt; at least now my sadness makes sense."

"What you're feeling is perfectly normal, dear. It's called post-traumatic stress, and it happens way more often than people realize. The important thing to remember is that it's *post*-traumatic. You've already made it through the hard part. You just have to wait for your emotional system to catch up. This thing with your friend might even give you a chance to speed up the healing process. It's an opportunity to take action. Now you can do something about your sadness by helping your friend."

Nina nodded. *Gonna find the person who killed her, at least.*

"So, you're still processing almost losing your dad. Your friend got hurt. And you're lonely," Norma summarized. "It will all pass, in time."

"Did I say I was lonely? I didn't say I was lonely," Nina objected.

"Oh," Norma said, chuckling. "My mistake."

"Eggs!" Russ said, shuffling down the hall. He yawned and patted at his hair, which stuck out everywhere. Then he lowered himself onto a seat at the table. He tried to spoon the eggs onto a plate, but his fingers couldn't grip the utensil.

"Your wrist is worse than you were letting on," Norma said firmly. "I think you need a doctor." She stared with concern at his bandaged wrist.

"I'm doing great," Russ told her. Nina watched him use his other hand to slip a pain pill into his mouth. "Has anybody seen the Whitefeather? I swear I left it in my closest but it's not there."

"It's with Norma's dresses," Ensine joked.

"You lost a gun? Isn't the Whitefeather your rifle?" Nina said.

"I didn't lose it. I put it in the closet and someone took it out. I think."

"Oy!" Norma said. "That was one of Clark's favorites. It's not safe to misplace guns! I'll report its disappearance to the sheriff. And I'll check the count in the ammunition safe to make sure it wasn't loaded."

"Everything is under control," Russ said, but he was still struggling to grip the spoon.

"Russ could probably be a little more careful at work too," Nina told Norma. Both women studied Russ's swollen wrist.

"He's doing great," Ensine said from the other room.

"Don't support his behavior," Norma told Ensine. "We don't like to see him hurt." She stood up and retrieved the orange juice pitcher from the fridge. "Do you have any idea how valuable it is to have a good woman caring about you?" she asked Russ as she poured him a glass. "And you're lucky enough to have two."

"And I love all three of you jerks," Russ reminded everyone. "Which is why I respect everyone's decisions." Russ glanced at the book in Nina's lap, "Even when they read things like *The Sheikh's Pregnant Prisoner.*"

"It's a good series," Nina said. "Is there any way to make him be more careful?" she asked Norma, earnestly.

Norma guffawed. "I'm afraid not. Russ is very much like his grandfather. Even in the months directly before Clark's death he was uncontrollable. He refused medical attention. He kept taking long walks at night. Sometimes he'd leave the hospital for hours on end and I worried he'd gone somewhere to die. But he'd always show up again—until he didn't." Norma stood up and walked to the other side of the kitchen. She washed a dish, staring at it intently. "We buried an empty casket." Norma shrugged, an awkward, forced motion. "He couldn't even die like a normal person. I never had a chance to—you know."

Ensine came into the room and kissed Norma lightly. "Who is supposed to be telling who about their problems?" he chided her.

Norma patted his arm. "No problems anymore, my handsome *amore.*" Norma turned away from Ensine to look directly at Nina. "The Wesleys are great men in many, many ways. But not all ways. You have to accept that they're going to take plenty of risks and make plenty of mistakes. If you can't, it's best to keep your distance because they can make a mess of things—"

"If I may present a counterargument," Russ started to say, but at just that moment, the orange juice slipped from his unsteady fingers. The glass broke with a jarring *crash*. They all watched as juice spread slowly across the table, soaking the napkins and the sausage and the eggs before sliding off the edge to form another papery, greasy, eggy puddle on the floor.

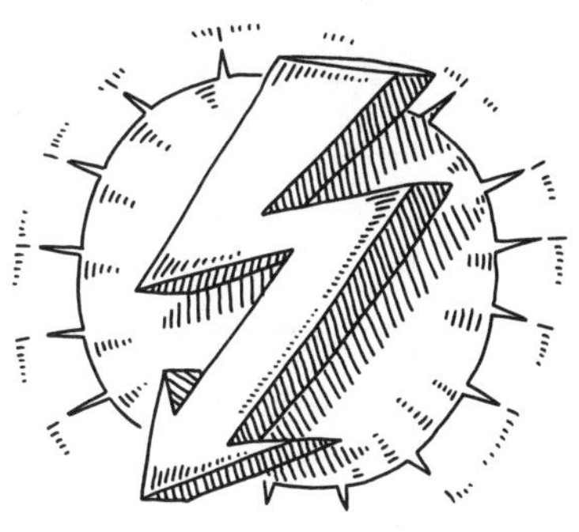

13
NINA

NINA WAS STILL THINKING ABOUT Norma's advice an hour later, when, for the second week in a row, she was on her way to work without Russ by her side. Aliens passed all around her, headed to their own places of business. Others, dressed more casually, carried shopping bags, likely returning from Alphane's commercial megatowers. SAS units marched through the crowds, keeping peace and regulating immigration in the busy galactic hub. Despite the loud and frenetic environment, Nina felt like she was only half there. Though they'd always had a contentious relationship, Nina was happy to see Atara waiting for her at the loading ramp of Bah'ren's newish ship.

"Still no luck lifting Russ's suspension," Atara said. "Bah'ren is dug in about it and she rarely backs down." Atara sighed. "It was so nice having another human around."

"Uhmm—"

"And if I'm being totally honest, a part of me feels really indebted to him for what he did on the *Flashaway*. He charged straight into the jaws of death—just to save me?" Atara laughed at Nina's offended expression. "And you were there too," she added.

"He'll be back in ten cycles. In the meantime, try this," Nina handed Atara her copy of *One Night with Consequences: An Innocent, a Seduction, a Secret.*

Atara recoiled. "I haven't read a book in—I don't know how long." Then she snatched it out of Nina's hand. "Why not? We're doing a fumigation today. It can't be more boring than that."

"I don't get it," Atara said, looking up from the romance novel. "Why doesn't she think she can effectively decorate his mansion? And why does she keep turning down a ride in his helicopter?"

"I haven't read it yet," Nina said.

Atara and Nina were in the subbasement of the *Aldersochi*, in a small, hard-plastic alcove separated from the main ship by a thick graphene door. Atara had slid one of the plates of plastic away to form a three-foot-wide bomb bay door. With the plastic plate moved, nothing separated them from the fields of crops rushing by fifty feet below.

"I don't think men really act like they do in this book," Atara said absently.

Nina kneeled on the floor; her hands splayed on the plastic. She watched the world stream by. The fields were sown with an alien crop, fat, bulbous fruit growing at the end of tall stalks of green. Even from their lofty position, Nina could see clouds of ugly, scary insects clustered around the circular center of the fruit.

She handed Atara a can of C09. Both women lowered their rebreathers onto their faces. Atara dog-eared her page then popped the cap on the C09. "Bombs away!" she said as she dropped the can through the opening. They watched it spin end over end before it landed in a cloud of gas. Atara raised her rebreather again. "Die, bug bastards," she called through the hole in the floor.

"We're going to do one more drop on the vertex," Bah'ren said via the comm.

"Everything okay?" Atara asked Nina. "You seem sad. More than usual."

"I'm fine."

"Talking about your problems makes them easier to process."

"I've heard that before."

"I'm a terrible listener," Atara said. "Which means I won't judge you or even remember what you said."

Nina laughed. "Actually, maybe you can help me. If someone dies in the Darkzone, what happens to their body? Does it get autopsied? Does anyone investigate?"

Atara blinked twice. "Without context, that's a terrifying question."

"Remember Jaq'li? We rescued her on the *Flashaway*?"

"The little Gnurian?"

Nina nodded, "She died. Out in the Darkzone. It must have been just a handful of hours after calling me for help during our mission on Xodli."

"Approaching vertex," Bah'ren said.

Both women lowered their rebreathers. "I'm sorry to hear that." Atara popped another can and dropped it through the open hatch. She seemed to be deep in thought. "To answer your question, nothing happens. There is no law in the Darkzone. If a decent person found the body they might notify her next of kin, but there's no investigation. Who would do it?"

"Me, I guess."

Atara watched the fields down below. "The old SOL Pest Control crew sure has been having a tough time lately," she added.

"What do you mean?" Nina asked.

"Lenus and P. T. Kling die on the *Flashaway*. Their robot workforce pilot program gets put on 'hiatus,' and a week later the entire IP crumbles under the extremely bad publicity. Remember that TEN-awtch we saved from the *Flashaway*'s Medbay? His name was Stormside. He died a couple weeks ago."

"How?"

"He'd been working a job with an industrial mining conglomerate. He fell into a Geo-therm pipe casing and it shredded him."

"The MUPmap is reporting that we got all the critters," Bah'ren said through the comms. "Starland, take us through one more pass while we verify."

"That's going to take an hour," Atara grumbled. "So boring . . ." She turned back to the book.

Quite a run of bad luck for SOL Pest Control, Nina thought to herself. She leaned out the opening in the floor and pulled closed the bomb bay doors. The *Aldersochi* banked left, and acres of green and yellow crops zipped by.

Nina tapped away at her transponder. She was going to text Russ but changed her mind. "Do you know anyone else from SOL Pest Control?" she asked Atara. "We saved ten of them, total. Did you happen to know any of the others' names?"

Atara shook her head. Into the comms she said, "Starland, what's the name of the guy we saved on the *Flashaway*? The one you did CERT training with? The Quen-to-tal?"

Starland's comm opened and they were hit with the discordant sounds of multiple babies crying. "Rendell Ploom," Starland said. She sounded exhausted. "Why? Also, he's dead." Without waiting for an answer to her question, she switched off the comm and the chorus of babies cut out.

"That's a lot of coincidences," Atara said.

Nina punched the search string, "Rendell Ploom, SOL Pest Control, Obituary" into the small screen on her wrist. She studied the results. "Aneurysm in his sleep," Nina told Atara. "Due to a previously undiscovered heart condition."

"Huh," Atara said, scratching at her chin thoughtfully.

"Is there a database somewhere that would have a log of the entire crew?"

"The MERC board would have it, but you have to be an admin to request that kind of information. You could ask Bah'ren . . ."

"It took Bah'ren five days just to get me Jaq'li's address. Would there be a record onboard the *Flashaway*? From the brief time SOL Pest Control owned the ship?"

"Nope. Although if any of them used the Virtual Training Room, it would have duplicated their biological information in order to run the simulations. That information is stored in a cloud database under Bah'ren's account, so we could probably access it from the VTR here on the *Aldersochi*."

"Can you show me how?"

Atara nodded. She rose to her feet and the two women climbed the hatch to the basement corridor of the ship.

"We're going to have to wait to use the room, though," Atara said while they walked. "Kendren has it reserved for personal time until four."

"What's he doing in there?"

"No idea, but I can guess. Kendren has been working out nonstop since his first small brush with fame. Whenever he's not in the gym, he's in the VTR recording himself practicing different facial expressions. I'd think it was cute if he'd actually helped on the *Flashaway* instead of hiding on the rental ship like a coward."

"Is coward the right word? Hiding isn't entirely unromantic."

"C'mon."

"I mean it," Nina said. "It implies that you care about something enough to stay alive for it."

Atara handed the romance novel back to Nina.

"Scans came back. We missed a batch!" Bah'ren's voice barked over the comm, jarring both women. "Everybody return to your positions."

"Seriously!" Atara said into the comm. "We are never going to leave this shitty farm planet. I got this," she told Nina, reversing course and heading back toward the subbasement. "Kendren, the romantic coward, can show you how to search the *Flashaway*'s VTR records. If any more SOL Pest Control are dead, we should probably stop considering it a coincidence."

When Nina reached the VTR, the observation windows were closed tight. The lights around the door glowed red indicating the training room was still in use.

Waiting outside, she was overcome with curiosity. She slid the observation window open a crack and peered inside.

Kendren was in a coastal simulation, sitting on a long dock, hanging his legs over the end. The bottoms of his feet dangled just a few inches above the churning ocean water. Far above his head, dark gray clouds hung in the sky. A light rain drizzled onto his hair and the back of his neck, but he didn't seem to notice it.

Nina watched him silently, struck by the realization that she'd found someone just as sad as she was. Kendren never looked up to see her watching. He had his elbows propped on his knees and his head buried in his hands.

14
RUSS

RUSS TRIED TO READ *The Sheikh's Pregnant Princess*, but it couldn't hold his attention. It was pretty obvious that the charming man Lauren had met in New York was not dead after all but was, in fact, the fabulously wealthy sheikh of Behraat.

I need to find a job, he thought as he put aside the book and rolled over on the motel room bed. Even though it was the middle of the day, his grandfather snored lightly in the bed on the other side of the room.

Russ could see Applebum moving around in the bathroom. Russ rose from the bed and padded over to the bathroom door. Applebum was standing in front of the mirror staring at himself. *Slightly unnerving*, Russ thought. When Applebum noticed him watching, he frowned, swiveled in a semicircle, and yanked the bathroom door shut. *No less unnerving*, Russ decided.

Russ wandered outside and called Lanie. When she answered, he could hear the sounds of an industrial blade whirring in the background and the fizzle-crackle of sparks.

"Russ! Is it something quick? We're in the middle of a job," Lanie shouted over the noise.

"This suspension sucks."

"Feeling restless?"

"Always. Got any more per diem work?"

"Gimmie an hour," Lanie said. "I'll see what I can come up with."

"You need me there today, maybe?"

"Sure. But can you—" In the background, the sound of heavy metals compacting together obscured Lanie's voice.

"Say that again. Lanie? You okay?"

"—come by in an hour. I'll have something for you."

Russ terminated the call, feeling relieved to have somewhere to go. He went back into the motel room and pulled on his shoes. Clark was suddenly standing behind him, fully dressed.

"There you are," Clark said. "I'm glad you're getting dressed. It's time to go see the man about the thing."

"Huh? What man?" Russ asked. "How long is it going to take?"

"We'll be quick."

Thirty minutes later, they were seeing a woman instead, a nearly naked Luzarian gyrating on a small stage in the back of a dingy bar. She had on a G-string and three diaphanous capes draped over her shoulders. Each cape was fully transparent, but through a trick of the light, or perhaps the unique nature of the cloth, the capes became cloudy whenever they overlapped. She was performing a masterful tease, looping each cape in rotating patterns to keep her nipples just out of view. Heavy bass thumped, shaking the stage under her feet. Behind her, neon lights flashed a credit icon across threadbare drapes whenever someone dropped her a digital donation. Each donation made her twirl her capes with more enthusiasm and less chastity.

"How long do you think this is going to take?" Russ asked Clark. "I've got to be at work in half an hour."

Up to that point, it had been a quick trip. The Waypoint at the Riverview Motel had transported them directly to Romcube Pleasure Satellite #1138 in the Loopanga Cluster.

They'd landed in a small, unmanned hub, then stumbled out onto the dirty, unkempt streets inside the manufactured structure. A thousand yards above, Russ could see the translucent roof of the cube shielding the five-square-mile complex from the black, starlit galaxy beyond.

Russ had been on edge even before they reached the club. The satellite was in complete disrepair. Many of what Russ would call the legitimate businesses—food stations, ship repair docks, clothing retail—were shuttered up, permanently closed for business. Their failed storefronts were empty, smeared with dirt and graffiti and awash in the neon afterglow of the signs from the neighboring businesses, all of which seemed to offer either massages, discount weapons, or off-brand pharmaceuticals.

"These cubes used to be a travel stop for folks on long journeys via the Dexadrive lanes," Clark explained as they walked. "Families taking trips and truckers transporting goods would dock here for a souvenir, a shower, whatever they needed. As I understand it, the Romcube brand was flourishing across the galaxies, kind of a hybrid rest stop and truck stop. But when Waypoints became the primary avenue for transportation, most folks stopped using the Dexadrive lanes and the Romcube brand fell on hard times." Clark paused to let three Gnurian youths pass by. All three were laughing; one was shaking a can of spray paint. "Since then, a different element has moved in."

They had only made it two blocks before Clark pulled them through the door marked "NeNe's Nearly Nude Review." It was sparsely populated, with only a handful of depressed-looking males alone at the other tables and on stools at the bar. Clark had led Russ to open seats in front of the stage.

"Why are we here?" Russ asked.

"That should be obvious," Clark said, not taking his eyes off the beckoning Luzarian. "I'm not going to miss a chance to see barely dressed beautiful women." Clark grinned. The Luzarian was bent at the waist, rotating her G-stringed booty in short ellipses around Clark's face.

"Grandpop, why won't you tell Grandma that you're alive?"

Clark glared at his grandson, the dancer's backside no more than six inches from the tip of his nose. "Do you feel like it's the appropriate time to talk about that?" Refocusing on the dancer, he raised a hand high to spank her but one of the bouncers yelled, "No touching!"

Russ exhaled deeply. He tapped at his transponder.

Russ: *It's worse than we thought it would be*

Nina: *where are you*

Russ: *(o)(o)*

Nina: *i hope thats an eyeball emoji*

Clark sat back in his seat and studied the drink menu.

"You two were married for over fifty years. You raised a family together, ran a business."

"My daughter birthed you and raised you, by herself," Clark said. "When was the last time you saw her? Or called?"

"Mom doesn't think I'm dead," Russ pointed out.

"I would be dead," Clark reminded Russ. "I was really dying. I made it into a CRC machine just a handful of days before my old ticker would have given out completely. I wasn't getting enough blood to my brain. I was hallucinating, every day. When I did stumble through a Waypoint, I wasn't sure it was all really happening. Half of me was convinced I was dreaming, or in heaven. But here I am. You don't just walk away from a second chance like that."

Russ shook his head disapprovingly. "Second chance for what? Romcube strip clubs? This place sucks." It wasn't helping his mood that whenever he raised his feet, the bottoms of his shoes briefly stuck to the stone floor.

"Do you know that CRC machines have a limit for how long they can fight off old age?" Clark said, suddenly.

"I guess they must, right? Otherwise, people would be immortal."

"But why?" Clark asked. "They can cure all manner of illness on the cellular level. Why wouldn't that extend to repairing all age-related damage?"

Russ shrugged. He didn't really think about that kind of stuff. All he knew was that if he could get access to a CRC machine, he'd climb in with his wrist broken and when he climbed out again, it would be as good as new.

"For as long as I've been in space, I've heard whispers that a UAIB shadow government keeps consumer CRC technology from reaching its full capacity because they don't want age-reversal technology to exist. It would be too disruptive. But other cultures—outside of UAIB space—don't have the same restrictions." Clark dropped his voice to a low hum so that Russ could barely hear him over the pounding dance music. "When you get to be as old as me, the idea of eternal life gets more and more appealing."

The song finished and the dancer sat heavily on the stage. She buttoned her diaphanous cloaks at the neck and checked the buckles on her five-inch heels.

A moment later, two other dancers, a curvy alien species that Russ had never seen before and a female TEN-awtch in a very risqué dress, approached their table.

"Our private escorts have finally arrived," Clark said happily.

"I'm not doing anything that involves champagne rooms," Russ told Clark as the TEN-awtch lifted his hand to her mouth and lightly kissed the tops of his knuckles.

She pulled him to his feet. "You won't be disappointed," she promised.

Clark must have seen the expression on Russ's face because he said, "Play along for just a few more minutes."

A new dancer took the stage, eliciting a spatter of cheers from the sparse crowd. Russ and Clark followed their girls through a different exit on the south wall of the club.

They walked down a hallway and passed another set of bouncers. This pair looked more professional than the ones in the main portion of the club. Where the others wore tracksuits, these had on pleated slacks and thin, bulletproof vests.

The escorts brought them to the door where the bouncers stood and the TEN-awtch dancer dropped Russ's hand. She turned back toward the main portion of the club without a word. The other dancer ducked slightly to kiss Clark on the cheek. "Nice to see you again Clarkie," she said. Then she followed her partner.

"Clarkie," Russ said.

The bouncers moved to let Clark and Russ through the new door. The room on the other side was large and full of machinist equipment. A handful of transponders in various states of modification and repair were scattered across a table. Several were attached to ad hoc machines, blinking with lights. In the corner was a bedraggled Waypoint. It had an Obinz stone cradle at the top but no stone inside. Several stones of different colors sat in a ring around the Waypoint's base. They were attached to the cradle by spiraling gray wires. A series of SAS unit bodies lined a far wall mid-deconstruction and reconstruction. Russ approached a tall black-steel cage, its door hanging open like a tongue. He ran his fingers along the bars, curious. They were ice cold to the touch. "Nina would love to see this place," he whispered to himself.

An alien sitting at a table in the center of the room smiled at them, warmly. He rose and crossed the room. "Show me your ears. Show 'em!" The alien said, ruffling Clark's hair. He was another species Russ had never seen before. He was thin, so thin his dirty T-shirt hung from his arm bones like a bathrobe. His head was oblong, ending in a protruding jaw that was almost canine. From the top of his head, thin feathers twisted in Art Garfunkel–style ringlets. Russ realized he was likely mixed race, the product of an elaborate process that could facilitate cross-species fertilization.

Clark pulled wisps of gray hair away from the top of his ears. The alien ran his fingers across Clark's ear, checking for a transformer.

"It really is you, you old sonofabitch."

"How you doing, Algadon?" Clark asked. He seemed more wary than jovial.

"Better than you are," Algadon said. "There's a bounty on your head. A big one. And I hear you've been looking for something that you can't seem to find. Why not ask your old friend Algadon for what you need?"

"You don't have it," Clark said.

"You won't know until you ask."

Russ pulled the two silver cubes from his pocket. "My grandpop said you would know what to do with these."

Algadon looked at the cubes. He took them from Russ and turned each over in his hand. Then he took an ultraviolet light from his workbench and shined it on one of the cubes. A series of glowing letters appeared. They spelled *Waymore Industries.*

"Where'd you get this?" Algadon asked.

"I found that one on the floor of a corporate office."

"Well, somebody is going to get fired. This is a Thufflin Box. It's used to transport information that is too sensitive to be stored in the cloud." Algadon shined the light on the second box. He spun it between his finger and thumb, revealing the writing: *Waymore Industries.*

"Are they the same thing? Duplicates?"

"Absolutely not. Each is one of a kind, holding its own unique secrets. They just came from the same place. Which also happens to be one of the biggest corporations in the universe."

"Dangerous," Clark added. "Can you open them safely?"

"Please," Algadon chided him. "Who are you talking to here?"

"A guy who works in the back room of a strip club," Clark said.

"I'll have the first one open in a hundred and twenty seconds," Algadon promised. "Or less." He hefted a heavy alien contraption onto his workbench. He opened two drawers before he found a series of electrode cables.

He wired them to the contraption then clamped their other end on either side of the Thufflin Box. Alien symbols began to appear on the contraption. Russ expected his nanotranspods to translate them, but the strange shapes never shifted into anything recognizable. The machine chugged away, and more and more alien symbols appeared.

Russ still had one hand on the bars of the cage. The metal was so cold his fingers were starting to go numb. "What's this thing for?" he asked Algadon as they waited.

"That little beauty is made of the densest metal blend in the universe. Something called Fromantium."

"Fromantium? Really?" Clark seemed genuinely surprised. He approached the metal and ran his fingers across it. "I've heard about this stuff. It's a whole new compound. How'd you get your hands on it?"

Algadon shook his head. "You're not the only one who gets to keep secrets."

"You can't turn on a single broadcast for more than five minutes without hearing about the possibilities of Fromantium," Clark told Russ. "It's supposed to open a new chapter of UAIB progress through the stars."

"They call that blend Triple-10K because it can survive heat up to ten thousand degrees, cold down to minus ten thousand, and impact up to ten thousand megatons." Algadon hummed a quick commercial jingle: "Make your way with Triple-10K." He looked up from his work, suddenly excited. "It's manufactured by Waymore. Do you think one of these cylinders has information about how to make it? If so, our financial problems—whether we have them or not—are long over." He went back to tinkering with the box, adjusting knobs and studying the symbols.

"This guy seems all right," Russ whispered.

"He's recklessly confident. Partially because he's got skilled bouncers outside. And that." Clark pointed to a wall-mounted laser weapon system above the door. "And those," he indicated two more, one above the workstation and another by the Waypoint. "But never assume you're safe—anywhere, anytime."

"Got it open! And it's less amazing than I expected," Algadon said, unhappily. "All this box contains is a series of documents relating to a Providence Travel Solutions cruise liner named the *Marcy Hedron*. Looks like it's blueprints for the ship, design schematics, crew rotations, security details, the location and code for every emergency Waypoint onboard, and a travel schedule. These are corporate secrets, I guess, but just barely."

Russ texted Nina: *I probably owe you seventy-five cents. My cube just had blueprints for a cruise liner.*

Nina: *woot! what was on mine?*

Russ: *About to unlock it.*

Algadon had already placed the electrodes on the second cube. The heavy contraption on his desk began to populate, but instead of colorful kanji, the words were red, and Russ could read them. They said: *Unit compromised. Disconnect! Disconnect!*

"Oh shit," Algadon said, ripping off the electrodes. He put his hands on either side of the contraption and yanked it apart. The screen went black, and Russ realized he had removed its power source. He pointed to the second cube. "Take this away. Take this and go. Right now."

"We should do what he says," Clark said. Russ's grandfather had already covered half the room, making a beeline for the door.

"What's happening?" Russ said. Instinctively, he drew his NoxFire pistol from where he'd been carrying it in his belt.

The Thufflin Box began to glow yellow, a bright light emitting from one end. "It's boobytrapped. We have less than five minutes before it relays our location to . . . someone."

The second cube turned yellow as well, emitting its own bright light. "What the fuck did you bring to me?" Algadon swore.

An Obinz stone at the base of the dormant Waypoint glowed faintly, as if energy was transferring from the cylinders directly to it. Russ took a step in that direction and the entire Waypoint started to hum. "Yeah, it's time to go," he confirmed.

"What are you doing? Don't activate the Waypoint!" Algadon shouted. The Waypoint was powering up on its own, adding its sheen of blue light to the red glow of the Obinz stone and the parallel yellows from the cubes. "Take these and leave my club. Now! Follow your kin."

"I didn't activate anything," Russ swore. He looked back at the exit door and saw Clark was gone.

"Then we're already dead," Algadon said as the first of seven armed men came crashing through the crackling blue light.

15
RUSS

ALGADON DOVE FOR A SWITCH on the wall and heaved it upward with both hands. Russ only had time to dive behind the heavy cage before the wall-mounted weapons systems began to discharge their own condensed light, disassembling two of the intruders.

The wall-mounted weapons flashed again, and a third intruder fell, his body split in half by a high-energy blast. Russ raised the NoxFire, but he held it in front of himself like a shield. He didn't know who these newcomers were, and thus far the only thing they'd done aggressively was die. He trained the NoxFire on the last man to come through the Waypoint, a RreRriaNnian who appeared to be their leader. The RreRriaNnian was larger than the others, larger than Kendren even, close to eight feet tall. He had a long black beard streaked with gray. The hair on his head was equally thick and equally wild, sweeping behind him like a mane.

While the others bobbed and weaved away from the lethal energy blasts, the RreRriaNnian stood tall.

"Shoot! Shoot him!" Algadon implored Russ as he dove for his own weapon.

The RreRriaNnian's eyes met Russ's, and he pulled a blade from a sheath on his back. It was long and hooked, roughly four feet hilt to tip. As the huge, gray-bearded alien gripped the weapon, the blade began to glow with heat.

Russ pulled the trigger. A few inches before the blast reached the RreRriaNnian, it deflected off course, burning a hole in the wall.

"He's the one who stole the Thufflin! I just work here!" Algadon implored as the graybeard dove toward him. The giant cut him down with a single flick of his wrist. Algadon had his mouth open to scream, but the sound couldn't move up past the widening gap in his throat.

Russ heard the bouncers come blasting through the back door. It had taken them longer than Russ expected, but he could see why. They were carrying condensed graphene shields, which they now held high in front of them.

"Self-destruct initiated in twenty seconds," the weapons systems warned, the digital voice blasting in stereo from each location where the weapons were mounted. "If you are a nonviolent entity, the makers of this recording strongly suggest you leave the area."

Russ crouched lower behind the dense metal cage and pressed his forearms against his face as the system counted. It said, "Eight . . . seven . . . six . . ." and a deathly quiet filled the room.

In the silence, Russ could hear one of the bouncers say, "W-we don't have any beef with you. We'll be on our way."

"A little too late for that," a man growled, his voice a deep baritone. Russ knew it had to be the RreRriaNnian speaking. Russ held his position behind the cage. He also held his breath.

"We don't want trouble," the bouncer tried again.

The giant had three men standing behind him, the only ones who had avoided the first volley of fire. The men stayed behind the RreRriaNnian, but they bounced on the balls of their feet, like dogs begging to hunt. Finally, one of the bouncers dropped his shield and raced back toward the door.

"Can we get him, Mr. Verch?" one of the thugs asked the giant.

"Yes," the giant told them.

The bouncer was only a handful of steps from the door, but the pack of aliens came after him with maniacal glee. They leaped past Russ's cover, hooting and hollering.

The closest to the bouncer was a Klung. Stabilizing the NoxFire and his broken right wrist with his left hand, Russ shot the Klung through the back of the knee. He'd adjusted the NoxFire blast radius down to a pinpoint, so all he did was sever whatever the Klung had for a tendon. The alien's leg gave out as he landed his jump, and he rolled to a stop, moaning. The second pursuer, a Gnurian, had made a corner turn to see where the blast had come from when Russ shot him through the hand, severing two of his fingers. His weapon went skittering away, firing as it bounced. The third, a thin Lixil pivoted and tried to jump behind the pile of disassembled SAS units. Russ shot him through the ankle as he dove, his severed foot flapping free like a flag. Russ could hear him screaming in pain.

The first bouncer cleared the room and was gone.

Russ stood from behind his cover and leveled the gun once more on the gray-bearded giant called Verch. The man grinned back.

"He's wearing a shield belt," the second bouncer yelled. "We've got to deactivate it."

"How?" Russ asked.

"Don't know. It's some kind of prototype. The glowing red button on the center of the belt might—" He wasn't able to finish his sentence. Verch was on him mid-breath, his hooked blade flashing. It cut through the man's shield, leaving a trail of molten fire dripping down the bouncer's arm. The bouncer screamed in the face of his own burning flesh, then went silent again as Verch's blade sliced his head from his shoulders.

Russ held the gun level, but Verch returned his gaze without an ounce of fear.

"Would it matter if I said I wasn't looking for trouble either?" Russ asked.

Verch shook his head with slow menace. But then his eyes shifted to the Thufflin Boxes on the workshop table. "Two?" He grunted in surprise. He approached them both, curious. He tapped a pattern on the base of each, and the devices stopped glowing. For the first time, he looked something other than fully confident.

"You can have those," Russ offered.

"One of them already belongs to me," Verch said. "I was using it to find you. You are Russ Wesley? Correct?"

"Negative," Russ told him. "My name is Randy Orangebutton."

"You have critical information that I need." Verch reached into his pocket and removed a small projector. A six-inch image of Russ's own face populated in the room. "You've been difficult to find. Your entire UAIB profile was wiped then reset. Most Waypoints don't register when you use them, and your transponder seems to be scrambled. It's almost as if you're an invisible man. Are you Mafia? Ex-military? Some kind of systems hacker?"

"I'm in Trash Remediation," Russ said. "Per diem. Currently late for work. I don't think I'm as important as you think I am."

Verch nodded. "You're not. Not directly, anyway." Verch tapped the projector, and a number of other faces flashed in and out of existence. Russ saw Starland, Atara, Jaq'li and Kendren as well as a number of faces he just barely remembered, members of SOL Pest Control. His blood ran cold when Nina's face flitted by. Verch kept changing the image until it settled on Applebum. The picture was grainy, likely a crop from a video. Even though it was zoomed in, Russ recognized the time and place of the photo. It was from almost six months ago. Applebum had a puncture wound in his shoulder that he'd gotten fighting Triwin aboard the infected *Flashaway*. In the photo,

Applebum was crossing the galactic bridge between the *Flashaway* and the *Numbawalla* helping the surviving members of SOL Pest Control flee to safety. "This is what I need to find," Verch said, nodding to the image of Applebum.

"If you're looking for a Tech12 SAS unit, there are literally hundreds in every major Waypoint hub across Alliance space," Russ pointed out.

"I'm looking for this particular unit," Verch said. "I believe he is traveling with you. Do you want to tell me where to find him? Or do you prefer to be tortured first?"

"Neither?" Russ suggested, raising the NoxFire.

Verch crossed the room, languidly. Russ fired, but the blast ricocheted skyward. He fired again, aiming for the same spot, hoping the first blast created a weak point. The shield held and the blast went bouncing away. Verch was almost in arm's reach, the blade in his hand twirling. Russ realized this was probably it. The end. He could allow himself to be captured and tortured, or fight back and die, ungracefully, in the back room of a strip club where the women were only nearly nude.

At the last minute, he dove into the Fromantium cage and swung the door shut. With his free hand he slid the key from the lock and tucked it into his pants.

Verch approached the cage, smiling. "Did you miss what my blade did to the bouncer's shield?" he asked, confidently.

Russ didn't say anything. He just shrugged, same as his grandfather always did.

Verch gripped the hilt until the blade glowed like molten lava. Then he swung it in the direction of Russ's head.

When it contacted the metal, the flame went ice cold and the blade spun away, burying three inches deep in Algadon's worktable.

Verch touched the metal of the cage. "Make your way with Triple-10K," he hummed under his breath. He stopped to think a moment, then he retrieved his blade.

Russ holstered his gun. He began to type on his transponder.

The giant put both his hands on the metal again, seeming to test if he could bend it. Then he leaned forward. The cage was seven feet high but only five feet wide, so when he smiled, Russ could clearly see that his teeth had been filed down into fangs.

Russ kept typing away at his transponder. He said, "I'm guessing you can't fire a gun with your belt-shield. The forcefield would probably bounce the blast backward and kill you. That's why you use the heated blade. It's hot enough to melt the forcefield? But not quite strong enough to slice through this lovely cage."

"Now that you've trapped yourself, I can just get my men to blow off one of your legs. I don't need to be in there with you to perform a little bit of torture."

Russ nodded. "Maybe. But I don't miss very often. Maybe I get my gun back out and kill the first man who leaves cover."

"Maybe that happens too," Verch said, unconcerned with that possibility. Being a huge, dangerous villain hidden inside an impenetrable forcefield seemed to give him a lot of confidence.

"Either way, if you could just hold off on making any kind of decision for a moment longer?"

Russ went back to typing.

"In the last, precious, pain-free minutes of your life, you're doing what?"

"Sending a message. There's something I need to tell someone. Just in case I do die."

"Why don't you tell me where I can find the Tech12? And save us both a lot of unnecessary violence?" Verch said.

"You're going to kill me no matter what I tell you," Russ pointed out. "Same as how you've been hunting and killing all the other faces on that little projector of yours. You killed my friend Jaq'li."

"The little Gnurian with the bad attitude?" Verch nodded curtly. "I liked her though. She fought to the end. Hopefully your last moments will be less violent."

Behind the pile of SAS units, Russ could still hear the Lixil groaning from his partially severed ankle.

Verch spun his blade on his open palm. After each rotation, he'd snatch it out of the air and his grip on the hilt would cause the blade to surge with heat and glow more brightly.

Russ kept typing.

"I am a little curious," Verch admitted begrudgingly.

"Almost done . . ."

"Who are you writing?"

"Just a friend."

"I think what you're doing is stalling," Verch said.

Russ was stalling, just as Verch had correctly diagnosed. He was hoping the bouncer or his grandpop would burst back through the door with reinforcements. As each second ticked away, a miraculous rescue seemed less and less likely. He looked down at the message he had composed to Nina: *Man named Verch killed Jaq. Hunting Applebum. Coming for you next. Please be careful. If I die, I want you to know being your partner was the best thing—*

Russ stopped typing for a moment, suddenly not sure how to finish the sentence.

"You don't seem scared of your own death," Verch said. He walked over to where the Lixil was still groaning next to the SAS units. He picked the man up with just his right hand and tossed him back through the Waypoint. He did the same for the Klung and the Gnurian. Then he picked up Nina's Thufflin Box and stuffed it in his pocket. He lifted and studied the second one, curious.

"I'm not scared of anything. Not even you," Russ said.

"You aren't afraid of dying?"

"I guess not. Life's pretty tiring."

Verch studied Russ. He nodded, a begrudging sign that he believed Russ's words. Verch scooped up the Gnurian's gun. As he lifted it, one of the Gnurian's severed fingers dropped free, thudding against the floor. Verch moved toward Russ's cage. "Let's make this a little fairer," he said.

Russ watched him push the red button on his shield belt. The forcefield surged into sight then faded away. "You deactivated your shield?" Russ said.

"Don't need it to shoot off one of your legs," Verch grunted.

Russ cleared the NoxFire from his belt, but his wrist was still broken. All the adrenaline in the world wasn't going to compensate for the lack of stability in his aim.

Verch kicked hard against the cage, rocking it backward and making Russ's shaky aim worse. The blast burst harmlessly into the ceiling. As Russ tried to level the weapon for another shot, Verch snaked his curved blade through the bars and sliced the NoxFire clean in half. Russ nearly lost his own fingers. The severed parts of the NoxFire splattered to the ground and smoked in a puddle at his feet.

"Fuck," Russ said. He pressed against the back side of the cage, his eyes drifting to the door. No one was coming to save him.

Verch kicked the cage again. Russ tipped backward. He threw himself forward to keep the cage balanced.

Verch transferred the Southern Blurn's blaster from his left hand to his right. He raised the weapon and took careful aim between the bars of the cage. Russ's head was bowed from his efforts to stabilize the cage. When he looked up, he could see down the long, wicked barrel of the gun.

Then, from the small space between the two men, Russ heard a familiar *cough.*

Someone is coming to save me after all, Russ thought.

Verch seemed to recognize the sound as well, because his face went as white as a sheet.

16

STEVEN APPLEBUM

APPLEBUM'S TRIP TO PORNHUB.COM had not gone well. In fact, it had totally rewired his understanding of all human sexuality. Based on the novels he read, he had thought sex was about being vulnerable for a loved one, about sharing the most intimate act possible to signify the depth of your feelings. In video after video, he'd learned that humans had sex to dominate and humiliate each other. Sometimes in large groups.

Less than twenty-four hours after discovering the internet, Applebum realized that he hated Earthlings. Books had convinced him of human virtue, but seeing their actual behavior on the internet told a completely different story. For the first time since he'd arrived, he actively wanted to leave Earth.

One way or the other, he promised himself he would never, ever visit the internet again—just as soon as mrnoonan2011 on the Reddit board /rFuturology admitted that artificial intelligence could be leveraged to effectively enhance fantasy worlds in the metaverse. They'd been arguing back and forth about it all afternoon in the comments section. Mrnoonan2011 was adamant that even advanced AI lacked true artistic merit, and it would never be anything but a very complex set of soulless computations.

To convince him otherwise, Applebum tried facts, case studies, statistics, six different types of logical fallacies, and even veiled threats, but mrnoonan2011 would not pivot from his unsupported core argument.

Applebum felt angry and unsettled in a way that he had never experienced before. He closed the www program and struck his right hand against his open palm three times.

While he was trying to put Nina's transponder back in the drawer, his finger grazed her digital address book, opening it by accident. His eyes landed on Nina's recent search query: Jaq'li K'l'w'qi'. 31534571 West Bollvel Avenue. Apartment 390.11K. Star's Crescent Nebula, Y Alpha Vixen Cluster.

Jaq'li was the young woman who had been murdered, Applebum remembered. His eyes drifted to the stack of mystery novels in the corner of the room. Then he slowly rose to his feet. *AI are more than a complex set of soulless computations*, Applebum assured himself.

He had promised Clark he wouldn't leave Russ's side. He'd promised Russ he would not leave the hotel room. But every single one of his emotional databases were strained to the point of collapse. He was acting irrationally, he realized, and he had to create a whole new database to store that sensation. That realization created two more emotions, "fear" and "excitement." Each new stimulus caused his feelings to tangle together and overlap. Earth's internet had reconfigured his entire emotional spectrum, and now each category was irremediably daisy-chained to the others.

He looked again at the mystery novels on the desk near the window. Unlike how he currently felt, heroic detectives were a study in emotional repression and moral simplicity.

Glancing again at the screen of the transponder, he began to interface with the Waypoint's location systems, homing in on Star's Crescent Nebula.

Ten minutes later, he slipped out of the tiny Waypoint hub less than two miles from Jaq'li's apartment. He kept his distance from the twin SAS units posted on either side of the transportation clerk. The SAS units stared ahead blankly and a twinge of "pity" shot through Applebum's cerebral circuitry, followed by "fury" and "helplessness." He knew he couldn't do anything for them. They looked the same as he did, but there had been a flaw in Applebum's manufacturing, which had eventually unlocked his ability to read and learn. His manufacturer, Waymore Industries, had recognized he was imperfect but not the extent to which he was truly special.

Unwilling to waste such an expensive unit, they'd leased him to an immigration satellite—which was where Russ had found him and accidently set him free. Not only could he not help his SAS brothers, Applebum needed to steer clear of other units or they would attempt to reconnect him to the central UAIB cloud server that controlled all their decisions.

He moved out the door and into the street, then quickly ducked into an alley behind a large pile of empty cardboard boxes. An unhoused Gnurian was already there, spread out on the ground atop a box. When he saw Applebum, he rolled on his side and muttered, "Take our jobs . . . who made who? . . . you robot sonofabitch."

Noting the man's condition, Applebum filed the slight under "understandable," and "irritating."

He peered out at the adjoining street. It was mostly empty, just a few men in brown jackets delivering packages. There was no good reason for an SAS unit to be traveling the streets, and he was sure to run into more effective resistance if he kept moving around without a better plan. He understood that he needed a disguise.

Applebum spotted an alien approach alone from the south side of the street wrapped in a long green hooded trench coat. It was a Pios, the only UAIB species to have shrunk, both in population number and geographical influence since joining the collective. Applebum had read that this was because of their extreme tendency toward kindness and civility. They were tall creatures with narrow, pointy shoulders flanked by bones that protruded from their backs, usually in the shape of fanned blades or curved horns. Pios were distant ancestors to a dangerous race called the Liafen. It was considered part of Pios culture to keep their shoulder blade bones covered as an act of propriety and to distance themselves from their far more malevolent kin.

As he approached the Pios, Applebum hoped what he'd read about the civility was true.

"Have I done something wrong?" the man asked. "My immigration paperwork is all in order. I have it here." The Pios popped open a briefcase and began to dig inside.

"That's not necessary," Applebum said. "I just need your trench coat." He tried to sound as official and robotic as possible.

The Pios was taken aback. "Why? What use could you have for it?"

Applebum had no answer to this question. *What would hero detective Sam Spade do here? He'd take the jacket by force or trickery.* "I can promise I won't perform any acts of violence on your person in return for the cloak."

The Pios frowned. "Pardon me for assuming, but is this a robbery?"

"It's an exchange. You give me the item; I give you peace and injurylessness."

"This trench coat was a birthday gift from my mother-in-law," the Pios said before pausing. He smiled a genuine smile. His teeth were long, crisscrossed, and thin, echoing his general physique. "But I dislike my mother-in-law." He shrugged out of the coat and handed it to Applebum. "I have to say, this is odd behavior for an Alliance-controlled robot. Are you sure we shouldn't consider this a robbery?"

"Would it help if it was?"

"I believe it would help me explain the loss." The Pios was using his hands to cover his shoulder blade bones, which fanned out beautifully behind his head.

"Then, yes, I am robbing you."

"Excellent," the Pios said. "A fine robbery!"

"Yours are a commendable people," Applebum told him. "Far better than Earthlings. Where is your home planet?"

"I'd rather not say," the Pios admitted. He walked around Applebum and continued hastily down the street.

Applebum wrapped himself in the trench coat, cinching it shut and pulling the hood up to hide his metallic head. The cloak was long enough to reach all the way to his ankles, hiding everything except his shining chrome feet. "Excuse me," Applebum shouted just before the Pios reached the corner. "I don't suppose your mother-in-law gave you those boots as well?"

Jaq'li's apartment was two floors down in the subterranean basement section. The door was locked. The robot lifted one of his new boots and kicked the door hard. It came full off the frame, collapsing backward in a loud crash. Applebum looked over his shoulder at the other doors along the basement floor. No one showed up to investigate. It didn't seem like the kind of place where people went out of their way to look for trouble.

He stepped inside to near total darkness. The unsettled feelings he'd had all morning were being quickly replaced by the thrill of the investigation. "The closed-up room was almost hot," Applebum said tentatively. Then with more confidence he added, "It was underground, so no light filtered in through the absent windows. The living room was long and depressing, with sparse metal furniture and plastic lamps and a budget food printer instead of a kitchen. The whole kit and caboodle depressed the hell out of Steven Applebum."

He moved down the long living room to a small closet. Inside were only two civilian outfits. One was a nice sports coat and slacks. The other was a jersey with Jaq'li's last name *K'l'w'qi'* hand-stitched across the back. Hanging beside the jersey were three jumpsuits in the orange of Ecosystem Preservation, each badly damaged by tooth and claw. "Yes, depressed," Applebum continued, checking the pockets of the sports coat. He was delighted to find a matchbook inside one of them, but it was all white with no writing. "Depressed that this was all a young chickadee like Jaq'li could afford. That her last days had been spent alone in this desolate place."

He moved into the small bedroom. He found the light switch on the wall and flipped it. The bedroom was in total disarray. It had been turned upside down. The mattress was moved from the bed and shredded. Jaq'li's pillows were turned inside out, and clothes were strewn in every direction. Someone with great strength had even dismantled a portion of the paneling off her walls. A tingling sensation raced down the neural network in his spine.

He was so distracted scanning his eyes over the mess that it took him a second to realize he was no longer alone. A chill ran through the room, the temperature dropping noticeable degrees. Something was standing at the cusp of the entrance, its bulk barely fitting through the doorframe. The thing was dark, twisted, and moving toward him. Applebum squared his shoulders to meet it.

A shadowy reflection stared back at him, and he thought for a moment that he must be staring into a horrific, primeval mirror. The thing lunged forward, a hulking mix of silence and shadow. A split second later, Applebum found himself fighting for his very life.

17

RUSS

VERCH'S HAND DARTED TO HIS belt and the shield shimmied back into place just in time. A fraction of a second later, a wicked throwing knife appeared in midair and bounced off his throat.

Verch drew his own blade, swinging it cold. For a moment Russ thought he hadn't had time to heat the blade, but it never ignited. He moved in disciplined arcs, slicing the curved metal every few feet. He clearly knew his enemy was invisible and he was striking out in an organized pattern. As he carved his way to the Waypoint, Russ realized Verch wasn't attacking the room, after all. He was fleeing. He stopped just short of the teleportation device, glancing around, haphazardly. "Nurcia!" he shouted. "I know you're here. I can hear that damned cat."

"If you know where I am, why can't you find me?" a silky-smooth voice said.

"I don't want to hurt you," Verch growled.

"That's why you were swinging your cute little sword all over the place?"

"It's past time we talked," Verch insisted. "Let's kill the human and sit down a minute to figure things out."

In response, another throwing knife bounced off the center of his forehead. "Run back to my mother, little lapdog," Nurcia said.

Shockingly, Verch complied. He exhaled, hanging his powerful arms by his side. Then he stepped into the swirling quantic pattern and was gone. A moment later, Nurcia Fragnar blinked into view. She was wearing a business suit, the gray sling cinched tight across her chest. Her neon eyes flashed and her unbound purple hair fell in wavy strands across her shoulders.

Russ carefully deleted the second half of his text. He studied it a moment: *Man named Verch killed Jaq. Hunting Applebum. Coming for us next.* He hit send. "How long have you been following me?"

"I haven't. I was following the trace on a Thufflin Box. It contains information about important Waymore assets." Nurcia glanced at the transponder on her wrist, then back at the Waypoint. "According to my tracker, the Thufflin Box left with Verch." Nurcia stroked her chin thoughtfully. "Why would he have stolen it in the first place? And brought it here?"

"I don't know. I just met him."

"Aldos Verch is the director of security at Waymore Industries," Nurcia said. "He's my mother's right-hand man. Her best henchman. He's fiercely loyal."

"He's got the Thufflin Box. I watched him stick it in his pocket just before you arrived."

Nurcia looked around the room before her eyes settled again on Russ. "I'm missing something," Nurcia said, "and I think it has to do with you."

"Verch stood fearless against the weapons systems, against me, and against the bouncers. He did that to that guy," Russ nodded to where Algadon lay on the floor, his throat cut. "But he ran from you like a scared child. I think I'm the one who's missing something."

Nurcia held up her pointer finger. "The doctrine of forceful control," she said. She held up her ring finger. "Also, Verch and I have a complicated history." She held up her middle finger. "And you can't kill the boss's daughter. No matter how hot your long metal sword gets."

They stared at each other for a minute. A cough filled the silence.

"You want to finally show me what's inside that sling?" Russ asked.

"Do we know each other that well already?" She bent over Algadon's corpse, running her hand along the blood on his perforated midsection. "Looks like there's some food for you here, baby," she said.

"Uhm— For me?" Russ said.

Nurcia undid the top of the sling. As she pulled it open, Russ could see it was lined with knives. The direct middle of the sling was knife-free and stitched into a small baby carrier. The baby carrier held what appeared to be a tiny long-haired kitten, its legs dangling through four precision-cut holes.

Nurcia drew the kitten from the carrier, and it batted a paw playfully at her chin. It sat dutifully in her palm as she leaned over to set it on the ground. The kitten bounded to the puddle of gore that had formed beneath Algadon's shoulders and licked at the blood.

"Not too many men get to see inside my sling," Nurcia said, playfully. "Or meet my Coffin Cat. You *can* come out of the cage now."

The kitten stopped slurping for a moment. It coughed, spraying blood on the floor. Then it turned and hissed at Russ, its furry chin dripping. Then it sunk its teeth directly into Algadon's carotid artery.

"I feel like staying in here a tiny bit longer," Russ said. "I call it the doctrine of self-preservation."

"That doesn't seem like your style," Nurcia said.

A moment later, both cat and corpse disappeared.

"Nifty evolutionary trick, isn't it?" Nurcia circled the spot where the corpse and cat had been. "What better way to enjoy a meal free from danger than by turning yourself and your food a color on the spectrum so rare that it can't be perceived by any of the species in the UAIB charter?"

"That's how you become invisible? Does it hurt, when he bites?"

Nurcia showed him the pointer finger on her left hand. A single drop of her blood pooled between two tiny fang holes. Her finger was calloused from what appeared to be many punctures. "It hurts every single time."

Nurcia turned her palm upward. Russ watched bloody cat footprints prance across the distance between them. When the footprints reached Nurcia, her hand bobbed in the air slightly. The cat appeared again, and she offered it her slender, purple index finger. The cat sank its teeth into her skin and they both blinked out of sight. When she spoke next, her voice came from behind Russ. "Why do you keep showing up in my investigation?"

"Just lucky, maybe," Russ said. He was trying to track her movements, looking for any clue to where she was. The air was still. Distant bass from the dance floor rattled the door in a staccato rhythm, but Russ couldn't hear any other sound.

Nurcia faded back into sight right next to the cage. The kitten poked its head out from the sling and coughed again.

Russ managed to not jump. He side-eyed her.

"Eventually that luck is going to run out. If I gave you two pieces of advice, would you listen to them?"

"I'm bad at taking advice," he admitted. "But tell me anyway."

"The first is to get as far away from all this as possible. There are complex wheels in motion. Things you can't possibly know, that will lead directly to your death. A lot of people involved have died already. I read your history, what little of it there is. You were working with Kendren Ockanian when he rescued that team from SOL Pest Control so many months ago. Nine of the ten people he rescued have died in the past three weeks. Including the one on the Waymore mining ship where we first met."

Russ nodded, trying not to think about the fact that Nina, Bah'ren, and Starland would likely be next. "Verch is killing them. He just admitted as much."

Nurcia sauntered to the left side of the cage. She wore a fitted business skirt that seemed tailored specifically to accent her long, purple legs. Russ had to lean to the right to follow her movements.

Nurcia grabbed the cold bars and leaned in, just as Verch had done. Her lips drew back from her teeth. "Verch doesn't do anything on his own. My mother must have sent him on those gory little errands."

Russ blinked back at her. He almost said, *So your mom is trying to kill me*. Instead he asked, "Any idea why?"

"Not yet. I'm trying to figure it out, but I have a lot on my plate."

"What's the second piece of advice?"

"Get your wrist repaired. You don't want to face off against people like Aldos Verch if you're not one hundred percent. I feel a little responsible because—you know—I broke it. I have a community CRC machine in my apartment building. It's just for tenants, but I bet I could sneak you in. We can even go now if you'd like."

"Your second piece of advice contradicts your first," he said.

"I didn't say it wouldn't," Nurcia told him. She smiled and her neon eyes flashed with mischief. Her beauty was undeniable, and when she smiled, something in him shifted, a first layer of critical resolve melting away. It helped that for the first time since he'd met her, her expression seemed fully authentic.

You do need your wrist repaired, Russ reminded himself.

Nurcia waited patiently for him to accept her offer.

"I'm late for work," Russ said, finally.

The kitten hissed at Russ, then coughed again. Its fur was still wet with Algadon's blood.

Nurcia's beautiful smile curled downward into a frown. "I live above the Skylounge on Gorrillian Green, if you change your mind."

She scratched under the kitten's chin, then wrapped her fingers across its mouth. Both of them disappeared. A moment later, the Waypoint fizzled and died, and the room was quiet.

Russ realized he was alone in the Fromantium cage. "Grandpop?" He called into the empty room.

18
RUSS

CLARK HADN'T BEEN TOO HARD to find. He was sitting on his bed in room 22 of the Riverview Motel, dealing a hand of solitaire. Nina sat on the other bed, her legs pulled tightly against her chest.

"Things were getting a little too heated for my taste," was the only explanation Clark had given. "Did Algadon survive?"

"I'm sorry, Grandpop."

Russ's grandfather's face fell. "A confident man in a dangerous lifestyle rarely makes it to old age," he said by way of eulogy.

Russ had been so relieved to see his grandfather alive and safe it had taken him a moment to realize Applebum wasn't in his customary spot in the corner next to the reading light.

"Where's Applebum?" Russ asked. "There are some dangerous people looking for him. This is not the time for him to be running around."

"What dangerous people?" Nina asked. "I didn't fully understand your text."

Russ told them about his experience in the Fromantium cage.

"And this Verch character admitted to killing Jaq'li?" Nina clarified.

"He did. And as much as said I'd be next."

"It sounds like there are dangerous people looking for *us*," Nina said.

"Nine of the ten members of SOL Pest Control are already dead."

"Nine? Are you sure?"

"You know the woman who tried to knock your head off in the Darkzone? That's what she told me."

Clark swung his legs off the bed and began to methodically pack his suitcase.

"Where are you going?" Russ asked.

"I'm moving to a different room. You should completely disassemble the Waypoint every night. Not that there aren't others, scattered around." He zipped up his suitcase. "Don't even think about going back to Norma's," he warned Russ. "If they come for you while you're there, it will put her in danger. Ensine is fine. He has that hard-light transformer. He can hide like a sonofabitch. Norma wouldn't understand what was happening, and she wouldn't last a second." Clark snapped his fingers for emphasis. He raised the handle on his suitcase and scooted out the door.

"Your grandfather is a coward," Nina observed as the door swung shut behind him.

"The doctrine of self-preservation," Russ said.

"Utter selfishness will only get you so far," Nina said.

Russ patted his waistband where he kept the NoxFire, remembering it was melted in a puddle. "Do you think Bah'ren would notice if we borrowed a couple of weapons from the *Aldersochi*? Tonight?"

"Give me fifteen minutes," Nina said.

"I'll come with you."

"She won't let you near the ship," Nina said.

Russ's transponder shook with an incoming call, distracting him long enough for Nina to step through the Waypoint and disappear.

With Nina gone, a creeping sensation of dread tiptoed down his back. He had an odd sensation of being watched. When he stared at Applebum's empty reading corner, it only served to make him more nervous.

Before he answered the call he texted Nina: *Be quick. Be careful.*

Nina texted back: ┌(^o^)┘

"You know how per diem employment works, right?" Lanie said when he finally answered. "If I say show up in an hour, you show up. Do some work. We pay you. It's not complicated."

"I'm so sorry," Russ said. "There was this cube—two cubes actually—and a giant, and this invisible cat . . ."

"Russ?"

"Yeah."

"Can you come to work tomorrow?"

"You bet."

"You won't miss?"

"Nope."

Lanie hung up.

Thirty minutes later, Nina returned with two stunsticks and an RNO-Tech rifle. Russ was relieved to see her back in one piece.

"Bah'ren was still onboard. I think she's working late to avoid her babies. I told her about Verch. She promised to warn the others," Nina said.

"Did you suggest a day or two off for the Intergalactic Exterminators? It would give everyone a chance to lie low."

"I suggested that. She reminded me not to be late for my shift." Nina bugged her eyes at Russ. "Let's make sure we get this stuff back to the *Aldersochi* before she notices."

Russ touched the crafted steel of the curved barrel, appreciating Nina's choice of weapons. He propped the gun against the bedside table. Together they disassembled the Waypoint, unlinking each tube and lining them up in order of height, then rolling them against the wall.

"I hope we're not trapping Applebum on the other side of the universe," Russ said. "He's not supposed to leave the room. He picked a bad time to break that rule."

"Have you noticed how he's been changing? Maybe *growing up* is a better word?" Nina asked.

"I caught him staring at himself in the mirror this morning."

Nina looked worried. "The beginnings of self-actualization?" she suggested. "Emotionally, I think he's entering adolescence. Teenagers are capable of just about anything."

"Teenagers do crazy shit," Russ agreed.

Russ stowed the last bar of the Waypoint and ran his fingers through his hair. "I'm going to stay here tonight," he decided. "No sense exposing Norma to additional risk."

Nina glanced around the small, messy motel room. She sighed. "I don't want to put my parents in danger either. You want the left bed or the right?"

"Whichever," Russ said.

Russ climbed onto the bed on the right side of the room. Nina carefully placed one of the stunsticks under each bed, then lay down next to Russ. She rested her head on her open palm, her big brown eyes staring into his. Then she rolled onto her back. She put her hands on her hips and stretched out her legs, pointing her toes.

She must have noticed Russ's eyes drifting once again to Applebum's empty reading corner because she reached across the bed and touched Russ's shoulder. "It's funny that you never worry about yourself, but you twist in knots worrying about me, Applebum, your grandfather, literally everyone else."

"Why do you think I've spent so much of my life alone?" Russ chided her. "Caring about people is exhausting."

"If he doesn't come back on his own, we'll find him." She removed her hand, yawned, and said, "I hate sleeping in my work clothes."

"Did I take your bed?"

"You took the unused bed. Your grandfather's been sleeping in the other one."

"I can switch," Russ offered. "But I kind of get the feeling the sheets aren't that clean over there."

"We can flip for it in a minute," Nina said. "I don't mind sharing right now." She yawned again. "So tired though . . . tough couple weeks." Nina closed her eyes, and Russ thought she'd gone to sleep but as he started to extract himself from the bed, she said, "At work tomorrow, I'll keep watch over Bah'ren and Starland. I'd hate to think of anything happening to all those beautiful babies." She opened her eyes again, drumming her fingers lightly against the linens. "After that we need to talk to the last surviving member of SOL Pest Control. Whoever they are."

Nina rolled back onto her side and Russ watched her close her eyes again. "Neither of us should have to sleep on dirty sheets," she mumbled. She inched forward half a body length and her long, tanned forearm stretched across Russ's chest. Her fingers wrapped around his bicep. "Goodnight, Russ," she murmured. He could feel her breath against his ear. A moment later her breathing evened out.

"Goodnight, Nina," he whispered.

Russ stared up at the asbestos patterns on the ceiling. He tried to close his eyes. He knew he couldn't miss another day of work at Intergalactic Waste Management, and he needed rest. Instead, he watched the door, waiting for Aldos Verch to bust through. *The rifle is useful, but maybe the stunsticks have a chance of short-circuiting his shield belt,* Russ told himself.

His thoughts were interrupted by a distant sound. It came from outside, somewhere in the parking lot. It could have been the creak of a car door opening. It could have been a Coke, thumping to the bottom of a vending machine. It could have been nothing, the product of his overactive imagination. What it sounded most like was the familiar, worrisome *cough* of an alien cat.

Russ rose to his feet and peered out the window. The parking lot was empty. The forest of trees to the north, barely visible in the light of the Riverview Motel sign, danced in the breeze, but nothing else moved. Russ closed the blinds. He slid the desk in front of the door. Then he returned to bed, Nina's arm immediately snaking back to rest on his bicep.

He lay and listened in silence, interrupted only by Nina's slow breathing. It wasn't helping him relax to have her curly brown hair cascading over his shoulder, her arm draped across his chest, and her generous breasts pressed snuggly into his side.

It took him a very long time to get to sleep.

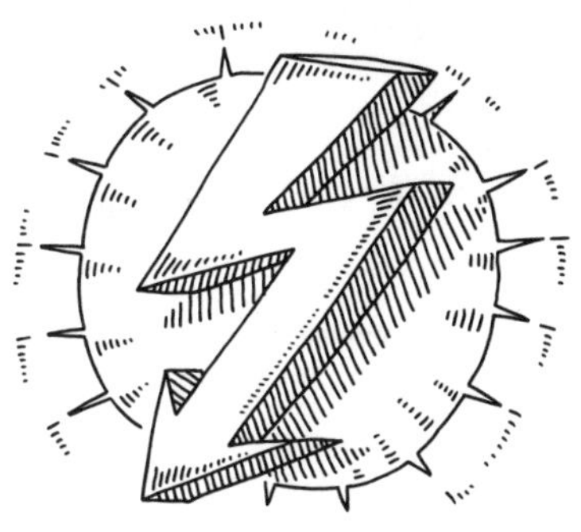

19
NINA

THE NEXT MORNING, NINA REGRETTED falling asleep. She had been tired, sure, but it was also an avoidance tactic. She hadn't thrown her arm across his chest just to tease him. She had wanted more, but something was instinctually holding her back. As she methodically put the Waypoint back together, she tried to sort through all her feelings about Russell Wesley.

Nina's dad had nearly died six months ago. Losing him slowly had been the most painful experience of her life. So much so that she still hadn't shed all the bad mojo.

Her emotional system was stuck powering itself with negative thoughts—Norma had described it as PTSD.

She could tell by the way Russ acted—by the way he made decisions—that he could die on any given day. Heck, he'd almost died the previous afternoon. A week before that in the Darkzone. And the week before that, hunting the Zypper, drunk, on Xodli. Now that she'd had a taste of what it was like to lose someone she loved, she was determined not to care deeply for a man who habitually put himself in grave danger.

Once the Waypoint was reassembled and powered up, she slipped into the bathroom to prepare for work. Through the bathroom doorway she could see that Russ had shimmied out of his T-shirt in his sleep. His arms and chest were bare; his shirt bunched around his neck. Dressed in her orange jumpsuit, but with the laces of her work boots untied and flapping, Nina found herself crossing the room to take a closer look at him. His chest was gorgeous. It wasn't the chest of a ridiculous Hollywood action hero, artificially puffed with protein powder and endless weight lifting. Instead, he looked like a real person, one who ate healthy food, spent time in the sun and the fresh air, and who moved his body for a living. He had a thin scruff of brown hair covering his abdominal muscles and his strong, athletic pectoral muscles. His shoulders were broad and his neck thick, his chin spotted with two days' worth of stubble—and his eyes were open and staring back at her.

When she met his gaze, he closed his eyes quickly. He stretched and rolled onto his side, turning his back toward her. But not before Nina caught the corner of his mouth twitch into a smile and his cheeks start to flush.

Without a word, she snapped on her transponder and disappeared through the Waypoint. If no one tried to kill her at work today, she still might end up dying from embarrassment.

"So, we're in danger of dying?" Atara asked as they armed themselves in the *Aldersochi*'s extensive weapons closet.

"Every day," Nina confirmed.

"No. I mean, Bah'ren said that you said that someone might be trying to kill us."

Nina tried to refocus. She had still been thinking of Russ's cheeky smile when she'd Waypointed out of the motel room before he "woke up."

"Nine of the ten crew members from SOL Pest Control are dead. Russ met the killer, a giant RreRriaNnian named Aldos Verch. He's probably coming for us next."

"Why?"

"We're still trying to figure that out."

"But no day off for us?" Atara said.

"The wheels of capitalism grind ever onward," Nina said.

Bah'ren came into the weapons closet, a pink and blue baby in her arms. "When do they get old enough to walk on their own? When? I demand to know," she said.

She put the baby on the ground, letting its feet touch first, but the little one's legs just folded under it and the baby sat on the cold graphene tile. Then it tipped slowly to the left until it was lying on its side, its face pressed against the floor, its eyes watching them far above. "Have some pride!" Bah'ren told it.

In response, the baby said, "Goo."

"Why are you both armed with guns?" Bah'ren asked Nina and Atara.

Nina was carrying the RNO-Tech rifle and the stunsticks she'd stolen the night before. She tried not to blush as she carefully put them back.

"Didn't you read the brief?"

Before her babies were born, Bah'ren had always briefed them in person, with videos, advice, and notes. These days, she just forwarded the mission parameters directly from the MERC board to their transponders.

"Of course we read it," Nina lied.

"Then you know we're relocating a massive fungus? How are the guns going to help with that?"

Grandveega Fungae, also called "the mold that ate the world," was big enough to deserve the name. It was in the middle of a dense swampland on the planet Fi9, clearly absorbing the swamp water into its porous skin. Its mass shimmered and grew with each droplet of liquid it came in contact with. In the absence of water, the mangrove-type trees around it were dropping yellow leaves, their roots exposed and brittle.

"How long has it been here?" Nina asked, breaking a thin dry branch from the nearest tree.

"Less than an hour," Atara said.

"Wowsers." By Nina's quick estimation, the fungae was thirty feet wide and three feet thick. Though classified as a mold, its skin felt unnervingly like flesh, aside from the Swiss cheese–like holes that pocked its surface. For a moment, Nina had been happy she didn't have to deal with any insects. But only for a moment. "Can't we cut it into more manageable pieces?" she asked into the comm.

Kendren was standing behind her. Nina lifted one of the edges while he crawled on hands and knees beneath. When she lowered the spongy corner onto his back, he stood up, bracing his open palms on the fungus's underside. A small wave of mucus membrane sloughed off the top and drenched both their heads.

Nina pinched her lips closed as mucus slid down her faceguard and rolled off the rounded filter on her rebreather.

"No," Bah'ren said through the comm. "Do not cut it. It reproduces via bidirectional regeneration. If you cut it in half, if you even break off a small piece, we'll have twice as many Grandveega to deal with."

Kendren took a step forward and the fungus split, tearing free a two-by-three-foot section. He raised his rebreather so his mouth was away from the comm microphone and said, "Shit." He heaved the broken piece atop the main portion and tried to squeeze them back together.

"If we move it, it just tears," Atara said from across the clearing. She held smaller chunks in each hand.

"I'm starting to get the impression none of you morons read the brief," Bah'ren grumbled through the comm.

As Nina watched, the two sections in Atara's hands began to flex and expand. Atara put them on top of the rest of the Grandveega and casually moved away.

"You've got to roll it, like a sleeping bag," Bah'ren said.

Starland appeared at the top of the onramp. She held a baby perched on each of her shoulders. Two more wrapped like koalas around each of her legs. "These four wanted to see the fungus," she called down to Atara, Nina, and Kendren. "Gosh, it's good to be outside, feeling the air on my skin again." Starland—and her offspring—were the only ones who didn't need a rebreather. Her smile was radiant. "I'll get the crane lift ready."

A mechanical hum filled the air as Starland rolled the crane lift to the front of the open hatch. The crane was on a two-girder frame with the hoist suspended between each girder. Three of the babies were now sitting on the bench seat next to Starland and the fourth was riding astraddle the hoist.

As the crane swung out over the Grandveega, the baby on the hoist cooed happily. Nina moved beneath, ready to catch it if it pitched off the end, but Starland was a master at manipulating machines. She glided the hoist smoothly over the large fungus. Then she tipped the crane sideways on purpose.

The baby fell through the air, struck the fungus, bounced twice, and erupted in happy giggles.

"This one is a born exterminator," Kendren said, lifting the baby off the mold and brushing the mucus membrane from its spotted yellow stomach.

Nina grabbed one side of the canvas tarp that hung from the end of the hoist and unfurled it to its full length. Kendren came to her side and helped her stretch the canvas the length of the Grandveega. Atara joined them. They kneeled together on one end of the huge fungus and began to carefully roll it onto the canvas, like they were storing an enormous and very fragile Persian rug. The crane lumbered overhead, its claw-like mouth open and waiting.

Once they had it packaged and stored, Nina took a seat on a crate in the cargo hold and watched the fungae pulsate in its canvas wrapping. Starland had left it attached to the crane hoist, and it hung suspended four feet off the ground.

The *Aldersochi* raised into the air high above Fi9, its Dexadrive engines whirred noisily, picking up speed.

Nina pulled the inventory console from the wall and lowered it onto her lap. The previous day, Kendren had showed her how to access the ship's intranet and scroll through the VTR records. She began to read everything she could about the health histories of SOL Pest Control. Only five of the members of the team had profiles uploaded, and the day before she'd managed to verify the deaths of three of them. After a few minutes of searching, she found the fate of the fourth. His death was listed as a "natural passing" from a previously undiscovered heart condition.

As she studied his health scans in the VTR profile, she noted no evidence of any latent biological weaknesses. *Guess it doesn't matter. Dead is dead. I just need to find something on number five*, she told herself. That profile was a Kyrillian named Josiv Drench. Intergalactic news archives didn't have any searchable information about his death. In fact, he was listed as an active crew member for a transportation security company called SavUQuik.

"Is Drench the last living member of SOL?" she asked the Grandveega.

The ship banked left and the Grandveega responded with a splash of mucus sluffing from its fleshy surface and spraying across the cargo floor.

"You prefer the company of the fungae?" Kendren asked, stepping into the cargo bay. He was so tall he almost had to duck the high, arched entry portals.

Nina smiled. "It's extremely interesting from a biological perspective. But, no, I was doing a little research on SOL Pest Control."

"The crew I heroically saved from the *Flashaway*?" Kendren said, grinning.

"Right . . ." Nina said. "You know anything about Josiv Drench? He's one of the people you saved." Nina tried to keep the sarcasm out of her tone.

"That guy's an asshole," Kendren said. "He sends me hate mail once a month like clockwork. Me. The guy who saved him. Sort of. If he's dead . . . that would be okay."

"Do you know anything about the company he's with? SavUQuik?"

Kendren smiled ruefully. "Makes sense he'd be there. Those guys are also all assholes. They're private. They used to run municipal contracts, but had their license revoked for constantly ignoring regulations—usually the ones that limited violence against UAIB species. You won't find Drench anywhere near here. SavUQuik works way out on the edge of the Darkzone."

Nina texted Russ: *josiv drench of savuquik. last member of sol. might be with you in the darkzone (⌐■_■)*

When she looked up from her transponder, Nina noticed Kendren was still standing in the doorway. He had already bathed and combed his hair. Sitting on a crate in her work coveralls, her curly hair crusted with membrane, she felt immediately self-conscious. Kendren, on the other hand, looked really handsome.

"I wanted to ask you something," he said. Kendren was usually bold to the point of indifference, so she was surprised at his tentative tone. "There's this stupid event coming up in a few cycles. It's a sports tournament for a game called Bootball. They're having municipal week, which is when travel tickets are half off if you're CERTified. Their way of showing appreciation for everything we do, or some shit like that. It's a pretty big production. They call it the party of the century but it happens, like, once per year. They close down the Waypoints and everybody has to ferry to the game on these huge, ridiculous party barges. It's been sold out for months, but I'm supposed to be a featured guest. They gave me two tickets, I guess because . . ."

". . . because you're famous now?" Nina said, teasing him.

"I am," Kendren said. "But only for a few moments. They will forget about me soon."

"It's still really neat to be featured at such a big event," Nina said.

"Right. Well, what I was wondering was, would you be willing to be my—my—uhh . . ."

Kendren trailed off. He was biting his lower lip, an unusually childlike expression for someone who was seven feet tall and close to three hundred pounds.

Nina's heart beat faster. It was the same sensation she'd ignored the night previous when she'd taken the chance and climbed into bed next to Russ. If she fell asleep to get out of it this time, she would have to topple off the crate and onto the hard metal floor.

Kendren started again, "What I was wondering was—"

"Who just made a Waypoint jump?" Starland's voice barked through the comms.

Kendren flinched at the sudden interruption.

Starland said, "Tell me one of my babies didn't just stumble through an intergalactic gate." Her voice took on even more urgency: "HUD says it wasn't an outgoing jump. It was incoming. Someone is on the ship with us."

"Bring us back down," Bah'ren's voice came over the comm. "Get us back to the surface. I don't want a stranger in my craft at twenty thousand feet. I'm remotely locking the weapons closet in two minutes. Arm yourselves and let's show this intruder why it's a bad idea to fu—"

"He's here!" Atara shouted into the comm. "In the engine room." Over her comm they heard a small explosion. "What in the hell is he—"

Nina's comm shut off. In fact, all their comms shut off. In the deathly quiet, it was easy to hear the first of the *Aldersochi*'s three Dexadrive engines sputter to a stop. Followed by the second. And then the third. And then Nina felt weightless, her body rising slowly into the air as the *Aldersochi* began its rapid, uncontrolled descent back to the surface of Fi9.

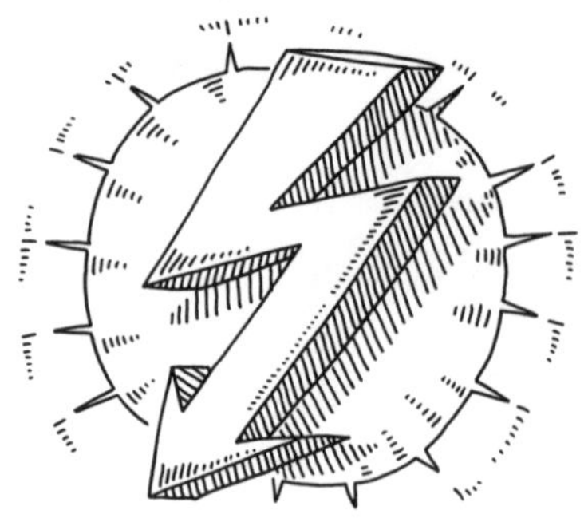

20
NINA

THE SHIP LURCHED, THEN STEADIED. "The emergency stabilizers have kicked in," Kendren said. "They will keep us afloat for ten, maybe fifteen minutes, then we're going to sink like a stone."

Nina could hear the wind whistling across the wings as the nose of the ship dipped downward. The emergency thrusters were firing, but they were made to stabilize the ship in zero-gravity space. They were no match for the full force of Fi9's gravity.

"Atara! Do you copy?" Kendren barked into his comm. There was no response.

The lights on Nina's transponder were out. Whoever hit the engines must have used something like an electromagnetic pulse. Nina hadn't yet learned what powered Dexadrives, but somebody knew, and they had the tech to shut them down.

"The Waypoint?" Nina asked Kendren.

He shook his head, and a new wave of fear washed over her. "The Neo-Brindle Pulse will have crippled it too."

"Do we have any EFlyers onboard?" she asked.

"No. We have two Stingers moored on the roof." The sounds of gunfire rang out on the other side of the door and down the corridor. "Get up there and see if they're functional," Kendren told Nina. "If the Pulse took those down as well . . . it's been a pleasure knowing you." He drew his weapon and tore down the hall.

Nina hesitated at the door. Then she grabbed a knife from the supply crate and sliced through the tether holding the Grandveega. The fungus thudded wetly against the ground and partially unrolled from the canvas. Nina dug her shoulder into it, slipping on the mucus but still managing to roll the fungus flat across the whole of the cargo bay. Using the knife, she began to slash at it like a lunatic.

Out in the hall, the sounds of combat grew louder. Nina yanked hard on the fire-control circuit. A pressurized metal drum on the ceiling tore apart as foam loaded inside forced its way free and covered the entire room with a blanket of greasy, fire-retardant froth. As it hit the fungus, it made a sizzling sound.

She dashed out of the cargo bay, headed for the weapons closet. From the corner of her eye she could see frenetic combat. Bah'ren was firing a six-piston STR Light Machine Gun. Even all the way down the hall, Nina heard the piston's whirring as the weapon poured high-velocity physical bullets from its twin barrels. Conscious of the danger of friendly fire, Nina dove around the corner and through the corridor leading to the weapons closet. She was relieved to find Bah'ren hadn't been able to lock it before the electrical systems went down. Inside, she found that none of the laser weapons were alight or functioning. Nina yanked her favorite combustion weapon off the wall, an American-made XM25 grenade launcher. She checked the load and ducked back into the hall.

The fight had made its way down the corridor. A giant of a man, with a flowing black-and-gray beard marched toward her. He held a flaming sword in his hand like the Archangel Gabriel. He was at least seven and a half feet tall, a wall of muscle and sinew. He wore the expression of a laborer, a man doing a job he neither liked nor disliked.

"Verch!" Nina called out.

Verch narrowed his eyes. His expression said, "How does this one know my name?" He was close enough Nina could feel the flame from his blade burning against her cheeks. She pointed her weapon past Verch and pulled the trigger, sending a 25mm grenade spinning behind them. The grenade was designed to explode in midair. When it did, the corridor shook and shrapnel pelted against Verch's back, but rather than knock him down, it bounced off like so many harmless pebbles.

Bah'ren turned the corner, swinging the stalk of her STR Light Machine Gun. The stalk smoked with fiery embers and melted metal. Nina realized the giant had cleaved it in half. When Bah'ren brought the stalk down on the giant's neck, the stalk bounced back with no effect. Kendren and Starland were right on her heels. Kendren was carrying Atara, unconscious, over his shoulders. He also had a fiercely wiggling baby draped over his left forearm. Starland had pulled a sorting cart from the cargo bay and had stuffed it full of four more babies. A fifth hung from her neck, its legs swinging like a pendulum with every hurried step she took.

Verch looked at the new arrivals and grunted. He marched past, leaving Nina untouched.

Bah'ren grabbed Nina's shoulders. "He's headed topside to cripple the Stingers," she cried. "We've got to find a way to get the babies to safety."

Nina realized the giant didn't need to kill them if a crash landing would do the trick. *And, it wouldn't raise any suspicion*, Nina realized. Same as all the other deaths. *Just another dead exterminator crew in an overused, underrepaired starship.*

She peeled to the left down a smaller repair access corridor. She hit the access ladder at top speed, huffing for breath. She scrambled up the rungs. There were maybe two hundred, but she didn't pause or dare look down. By the fiftieth rung, her arms were throbbing. A hundred more and she felt like they might rip clean off. With the last of her strength, she popped the repair hatch and pulled herself up onto the roof.

The atmosphere howled against the sides of the sinking ship. A pair of small emergency thrusters were mounted on the underside of the wing to her right. They chugged valiantly, but the moment she got her feet under her, one of them belched smoke and sputtered to a stop. The *Aldersochi* tilted a few feet to the left, sending her back to one knee.

On the far side of the roof, Nina could see the orange flame of the gray-bearded giant's sword as he climbed the ramp separating the roof from the main corridor. He was at least fifty feet away, and Nina now stood between him and the two Stingers. They moored on either side of a sweeping dorsal fin that extended half the length of the roof. Nina raced up the fin, gripping the metal handrails to keep herself steady. She climbed into the closest open-faced Stinger and pounded her fist on the power button. Nothing happened. She shook the control screen and threw every physical button she could find. The Stinger's battery was dead. Whatever a Neo-Brindle Pulse was, it was strong enough to reach this smaller craft.

Nina jumped out of the first Stinger, dancing straight across the metal handrails and hurtling herself into the second, tearing the knees off her orange jumpsuit as she landed. Verch was running now. He had impossible dexterity of movement, sprinting on the trembling roof of a ship actively falling through the sky. He was thirty feet away, then twenty, then fifteen. His mouth set open as he ran, and Nina could see his fang-like teeth.

She pounded her hand on the power switch. This Stinger lit up. "Battery is below 50 percent," it announced. "Entering power saving mode." Nina punched at the screen, trying to disengage the docking protocol. The screen locked, let out a long beep, then slowly rebooted. She glared at it, hating technology, willing its lowest-bidder processor to reload faster. In her periphery, she could see Verch growing closer and closer. And then he reached her.

Nina yanked the grenade launcher free from where she wore it across her back. Just ten feet to her left, Verch saw the weapon and skidded to a stop. He stood straight, a wicked smile gleaming between the bushy fibers of his thick beard. He seemed to be inviting her to fire directly into his chest.

Nina pivoted to the left and fired. The grenade *wumped* out of the barrel in a high arc, soaring well over the giant's right shoulder. It landed, unexploded, on the roof thirty feet away. Nina shook her head ruefully. Nothing was working like it was supposed to.

Both she and Verch watched as the grenade tumbled in short skips and hops to the end of the wing, pushed by inertia and pulled by gravity. When it finally reached the emergency thruster, the intake sucked it directly into the engine. Only then, finally, did it explode in a spectacular ball of flame.

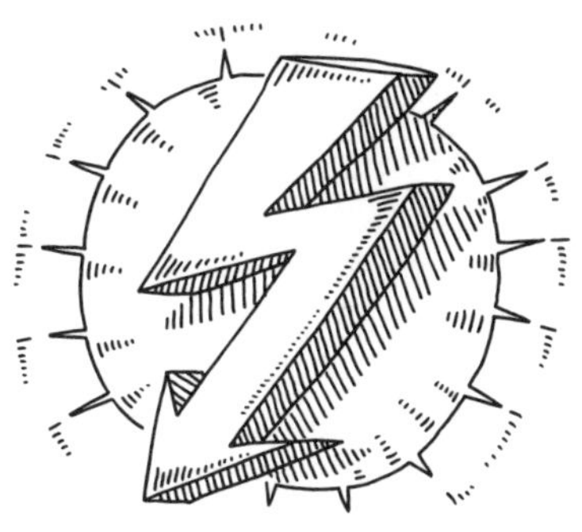

21
NINA

THE GRAY-BEARDED GIANT WAS THE first thing to go. When the last left-side emergency stabilizer blew, the ship pitched 180 degrees downward. The giant went sliding away, struggling to free a portable Waypoint wrapped around his waist as he skipped off the side and out into open air.

The remaining two emergency thrusters on the right wing went next. Under the increased burden of the entire ship, they threw up their hands and quit. The ship righted itself a moment, hanging suspended in the air, and then the nose pitched downward one last time. The *Aldersochi* barreled through the sky on its final, wild ride back to the surface of Fi9.

Still crouched in the Stinger, her hands clutching both sides of the control screen, Nina watched the ground below growing perilously closer. The greens and browns of the planet were blurry at first, but as they rapidly approached, she could make out a mountain and a thousand mangrove trees littered along the ridge of a twenty-mile bayou.

She was worried if she waited any longer, she would begin to see the mangrove branches, then leaves, but the ship was traveling at such velocity that she dared not let go of her grip or she'd be sucked overboard just like the giant.

Her curly hair was blowing everywhere, making it tough to see when the access ramp opened again and Starland walked out onto the roof. It seemed a wanton disregard for physics, as she picked her way carefully across the expanse. Starland moved laboriously, lifting one heavy foot at a time. Nina realized she was wearing gravity boots.

After she had tested the process, Starland gestured back where she'd come from and Bah'ren and Kendren followed wearing their own boots and carrying a still unconscious Atara and nearly half a dozen babies.

At the rate they were falling, Nina figured they had about eight minutes before they smeared across Fi9. She clutched the control panel, wishing the rest of the crew would move just a little bit faster.

When they finally arrived, Kendren scrambled into the Stinger and the others hoisted babies into every available space. Stingers were two-man recon vehicles. They had a convertible, open-topped design, with a long bench and a lock bar running the length of their center. Starland climbed into Kendren's lap, wrapping her legs around his waist and her arms around his chest. He carried Atara across his broad back. Nina was in the second seat helping Bah'ren stuff cooing babies all around her.

The screen on the Stinger was once again operable. In heavy red letters it flashed the message: *Critical Warning: Maximum weight exceeded. Critical Warning: Maximum weight exceeded. Battery critically low.*

Nina swiveled to her right as best she could in the crowded space and began to unlatch Kendren's gravity boots.

"Are you trying to kill me?" he shouted. His eyes were full of fear, but he couldn't do much while holding Atara in a fireman's carry and with Starland wrapped around his midsection.

Nina shook her head and put the boot on her own foot. It was at least five sizes too big.

The ground raced toward them at an alarming speed.

Bah'ren managed to fit the last baby between Nina's legs. She saw the message on the screen. "Go on! Get moving," Bah'ren said, resigned. "It won't take any additional weight. I'll get back inside and try to land safely."

"You won't," Nina said, buckling into Kendren's second boot. She vaulted out of the Stinger, making space for Bah'ren. "The kids need their other mother," she said. "If I'm alive when I reach the ground, I want my pay restored."

Bah'ren nodded, but her face was pale. She had trouble meeting Nina's eyes. "T-thank you," she said, her voice nearly lost in the sound and fury of their descent. She seemed to have already accepted that whoever was left behind would most certainly die.

Bah'ren took Nina's place in the driver's position and unmoored the Stinger. Nina was already making her way back inside the ship as the Stinger lifted free from its tethers. She turned, briefly, to watch it disengage. It seemed to fly away, but it simply held its altitude, while Nina and the *Aldersochi* dropped beneath.

I'm doing Russ stuff, Nina chastised herself. *This kind of shit is why I can't fall in love with Russ. And now I'm doing it.*

She had kicked off the gravity boots and dead sprinted down the main corridor when she spotted the small orange, yellow, and purple baby sitting happily on the ground outside the weapons closet. It was the one who had ridden the crane earlier in the day, the one with the spotted yellow stomach.

"Not going to judge," Nina muttered as she scooped the baby up and bolted through the door to the cargo bay.

The fungae waited for her inside, huge and pulsating. It had "eaten" every bite of the fire retardant, doubling, then tripling, in size. The pieces Nina had cut free were already expanding, pushing themselves against their mother, mucus membrane sloshed across the floor, carrying clusters of polyps up and over Nina's cotton socks.

The ship must have reached maximum velocity. She could hear the wind whistling loudly over the central fuselage.

With her nose pinched and her left arm cradling the baby, she dug a big scoop out of the side of the fungus. The outer layer felt like flesh, but the inside had the same density and general texture as sponge cake. She dug a bigger scoop, tearing away huge handfuls. Then she pushed her right fist through the middle. She followed it with the rest of her body. The fungus was at least seven feet thick now and growing bigger by the second. She took a last deep breath, said, "You're an idiot for thinking this would ever work," then wiggled her way deeper. The baby in her arms giggled, mucus dripping down its face.

When Nina reached two-thirds of the way to the center, the mold opened up, revealing a Nina-sized spongocoel in the center. She burrowed toward it, clawing through more spongy skin and slippery membrane. She waited there in the hollow center, cradling the baby to her chest and willing the Grandveega to grow even larger.

Her transformer booted back to life, and she realized the effects of the Pulse were fading. Figuring she had about ten seconds left to live, Nina found herself tapping out a quick text message to Russ: *thank you for saving my dad*

She erased that message and wrote: *u have been the best thing about my life since the day I met you <3*

She looked at the heart symbol, erased it as well, and started to write l-o-v-

And then the *Aldersochi* hit the ground.

The impact was deafening as the three-story ship pancaked into two stories, then one. In a shattering of pain, Nina felt her collarbone snap. The air filled with the sounds of metal and graphene debris raining down on Fi9 like demonic hail. What was left of the main engine exploded, setting off a chain reaction and blowing the second engine, then the third. There was a great groaning of metal, and the structure tipped forward and collapsed farther into itself. The cargo bay pitched almost vertical, which sent Nina sloshing forward down the fungae tunnel she had carved, the baby squeezing free from her arms.

She waited for death, for some huge chunk of burning slag to slice her into ribbons. But she might as well have been in utero of some giant, broken-winged bird.

The shifting subsided. She groped around blindly inside the sponge-like fungus, trying to feel for the baby. The fungus was still expanding, absorbing anything porous that it came in contact with. She was no longer worried about crashing, but now suffocation was a real possibility.

The screen on her transponder had smashed on impact but it rebooted once again; ambient light filling the small channel. Her message to Russ was gone.

In the new light, she realized that the baby was six inches in front of her, lying on its side. Its eyes fluttered open. "Goo," it said.

Nina brushed the mucus membrane from her own eyes. She was so relieved that tears were running down her cheeks, the fungus absorbing them as quickly as they appeared. "So much goo," she told the baby. Then she scooped it against her chest and began to carve her way back to the surface.

Nina felt a deep, throbbing sensation—like someone was stabbing her just below the neck—as Starland and Kendren grabbed her arms and pulled her free from the grip of the Grandveega. The pain was easier to manage as the others hooted and cheered her name, doing their best to clear the slime from her face. She realized the stress that had been hanging on her shoulders so long was gone. As they cheered, hugged and thanked her, she was filled with a rush of adrenaline stronger than anything she'd ever felt. *Is this why Russ does it?* she wondered. Kendren wrapped her in a strong hug, causing a spike of new pain from her collarbone, but she was grinning so broadly that she hardly noticed.

The baby with the yellow spots had a smashed nose. Nina held it close as they moved clear of the wreckage and sat side by side on the roots of a giant mangrove tree. Small rivers of yellow blood ran from the baby's nostrils and veered left across its upper lip. Nina dabbed at it with the sleeve of her jumpsuit, trying not to move more than she had to.

Bah'ren and Starland went down the line, checking the other babies for injuries. Atara was finally awake. She put her arm around Kendren's shoulders, and they watched the *Aldersochi* burn and collapse in on itself again and burn some more. The baby with the smashed nose sang a woeful dirge for the lost ship.

After checking the last child, Bah'ren called an exterminator friend at Kwiky Pest & Nuisance, taking careful steps into the six-inch deep turbid water of the bayou. "All we need," she explained patiently, "is a lift home, a few hours in the CRC machine for half the crew, and help disassembling what is quickly becoming an army of enormous, fiery Grandveega."

"We've got insurance, right?" Nina asked, looking out over the burning wreckage.

"They'll fight us for every penny," Starland said. "I believe the Intergalactic Exterminators are going to be out of business for a little while."

"It will be nice to have a paycheck, though," Nina said. "Eventually."

"So that was the guy who wants to kill us? Didn't seem that tough," Starland said.

"It would have been nice to have the day off," Atara said. "Maybe we would have avoided some of this." She munched on pain pills, her hand resting on her injured thigh.

"Any idea why he wants us dead?" Kendren asked Nina.

"Not entirely." Nina watched the flames from the ship climb toward the sky. "But it looks like I'm going to have more free time to find out."

Starland hugged Nina for a third time. "You kept my family together. I won't forget it," she said. Nina smiled as she felt the return of a kind of heroic euphoria permeating her brain. The sensation made her feel lighter than she had in weeks, maybe months. Energy tingled across every one of her nerve fibers.

Starland took the baby with the smashed nose and held it against her chest until it finally stopped singing its sad lamentations. Starland sighed, an unexpected look of peace descending onto her face.

Nina was shocked to realize that Starland was happy—and not just about having survived the attack. She looked closely at the other woman for the first time in a while. Starland had deep bags under her eyes, and her normally vibrant skin was a pale yellow. The scales on her head, which she wore trimmed tightly, were long, chipped in some places, and uncut in others. Her fingernails—a point of pride for the lizard-like TEN-awtch—were bitten down and broken.

Nina suddenly understood Starland's relief. She would no longer have to work a fifty-hour week and raise her six children at the same time.

"It's TEN-awtch custom not to name our children until life provides an appropriate inspiration," Starland said, thoughtfully. "I didn't have a name until the age of three when our family was visiting Torntula—a planet with almost no atmosphere—and I was nearly killed by a meteor fragment the size of a dinner plate." Starland studied the baby's broken nose. A broad smile crept across her tired face. "I think we will call this one Serendipity."

22
RUSS

"WHO'S THE NEW GUY?" a rough-looking Zanglorian asked, stabbing a thumb in Russ's direction.

"That's Russ Wesley," Lanie said. "He's per diem." Lanie stood beside Linnie in front of a small scrum of trash collectors. Linnie kept her arms folded across her thorax, barely speaking, while Lanie used a laser pointer to identify space trash on a holographic 3D map. "Routine cleanup day," she told the crew. "Sensors show the remains of a minor moon here," she tapped at the screen. "Providence wants any rock over one thousand feet in circumference cut up and hauled away. At that size, it's a danger to their cruise ships. However, we've been asked to use our judgment and leave some of the wreckage arranged"—Lanie blushed, reading from a direct quote—"as cinematically as possible."

"What a bunch of bullshit," a small man standing next to Russ said. He was no more than two feet tall and covered, head to toe, in coarse hair. Russ had caught a glimpse of him on his first day on the *Nightfire*.

Up close, he looked a little like someone had made a Muppet out of the leftover parts from all the other Muppets.

Russ nodded. "Total bullshit," he agreed, speaking only loud enough for the small, hairy man to hear.

"You're total bullshit!" the hairy man said, circling away from Russ to stand on the other side of the room.

"Ignore that," a Klung standing beside Russ told him. "That's RK. He's a Plutorach"—the Klung's face lit up with a realization—"from your solar system! They're notoriously ill-tempered."

"Real sorry about what we did to you guys back in '06!" he called after RK, sharply.

Lanie gave him a quizzical look, then returned her attention to the 3D map. "About a quarter of a parsec, down, we've got the main focus of today's cleanup. Part of an abandoned space station has drifted onto Providence's predetermined route. All that's left is the foundation, less than a hundred thousand square feet, but we've got to get rid of it. One team will use the *Lumina* to paint her up, and once the *Nightfire* cuts her into manageable pieces, the rest of you gearheads will help Linnie and me navigate the pieces into the compactor."

"Who gets to pilot the *Lumina*?" the Zanglorian asked.

Lanie nodded in Russ's direction. "I thought we'd let the new guy do it," she said.

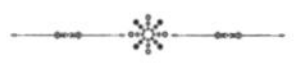

The engines fired and the small Lumina starship rotated in a quick circle.

"See the bar near your feet? The long red one?" the Klung strapped tightly into the cockpit next to Russ asked.

Russ glanced down at the bar. Emergency Use Only was written in bright red paint along its length. "The emergency one?"

"Yeah! Kick it! It'll release the ship's main gyroscope."

Russ yanked the driving yoke left and the ship did another three-hundred-and-sixty-degree rotation. And then another. A set of tools lifted off the control panel, paddling the ground with each rotation. On the third rotation, he kicked the Emergency Use Only bar and the ship tucked its shoulder and did a full cartwheel. The hair on Russ's head rose up at the same time as the goosebumps on his arms. A thousand feet in the distance, a huge slab of frozen, derelict space station went from eye level to far above their heads to way down below their feet. The stars and the sun moved with it. Russ's small craft tumbled with such velocity that he instinctively took his hands off the yoke to grip the straps of his chest harness. The tools spilled over the dash, scattering to a stop as the ship autonomously engaged its thrusters and finally regained its equilibrium.

"Awesome!" the Klung said at the same time as Russ said, "Pretty rad!"

The Klung was named Trellinanium ViV Klurppewpuu, or just Trell. He was hairless with light gray skin and long darker gray lines running in zigzag patterns everywhere his skin was visible, including his cheeks and forehead. Russ couldn't tell if the lines were species specific, if they were tattoos, or maybe battle scars. In contrast to his skin, his teeth and irises were gleaming white and his pupils glowed with a faint yellow intensity.

Trell jumped back into the pilot's seat and took the yoke. "Full rotations are easy, but an ass-over-elbows cartwheel? That takes some mastery. Good first day."

Russ gathered up the spilled tools, taking a moment to straighten his yellow jumpsuit and study the badge on the arm that read Intergalactic Waste Management, LLC. "Mastery of what?" Russ asked. He had been just ripping the yoke around like an angry baby.

"Of general chaos," Trell said, without further explanation. "Tell me again how you got the job without being CERTified for Trash Remediation." He had had trouble accepting that Russ was only allowed to drive. Especially because Trell's specialty was piloting, and Russ had never done it before.

"Lanie and Linnie are friends of mine. And I'm CERTed for pest control, so if we do run into an infestation—"

"In the vacuum of space?"

"Bugs can live off astral gases," Russ said.

"Astral gases," Trell repeated, chuckling.

"In the meantime, you're supposed to show me how to fly. I've piloted a few Stingers planetside on exterminator missions . . ."

"The physics are completely different," Trell said. "And it's not just about flying. The junk pilot has the most important job." He punched on his comm and said, "Trell and Russ ready to paint. Let us know when to start."

Linnie's voice came back over the comm. "We're delayed. Having a little trouble getting Fat Sister to spin. She keeps seizing up; her sensors are registering an organic on target location. Hold on the paint."

"Copy," Trell said into his comm.

Russ looked out the starscreen at the derelict trash floating in the distance. At one point, it had been the foundation of a large habitable structure, but it clearly hadn't been in operation for a while. Now, it was just twisted metal and slag. Its colors were faded and more than half of the structure—the part that was floating on the far side of this star cluster's sun—was encased in ice.

"Lemmie drive again," Russ said, and Trell gave him back the pilot seat. The other man had drawn a small tube from his pocket which Russ thought were pain pills. Trell raised the tube to his face and sucked on it. Russ realized it was a battery. "Klung really feed on electrical energy?"

Trell nodded. "Still hungry," he said, grinning. He put his hand on the dash of the small craft. For a moment the lights dimmed, and Russ heard a hissing sound. The lights came back to full power and Trell belched.

"That's fucking cool," Russ told Trell as he slid the craft's single, movable engine to the left side and hit the accelerator. He and Trell slid sideways through the void.

"Better to stay in the shade," Trell told him. "Battery drains faster over here on the sun side." He belched again. "And we want to save the battery for . . . lots of reasons."

"What happens if you absorb too much? Would you get fat?"

"Nothing like that. If we eat too much, it just diffuses out of our molecules as released energy. When we want to shame overeaters, we call them heat banks, or sometimes just hot tots."

The comm reactivated, and Linnie said, "Lanie confirmed Big Sister's automated failsafe is seizing up. We ran another scan and got a faint hit on a sentient species."

"Who would be camping out on that big pile of junk?" Trell asked. He gestured to Russ to draw the *Lumina* in closer to the derelict trash.

"Whoever it is, they're registering as 'other.' Meaning they're not part of the UAIB charter. Of course, that describes Russ, so it could be anything, even an Earthling. Disembark and run a hand-scanner on any structure with enough integrity to hold an organic."

"Copy that," Trell said.

"The organic could also be dangerous. You're authorized to call for security backup at your discretion. The Providence Travel Solution's cruise liner is right on our tail, so make it quick."

Russ gave the small *Lumina* starship more thrust as they rocketed toward the derelict structure. His transponder screen lit up with a message from Nina: *josiv drench of savuquik. last member of sol. might be with you in the darkzone* (⌐■_■)

"Do you know a security team called SavUQuik?" Russ asked Trell.

"We're not calling them," Trell said firmly. "I'd call SecureMore or even Hard-n-Fast-Shield-Guard before SavUQuik. Those guys are a bunch of assholes."

Russ looked at his transponder again. "Naw, let's try SavUQuik. Just to be safe," he said.

"Not for any other reason?" Trell asked.

"Just to be safe," Russ said again. They were nearing the derelict station. Russ searched the digital dashboard for the docking controls.

An odd expression passed across Trell's face. "What else do you know about the Klung?" he asked.

Russ turned and faced his copilot. "I know Klung keep mostly to themselves. Some even live the life of hermits—I kind of assumed it was because of the electricity thing."

"Klung self-isolate because we're fiercely empathetic. We draw emotions toward us in the same way we draw electricity. In fact, for Klung, emotions are just more electrical impulses diffusing out of the people nearby. In the company of one or two others, it can be a pleasant sensation, especially if those people are positive and kind. We literally eat their feelings. It's why I like working for Lanie and Linnie. They're sweethearts. In the company of a crowd, or even just a single jerk, we can get overrun with negative emotions and lose our shit." Trell scratched at his gray cheek. "The assholes in SavUQuik will give me a headache before they even open their mouths."

"Let's call them anyway," Russ said. "To be safe."

"Another part of being empathetic is we can tell when someone is hiding something. The energy is different."

Russ sat in the pilot's chair for a moment, considering this information. "That's a cool trick," he said.

"I can't tell why, but you're not being honest with me," Trell concluded.

Linnie spoke over the comm: "The cruise liner is almost here, so we're overriding Big Sister's safety controls. We're going to spin her up while you're still onboard. With the safety protocols off, this is going to be a little more dangerous than usual."

"How long do we have?" Trell asked.

"Twenty minutes," Lanie said. "Make sure you're ready to paint by then." The comm crackled, then fell silent.

Russ considered explaining the whole situation to Trell. Instead, he opted for a safer and faster approach. "What if I paid you a thousand credits to 'empathetically' go along with what I need to do?"

"There's a lot of good energy flowing outward from your thousand credits," Trell said.

Losing the money stressed Russ, but he pushed the credits to Trell's transponder. It was the entire day's per diem, the equivalent of five hundred Earth dollars. It seemed worth it if it would protect him and his friends from Aldos Verch.

"Your credits bought you twenty minutes. Come aboard. Don't come aboard. Call security. Do whatever it is you want to do; it just better not get me fired," Trell told him.

It took eight of the minutes for Russ to inflate the dock and for him and Trell to dress for the spacewalk. Onboard the derelict station, it was cold as a witch's teat.

Even on the sun side, even through the compression gear, the heavy-duty rebreather and thick magnetized boots, Russ was quickly losing feeling in his fingers and toes.

"L-let's call Transport Security now," he said through chattering teeth.

Trell punched a series of codes into his transponder. While he did, Russ picked his way through the twisted metal of the broken corridors. He ran the biologic hand-scanner on anything he came across. His magnetized boots clanged heavily against the metal structure, an odd contrast to the weightless sensation permeating the rest of his body. Conscious of time running short, his eyes searched the endless horizon of space, looking for the SavUQuik ship.

He passed two domiciles that had seemed intact, but up close it was clear that their starscreens were compromised. The hand-scanner stayed dark. Russ trudged forward to the next domicile and found it sealed up tight. He ran the scanner across the length of the door. It blipped, faintly, but not strongly enough to register a definite location. Russ moved to the starscreen on the side of the domicile. It was covered in latex-style black paint. Russ picked at the edge of the paint, still scanning the horizon for SavUQuik. He put both his hands against the glass and peered through the tear in the paint. He saw a flicker of movement inside. He looked again, willing his eyes to adjust to the very low light.

Trell was just a few steps behind him. The Klung disengaged the manual release lever on the door, happy to find its pneumatics were still working. "Come help me get this open," he told Russ.

Russ stood back a moment, letting sunlight trickle into the room from the hole in the latex. He dug at the paint, trying to make the opening larger. As he worked, he caught the briefest motion on the other side of the starscreen. The thing inside was visible just long enough for Russ to register what it was—the face of a child staring out at him, eyes heavy with worry. The child drew back into the darkness, disappearing again.

"Never mind. I got it," Trell said, yanking hard on the lever.

"Stop!" Russ shouted through the comm. "There's a kid inside!"

23

RUSS

TRELL TOOK HIS HANDS OFF the door lever. The Klung reversed the polarity on his gravity boots, suddenly drifting weightless. Once he'd cleared the roof, he reversed the polarity again and zipped back to the surface like a homing missile.

Russ kept digging at the paint until a two-inch-wide chunk of latex came free. Peering through the widened opening, Russ got a better look at the young boy huddled inside. He was no older than six or seven and trembling from the cold. His eyes were fixated on the roof where Trell's metal gravity boots shook the ceiling with each heavy step.

"He's really young," Russ said through the comm. "I don't recognize the species. Looks like he's scared to death."

"Is he wearing compression gear?"

"No. He's freezing in there."

"If we break the pressurized seal it's going to get a lot worse. Outer space will swallow him whole."

Russ held his transponder to the small opening. Light from the digital screen flooded the darkened room, and the kid looked fearfully in Russ's direction.

"Put on your gear," Russ said, pantomiming pulling on a helmet and rebreather. "We're here to rescue you."

The child shook his head vehemently.

A ship appeared high above their heads. It was a gray-and-blue fighter with an enormous chrome shield badge on the side. Stenciled in the center of the shield in large red letters were the words *SavUQuik*.

"Put on your helmet," Russ pantomimed. The boy just covered his head in his hands. "Why would he be here?"

"His parents are probably pirates. They stick him here while they go to work, like a dark and very cold daycare. The little guy was either too frozen to show up on the initial heat scan, or they've used some kind of tech to mask his location."

"It's crazy-lucky Big Sister sensed him," Russ said.

"That shit is state-of-the-art," Trell said, moving next to Russ and peering through the window. Trell took his hands off the window and backed away, almost like someone who had run across a rattlesnake. "Oh no," he said.

"What is it?"

"That's a Liafeen," Trell said.

"I don't know—"

"They're the scourge of the known universe. Bringers of death. Uhh . . ." Trell kept thinking, but his eyes, and concentration, were focused on the window. ". . . destroyers of everything."

"This little guy?"

"He shouldn't be anywhere near the border of recognized UAIB space."

Russ looked through the window one more time. The child appeared somewhat humanoid: two arms, two legs, two eyes, one nose, a mouth. But looking closer, Russ could see skeletal bone rising from the boy's shoulders and fanning out, like jagged knives. At his neckline, the bone disappeared back into his flesh, but Russ could still see the outline of it, on his arms and chest, stretched tight against his thin white skin. The Liafen wore their skeletons on the outside of their muscles and tendons.

"I am in the presence of a master of general chaos," Trell said, as if something had been confirmed. "This kid could cause an international incident. Freezing to death might have been a better option . . ." Trell looked skyward as a tether hook fired from the throat of the SavUQuik ship and buried deep in the floor fifteen feet to Trell's left. The base of the ship slid aside. Four humanoids stabilized themselves to the tether hook and came blasting toward them. The newcomers had names and call signs emblazoned on their chests. The first in line was *Ranyard.* Beneath his name in a bolder cursive font it said *CannonWulf.*

Normally, Russ would have found it obnoxious, but it was pretty helpful considering the circumstances. The suit of the fourth man to touch down bore the name *Drench: FeebleCock.*

Trell moved away from the window to shake Ranyard's hand and then gestured with his fingers, 2-4-5-1. It was a signal to switch to channel 2451 on the comms. Both men did, and Russ followed suit.

"What's the situation?" Ranyard asked gruffly.

"We've got a cruise ship due at this location in less than ten minutes. We're scheduled to scrap this heap, but a biologic showed up on a last-minute scan." He nodded to the door. "There's a kid in there. He's not wearing the proper gear to survive if we depressurize the cabin, so we're not sure what to do."

"We need to get this junk removed before the cruise ship comes through," Ranyard said.

"Right," Trell said, patiently. "But there's a kid inside."

Russ noticed Trell was purposely avoiding mentioning the kid's identity. He also realized Trell had moved away from the window to keep SavUQuik from glancing inside.

"How the hell did he get in there?" Ranyard was looking at Trell so Russ couldn't see his face, but he knew the expression. He'd seen it every time he'd pushed against an authority figure, which happened, well, every time he encountered an authority figure.

"We think his parents left him here while they went to work."

"Yeah. Work," Ranyard huffed. "He's an illegal and he has no authorization to be onboard this craft."

"It's the Darkzone," Trell reminded him. "Nobody has authorization to do anything, and it's impossible to be illegal in a zone without government or laws."

Ranyard began to talk about the importance of his oath to "provide safety and keep order" for all Providence Travel Solution's routes. Russ tuned him out, literally, changing the comm channel. Ranyard's lawful evil existence was digging directly into every one of his nerve endings. He turned to Drench and used his fingers to flash the numbers 1-9-9-2.

"What's up?" Josiv Drench said on the new channel, looks of annoyance and curiosity sharing space on his face.

"I'm Russ Wesley," Russ told him. "I think we met before, onboard the *Flashaway*. My crew saved you."

"Saved us?" Drench corrected. "You mean right before our business went under, I lost my job, my wife left me because my name was attached to a huge, viral embarrassment, and I had to come out to the middle of nowhere to work with these assholes? Oh! And, every time I close my eyes, I see huge insect swarms of death buzzing just behind my eyelids, and it makes my hands shake when I try to hold a weapon. Or a spoon to eat the cereal I can barely afford? Great save. Thanks."

"You're welcome?" Russ said, understanding quickly why Drench had bothered to send Kendren hate mail.

"Do you see the call sign they gave me?" Drench asked, gesturing to FeebleCock.

“I assumed that was some kind of bird of prey.” To his left, Trell was purposely positioning himself to block the blackened starscreen while Ranyard stood with his arms crossed over his chest. “Have you heard what happened to the others on your crew?”

“The industrial accident that got Stormside? I heard about it,” Drench said. “Savage way to die. I thought it might be suicide, considering.”

“Not just Stormside,” Russ said. “Jaq’li K’l’w’qi’ showed up dead on a derelict ship shortly after sending my friend a distress signal. Rendell Ploom had a heart attack. Everybody else is dead. All nine of the crew. Everyone except you.”

Drench exhaled noisily. “I get it,” he said. A look of relief seemed to wash over his face. “What do you want from me?”

“What do you mean, you get it?”

“Someone is killing the crew,” Drench said, untroubled.

“I want to find out why.”

“I have no idea.” Drench leaned backward, chin pointed to the darkness overhead, his gravity boots the only thing holding him upright. His hands rested on his hips.

“It might have something to do with a rogue SAS unit. Does the name Aldos Verch mean anything to you? He’s the director of security for Waymore Industries,” Russ told Drench.

“Our current employer?” Drench thought for a moment. “Waymore is shady as shit. They’re capable of it. Especially because they’re circling the big corporate black hole, if you know what I mean.”

“I don’t, exactly. Hold on a sec,” Russ said. He could see that Trell and Ranyard were struggling for control of the manual release lever. Trell was looking in Russ’s direction, his face full of grim tension.

Russ walked over to the window. His heavy gloves found purchase, and he managed to peel back a large strip of the black paint. The boy inside still had his head buried in his hands; his sharp shoulder bones pointed in Russ’s direction.

A few feet away were the remains of an oxygen transportation unit. Russ put his hands around a metal pole that was jammed into the system. He had to leverage his foot against the unit's centralized processing core, but he managed to wiggle the pole free. Then he swung it hard against the window—a difficult task in zero gravity. The impact made the boy jump to his feet.

Russ stabbed at the window. A small hairline crack formed on the outer pane of the dense plastic. Russ raised the pole over his head, positioned to take a second swing, though he had no intention of doing so. Inside, the boy ducked behind a crate. Russ thought he might be cowering back there, but a moment later the boy reappeared, a functioning rebreather on his face.

The boy pulled his hood up and sat in the darkness, legs shaking.

Russ pointed to Trell, gave the thumbs up, and turned back to Drench. "Start talking."

Russ could see a wild expression on Drench's face. "First, I need you to do something for me. I'm going to push my mother's information and forty-four thousand credits to your transponder. Use 90 percent of the money on a life insurance policy in my mother's name. Insure me against all types of death. An umbrella policy. Do it tonight. Use Starlight Banc, they give shit returns, but they also don't ask a lot of questions. Keep the rest for yourself, but please, don't keep it all."

"Don't you have any other friends that could maybe—" Russ started to object but Drench clicked his wrist against Russ's transponder, and it lit up announcing the credit transfer. Over Drench's shoulder, Russ could see Lanie and Linnie's ship, the *Nightfire* looming closer. The huge saw they called Big Sister was extended high above the ship on its articulating polymer and graphene arm. The blade was spinning. If he went back to their main channel, they'd probably be demanding answers.

Russ glanced at Trell and saw the Klung was nose to nose with Ranyard, their face shields and rebreathers nearly interlocked. The other two members of SavUQuik, FireLilly and LazerTank had positioned themselves behind Trell, their hands on their weapons. Ranyard's gun was holstered, but he was yanking the manual release on the pressurized door. Trell was glancing at Russ, his eyes imploring him for help. He looked like he had a terrible headache.

"Stay on this channel," Russ told Drench. Then he switched back to channel 2451. Ranyard had yanked the door free with the manual lever. Trell rushed past him to wrap the boy entirely in a foil blanket.

". . . pirates, no matter how young, are the jurisdiction of Transport Security," Ranyard was shouting.

"I can read every emotion on your face," Trell swore. "I know you plan to dump this kid at the nearest immigration outpost. Or worse."

"That's the proper protocol. I'm not leaving without that illegal in my possession," Ranyard insisted.

Russ knew these types, and he knew the minute they saw the boy was a Liafeen they'd get grim, resolute, and bloodthirsty. He left Drench and headed laboriously back toward the docking bridge. He knifed passed Trell, Ranyard, FireLilly, and LazerTank and scooped up the kid, the blanket held securely in place. He headed back toward the Lumina switching to channel 1992 as he walked.

LazerTank grabbed at his shoulder, but Russ slipped out of his grip. He reversed the polarity on his gravity boots and leaped through the darkness, just as he'd seen Trell do.

"They're pretty pissed at you right now," Drench said.

Russ was too busy flying to answer. If he hadn't been clutching the child, his arms would have been spinning in panicked windmills. After he'd traveled about thirty yards, he reengaged the boots and came crashing down beside the docking bridge. The landing shot pain through his feet, legs, and hips. It also sent a particularly strong jolt through his broken wrist.

Russ ignored it as best he could. He looked down at the boy. Through a gap in the blanket and the boy's rebreather mask he could see his lips were deathly white. The boy's eyes were full of fire, but the extreme cold was draining the fight right out of him. He clung to Russ's bicep with both his small, bony hands.

"Why is Waymore circling the drain? Does it have to do with an SAS unit? Tell me everything, quickly. Or I'm keeping the forty-four thousand."

"It has to do with a lot of SAS units. And Fromantium." Drench hummed a moment, "Make your way with Triple-10K."

"I know it."

"It's crap metal. Waymore is leveraged out the ass on manufacturing. They have contracts for interstellar space stations, prisons, and a whole bunch of Fromantium-built SAS units you seem to want to know about. Yes, it performs to its specifications. It also completely dissolves in salt water. Waymore's scrambling to keep the UAIB Construction Committees in the dark, but it's only a matter of time before it leaks and the whole house of cards comes tumbling down."

"That doesn't explain why SOL is being hunted," *or Applebum*, Russ almost added. Over his shoulder, the *Nightfire* loomed large, the giant blade from her roof spinning so fast the rivets in the metal were blurred into a single disk of death.

He climbed up the loading hatch of the Lumina. The boy's chest was heaving. He sat the boy as close to the heat of the engine as he could. Trell came up the loading ramp right behind them. The three members of SavUQuik were right on his tail, so Russ deflated and disengaged the docking bridge.

The bridge separated immediately, sending SavUQuik drifting untethered into space. They flailed awkwardly. LazerTank tried to dive back to the derelict space station, while FireLilly and Ranyard made frantic breaststroke motions, attempting to swim to the Lumina. Physics and the now-partially-inflated docking bridge were working against them. The bridge wrapped around their feet, pulling them farther from their respective destinations.

"Come pick up your people," Russ told Drench. "They're ruining our docking gear." He switched back to the main channel for Intergalactic Waste Management.

Lanie's voice came through loud and clear, "Where the hell are you guys?" she shouted. "This is no time to screw around. The cruise ship is right on our ass."

"Hey Lanie," Russ said.

"Why did you switch comms?" Lanie asked urgently. "Is this the kind of shit that got you canned from the IEI?"

"We're painting the lines now," Russ promised.

Trell plopped into the bucket seat and fiddled with the controls. Russ strafed left until they reached the far side of the derelict station. As they moved, the onboard computer measured the length of the space junk populating a 3D image on Trell's HUD.

Trell studied the measurements and then he began to run the laser lengthwise down the floating space station. He was marking lines every two thousand square feet. In a twisted way, he was prepping it for surgery.

"Russ, tell me what's going on," Lanie demanded.

"Hold one moment," Russ told her calmly. He switched back to channel 1992, then glanced at the huge, spinning blade. It appeared even more terrifying up close, ripping through metal and slag straight along the lines Trell had painted with the laser. "You better get off that station," Russ swore at Drench.

"Working on it," Drench said. "Get that insurance policy to my mom." For the first time, Drench's voice had confidence though he was huffing from the effort of pulling the deflated docking bridge back onto the derelict space station. The other three members of SavUQuik hung on for dear life. "If I'm still alive, I'll have more information for you once I confirm she has the policy."

"I'll get you insured," Russ promised. He paused a minute to text Nina a message: *Spoke to Drench. Waymore Industries again*

There was a hissing sound, and his transponder went blank. The lights in the ship dimmed, then shut down entirely, along with the control board, the HUD, and the comm system. Russ glanced back at Trell. The Klung was sucking the energy dry from everything around him, and the excess heat was emanating from his pores. He held the frozen, shivering boy against his chest as heat traveled in waves over his entire small body. As the heat washed over him, the boy regained some of his color. He hissed and clicked in a language beyond the capabilities of Russ's nanotranslator.

Through the starscreen, Russ could see the first glimpse of the Providence Travel Solutions cruise liner as it appeared across the horizon. Against the deep black backdrop of space, it looked like a garish floating castle, bloated and shining.

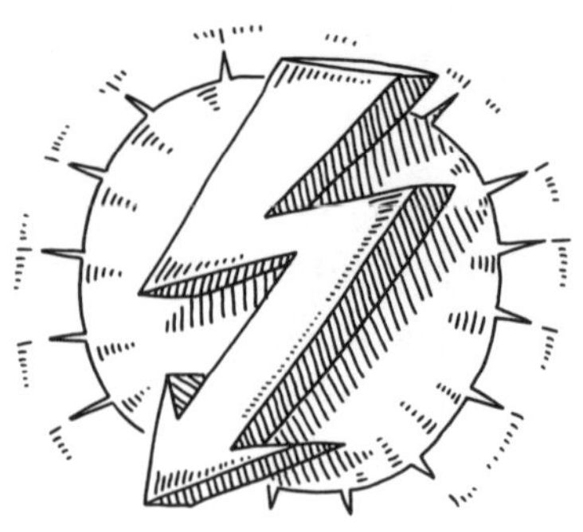

24

NINA

KWIKY PEST & NUISANCE HAD a small CRC machine in an even smaller Medward. Nina thought that the Intergalactic Exterminators were a cheap operation, but the Kwiky Pest & Nuisance ship made the *Aldersochi*—before the crash, anyway—look like Shangri-la.

Nina had yet to figure out how CRC machines worked, exactly. As best she could tell, they were very advanced organic 3D printers. They would recreate lost tissue, muscle, and bone, then stitch their subject back together whole. It was the same kind of machine that had saved her father's life and cured Clark of his heart condition.

There was no door separating the Medward from the main corridor, which didn't allow them much privacy. Atara either didn't notice or didn't care, slipping entirely out of her clothes. She stood nude in the center of the room, letting the CRC machine prick her finger for a DNA sample. She had the kind of body that no one in their right mind would be ashamed of. Nina heard her own chaste, guileless mother's voice in her head as she looked at Atara: "That girl has a fantastic figure."

"Do you think this thing cures PMS?" Atara asked as she rolled onto the repair tray. As she positioned herself on her back, Nina caught sight of the large burn on her thigh.

"He wasn't trying to kill me," Atara explained. "I tackled him, and the heat blade hit my leg in the process."

"I don't think he wanted to leave any trace that he'd been there," Nina said. "That was supposed to look like an accidental crash. I think we're being silenced by somebody."

"We should probably find out why," Atara said.

Nina examined Atara's injury. "I've seen that burn before," she realized. "Twice now. It was on Jaq'li." She did a small circle, hopping with excitement. "It was also on the arm of Jaq'li's neighbor. The person who gave me the Thufflin Box that led Verch right to Russ. At the time I thought it was a rash!"

"I'm not sure what you're talking about," Atara said.

"Sorry," Nina said. "The big guy with the flaming sword. He's been busy." Nina shook her head sadly. "Pretty sure he's searching for Applebum, or maybe murdering enough people to try and draw him out of hiding."

"What the heck is an Applebum?" Atara asked. As the tray rose up into the machine, Atara kept speaking, her voice muffled by the cocoon-like device. "Hey, I want to apologize for something."

"For what?"

"Just how I've treated you. Pretty much since you signed on to the crew."

"It's okay. Newbies always get hazed a little," Nina said with as much sincerity as she could muster. She'd been able to tell Atara didn't like her from the get-go and had never been able to pinpoint exactly why.

"There was a Kyrillian girl a lot like you that ran with our crew last year," Atara continued. "She was beautiful. Just striking. It allowed her to get everything she wanted, but it also kept her from ever being tested. She pretended to be tough, but she was soft."

"Where is she now?"

"We were doing a routine search-and-destroy on Olivian-12 and she stumbled into a cave-hive of carnivorous Hhzzees. We eventually found her skeleton, but we couldn't safely extract it from the hive. She's probably still there, actually."

"Wonderful," Nina said.

"You've always reminded me of her, from the minute you stepped onboard the ship. Pretty girls never realize how the world bends around them. I doubt you even notice how many breaks you get."

Nina didn't say anything. She stood beside the CRC machine, frowning. "This is sounding less and less like an apology," she said, finally.

"It's an apology and a compliment. This part is. Because I was wrong. You don't remind me of that Kyrillian girl anymore," Atara continued. "You're a survivor. Smart as shit. And now you're a hero, too. Bah'ren wouldn't have gotten off the ship alive. She'd have died with little Serendipity clutched in her arms. Hell, you saved all of us."

The repair tray clicked into place and the heavy internal printer arm began to gyrate so much that conversation was no longer possible. The machine shifted and rumbled, digging out the destroyed flesh on Atara's leg and replacing it, layer by layer.

Once again, Nina felt that heroic euphoria coursing through her system. She had convinced herself that she didn't need Atara's validation, but that didn't explain why it felt so good to have it. "I'm starting to understand Russ's risk-taking a little better," she mumbled.

Nina's transponder suddenly brightened with a message, as if Russ had heard her speaking his name. All his message said was:

Spoke @32 Drench.@. Waaa77ymore Indust__09.

Nina sat next to the CRC listening to it stitch Atara's leg back together. She was deep in thought.

A few moments later, Kendren came strolling down the hall. "I get it now," he said. "Some of the crew were joking about coming down here to supervise. I see why." Kendren ran his finger down the door frame. It looked like it had housed a door at some point, long ago. "Are you going in the machine next?" he asked. "I will stand here and block the view of your naked body with my broad back and shoulders. I know you Earthlings value your physical privacy."

"Thank you," Nina said. She looked at the message on her transponder again. "What do you know about Waymore Industries?" she asked Kendren.

"They're one of my sponsors." Kendren pointed to a large patch on his jumpsuit. It was a blue circle with the word *Max-Im-Ize* written inside. "It's funny because growing up I hated these bastards. They're run by a bunch of Divians, but they do their manufacturing on other planets to minimize their home planet of Ren'Div's exposure to pollution-created climate change. Growing up, we had a Waymore SAS factory on my home world of Fidrrarrbore. Practically everyone worked there, including both my parents. The whole town smelled like metallic farts. One of my cousins died of lung rot, though it was never officially linked to the factory. Now they pay me three hundred credits a cycle to wear this badge." Kendren was silent for a moment. He tore off the badge and tossed it to her. "I don't think I want to wear it anymore, though," he said.

The CRC arm stopped jiggling with a hiss. The repair tray holding Atara began to lower back to the floor.

Nina stuffed the badge in her pocket. She unzipped and stepped out of her orange jumpsuit and the tank top and spandex shorts she habitually wore underneath.

Her collarbone ached as she stood there in just her granny panties and unmatching Amazon-essentials bra.

Kendren was watching her closely, a neutral expression on his face. She almost said something snide like, "Is this how you protect my privacy?" but his neutral expression slipped, and she caught another glimmer of tender sadness in his eyes.

Nina slid out of her underwear. *If Atara's right, I'm casting some sort of spell over him by doing this*, she thought. Feeling his eyes on her skin, the adrenaline that had been carrying her forward the whole, wild day surged through her brain again. *If Atara is wrong, at least I can cheer up a fellow gloomy.* She took off her bra, whisking it from her body like a sculptor removing a drop cloth to reveal their prized work.

She stayed in full view of Kendren for ten electrifying seconds, then turned and reached a hand up to help Atara down from the tray. Then she took her place.

In the tray, she thought of Kendren's behavior just before Verch attacked, the way he'd been standing awkwardly, how he'd combed his hair and put on his nice clothes. As the tray began to raise into the CRC's cocoon-like chamber, she took another quick glance in his direction, expecting he would still be studying her naked body, getting a last quick look before she disappeared into the relative modesty of the device.

Instead, he was kneeling, head bowed. She realized he was tying his shoe.

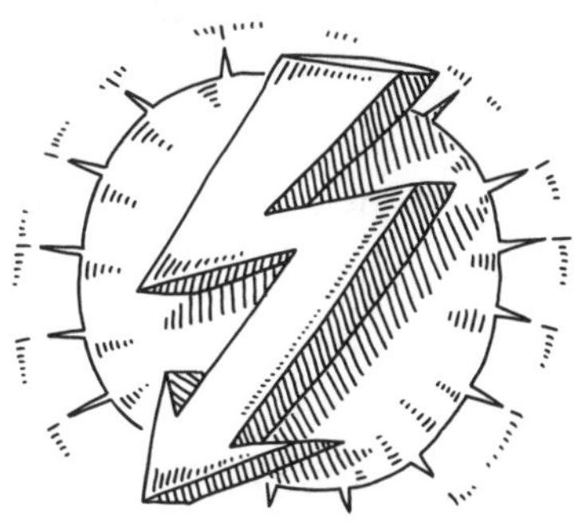

25
NINA

"THE SHIP'S GONE?" RUSS ASKED. "The *Aldersochi*? The new ship?" He was sitting on the single bed they had shared the night before. Having a Waypoint in the closet meant maid service was out of the question, but so far neither of them had lugged Clark's sheets out to the coin washing machine on the far side of the motel pool. To be fair, Nina hadn't even had time to clean herself up. The CRC machine had repaired her collarbone, but it had left her hair crusted into a shape somewhat resembling the Eiffel Tower.

"Verch took down the whole ship. Right before I pitched him off the roof," Nina said.

"Did he die?"

"Can't say for sure. I piloted the Stinger around the perimeter of the grove trying to estimate where he would have landed, but I didn't find a body. Hopefully he was impaled on a mangrove root just out of my line of site."

"We should still disassemble the Waypoint at night."

Nina touched the top of her curls lightly but knew immediately that patting it down into a respectable shape wasn't going to happen without a long shower. "Is Applebum still not back?" she asked, glancing around the motel room.

Russ shook his head, his mouth pushed into a tight line.

"I'm going to wash my hair. Go get your grandfather and catch him up on what's happened. We've got to figure this all out. Then we have to find Applebum."

Nina rinsed her hair carefully. If even a speck of Grandveega was still on her head, Evanstown, Wyoming was about to have a terrible plumbing problem. When she finished, Clark and Russ were waiting. Clark, wearing just a tank top and sweatpants, was manspread on his old bed.

"You pay wage taxes on every life insurance premium you buy. The purchaser pays the tax, prorated on the total amount," Clark was explaining to Russ. "If you buy it for forty thousand, they'll dock your paycheck a thousand a cycle for four cycles. It keeps people from opening a bunch of toxic policies. Or insuring, then murdering, their spouses. Drench was probably counting on you not knowing that. That's why he gave it to you when he could have just as easily done it on the ride back home. If those credits are hard marked as a loan, that will cause even more trouble."

"I don't know anything about any of that," Russ said. "But I made a promise to buy the policy tonight."

"I know you had good intentions—that you still have good intentions—but he's trying to take advantage of you. The best thing you can do is let me flip the money. We could clear at least twenty-five thousand from a just slightly illegal check cashing service. We give ten to Drench's old lady and keep the rest as a service fee."

Nina wasn't sure what they were talking about, but she had yet to see Russ say no to his grandpop, no matter how bad the older man's ideas were.

"He won't give me more information without the policy," Russ said impatiently.

"What else does he know?"

"If I knew that—" Russ spread apart his hands. "What's the best way to do it that still involves me keeping my promise?"

"I can check the credits for hard marks," Clark said. "And I can buy the policy through a proxy. It will take a while, and it will cost a percentage, but if I get started right now, I might be able to pull it off by tonight."

Russ tossed his transponder to Clark and the older man tapped at the screen greedily.

Nina cleared her throat, and both men turned to look at her. "I had a few ideas while I was cleaning up," she said. "Tell me what you think of this. We know that Waymore Industries has invested a fortune in Fromantium, and it's about to blow up in their faces. But they're a huge company. They're not going to just roll over and die. What do they do?"

Russ blew air out of his cheeks. "Murder a bunch of low-level municipal workers?"

"Because they're looking for . . ." Nina gestured over to Applebum's empty reading corner.

"They're looking for an SAS unit. One special enough that it can learn on its own," Russ said. He had clearly already reached this conclusion himself.

"One that they already manufactured but lost track of when it disappeared from the immigration satellite where'd they'd stashed it. If they could find the unit and reproduce the flaw, they could manufacture an army of sophisticated, brilliant machines. I can't think of a better way for an ailing company to reverse its fortunes."

"Except a robot that can learn is against intergalactic law," Russ reminded her. "And even the dumb ones aren't allowed in the workforce—except for jobs related to immigration enforcement."

"Only poor people and fools care about intergalactic law," Clark pointed out, shaking Russ's transponder in his hand, the screen open to his banking application. Clark looked back at Nina. "And corporate monoliths have a way of changing the law when they put their minds to it."

Russ's pupils danced back and forth. His face was full of worry, and she realized it was for Applebum.

He said, "Somebody remembers the critical flaw in Applebum and says, 'We've had this tech all along.' But Applebum deleted his manufacturing file months ago when he rescued me from getting mind-wiped."

"They start to look for him, but his file is gone. They couldn't possibly predict he's hiding in a motel room on a Podunk, Tier Nine planet. With his location hidden he should have been untraceable. But then . . . how did they find him?" Nina said.

"The news story. The rescue onboard the *Flashaway*."

"A story that featured SOL Pest Control and the Intergalactic Exterminators," Nina finished. "But Verch didn't even try to torture me for information."

"He wanted to torture me," Russ said.

"He walked right past me in the corridor. He just needed us dead."

"They already have Applebum," Russ realized. He leaned back, his fingers intertwined beneath his head. "Shit!"

"There's still so much we haven't figured out." Nina went to peer out the motel window. She picked up Applebum's copy of *The Maltese Falcon* and studied its well-worn spine. When she turned around again, Clark was still tapping at Russ's transponder. "Are you sure you want to give him free access to everything on your transponder?"

Clark grinned and said, "You leave your transponder unlocked in my motel room every night. Heck, Applebum uses it to watch YouStar videos when he thinks I'm asleep."

Nina shook her head like she'd been slapped. "Applebum uses it?" She flicked her fingers across the screen of her transponder. She scrolled past all the searches she'd made while she awaited rescue on Fi9, the YouStar tutorial she'd watched to learn how to pinpoint the SOL health records from the VTR, even a small Earth article she'd read at lunch entitled, "The Sexiest Pajamas of 2025." Finally, she reached the first log that she didn't recognize. "Applebum looked up Jaq'li's address and searched out the fastest way to get there without using any major hubs," she told Russ.

"What are we waiting for?" he asked her.

There was only a single spaceclerk at the Waypoint hub on Star's Crescent Nebula in the Y Alpha Vixen Cluster. He seemed annoyed that they weren't moving faster.

As if he had anything else to do.

Outside, the street was nearly empty aside from a man in pants and a T-shirt pushing a sled full of packages on a motorized cart. Nina spotted unhoused people moving around in the alleyway and smelled the pungent stench of urine on the sidewalk as she and Russ followed the map toward Jaq'li's apartment. "Jaq'li was very lonely here," she told Russ. "She said nobody ever went outside unless they absolutely had to."

"Seems like it," Russ said. He kicked a loose section of road, and an entire five-inch piece broke off. "Whoops," he said, trying ineffectively to push it back into place with the bottom of his boot.

When they finally arrived at Jaq'li's apartment complex, they found the door kicked completely off its hinges.

Nina knocked on the door of the neighbor who had given her the Thufflin Box. The small viewing panel slid aside and the same bedraggled Romgulang stared out at her. When she recognized Nina, she slid the viewing panel back closed, but not before Nina could catch another glance at the burn she had across her forearm.

"I know how you got that burn," Nina called through the door. "Giant dude with a flaming sword. Looks like one of the archangels who lost the war in heaven."

There was silence, then the Romgulang's voice came through the door, "I don't know what that is. But I am surprised you're still alive."

"Can we ask you a few quick questions?" Nina asked. "Did the giant give you the Thufflin Box? If so, what did he ask you to do with it?"

"He said to give it to anyone who came asking about Jaq'li. He said to call him when I did and he'd bring another, in case anybody else came looking."

"Did he?"

The viewing panel opened, and a new Thufflin Box came spitting out, rotating end over end until it hit the wall and fell down to the floor. Nina left it there. Russ stomped on it with his boot.

"Do you know what he wanted?"

"The muscle-bound murderer with the flaming blade that fried my arm just to show me how serious he was? That guy?"

"Yeah."

"I didn't get a chance to ask." There was a pause and then, "If I come outside, will you stop yelling through the door?"

"Of course," Nina assured her.

They waited. Then they waited more.

"She's definitely not coming out," Russ observed. "She's probably fleeing out the back." He struck the viewing panel hard with his palm. It gave slightly. He struck it again. The cheap hinges bent, and the panel dropped a quarter of an inch.

Nina peered through the gap. The Romgulang had opened a subterranean window on the far side of her apartment. She was wearing high heels, a garish printed crop top, and small miniskirt. Despite the restrictive movements of the tight skirt, she climbed halfway out, managing to throw her right leg over the top of the window ledge.

"She's not gone yet," Nina said. The Romgulang dropped through the opening and out of sight. "Okay, now she is."

They moved on to Jaq'li's apartment. The living room was bare. Either thieves had come through the broken door and carefully removed anything of value, or there had been nothing of value to begin with.

Nina found a jersey in Jaq'li's hall closet and was slipping it over her own head when Russ called out, "In here!"

She hurried into Jaq'li's bedroom. It was torn to shreds. The paneling on the walls had been ripped down and thrown around the room. The bed was in pieces, and the closet door was broken into three jagged panels.

"Somebody tossed the place," Russ said.

"It's fight damage. Look." Nina pointed out the tear marks in the paneling. "Somebody ripped this down and then hurtled it." She leaned backward against the three broken panels of the closet door. "And somebody heavy was tossed here. They hit with enough impact to smash straight through this door."

Russ grew quiet, preoccupied. The ground was covered in the inverted remains of the pillows, linens, and mattress. He dropped to his knees and started to rummage through the debris.

"What are you looking for?" she asked him.

"Something to reassure me that my friend isn't dead." The moment he said it, his face fell even further. He raised his right hand from out of the feathers and torn linens, and Nina saw he was holding another right hand. It was the hand of a Tech12 unit. "Fuck," Russ declared as Nina dropped down onto her knees beside him, and they both began digging more rapidly.

When they were done, they had found both of Applebum's hands, his right arm, a portion of his left leg, and his pelvis. Russ was stoic as they grimly piled up what was left of Applebum's severed body. Nina was pretty sure he was trying not to cry. She didn't feel so great herself.

"His head is not here," Russ said hopefully. "Or his chest. I think most of his neural network is stored in his spine. Right?"

"He could still be alive," Nina said. She hugged Russ, remembering how important his hug had been when Jaq'li had died. For a moment, they stood together and she could feel his heartbeat against her chest. Russ disengaged.

"He doesn't do Waymore any good dead. If our theory is correct—" Nina told him as he continued to scour the room.

Russ pulled apart the remains of the closet door, his eyes searching the floor inside. "Wait a second," he said. He leaned down and picked something up with his right hand. It was yet another right hand.

26

RUSS

SOMBER, THEY STOOD TOGETHER BEFORE the single Waypoint on Star's Crescent Nebula. The spaceclerk looked at them expectantly. He seemed ready for them to jump back to wherever they had come from. Russ hoped the clerk wouldn't say anything about the heavy bag full of robot parts he was carrying.

Nina stood at Russ's side in Jaq'li's jersey. Russ was too distraught to notice how cute she looked in it.

"That second right hand. It was cold to the touch," Russ whispered. "Pretty sure its Fromantium, which would explain why Applebum lost the fight." Russ's voice betrayed him, cracking just perceptively between the "fi" and the "ght."

"You doing okay?" Nina asked.

"Yessir. Just fine."

"Do you remember what Applebum did when he learned Jaq'li had died?"

Russ shook his head, not trusting himself to speak.

He didn't need to. Without another word, Nina turned and hugged him.

"Are you guys leaving soon?" the spaceclerk asked.

"Sorry to be taking so long," Nina told the clerk. "I'm sure Applebum is still alive," she whispered.

"How could he be? We've got most of him in this bag," Russ pointed out. Impossibly, his voice betrayed him again, breaking between "ba" and "g." If he had a moment to collect his thoughts, he would have to figure out why Applebum's death was hitting him so hard.

"He doesn't do Waymore any good if he's dead." Nina kissed Russ on the cheek. Then she kissed him on the other cheek.

The sudden affection did not make Russ any less confused. Russ wasn't sure about much, but he was sure about one thing, and that was that women liked men who were macho and took huge risks. Men who rode around on motorcycles and intimidated other, smaller men. Men who controlled their emotions and who utilized energy generating outward from their enormous testicles to keep everybody they cared about safe. Women didn't like men who need consoling when they lost their robot companions.

"What's gotten into you?" he asked Nina. "You've been kind of different since you got back from work today." He waited patiently, hoping she would kiss him again. The edge of her lips had brushed against the edge of his.

"I'm beginning to understand why you take so many risks," Nina told him. "One, it's exhilarating. And two, you're so busy staying alive you don't have any time to think about your problems."

Russ grunted. "It's cheaper than therapy."

Across the small hub, the spaceclerk drummed his fingers on his desk.

"Take it easy," Russ told him. "She's never kissed me before. I want to savor this for a second."

"It was just on the cheek," the spaceclerk grumbled.

"True," Nina said. She stared at Russ for a moment. She cocked her head slightly and her eyes fluttered. Her lips were just a few inches from his. Russ forgot about Applebum. He forgot about being sad altogether. He moved his mouth slightly closer to hers. It didn't take much. Their lips were already nearly touching. Nina opened her mouth . . .

"Do you think you could be more careful?" she asked. Her voice was so soft it was almost imperceptible, but she was close enough that he could feel the words on the edges of his cheeks.

"How do you mean?"

"Do you think you could be safe? I get why you do it, why you take chances . . . but I want you to stop." She moved her head slightly to indicate the bag of Applebum parts. "Someone is actively trying to kill us. Can you not do the job for them? At least?"

Russ processed the question. "Yes," he said, after a short pause. "I can be more careful." The pause—just a brief second of time—said more than words. It was enough for both of them to know he was lying. Nina sighed, stepped away, and turned to the spaceclerk.

"Whoa! Thought you really were going to kiss him," the clerk said.

"You can send us home now," Nina said, quietly.

Once back at the motel, they dutifully disassembled the Waypoint and rolled the component bars against the far wall. Russ did most of the work because Nina could barely keep her eyes open. She took apart a few of the bars and then flopped on the bed.

Russ glanced at her and thought about what had happened moments before. Then he placed the bag of robot parts next to Applebum's books. He put his hand on the bag. "Applebum doesn't do Waymore any good dead," he reminded himself.

He stood up and turned again toward the single clean bed where Nina lay on her back, her arm over her eyes. He sighed.

"I really hope my grandpop got a room with two queen beds and not a king."

"Why is that?"

"I'm going to stay with him tonight. I'm too sad and grumpy to be in decent company." Russ pulled open the door and stepped outside. He looked across the courtyard and the algae-filled pool. He couldn't stop himself from adding, "Plus, it's *safer* if we split up. I'll listen for trouble in your room and you listen for trouble in mine."

"I-uhh . . ." Nina started to say. She was slowly sitting up from the bed.

Russ stepped outside and pulled the door shut behind him. He stayed on the stoop long enough to hear Nina approach the door. He could sense her standing there, just on the other side. Then he heard the door lock with a *click*.

Light rain drizzled on his head and shoulders as he crossed toward his grandfather's room. Inside, Clark was snoring loudly on the king-sized bed in only his tighty-whitey underwear, his legs spread open, gnarled, curly white thigh-hair pointed in Russ's direction. Next to Clark was a sheet of paper where'd he'd been jotting down numbers. Russ stared at the paper, but he couldn't make much sense of it.

Russ snapped a pillow from the bed and curled up on the floor. The threadbare carpet smelled like animal musk. Out of the corner of his eye he caught sight of the clock on Clark's end table. It was two a.m. Yawning, Russ remembered that he'd agreed to work with Lanie and Linnie again, per diem, in six hours.

He listened to his grandpop snore. Russ had idolized Clark during his youth, but the old man seemed quite a bit different when viewed through the eyes of an adult. These days, Russ could still see the passion he'd always admired. It drove Clark to discover new secrets and explore new lands—but that passion could also be described as selfish dedication to avoiding any and all personal responsibility. Had his grandfather always been like this? Had Russ modeled his own life after a man who was, not a villain exactly, but still somehow the opposite of a hero?

Maybe I'm being too harsh. It's been a frustrating day.

Russ was drifting off to sleep when his transponder lit up. He fished it out of his pocket, pushing back against the sadomasochistic urge that it be a text from Nina.

Ω: *Wh3r3 am I?*

Russ: *Nina?*

Ω: *Back onlin3, but, where's h3r3?*

Russ: *Who is this? How do you have this texting program?*

Ω: *Bad1y Hurt. Pl3as3 find m3*

Ω: *Com3 and find m3*

Russ: *Applebum? Is this you? Please tell me this is you . . .*

Russ waited and watched the screen, holding his breath, but the next text message never arrived. Not even ninety minutes later when he gave up spamming messages to the mysterious sender and finally let himself lie back and close his eyes.

27
STEVEN APPLEBUM

THE WALLS WERE GRAY AND bare, artless and industrial. Applebum could hear large machines whirring on the other side. The room was completely empty—no bed, no bookshelf, no anything. It was actually more of a closet, less than six-by-seven feet in total. Applebum tried to stand, but he realized his legs were gone. He humped himself into a sitting position, using the wall to keep steady. In a flash of memory, he recalled his leg getting ripped off by a powerful SAS unit. It had launched itself at him in a flurry of coordinated strikes, its body dense and powerful.

Uninvited, he had another flash of memory, the robot clamping its strong hands onto his arm and tearing it from its socket. Applebum raised his other arm to his face. He was relieved to see it was still there, but it stopped at the wrist. He considered filing his emotional response under "deep panic." Instead, he severed access to his entire emotional matrix. Voices were coming from down the hall. He heard the door to his closet being unlocked. Slumping back to his previous position, Applebum fixed his eyes at a single point on the wall and held perfectly still.

“This is it?” a giant RreRriaNnian with a long gray beard said. “This is what I killed all those people for? It doesn’t look like much.”

“That’s because you haven’t seen the scans of its cerebral core,” a tall Divian standing next to him said. She was older, her skin a deep, almost regal, purple color. When she spoke, her voice rumbled with gravitas, like a stage actor’s. “The local R&D specialist couldn’t make sense of the scan results, much less reproduce them. I’m going to need you to eliminate him too. This evening. I asked him to work until seven.”

The RreRriaNnian nodded. “Send me his file.”

“I’m going to crate this SAS and ship it to Station 5 to see if their equipment can get a clearer scan. We’ve also called in one of Waymore’s best AI engineers to assist. I’d like you to meet him there and supervise his inspection. Be ready for any additional collateral afterward.”

“The collateral problem is getting bigger no matter what I do. Your daughter continues to get involved,” the giant said. “She compromised my work with one of the adherents, and I found her digital signature all over the contents of a very concerning Thufflin Box. She also attempted to access this SAS unit’s original file.”

“Nurcia Fragnar shouldn’t be trusted anywhere near this SAS unit,” the Divian said curtly. “One would think that Providence’s best public relations executive would be a better decision-maker, but she most definitely is not.”

“You’re too hard on her,” the giant said matter-of-factly. “You’ve got her exiled to a crappy subsidy, babysitting tourists through the edge of civilization—”

The Divian interrupted the giant. “Someday, when Nurcia has all the bad decision-making out of her system, she’ll get more responsibility. But it won’t happen until she’s ready for it.” The woman studied the giant for a moment, her eyes boring into him. “Leave her to me. You’re too emotionally compromised to be trusted around her anyway.”

The giant hesitated, then nodded again. He crouched directly in front of Applebum, his eyes furrowed with concentration. “If this thing can do what we think it can do, why are we being so quiet about it? With everything going on with Fromanti—”

The Divian held up her index finger like a schoolteacher, interrupting him again. “Don’t say that word.”

“It just seems to me that this technology could save Waymore,” the RreRriaNnian said.

The Divian took a step forward and patted the crouching giant on his thick gray hair. “I’m glad you’re on my side,” she said. “I can’t tell you how much your unceasing loyalty has meant to my personal success at Waymore. You’ve defended me from alien threats, from assassins, from my own stupid mistakes.”

The RreRriaNnian’s eyes narrowed. Applebum could tell that the compliment made him nervous, as if her speech was about to conclude with a bullet to the back of his head. Instead, the Divian held her hand under the RreRriaNnian’s armpit and pulled him gently to his feet. “You’re also extremely lethal,” she said chuckling. “When I need you to be.”

Now it was her turn to crouch directly into Applebum’s line of view. Her face was inches from his and he could see multicolored neon light swirling through her irises. “But I’m starting to realize that this SAS unit—sitting alone in this darkened clean room with its one arm and no legs—this is by far the most dangerous thing either of us has ever laid our eyes on.”

A few hours later, the RreRriaNnian returned and packed Applebum into a large crate. The giant had blood smeared on his hands, so he kept losing his grip as he lifted Applebum into place and lowered the lid. Applebum heard the giant's heavy footsteps thud out of the room and he heard the door slide shut.

He waited, packed in a crate. He waited so long, he felt his restlessness start to shift into insanity. He craved reading, and art, and YouStar, but all he could do was stare at the lid of the crate. *What would Sam Spade do? What would Hercule Poirot do? I. M. Fletcher? They weren't ever in this situation because they would never allow themselves to be so defenseless.* Applebum did not belong with them. And it was all fantasy anyway.

He felt such crushing helplessness that he severed the internal connection to his own sense of time. The wait was still interminable. The fact that he was still experiencing emotional responses made him both curious and worried. Of course, he didn't know what to do with those feelings—he had nowhere to put them.

Hours, days, or weeks later, he heard the door slide open again. He saw the giant's meaty fingers hook under the lid and pull it open. The giant's face peered over the edge of the box, his beard stopping just inches from Applebum's forehead. "He ships out in an hour. You almost missed him," the giant told somebody. "Tell me again why I'm risking my job and one hell of a pension to show you this? If someone finds out you were here, I'll probably be the one to kill you."

He heard musical laughter and a feminine voice say, "You couldn't kill me."

"I could, and would, if you mother asked me to," the giant swore. "I believe her exact words on the subject were, Nurcia Fragnar can't be trusted anywhere near this SAS unit.'"

"And yet you're letting me near it. That's so romantic . . ." A second face appeared beside the giant's. It was another Divian, remarkably similar to the one Applebum had seen days earlier. He knew they must share some genetic foundation. This new Divian, Nurcia Fragnar, reached down and dragged her fingers across Applebum's cheek.

Her other hand was resting on the giant's shoulder. "I'm not only near it, I'm touching it," Nurcia said. Her voice was playful and teasing, but as she looked down at Applebum, he saw a deep intensity in her eyes.

The giant must have also sensed her intensity. He swallowed, then turned to look at Nurcia, his eyes studying hers. Both their faces floated above Applebum's head like giant moons. "That's enough," he decided. "Probably too much." He lowered the lid closed and latched Applebum back into his box.

28
RUSS

"IT'S A SLUDGE DAY," Lanie said, and the rest of Intergalactic Waste Management groaned.

"I wore my new jumpsuit!" a TEN-awtch named Alleyborne groaned.

Russ looked down at his work boots, which were already caked with mud. They'd been clean the night before when he took them off for bed. Clark must have worn them out in the rain in the middle of the night for some reason.

Russ had been at work less than an hour, but he raised his transponder and checked for a response from his anonymous texting partner for what felt like the thousandth time. The message blinked empty, just as it had since the middle of last night.

"No laws in the Darkzone," Linnie reminded them all. "Nothing to stop UAIB businesses from transporting their hazardous runoff out here and dumping it wherever they please. We're processing what we can and moving the rest outside the cruise ship path. Observe every hazmat-handling protocol," Linnie reminded them. "No shortcuts."

Russ and Trell left the briefing room and moved down a long corridor. “What happened to the kid?” Russ asked Trell out of the corner of his mouth. “Did you find a safe place for him?”

“Yeah, thanks for leaving that whole problem to me—” Trell began.

Before he could finish his sentence, RK came up behind Russ. Just to be an asshole, the Plutorach zagged in front of him and then slowed enough that Russ had to slow down too, or he would have tripped over the much smaller man.

Russ sighed. He held RK steady by the top of his head and wiped his boots on the small man’s hairy backside.

RK squeaked, dried mud clumped on his back. He wormed free from Russ’s grip and hustled away, shaking his fists and shouting, “You’re bullshit!”

“Glad to see you’re making friends with the crew,” Lanie called through the open door of the briefing room.

Russ gave her a thumbs up.

Once RK had scrambled out of earshot, Trell whispered, “The kid is still onboard. I put him in an auxiliary storage room off the cargo bay. But I don’t know how long he will stay in there. And if he comes out—it’s doomsday for us and him. We need to use the MUPmap to scan for habitable planets nearby. If we find one safe enough, we can drop him there during lunch break. There’s only one problem.”

“What’s that?”

“Odette is our navigator. She’s spectacularly beautiful, but she’s also stickler for the rules. And she’s a Klung, like me.”

“So, she’ll know if we lie to her,” Russ said. “You Klung are worse than SAS units and their honesty protocols.”

Trell looked offended. “You really mean that. The Klung are a frangible and beautiful people. It’s not our fault everyone else is full of shit. Also, under absolutely no circumstances can we tell Odette the truth about why we need to use the MUPmap.”

The *Nightfire* MUPmap room was arranged a lot like a VTR, with padded walls and ceilings. A 3D hologram—this one of the entire universe—hung suspended in the open space. Odette stood in the middle, holographic light reflecting off the sparse angles of her body. Beneath the glowing layer of light, Russ could see she was hairless, with faintly gray skin that matched Trell's. Also, like Trell, she had jagged, darker gray lines running in zigzag patterns across her skin, albeit her line patterns were much different from his. From across the room, Odette's yellow pupils shone behind a pair of tear-drop spectacles.

"Hello?" she said.

"I'm Russ," Russ said, charmingly. "I think you already know Trell. We were wondering if you could do us a favor?"

"That depends on what it is," she said. She spoke in a flat cadence and didn't alter her expression in any way. Russ had trouble picking up on any kind of emotional response.

"Isn't she great?" Trell whispered.

"She's really hot," Russ lied, for the sake of his new friend.

"I can tell you think you're lying," Trell reminded him. "You'll have to do better than that with Odette. Also, calling a Klung hot is a grave insult."

"She's . . . whatever the right compliment is," Russ corrected as they approached the center of the room. Before they reached Odette, Trell pivoted left, moving to stand against the far wall. Confused, Russ followed. "What are you doing?"

"Klung always know how other Klung feel about them. We can sense each other's dominant emotion. If I get any closer, she will know I find her extremely attractive." Trell widened his eyes and bit the corner of his lip.

"Is that bad?" Russ took a quick glance at his transponder.

"Maybe? Maybe not. Staying away is an indirect, far more romantic form of flattery. It is simultaneously coy and a blatant admission that you have something to hide. The most sensual possible combination."

Russ grimaced. He wanted to check his transponder again but forced himself not to. "We came in here to help the little alien kid hiding in the closet, not get you laid."

"It is possible to do two things at once."

Russ looked at the huge map in the center of the room and a thought occurred to him: *This could be really helpful if you're looking for somebody.* His eyes moved to Odette. She was minding her own business, so he turned back to Trell. "How am I supposed to get her help if I can't lie to her and I can't tell her the truth?"

"Ask yourself this," Trell suggested, "What form of communication is never a lie?" Without providing an answer, Trell took Russ by the shoulders and turned him toward Odette. He gave Russ a shove in the middle of the back.

Klung express romantic interest by avoiding the person they're interested in? Russ thought as he approached Odette. *I'd be amazing in this culture. So would Nina.*

"I was hoping to use the map," Russ told her.

She studied him carefully. "The MUPmap is for official mission use only."

"This is official," Russ started to say, but Odette arched a brow under her overlarge glasses, and he knew immediately that she'd register the lie. "Officially a request by me to use the map," he concluded.

"Well, it's still officially for official mission use only," Odette informed him.

"I would be very happy if you'd run a scan for me," Russ told her.

"Why?" Odette asked pointedly.

"It's good to be happy," Russ said.

Odette nodded. Russ knew she wouldn't challenge that awkward logic. Mostly because she didn't need to. "Still for official use only," she said.

Russ looked over at Trell who waved politely. *What form of communication can never be a lie? Silence? Yes, but that wouldn't help. What else is never a lie?* Russ asked himself. And then he figured it out.

"Can the MUPmap tell us if there are any habitable planets nearby?" Russ asked.

"Of course it can," Odette said.

"How does it do that?"

"It's a state-of-the-art navigational tool with a database built from crowdsourcing and Multi-User-Protocol scanning algorithms. It can filter by atmosphere, planetary rotation, gravity scale, apex, secondary and tertiary predators, weather patterns, principal biospheres and plant life, principal rock and mineral formations, even frequency of natural disasters. It's been one of the honors of my life to run it for the Intergalactic Waste Management LLC." Odette's emotions were still muted, but just by the small shifts in her tone, Russ could tell she was excited by the MUPmap's capabilities.

"Can it search by alloy? Could it, for example, find an SAS unit based on its build and material makeup?"

Odette considered the question for a moment. "I believe it could. But there are millions of SAS units from each generation. It would be difficult to parse out the useful information with such search parameters."

"And what would this amazing machine say about nearby habitable planets?" Russ asked, trying to transition as seamlessly as possible to his other major problem.

"Why do you want to know?"

"Is it so important to answer that?"

"What if I say it is?" Odette's eyebrows arched, just a fraction. She showed no other emotion.

"Why don't you tell me?"

Odette smiled and gave a small shrug.

Russ realized she'd caught on to his gambit. The answer to Trell's riddle, what form of communication can never be a lie . . . was no answer at all. It was a question. Unfortunately, while he'd made some progress sticking to questions, Odette now seemed to be volleying them back to him in equally obtuse and unhelpful ways. He tried one more time:

"What if I told you it *was* official business?"

"If it is, why don't you tell me?" Odette's yellow eyes shone at Russ, reflecting the light of the holographic map.

Russ rubbed his temple. There was only one question left to ask, but he was pretty sure it would work. "What if I gave you a thousand credits?"

Odette frowned. Then she nodded, just slightly.

Russ opened his banking app and prepared to push the credits to her transponder. The screen blinked red, and a message flashed Insufficient Funds. He tapped on the icon to see his balance and his heart sank. Yesterday, just before he'd handed his transponder to his grandfather, he had had slightly more than forty-eight thousand credits, including Drench's forty-four thousand. Now, his balance read zero.

A moment later a text appeared.

Ω: *STATION 5! STATION 5! WHY HAV3N'T YOU FOUND M3?*

29
CLARK

CLARK WATCHED NORMA'S OLD MERCURY Tracer amble into the back parking lot of the Riverview Motel. Even though he knew she wasn't inside, the sight of it still made his heart swell.

That feeling evaporated as the door swung open and old Rufus Ensine stepped out. Clark's romantic rival had a crooked smile on his face as he crossed the parking lot and ducked into Clark's motel room.

"Why did I have to park in the back?"

"Nina is at the pool. She's been lying on the lounger all day." Clark peeked through the window toward the pool. He could see Nina was still out there, tanning and scrolling intently through her transponder.

"Why isn't she at work?" Ensine asked.

"Somebody sabotaged their ship. She'll be around for a while. That's why I told you to only come by at night."

"Does it have anything to do with us? The ship being sabotaged?"

Clark shook his head. "Russ and Nina don't even know there is an us. I'd like to keep it that way . . . forever."

"You called me," Ensine reminded him. "What's so important that you had to see me in broad daylight? With Nina right outside?"

"I've got a lead and the money to pay for it." Clark whispered. "But it's time sensitive."

"You found the missing Obinz stone?" Ensine asked.

"Nope. The other thing."

Ensine perked up. Clark could see he was trying to hide his interest, "What did you learn? Tell me quickly."

"There's not enough time to tell you," Clark grinned. "Follow me to the Waypoint and I'll show you."

They exited the Waypoint onto Triameed, a small moon rotating around the tourist-friendly planet Ekho. Clark was hit with a fit of coughing. Once it passed, he looked out the starscreen at the vast oceans of moon rock on every side of the small travel hub. Far below, Planet Ekho slowly rotated, its twin metropolises so filled with light pollution they were visible from orbit.

Ensine approached the spaceclerk.

"Where can I reroute you, fine sirs?" the clerk asked. "Southern Ekho has many delightful sites and a mostly agrarian landscape. It's clean and peaceful with lots of great places to eat. Northern Ekho is less calm, but with a much more upbeat and fun atmosphere that can—"

"We were thinking of staying on Triameed," Ensine interrupted.

"There's nothing on Triameed," the clerk explained patiently. "Just me and this humble outpost."

"Are you sure?" Ensine removed a coin from his pocket and spun it on the clerk's desk.

The clerk grabbed the coin, bit into it to test its legitimacy, then handed it back to Ensine.

"Next time, just lead with the coin," the clerk said smartly. Ensine touched the man's transponder with his own and they both lit up with a credit transfer. The clerk rolled his chair out from behind the desk and opened the floor paneling directly beneath it, revealing a staircase leading into darkness. Ensine gave a quick salute and went down the steps. Clark moved to follow, but the spaceclerk blocked his path. "He only paid for himself," the clerk told Clark.

"Of course he did," Clark said. They tapped transponders and the clerk nodded.

"Welcome to the Night Market," he said.

"You shouldn't be drinking. We need to keep our heads clear," Clark told Ensine, taking the Maxibrew out of Ensine's hand and lifting it to his own mouth.

Ensine had discovered Clark was alive in this very spot two months earlier. They had been both headed for the same black-market jewelry stall. Clark had been inquiring about the Obinz stone, Ensine had been picking up a bracelet for Norma. When they recognized each other, only one punch was thrown, and Clark's aim had been bad enough that Ensine hadn't bothered swinging back.

They accidently met again when Clark slipped over to drink at the Banville Blitzkrieg Bar where he'd thought no one would recognize him. Ensine, six beers into a thirty-beer night, had been the only one to do so. And that was when they had begun to talk about what Clark had been doing since his death. *I've already loaned Ensine my wife*, Clark rationalized, *why not share everything else*?

A strange alliance had been formed at the Blitzkrieg that night between a half-drunk old man and a very-drunk old fish.

The Night Market was full of shady-looking people milling all around the hollowed-out tunnel system, visiting different booths and semipermanent storefronts. Clark saw a booth selling modified RNO-Tech rifles, "Governor's off these babies," the unwashed, mangy Plutorach salesman said when they made eye contact. "On maximum setting, they can shred through anything short of Fromantium." The salesman moved with them as they walked, shuffling sideways. "But they show up as clean, registered, and legal on all government scanners. Guaranteed!"

In another booth on the other side of the broad tunnel, a salesman held a large digital sign. It was a menu, advertising Maxibrew, Desert Wine, and something called Saint-Oat's-Bubbly. When that salesman caught Clark looking his way, he quickly flipped over the sign, giving Clark the briefest glance at the other side. Clark caught the words, "Toer Flesh! Delightful taste! Any Cut to Order!" before the man quickly flipped the sign back again. The salesman grinned at Clark and arched his eyebrows suggesting other, even more illegal, foods might be available upon request.

"Will you at least tell me who we're meeting?" Ensine asked.

"A female. Kruxfasian. About twenty-five. Plain features. Missing half an antenna."

"Why does she matter?"

"She has the paste," Clark whispered. "At least, she claims to have the paste."

The words stopped Ensine completely in his tracks. "Unlikely," he said. "A twenty-five-year-old Kruxfasian has illegal Liafen technology? Technology we've scoured numerous planets and back-alley flea markets like this one for, without even a trace of success."

"My sources tell me she has the paste," Clark promised.

"Not Algadon, I hope. He's full of crap half the time—"

"No, not Algadon," Clark promised, sadly. They had arrived at a nondescript gray tent. Unlike the others, it had no signage. The flaps were pulled down, and it appeared completely unused—usually a sign you were about to buy something good.

Ensine balked before lifting the flap and stepping inside. "Is there any reason to believe she might have what she says she has? Any evidence? Proof that she has made contact with Liafen, much less done business with them?"

"No," Clark said. "Not exactly."

"And how much is she charging? You haven't done a job in months. How could you possibly have the money for something like this—"

"I've got forty-four thousand," Clark assured him. "But she didn't seem that interested in the money."

"Then what does she want?"

"Just your hard-light transformer," Clark said.

Ensine swung his fist in an arc, aiming directly for Clark's nose. Ensine was a CERT trainer, a specialist in hand-to-hand combat, and in much better shape than Clark. Fortunately, the punch was a reckless knockout blow, swung with all the strength and vigor he could muster.

Clark managed to get just out of the range. Then he dove forward at Ensine's knees. The two old men toppled into the tent, disappearing behind its heavy flaps.

30
RUSS

"YOU SHOULD HAVE WOKEN ME the minute you got the first message," Nina said. She dog-eared her book and folded her legs to make room so Russ could fit at the end of the motel pool lounger. Russ had spent the last eight hours piloting the *Lumina* around a lake of galactic sludge while Trell vacuumed it drip by drop into puffy hazmat sacks. He was tired, but seeing Nina relaxed and happy on the pool lounge gave him unexpected energy. He handed her his transponder and she studied the mysterious two a.m. text exchange, her eyes darting back and forth in front of the small screen.

"Have you got any response? It looks like this is only going one way . . ."

"No, yeah. I can't tell. One way, I think. The signal's really spotty. I got another message at the start of the workday." Russ scrolled to the final message and showed it to her. "But nothing since."

"The signal gets interrupted by galactic interference. I'm guessing the rotation of certain planets. Or meteor storms of particularly dense metals." Nina studied Russ's face. "There's really only one person these could be coming from."

"You think it's Applebum?"

"Your grandpop said Applebum used my transponder every night. He could have copied the texting protocol into his own system. I believe he just needs to stare at code and he can program himself. It's alarming when you think of the implications."

"I just want to find him," Russ said.

"We won't stop until we do." Nina stood up from the lounger and stretched. "Now that I've had a little rest, maybe I can actually start thinking straight again." She turned to Russ, her mouth dipping slightly. "Drench is dead. I put a tag on any news articles with his name. His compression gear failed on a spacewalk. They found him frozen to death, without a rebreather, still tethered to the back of the SavUQuik ship."

"Verch." Russ said. "That means we're next."

"At least your grandpop got Drench the life insurance," Nina said. "His mom will be well taken care of."

Russ grimaced. "Clark cleared out my account. All of Drench's money and my small savings. I'd be very surprised to learn that he used it to buy life insurance." Russ could hear the frustration in his own voice.

To Nina's credit, she avoided "I told you so." "Are you okay? Have you tried to get it back?"

"He's not in his hotel room. He may be gone forever." Russ realized he was gripping the metal pool fence hard enough that the rusted underside was cutting into his hand. "You told me not to trust him. I should have listened—you know my dad wasn't around when I was a kid and my grandpop, he—" Russ didn't finish the sentence. He couldn't find the words.

Nina tapped his bicep affectionately. "There's no shame in trusting the people you love. Until they betray you. You won't trust him again, right?"

All Russ said was, "I'll find a way to make it right with Drench's mom, somehow."

Nina leaned against him, resting her head between his shoulder blades. She hadn't touched him like this . . . ever. He felt his grip on the railing loosening a bit. She pushed his right side to spin him around in a small circle to face the pool.

"We're poor. We lost our jobs. The people we care about are either robbing us or disappearing or both. And the pool water is green." She pointed to the algae with her toe. "I wish the pool were at least blue."

Russ laughed. He couldn't help himself. "We could use a victory," he said. "Grab your keys. I've got an idea."

Russ noticed that Nina always drove with the window open. Her hair whipped all around, almost moving to the beat of the Old Crow Medicine Show song playing on the radio. She drove them up Highway 89 toward Medicine Butte. The radio signal, beaming all the way from the border of Utah, cut in and out as they rode the switchbacks.

Beautiful landscape raced past on either side, rolling hills and tall pines. Russ was from a big city, and he was still getting used to open spaces. He'd driven across much of the US—and now he'd seen half the universe—but there was a beautiful serenity to Wyoming that he hadn't been able to find anywhere else.

They wound upward on the dirt access road, Nina's old Ford F150 bumping along gamely, until they came upon the cluster of shortwave radio towers, honeycomb shaped television towers, and wantonly phallic cell phone towers. Each was wrapped in a wooden frame to protect it from snow damage in the winter.

"Why did we come up here again?" Nina asked.

"You said the transponder signal can get blocked. Seems like we should get as high up as possible."

Nina looked side-eyed at Russ. “We could have just Waypointed to a space station orbiting near the center of multiple civilized galaxies.”

Russ grinned sheepishly. “My grandma also said there’s a really beautiful view at sunset.”

“I think I saw your grandma’s car at the Riverview Motel!” Nina told him. “I spotted it driving away a week ago and I think I saw it drive by again today.”

“How is that possible? Norma can’t know Clark is still alive. Can she?”

“I don’t think she does,” Nina said.

“Who else would drive her car? Not Ensine?”

“I’m worried it might be.”

“Ensine and Clark working together—that would be a disaster.” Russ ran his hands through his thick hair. He began to think back through the conversations he’d had with Ensine lately, trying to decide whether Ensine had ever said anything that hinted he might know Clark was still alive.

Nina seemed lost in thought as well. She was looking through the windshield at the communication towers. “This mountain’s called Medicine Butt,” she said absently.

“Is that the real name? Medicine Butt? You Evanstown types are pretty weird. I think it’s butte.”

She climbed from the truck. “In high school we called it butt. I still hear it that way in my head. See that peak over there? That’s Humpy Peak. Don’t ask me what the high school kids called that one.” Nina lifted herself onto the hood and rested her feet on the truck’s front bumper.

Russ joined her. They sat shoulder to shoulder, admiring the view and the bright oranges and yellows of the setting sun. The engine was still warm, heating the hood against the night air. “This is the highest point anywhere near Evanstown. I figure we attach the transponder to that big cell tower”—Russ pointed—“and who knows, maybe—”

"It's not going to work," Nina said. "If the problem was something as simple as elevation or amplification, you'd get messages the minute you jumped onto the *Nightfire*."

Russ was silent for a moment. He was staring down at his transponder.

"But it's still a good idea—" Nina was saying, obviously just to be nice. Russ held up the transformer, trying not to be smug.

Ω: *CAN YOU H3AR M3? RUSS?*

He tapped quickly at the screen.

"C'mon! Really?" Nina said, shocked.

Russ: *Applebum, can you read this?*

Ω: *PL3AS3 COM3 AND FIND M3*

Russ: *Are you getting my messages?*

Ω: *IF YOU CAN R3AD THIS, PL3AS3 H3LP. I'M IN A LAB. A WAYMOR3 RESEARCH LAB. STATION 5.*

Ω: I *CAN S33 3NOVA TR33S OUTSID3. PLANT3D IN A LIN3*

Ω: . . . *BANN3R B3HIND THE TR33S. GR33N AND BLU3. WORDS AR3: PARK UNION BRAWL3RS.*

Ω: *NEXD ELP. PL3AS3 COM3 AND FIND M3*

Russ: *We will find you. I promise. Sit tight, buddy. We're on our way.*

Still shoulder to shoulder, Russ and Nina stared down at the transponder, but no more messages came. "You are so weirdly lucky," Nina said, finally.

"A master of general chaos?" Russ suggested.

"Not a bad term for it." Nina scrolled back through the messages. "We have three clues: Research Station 5, Enova trees and a Park Union Brawler's banner."

"They're a Bootball team," Russ said. "Out of the Triple S Star Cluster. They aren't one of the bigger squads and mostly only play regional games."

"That will narrow it down," Nina said.

"It might be all we need. Lanie and Linnie have a state-of-the-art MUPmap on the *Nightfire*. It has a filter that will organize planets through any number of data analytics. There's this stick-up-the-butt technician guarding it, but she got off work the same time I did."

"What are we waiting for?" Nina asked. She had left her keys in the car, and the radio station belched back to life, playing a solemn late-period Waylon Jennings ballad.

"I really want to find Applebum," Russ said truthfully. He yawned so wide his jaw nearly locked. "But can we wait three minutes?"

"For what?"

"Just until this song ends, then we can get right back to work." Russ nodded toward the setting sun. As it lowered behind Humpy Peak, its rays caught the evening clouds, infusing them with streaks of orange and red and a pale violet. Russ heard Nina gasp at the sight, and they were both quiet again. She learned sideways, her shoulder pressed against Russ's. They were keeping each other upright.

When the song ended he hopped off the truck. He put his foot on the bumper to help Nina down. "Ready to check out Odette's MUP-map?"

Nina nodded. "Three minutes of perfect," he heard her say quietly, her eyes still studying the beautiful sunset.

"I just need to grab some sandwiches from Bum's Sam'wich Emporium before we go," Russ said.

31
CLARK

ENSINE'S FACE WAS BRIGHT RED, glowing even in the darkness of the tent. Clark had thrown them both off balance and even managed to free the hard-light transformer from Ensine's ear. The other man transformed in his grip, his skin going from flesh to scales and becoming considerably harder to hold onto. Ensine reserved his hips, swung his body around for greater leverage, and pushed Clark's face into the dirt floor.

Clark flopped forward, rolling awkwardly to his feet and backing up until he felt the cloth of the tent wall against his shoulders.

Ensine rose, a look of tremendous determination on his face, his scales glittering in the faint light. "Give me back my transformer," he demanded.

"Is this all part of the negotiation process?" a female voice said.

The men turned to see the female Kruxfasian. Clark hadn't noticed her before, but she was suddenly standing in the corner of the tent, watching them. Just as he'd been told to expect, one of her antennae was half gone, the other disappearing into the top of the tent's ceiling. Clark tossed her the hard-light transformer, and she slipped it into the folds of her coat.

"No!" Ensine insisted.

"These hard-light transformers are harder to find than they used to be. And I happen to need one quite badly," the Kruxfasian said.

"Give it," Ensine said, holding out his palm.

She turned to face him. "You're Major Rufus Ensine, late of the 4029th Naval Command. It's a pleasure to meet a war hero." She pivoted to Clark. "And you're Clark Wesley, a professional criminal and general miscreant. You're wanted in six star clusters."

"A few more than that," Clark said. He felt a chill run through his body. All he had done to shield his travels, and this adolescent Kruxfasian knew his and Ensine's names?

"Who are you?" Ensine asked. He took a step toward her, so they stood chest to chest. It looked like Ensine was going to grab her by the sides of her head, but instead he flicked his fingers, knocking a transformer off her right ear.

The Kruxfasian held her ground and didn't flinch. As the transformer spiraled to the ground, her insect body shimmered away, replaced by the most beautiful Divian Clark had ever seen—and that was saying something. Her purple skin shimmered, reflecting a new color in Ensine's mirror-like scales. Her wavy purple hair fell over her shoulders. She had the lean muscles of a dancer—or a fencer. She was dressed professionally in a pantsuit. A sling hung across her chest.

Even Ensine was taken aback. No longer in disguise, they were now the same height. He took half a step away from the exotic Divian. "How do you know who we are?"

"It wasn't hard to put it together," she said, nodding to Clark. "I've met his grandson Russ several times. After the ambush at NeNe's Nearly Nude Revue, I followed him through the Waypoints back to Earth."

"I told him to disassemble the stupid thing!" Clark cursed.

"I know you did. I was in the room when you said it. I couldn't stay long without revealing I was there, but it wasn't hard for me to put the other pieces together. What do you know about the robot? You call him Applebum? What's so special about him that my mother would be killing everyone who came in contact with him?"

Clark laced his fingers behind his head and leaned back, closing his eyes. He let the disappointment wash over him. He understood what her questions meant. This wasn't a legitimate illegitimate business deal. "You don't have the Liafen repair paste? This is just another trap?" he said, tiredly.

The Divian smiled. "No. The deal is still on. I just find your grandson . . . fascinating. And he's right in the middle of something that involves my mother and the SAS unit." The Divian looked at Clark. Her features were almost impossibly symmetrical except for her oversized almond-shaped eyes. "The repair paste was a genuine offer. It has already been delivered to your motel room."

"How could you possibly have gotten your hands on something so rare?" Clark asked.

"I have powerful friends," the Divian said. "I don't want you to forget who got you the paste, in case there's anything else I need from you."

Clark nodded.

"The deal is not on," Ensine interrupted. He seemed to be fighting to keep his voice level. "That hard-light transformer is not for sale."

Without the hard-light transformer, Ensine couldn't live comfortably on Earth. Without it, he would have to be honest with Norma about who and what he really was. Clark considered that aspect of the deal a nice secondary benefit. "You stole my Obinz stone and traded it for that transformer. It practically belonged to me already," Clark snapped at him. "We needed the paste more than we need the transformer."

"No, we don't," Ensine said firmly.

"Our problems are about to be over! Once we find that Obinz stone—" Clark coughed violently.

A look of sympathy crossed the Divian's face. "I hope the repair paste works like you want it to," she said. "Do me a favor. When you see Russ again, remind him of the advice I gave him at NeNe's. It's important that he follow it."

Before Clark could answer, Ensine lunged at her, his hands clutching at her business jacket.

The Divian spun out of his grip and punched him hard in the chest, sending him back across the tent.

He dug in his heels and lunged toward her once more, his arms spread wide.

Just as he reached her, she blinked out of sight. Ensine glanced around the darkened tent, frantically. Then he spun on his heel and kicked down the support beam in the center. The tent collapsed. The tent fabric, heavy and caked with dust, sent Clark down to a knee, coughing.

For a moment, he and Ensine could both see the outline of the Divian as the collapsing tent clung to her invisible body. Ensine dove toward her, but she shuffled in the other direction.

A second later, the edge of the fallen tent lifted, then dropped closed again. Ensine army-crawled rapidly in the same direction.

Clark followed more slowly. When he finally got out from under the heavy material, he was greeted once more by colorful sights and raucous sounds of the Night Market. The nearby tents were full of people buying, selling, and negotiating.

The Divian was nowhere in sight. Ensine darted around the open space grasping at empty air.

32

RUSS

RUSS AND NINA HUSTLED DOWN the darkened main corridor of the *Nightfire*, a large sack of cheap sandwiches flung over Russ's shoulder.

"Should I ask why you bought ten seventy-five cent sandwiches?"

"It's nothing dangerous," he promised.

"Sure," Nina said.

They reached the MUPmap room. It was windowless and awash in darkness. Nina felt her way along the wall to the left while Russ moved to the right. She must have found the switch, because the lights came on and the map began to populate in the middle of the room. First, a cluster of swirling galaxies rolled into place like neon clouds blowing across the horizon.

The "clouds" anchored into position and the map conjured other astronomical objects: stars, planets, asteroid fields, confetti-like spattering of neon space dust, and inky splotches of celestial energy. For a moment, it seemed like the map was glitching. On the far corner of the room, it darkened and deepened, and an unidentifiable object loomed over an entire quadrant.

Then it was gone. While Russ had been lost in the splendor of all mapped existence, Nina had been figuring out how to zoom in using hand gestures. She focused on one galaxy and zoomed in even closer. Russ realized she'd narrowed in on Earth. Russ moved to the center of the map, and he was close enough to see thousands of man-made satellites floating around the edges of the sphere. They formed a sloppy halo, like Earth was Saturn's diuretic younger brother. He cupped the moon between his palms.

Nina was poking away at the map's control board. "Give me a second to figure out this navigational filtering system." She moved her hands around, seeing how the map reacted to each motion. Russ watched her, Mars sliding back and forth between her palms. When she glanced up at him again, Olympus Mons reflected in her dark brown eyes.

"Take your time. I'll be back in a second," Russ said.

It was cold in the ship at night. He rubbed his arms to stay warm as he hustled down the corridor heading farther south. He passed the mess hall and the comms center.

The door was ajar to the bunk room, and he could see hairy RK curled up in one of the top bunks. The little man snored with ruthless gusto. Russ ducked into the room and swiped RK's small jacket and boots from atop his personal locker.

Moving as quietly as possible, he made his way to the cargo bay, slid aside a heavy crate, and pulled open one of the larger storage lockers. After work hours, the cargo bay was lit only by faint running lights along the floor. They didn't produce enough ambient light for him to see more than half a foot into the locker.

But he sensed, as much as heard, a shifting of position, and the air was filled with a guttural clicking sound, like the warning of a threatened animal. "Boots. Jacket. Sandwiches." Russ whispered, throwing each item inside. "Are you doing okay in here? We have plans to get you planetside. If Nina figures out the MUPmap, we we'll have a planet to take you to tomorrow."

He waited a moment and a low, rasping wail emitted from the closet. "Charrrllliiiieee," the boy moaned. The hair on Russ's arms stood up. He quickly sealed the storage locker door and pushed the crate back in place.

"I think I figured out the filter," Nina said as he reentered the navigation room. The map zoomed out to Earth's entire solar system. Splotches of dark blue began to form on several of the planets. Big areas of color and hundreds of smaller specks appeared and spread across Earth, Mars, and Pluto. "Blue is power generating on the quantum level," Nina explained. "The little dots are Waypoints—the bigger blue splotches are mostly dense industrial areas. Not a lot of those in this cluster."

Russ orbited Pluto. It was the only planet in Earth's system with any large blue splotches. He could almost identify where Pluto's major cities were, based on the color. "I hate Pluto so much," he muttered.

"Strange take," Nina told him.

"Can we filter the map based on land use? Say, focus only on land owned and leased by Waymore Industries?"

Nina fiddled with the controls and the map changed. "I can do even better than that." Suddenly the planet Ren'Div was floating in the center of the room. Despite being gigantic, and the capital planet of the entire UAIB, it had fewer thick blue splotches than Pluto. Another planet appeared beside it, and another, and another. "These are the planets where Waymore Industries has either research and development laboratories or large-scale SAS manufacturing."

Russ looked down the line. "And now Enova trees?"

Most of the planets disappeared, leaving four.

Russ approached the third one. It was labeled Beta-9. Something about it bothered him, and he realized what. It had no glowing blue landmarks—no working Waypoints at all. "We can probably rule out this one—" he started to say. "There's no planetside transportation."

Nina refreshed the filter, but there was still no sign of the blue lights that indicated quantum power. She zoomed in on the center of Beta-9, and a map of major points of interest began to populate, each adjourned by a series of icons. Icons in the shape of crisscrossed tools seemed to denote manufacturing, along with icons of a credit symbol, likely for shopping zones, and icons of a bed, either pointing out lodging or residential districts. All the icons blinked in alternating patterns with a series of red X's. Nina scrolled through the 3D map until her fingers highlighted the Waymore Industries Research and Development lab. It glowed a distinct orange to indicate the presence of dense metals, but even the icon of the lab was covered by a blinking red X. "Everything is closed." Nina observed. "And I think the whole planet might be synthetic. That's why the entire thing glowed when I filtered by Waymore-owned property. It's a corporate biosphere, and it seems to be offline. Why would an entire synthetic planet be shut down?"

"To hide something?" Russ suggested.

"Or to prepare for something," Nina corrected. She studied the map more closely.

Russ noticed one icon not blinking red. Near the center of the biosphere, no more than a handful of miles from the Waymore R&D lab, was the floating icon of a helmet. He could see a face mask attached to the underside of the helmet. When he reached out and touched the icon, a dialogue box appeared: Mulgrew Melville Memorial Stadium. Home of the Huvvel Vaquals and the Intergalactic Bootball Tournament.

"The Vaquals play the Park Union Brawlers in the first round of the tournament. This is where he is," Russ said. "This is where we need to be."

Nina nodded. "I think you're right. The tournament is just a few cycles away. That complicates things."

"It probably explains why the Waypoints are all closed. Travel is restricted, maybe to prevent gatecrashers or just to make it more exclusive," Russ guessed. "Or to give people an additional day or two to party?"

"I think all of those reasons."

"It might work out perfectly," Russ said. "We go see the game. It gives us an excuse to be planetside and a crowd to distract Waymore and any local security force. We just need to scrounge up enough credits to afford a seat. And a large enough portable Waypoint to get Applebum back home."

"The tournament starts in three days. And it's totally sold out," Nina said. She hesitated for a moment. "But I know somebody who has an extra ticket."

"Would they give it to me?" Russ asked.

Nina shook her head. "It's Kendren. I think he was getting ready to invite me, just before Verch attacked the *Aldersochi*."

Russ frowned. Kendren was a veritable hulk of oozing testosterone, and he'd seemed mildly interested in Nina for almost as long as Russ had known her. "Waymore Industries owns this entire planet?" he asked.

"Yes."

Russ closed his eyes and rubbed his temple. "I think I know someone who will take me too," he said, not totally sure how he felt about the idea even as it left his mouth.

33

RUSS

"UNCLASSIFIED PLANET X-ERO 408A?" Trell asked. They had been midway through the next day's work shift before Russ found a good time to tell Trell about the planet he and Nina had found on the MUPmap.

He'd asked her to filter out a habitable planet along the *Nightfire*'s cleaning pattern in the Darkzone.

"It's got oxygen, plants, and protein-based life forms. Perfect for the scary little kid in the closet. He can hunt and eat to his heart's content," Russ told Trell.

"We'll move Charlie tonight then. Just as soon as we finish . . . this," Trell gestured out the starscreen. They were alone in the *Lumina*. A cluster of about thirty basketball-sized rocks floated by, glowing a faint, electric silver.

"Did you name the spooky Liafeen kid Charlie?"

Trell nodded. "It's what he sounds like he's saying when he's nervous, or angry."

"You two are drifting away from the rocks," Lanie's voice prompted over the comm.

"Blame the pilot. He's CERTified for pest control," Trell told her.

Russ cupped his hands over his eyes and stared at the electric silver rocks now floating a hundred yards to the left. He pushed the ship in their direction. "Any reason we can't just vacuum these rocks like we did that globby lake? Or grab them with that huge claw on top of the *Nightfire*?"

Trell pulled on the legs of his compression gear, looking out over the cluster. "This tiny meteor storm is super-condensed potassium, powered by a cocktail of stellar remnants, cosmic dust, and gases. Not only is it radioactive, but each rock will discharge a strong electrical current when it comes in contact with a metallic conduit. If a Providence Cruise ship sailed through this, she would sail out the other side with ten or fifteen holes popped in her hull. Lanie and Linnie will use the claws eventually, but we have to insulate the rocks first."

Trell handed Russ a three-by-three-foot box, then popped the top. Inside was a stack of polymer bags folded neatly. Trell attached a long, woven graphene tether to his waist. He took the box back from Russ and attached it to the tether as well.

"Wish I could help you with this," Russ said.

"Even a basic Trash Remediation CERT doesn't cover this level of hazardous waste disposal. It's only for us grizzled veterans. Just keep the ship close enough for the tether to reach that farthest rock." Trell was dressing very slowly, checking and rechecking the seals on his suit. "We've got to get Charlie out tonight," he said, changing the subject. "I doubt he'll sit quietly in that closet for too much longer."

"What would happen if someone finds him before we can get him off the ship?" Russ asked, curious.

"That's one of those UAIB secrets you don't ever hear about. And if you want to live with a clear conscious, you don't ask about it either. The UAIB is, by nature, mostly benevolent."

"Not if you can't ask questions about their immigration policy," Russ clarified.

"With the Liafen, it's not an issue of immigration. Haven't you ever wondered why all seventy-three species of the United Alliance of Intelligent Beings can work together without squabble and greed? How they can share technology and a free market with minimal infighting? Even our organized crime is . . . pretty mellow. It's because there's a boogeyman out here in the Darkzone. A species both violent and thirsty for expansion. A species so scary that seventy-three other species play well with each other just to keep them at bay."

"The Liafen."

"Yessir."

"Maybe we shouldn't save him?"

"What's the alternative?"

Trell finished suiting up, taking his time pulling his gloves on and carefully examining the seal between the gloves and the sleeves. He glanced at Russ and said, "You're wondering why it's taking me so long to get dressed?"

"Yep."

"Remember, the potassium is charged with electricity. In very small amounts, it is considered a Klung delicacy. But if I make noninsulated contact with a rock of this size, it would completely overwhelm my biological systems."

"It would knock you out or something?"

Trell shook his head. "It would kill me. I'd go supernova."

"That's why RK was giggling when he gave us our assignment this morning?" Russ clarified. "Because this job could literally kill you?"

"RK is an asshole," Trell confirmed.

"Let's skip it," Russ suggested.

Trell shook his head. "I have a son back on my home world. He lives with his mom, but I have to stay employed to keep the money coming in for the family. I think it's why I took pity on Charlie. I'm trying to shake off the guilt I feel for not being able to do more for my own kid."

"You and his mom divorced?"

Trell shook his head. "There's not even a word for marriage in the Klung language, much less divorce. Do you know what would happen if a pair of sensitive empaths tried to cohabit? It would be an endless cycle of hurt feelings. Klung know better than to get caught up in that nonsense. But we try to stay close for the sake of the child, and we always split financial responsibility. You already know I'm attracted to passionate women—"

Russ blinked in surprise. "You mean Odette?"

Trell nodded. "My ex-mate is twice so. Unfortunately, she struggles to hold on to employment. And the Klung economy is in constant flux." Trell brushed off his problems with the wave of his hand. "So, I'm out here in the Darkzone, making a living and tolerating assholes like RK and shit jobs that might kill me. Don't feel sorry for me. I can tell you're feeling sorry for me."

"I'm not," Russ lied.

"Are all my vitals registering properly on the HUD?"

"Yep," Russ said, starting to pull on the spare compression gear. "Now take the suit back off. You're wearing my favorite helmet."

A few minutes later, Russ was fully suited up and climbing along the metal handrails to the front of the ship. He leaned his back against the starscreen and stretched his legs over the *Lumina*'s long nose, making sure not to block the reaction control vents. Far on the visual horizon, the distant spirals of a pinwheel galaxy blinked pale pink against a backdrop of deepest black. "This is a better seat anyway," Russ said into the comms.

Trell engaged the thrusters, slowly motoring the Lumina that direction. "Thank you," Trell told him.

"Have you ever been to the Skylounge on Gorrillian Green?"

"Don't go there. That places sucks," Trell said.

On its slow trajectory, the *Lumina* reached tether length from the first potassium rock. Russ raised the lid of the box and took out a polymer bag. He unfolded it, taking a moment to determine which end opened and another moment to roll the sides together enough to separate them. Then he floated toward the closest rock and let the bag swallow it whole. Even in the bag, the rock zapped the shit out of him.

"Ooouch! You said these rocks only zapped metallic conduits."

"I don't know Earthling biology!" Trell swore. "Do you have internal metallic parts?"

"There's iron in my blood," Russ realized. He bagged another rock and once again it zapped him, hard. The electrical charge ran through his entire body, making his legs kick like a patellar reflex. *"Sonofabitch!"*

"Don't touch the rocks," Trell advised. "If you touch one that's not in the complex polymer bag, it will knock you unconscious. At the very least."

Russ's hair was still standing on end when the workday finally finished. He felt energized, literally. Trell escorted him, at a distance, to the Medbay where a TEN-awtch in a white lab coat hooked him to a series of capacitors and did a deep dive into his vitals. His teeth felt hollow.

"Everything okay?" He asked the tech as she looked over the results.

"Ehh," she said, noncommittally. She handed him a fresh roll of pain pills. "Your wrist is broken," she added. "Get in the CRC machine."

The tech helped Russ undress and climb into the CRC. Its untarnished metal gleamed.

When the machine spit him back out, Russ flexed his wrist, marveling at the repair job. The tech was gone, but Trell waited next to the machine. "The tech is off duty," he said. "It's closing time." They headed out of the Medbay in the direction of the cargo bay.

"When I was in the hold this morning, I spotted a rectangular crate. I think it was left over from a rifle shipment. Charlie should fit inside, and it will be light enough for us to carry up to the *Lumina*," Trell said as they hurried down the corridor.

"It's a bit early still," Russ suggested, checking the time on his transponder. "The members of the crew that live onboard are awake. They're probably eating dinner."

"It will take a while for Charlie to understand the plan. If he makes a big racket, we can wait until everyone is bunked up. No harm in getting ready while we wait."

The door around the cargo bay was lit by a ring of red light to indicate the presence of hazardous waste. Russ and Trell ignored the warning and slipped inside. The insulated potassium rocks were bagged and stacked in the corner. Russ spotted the rectangular box and used his knees to push it close to the storage closet while Trell cleared the crates they'd used to block the door.

Trell pulled the door open and light flooded the small space. Russ's heart went out to Charlie when he spotted him hunched in the corner, his knees tucked to his chest. At least he looked a little bit warmer, dressed in RK's child-sized boots and jacket.

"Hey there, little guy," Russ said in his calmest voice.

A low, keening moan escaped the closet. "Chaaaarrrlllliiiieee . . ."

"Everything is okay, Charlie," Trell said, taking a step into the closet. "We just need you to climb into this comfy box, and then we can take you to a big beautiful planet with lots of places to run around and live whatever freaky lifestyle you want to live."

". . . Charrrllliiiee . . ." It was more a wail than a moan now.

"That sound scares the shit out of me," Russ admitted.

"It's fine. Everything is fine," Trell told the Liafeen and Russ. He took a careful step forward into the storage closet. Then another. Then he reached his hand out and put it gently on Charlie's shoulder. "Everything is fine," he reassured Charlie.

The Liafeen stared at Trell's hand with wide, dark eyes. Russ saw the boy's lips draw back from his teeth, which gleamed white in the faint light.

"Trell . . ." Russ said.

"Everything's fine," Trell assured Russ, and maybe himself as well. He took the boy by the crook of his arm and pulled him gently from the closet.

". . . Charrrrrlllliiii . . ." the boy hissed, holding his hand up to shield his eyes from the bright ceiling lights. Even from a distance, Russ could see the boy's dark, black pupils contract to half their size, but it didn't seem to help. He raised a second clawed hand for further protection.

Russ hustled over and dimmed the lights. Then he opened the crate. There was a single rifle inside, wrapped in plastic. He laid it carefully on the ground. He smiled at Charlie and pointed cheerfully inside.

Trell was able to bring Charlie to the edge of the crate, but when he indicated the boy should climb in, Charlie hissed and cantilever bones on his shoulders extended three inches, like the hackles of a cat rising to meet a threat. Russ was fixated on the bones themselves. They were dense and jagged, resembling sharp, thick coral. The way they moved in and out of the boy's body, ripping new holes in his flesh—it was even more terrifying than the wail.

"He's not going in the box," Russ pointed out.

"I think you're right," Trell said. "Or maybe he won't get in alone." Trell looked around the cargo bay, his hands on his hips. His eyes fell on a larger box. He veered over to the wall to grab a motorized handcart and slid the cart under the new box. Pausing to rummage around inside, he withdrew packages of ammunition and set them on the floor. Then he motored the larger box over to where Russ stood uneasy beside the Liafeen. "The blue button is forward, the red is reverse," he told Russ, indicating the hand cart. Then he climbed into the box, a wide smile on his face. "See," he told the Liafeen. "There's no harm in the box. It's actually quite comfy."

The Liafeen's wide eyes narrowed slightly. He took a step toward the box and wrapped his sharp gray claws around the edge. A low trill came from deep in his chest.

"I don't know . . ." Russ said.

"I'm an empath," Trell reminded him. "I can tell the boy does not want to hurt me."

"Don't need to be an empath to know this kid is scary as all hell," Russ said.

"Relaxed vibes," Trell reminded him. He looked at Charlie and tapped all ten of his fingers against his chest.

To Russ's surprise, the Liafeen tentatively lifted one leg over the edge of the box and climbed inside. He lay beside Trell. After a moment's uncertainty, he nuzzled his head against Trell's chest.

"You're doing great," Trell told him. He nodded to Russ. It was nonverbal permission to lower the top. Russ grabbed the lid of the crate, but before he had pushed the top all the way shut, the cargo bay door slid open. He'd left a single set of lights on above the door frame, and a small, hairy shadow cast across the room.

"Assholes!" RK shouted from where he stood in the door frame. "What's this? Freaky! Child-molesting perverts!" The little man's voice squeaked, which gave his angry epitaphs a peculiar dissonance.

"The cargo bay is closed," Russ yelled at RK as he stormed across the room on small legs. Russ positioned himself between the crate and the advancing Plutorach. "Keep calm and we'll explain!" Russ said.

"Perverts!" RK shouted again. "Dressed your little victim in my jacket! My boots! Sick fantasy! Sick assholes!"

"Let's be a little quieter," Russ hissed.

From inside the crate a moan escaped, "Chaaarrrllllliiieee . . ."

"Lift the lid please," Trell said, somehow keeping his voice low and even. "Get me out. Quickly."

"Charrrrrllliiieeee . . ." another loud, low moan emitted from inside.

Russ lifted the lid.

The boy stood up and turned his shoulders square toward RK. Trell took the opportunity to scramble backward, extracting himself from the crate and stumbling to the floor.

Russ put his hand on the rifle, using his fingers to tear at its plastic wrapping.

"Liafeen!" RK screamed, spit firing outward from his open mouth. "Goddamn *Liafeen*!"

The door to the cargo bay was still open, and Russ could hear footsteps advancing from way down the hall.

RK leaped forward and struck the boy hard on the chest. Then he punched him across the jaw with a small, closed fist. He leaned over and raised his left pant leg. He had a wicked three-inch blade strapped to his ankle.

"Knife!" Russ warned Trell. He only had the gun half unwrapped. In the rushed, tense atmosphere, it seemed impossibly complicated to free the rifle any farther.

With surprising speed, RK cleared the knife from its sheath and sliced it across Charlie's throat. Where the knife hit, the boy's flesh slid away, blood following the blade's path in a spray of color.

Charlie didn't flinch. The blade hadn't gone more than a centimeter deep before it struck the dense skeleton just beneath his skin. The flesh fell away revealing stark-white bone, thick as a steel door. More of the same dense bone raised high from Charlie's shoulders and back. At first, the bones jutted out three inches high, matching the length of RK's blade.

But then they doubled in length and doubled again. Charlie seemed in pain as the bone ripped from his skin. His eyes were red and pinched. It looked like the twin legs of a malformed, thirty-pound spider were birthing from his shoulders and back.

Then the monstrous spider legs hinged forward on ragged ball and socket joints and pointed at RK.

Foolishly, courageously, RK struck at the new limbs with his small knife.

Charlie retaliated. The bone jutting from his shoulders flashed forward, finding purchase in RK's hairy flesh. One dense javelin ripped through his shoulder only to exit beneath his right shoulder blade. The second punctured his neck, mercifully killing him. The first struck again, ripping into his thigh. The second through his stomach. The first went directly through his heart, carrying the organ with it on its exit trajectory.

The Liafeen moaned, flexed the muscles in his arms and shoulders, and disgorged his new limbs outward, tearing RK to pieces. Clumps of hairy, wet skin and bone splattered in every direction.

Russ was still clearing RK from his eyes when Lanie and Linnie came sprinting through the door, weapons drawn. They leveled their rifles at Charlie and opened fire. The bullets drove chunks of flesh from his body, but his skeleton, now a genuine exoskeleton, stood strong against the concussion blasts. The two bone blades folded forward to protect his eyes.

When they stopped firing, Charlie looped one leg over the side of the crate, then the other. Then he crossed the short distance between himself and the twin sisters. Lanie drew a stunstick from her back and it crackled with electricity.

Up until that moment, Lanie and Linnie had been the toughest sentient species Russ had ever encountered. They were seven-foot-tall insects with jointed arms and legs covered in tibial spines. Their powerful thoraxes jutted out like a barrel chest and their wide forearms and thighs acted as thick organic shields. Unlike a rock-covered Bryn-Tyr, they were quick as lightning and impossibly agile.

As Charlie approached, bone blades whirling from his shoulders, Russ saw the twin sisters take a step backward. A look of stark fear crossed over their features. And then he was on them, bones whirling in a quick blur. Lanie raised the stunstick to block one of his strikes and the bone sliced through the dense, metal material, striking down hard against her forearm. Streams of yellow blood splattered out from the impact point.

Russ tossed aside the half-unwrapped rifle. He rushed over to the bags of potassium in the corner, selecting one just about the size of a basketball. He shucked the potassium free from its polymer wrapping. "Trell, hide!" Russ yelled.

Trell tore his eyes from the fight and saw Russ, standing above the bare potassium. He dove into the open door of the storage closet.

"Charlie!" Russ shouted, and the boy turned. Electricity was coursing through Russ's entire body as he lifted the rock and in the same motion, pushed a two-handed basketball pass right into Charlie's midsection. The small meteor broke against Charlie's exoskeleton, exploding the boy off his feet and sending rock fragments popping like fireworks throughout the cargo bay.

When the fireworks stopped, Charlie lay face down on the floor, moaning softly, ". . . arli . . ." Russ lay a few feet away, his body wracked with involuntary spasms.

Lanie and Linnie were huffing on the ground bleeding from many cuts both shallow and deep. The two sisters looked around at the destroyed cargo bay, unwilling to accept that the sudden, violent threat was neutralized. Lanie approached Charlie, her gun trained on the base of his skull.

Linnie's voice was full of worry. "Don't get any closer, sis. Please. That's a Liafeen."

Lanie looked at her sister. "You okay?"

"Yeah. Couple more seconds though—"

Russ had managed to roll onto his back. The spasms were starting to subside. Four jet-black insect eyes settled on him where he lay.

"Is that RK on the ground?" Lanie asked.

“Here? Yeah. And over there by the wall,” Russ said, pointing. “Can I help either of you get to the CRC machine?”

“Is this your doing?” she asked, ignoring his offer.

“Remember that lifeform Big Sister sensed on the derelict space station—” Russ started to say.

“It’s my fault,” Trell said, stepping back out of the closet. “We found him on the space salvage and I—”

Russ looked around the destroyed room. His eyes drifted over some of the bigger pieces of RK. “He’s lying, Trell’s lying.” Russ said from the floor. He raised a hand. “I caused this.”

“SavUQuik is already on the way,” Lanie cautioned. “You two clowns better get your story straight before they arrive.”

Russ managed to climb to his knees. He smiled a crooked smile at Trell. “It’s entirely my fault. Trell wasn’t a part of it. I found the boy among some space trash and took pity on him. I’m not from around here. I didn’t realize what he was.”

Trell opened his mouth, but Russ spoke over him. “Trell just wandered in here with RK. They were both responding to the noise, same as you.”

Lanie looked at Trell, then she looked at Russ. When neither of them said anything else, sadness fell over her insect features, replaced quickly by an expression of simple clarity. “I probably don’t have to tell you. Right, Russ?”

“I’m fired?”

“You’re in the final seconds of your final per diem contract,” she confirmed. “Get the hell off my ship.”

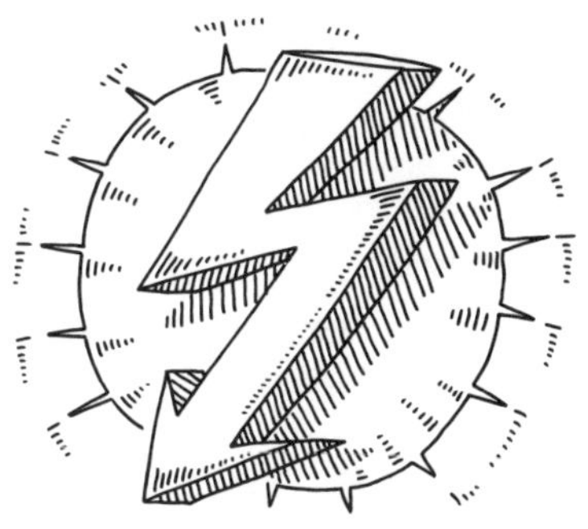

34

NINA

NORMA ANSWERED THE DOOR, HER hands on her hips. Her shirt bore the image of an open book and the words "Explore Every Mysterious Universe." "What a pleasant surprise," she said. "I have more books!" She scuttled away and came back with two romance novels, *Shipwrecked with Mr. Wrong* and *Mission: Soldier to Daddy.*

Nina took them graciously. "I was hoping to talk to Ensine," she said.

Norma screwed up her face. "Then I have some bad news for you. He's sick. He thinks he might have COVID. He won't let me within twenty feet of him."

"Does he need a doctor?"

"He doesn't seem that bad. But he is acting very strange. He's on edge. More nervous than I've ever seen him. I hope I'm not in love with a hypochondriac." Norma pointed a thumb toward the backyard. "He's by the river. Don't say I didn't warn you."

Nina found Ensine stretched out in a hammock about two hundred yards behind Norma's small cottage. He had strung it between two lodgepole pines not fifteen feet from the edge of where the Bear River ran past the property line. The river banked east against a cluster of rocks, and spray from the rocks misted onto the hammock, keeping its hemp rope permanently waterlogged. Ensine was also covered in mist, his back turned to the river to shield the book he was reading from the same fate. He didn't seem sick, but he jumped at the sight of Nina.

"You should stay away from me," he told her miserably. "I'm sick."

"I'll take my chances."

"Suit yourself. What do you need? Did Russ finally get his wrist repaired?"

"I came here to talk about Russ's grandfather, Clark Wesley."

"Norma's dead husband?" Ensine asked innocently.

"Is he dead?" Nina asked, her head cocked to the side.

"I think so?" Ensine said, tentatively. "They had a funeral, right? I'm dating his widow." Ensine was swinging gently in the hammock. Nina put her hand on it and held him to a dead stop. Ensine sighed. "Ahh screw it," he said. "Touch my arm."

Nina put her hand on Ensine's arm. She could feel the small ridges of the scales that covered his entire body and it made her gasp. Ensine was wearing a standard, legal transformer, which altered his appearance but did nothing to fool the other senses. It was significantly less convincing than his hard-light transformer, which bent light to mimic the sight and texture of the illusion it cast. "What happened to your other transformer?"

"Clark sold it," Ensine said sadly. "I desperately need to find a replacement. If Norma touches me when I'm like this—"

"Why did you let him?" Nina asked. "What's he up to?"

"You won't believe it."

"Try me."

Ensine looked toward the river, then toward the cabin. He breathed deeply from the misty air. "When you get to be my age, and Norma's, and Clark's, you start to think about your own death quite a lot. We Blurn live a hundred and ten years on average, but the last couple decades are not our finest. Our bones are hollow, and ten decades of gravity, especially gravity as dense as Earth's, grinds us down. Most Southern Blurn live the end stages of our lives exclusively in water. It eases the pain, but we also lose access to all the sights, sounds, and pleasures of you land animals. For me, it would mean I lose Norma." Ensine was usually cheeky—it was tough to get him to take anything seriously, but when he said Norma's name, his voice was full of emotion. "You have to understand that the opportunity to reverse the aging process, to avoid it altogether, it's very appealing." Ensine grinned, but the edges of his mouth were turned slightly downward. "No matter how farfetched it seems."

"I don't understand. You and Clark are going to cheat death? How is that possible?"

"It's probably not. When Clark approached me with his harebrained scheme, I turned him down flat. But the more I thought about it, the more I told myself, 'Why not give it a try?' Of course, if I'd known it involved stolen military hardware from distant planets and my hard-light transformer . . ."

Nina took the book from Ensine's hands and closed it gently. It was a mystery novel by an author she didn't recognize. Two skeletons sat back-to-back on the cover.

She tapped Ensine lightly on the head with it. "Start from the beginning."

"About two months ago, Clark Wesley sidled up next to me at the Banville Blitzkrieg Bar. He told me what he'd been up to, and I didn't believe a word of it. He's very much the opposite of Norma, so it's hard to trust anything he says. Still, he claimed he needed my help. He knew I sometimes, uhhh, operated outside of the UAIB Shared System of Civics. He wanted me to use my illegal connections to get him something."

Nina's impatience must have shown on her face because Ensine began to speak more quickly.

"CRC machines. Carbon Repair Chrysalises. They can recreate damaged parts of the body, everything from skin to internal organs. They're beautiful machines. So why can't they stop the effects of aging? What is aging other than the creeping hand of death slowly breaking down your cells? A CRC machine healed your father's liver! Why can't it do that to the aching joints in my hands? Or my knees?"

"I thought about that the first moment I discovered the technology," Nina admitted. "There are two central reasons. One, it's illegal. The UAIB charter protects against disruptive technology, and granting eternal life would be a pretty big disruption."

Ensine waved his hand through the air. "A charter isn't going to keep people from doing something like that. The rich? Those jack-offs wouldn't let a charter slow them down for even a minute."

Nina nodded. "It doesn't matter anyway. CRC repair paste isn't the same as the body's organic tissue." Absently, Nina touched the spot on her back where a Tharcus had shredded through her skin and the CRC machine had stitched her back together. "The body will only accept so much repair paste masquerading as real cells before it shuts down entirely. The percentage is different for every species, but I think the maximum threshold is generally around 46 percent."

"There's a legend of a Kruxfasian who claimed a 67 percent paste to original cell ratio." Ensine interjected. "They called him Stickybones, and he was a minor celebrity for a while, but a news station eventually scanned him without his permission and the real number was closer to 54 percent. Still impressive, but he died within a year." Ensine moved the hammock again in slow rotations. "What people often forget is that the seventy-three sentient species in the UAIB charter are not the only sentient species in the universe. There are hundreds of worlds unrecognized by the Alliance, for a variety of reasons, including Earth. The granddaddy of the unrecognized is a species called the

Liafen. They're imperial warmongers. Scary motherfuckers. I fought against them as part of the 4029th Naval Command back in the Second Intergalactic War. Have I told you about those days?"

"Clark's plan?" Nina reminded him.

"Right. So, the Liafen can't invent for shit. Given a thousand years to do the research, they couldn't invent a clock radio that worked properly. However, they are good at taking existing technology and improving it, especially military technology like the Carbon Repair Chrysalises. First thing Clark told me when he found me at that bar is that the Liafen are starting to show up again. They've been spotted on the cusp of UAIB space, usually in small numbers, never violent. But they're there. And that means war is coming. I have reason to believe that Liafen agents have been making inroads with both legitimate corporations and the criminal element in UAIB space."

"And Clark wants their technology," Nina concluded.

"Clark claims to *have* their technology. A CRC machine that can fuse up to 81 percent paste before the body rejects additional repair. Think about it. I could replace everything except my forearms and my ankles. I can live without those! Maybe forever?"

"Clark claims a lot of things," Nina cautioned. "Even if the technology existed, how could an old, broke Earthling get his hands on it?"

"Clark claims a lot of things," Ensine confirmed. "He said some very dangerous people traded for a Liafen CRC, and he snuck it out from under their noses. I did a little investigating, and there is a considerable bounty on his head. To a certain degree, his story checks out." Ensine's fingers touched his ear where he wore the standard, legal transformer. "Clark has also managed to get his hands on the repair paste that runs the machine. I was with him when he got it."

"He's immortal? That's just what we need."

"No. For some reason he still needs the Obinz stone. The one Russ found in the closet so many months ago? Maybe it's the only thing with enough power to run a Liafen CRC—I don't know why he wants it so badly but he's come into a lot of money, forty thousand credits. It's only a matter of time before he buys his way back to the Obinz stone too . . ." Ensine looked Nina in the eyes. He seemed to be trying to measure if she understood how it felt to be old. How it felt to see the finish line not too far off in the distance. "Could you do me a huge favor?"

Ensine's face was so earnest Nina almost automatically agreed, but then she caught herself. "Maybe?"

"Could you not interfere with his plan?" Ensine asked. "Could you just . . . let him try?" Ensine's tone was almost pleading.

"Rufus, it's likely none of this is true." Nina used Ensine's first name to comfort him. She could tell how badly he wished that Clark had an almost-functioning fountain of youth stashed somewhere. If he didn't, and he probably didn't, it was a cruel trick to get old Ensine so excited about it.

Ensine nodded. It seemed a tacit admission that she could be right. Slowly, he picked up the book again. "I never thought I'd like reading," he told her. "But this, with this and this," he pointed at the book, the river and the hammock, "This is as close to God as old Rufus Ensine is likely to get. Another twenty years here, with Norma by my side, missing only our ankles and forearms?"

Nina squeezed his shoulder. His scaly skin contracted, then expanded under her grip.

Ensine looked at her, hope alight in his eyes. "It'd be heaven, Nina. Another two decades of heaven. I don't care if it's a longshot. It's worth taking."

35

RUSS

THE SKYLOUNGE ON GORRILLIAN GREEN was awash in pastels. The sixteen-by-sixteen-foot floating sign that hung above the entrance was in glowing blue pastels. The moving walkway beckoning him inside glittered with cream and diamond-white pastels.

Russ couldn't stop his hands from clenching and unclenching even after taking two pain pills. He wasn't sure if it was from residual contact with the potassium rocks, his familiar unemployment status, accidently betraying Lanie and Linnie, or catching a glimpse of the cruel satisfaction on Ranyard: CannonWulf's face when he wrapped Charlie in a detention blanket and loaded him onto the SavUQuik ship. The sidewalk rolled forward so gently it took Russ a little while to realize he was moving. He stood stationary, but the ground urged him toward the establishment, a long pale-red pastel bar slowly creeping into view.

Russ walked backward, keeping pace with the moving sidewalk. He could see an enormous studio apartment above the Skylounge, brightly lit and fully visible through floor-to-ceiling windows. Nurcia was inside, perched on the back of a couch cushion, wearing a bathrobe and combing out her long hair. It cascaded over her shoulders, layered in three different shades of purple.

Russ tried to ignore his own voyeuristic thrill. While he watched, another Divian woman approached Nurcia from out of view. Confused, he realized the other woman was also Nurcia Fragnar. This new Nurcia was wearing a cocktail dress. Nurcia in the bathrobe looked at her finely dressed doppelgänger with an expression of both wonder and satisfaction. She reached out and touched her other self, running her hand along the other Nurcia's forearm before rubbing her fingers across the material of the dress.

After a moment, the Nurcia in the cocktail dress reached up to her ear and removed a transformer she had there. Her appearance changed, shifting into the visage of a slender male Lixil, his greasy hair clumped in unwashed bangs on his forehead. The cocktail dress was gone, replaced by work pants and a course linen work shirt. The man waved his hands like a magician and grinned. Nurcia in the robe laughed happily. Russ could see the Lixil was missing teeth and only had two out of four fingers on his right hand. "That guy looks sinister as fuck," Russ said under his breath.

Nurcia nodded in approval and tapped her transponder against the Lixil's transponder. The Lixil gave a mocking bow and walked back out of view. Russ let the moving sidewalk carry him into the lounge.

Inside, a three-member band plucked at string instruments. The musicians were all TEN-awtch women, lean with crisp black suits and immaculate skin, the scales on their heads combed carefully forward in matching hairstyles. Their instruments reverberated with each pluck, sending out delicate aural vibrations. The sound wasn't music as much as it was a mood. Every person within view was carefully primped, plucked, and pruned. Every ear had a transformer glittering from the top of the lobe, some of them ornately decorated with jewels or sparkling plated gold. He idly wondered what the crowd would look like without their technologically created beauty and youth.

Russ passed a noisy flock of Sikkie-Bruzz standing beside the front door, their tropical colored clothes tailored and tapered, their feathers peacocked, their heavy wallets molting. *Sesame Street, 90210*, Russ thought, as he weaved between and around beautiful, well-dressed narcissists.

"I told you this place was going downhill," a woman near the window said.

"Did you see the pink fleshy guy?"

"Remember when the Skylounge had standards?"

"It's like this everywhere now. I hate it."

Russ looked around for the pink fleshy guy. He spotted him in the mirror behind the bar, its frame branded with the words Chenul: Refined Wine for Society's Best.

Aside from decorative transformers, the style of the day was high waists. Women wore plastic pantsuits pulled up above their chests, while men's pants crested at the shoulder, looping over each deltoid like shiny, pleated overalls. Many in the crowd snuck glances at Russ, appraising his bland Earth clothes with casual dissatisfaction. Russ knew he was in a bad mood—maybe homicidal would be a closer descriptor—but he hated every person in the large, crowded room. As far as he could tell, the Skylounge was stuffed to capacity with social vampires who fed on each other's envy in much the same way a Klung absorbed electricity. He wiped his hands on his not-that-recently-washed blue jeans. The bartender was at the other end of the red pastel bar top, stacking cups and chatting with other customers. He quickly served drinks to three Gnurians in neon puffer jackets, even though they hadn't been there long enough to order.

Russ leaned across the bar, waving at him. "Hey, man. Hey! Is there an elevator or something? I need to meet somebody who lives on the next floor up. And I could use a drink."

The bartender ignored him, hovering around the three young Gnurians, smiling and wiping the bar with a wet rag.

"Hey there!" Russ tried again. "I said I could use a drink. What do you have that's really strong?"

The Gnurians in the puffer jackets moved on. The bartender kept idly wiping the counter, purposely avoiding Russ. Russ wondered what would happen if he lunged over the divide and drowned the man in his own beer tap. Not that there was beer in the tap. Russ suspected that the taps ran with the spilled blood of the proletariat.

Russ's fists continued to clench and unclench. His eyes were drawn to a tall female Divian standing alone out on the patio. She looked very similar to Nurcia. "So many Nurcias," Russ mumbled, but as the woman turned to blow smoke from an electronic cigarette over the metallic balcony rail, Russ could see that she was older, though it was impossible to know by how much. Her transformer glittered under a silky headscarf. While Russ watched, a tall figure ascended the stairs on the far side of the patio and stood beside her. The newcomer wore a business suit. He had his wild hair tamed back, his thick gray beard twisted into six-inch braids. He was cleaned up, almost presentable, but it was undeniably the murderer Aldos Verch.

Russ instinctively lowered his shoulder and covered his face with his hand in case Verch glanced in his direction.

Verch and the Divian conferred on the patio. The Divian's body language indicated authority and intent. Verch seemed to be listening to her carefully. He objected to something she said, but she shook her finger in his face, and he nodded gravely. Russ saw a statue in the corner he could listen behind. He took a step toward it but was stopped by a hand on his shoulder.

"Not exactly your kind of place, is it?" a familiar voice said.

He turned to find Nurcia smiling back at him, her beautiful neon eyes alight. She had gotten dressed, pulling herself into a pair of sparkling silver pants that cinched tightly just below her collarbone. Her hair was still slightly damp. She wasn't wearing a transformer, which, in this context, seemed like a casual flaunting of her natural beauty.

"Not too many CERTified types here," Russ grunted.

"Why are *you* here?" Nurcia asked.

"I was looking for you."

"That's flattering," she told him. "I guess you're not taking my advice? To stay out of this whole mess?" Nurcia caught Russ glancing back toward the balcony. She followed his gaze toward Aldos Verch and Russ saw her eyes narrow with resolve.

"I came here because you invited me," Russ said. He didn't have to fake the indignation in his voice. He'd had no idea that Verch would be on Gorrillian Green. "I've been trying to gain a little culture. Not this kind of culture." He pointed a thumb toward the three-member band. "But I do like Bootball. I'm pretty excited about the Mulgrew Melville Memorial—"

"—but it's been sold out for the last thirty cycles," Nurcia finished. She took one more look at Verch, standing with the older Divian, then turned back to Russ. "The Mulgrew Melville isn't just a series of athletic contests. It's a whole Providence Travel Solutions experience. The entire biosphere is shut down, and the only way to get planetside is via one of our cruise liners."

"Sounds pretty fun though," Russ said, smiling. "Can you get me a ticket?"

"The charter leaves tomorrow. You're not giving me a whole lot of advanced warning." Nurcia held up a finger. "One second . . ." She knifed through the crowd toward Verch and the older Divian. Russ instinctually followed.

Seeing the older Divian up close, with her high cheekbones and almond-shaped eyes, the resemblance to Nurcia was undeniable. This had to be her mother, Leyonella Fragnar, CFO and ranking member of the Board of Directors of Waymore Industries, among other things.

". . . some things are more important than financial solubility," Leyonella was saying. "We're going to put our resources in another direction. And that's my final decision. Make your way to Station 5. If you don't want to travel on the *Marcy Hedron* with me, you can take my personal cruiser. Either way, get there as quickly as possible . . ." Leyonella saw Russ and Nurcia approaching and trailed off.

Verch had his back to Russ and Nurcia. "Why don't we just get Waymore to reactivate an on-site Waypoint?" Verch grumbled. He must have seen the look on Leyonella's face because he stopped talking and did a slow turn to stand face-to-face with her daughter.

"What are you talking about?" Nurcia asked, innocently.

"Nothing. We're finished talking, I think. Are we finished?" Verch asked Leyonella. His eyes shifted back and forth between Leyonella and Nurcia. Whenever they landed on Nurcia, Russ thought he saw Verch's cheeks flush red behind his heavy gray beard.

"You may go," Leyonella told him.

Verch rose up to his full height and walked stiffly back toward the stairs. "What are you doing here?" he muttered when he recognized Russ. "You trying to make it easy for me to finish my list?"

Russ didn't answer.

Verch tapped him on the bicep as he moved past. It wasn't aggressive, just a gentle promise of future violence. "See you soon."

"Who are *you*, exactly?" Leyonella addressed Russ.

"That's Russ Wesley," Nurcia interjected. "Trash remediation technician. Tier Nine planet dweller. Human. Hero. He's also going to be my date to the Mulgrew Melville Bootball tournament." Nurcia said the last part loudly, and Russ caught Verch's shoulders tense as the giant walked slowly down the external staircase.

"I am?" Russ said. "Cool."

Nurcia seemed to be waiting for that last bit of news to shock her mother. She glanced toward the staircase, but Verch had already disappeared from view.

"We need you to get us two tickets. And a suite on the ship."

For a moment, Leyonella didn't speak, but she looked Russ over, head to toe, an expression of gross dissatisfaction on her face. "I will arrange for two more tickets. I already planned to be aboard. We can travel together as one big happy family," Leyonella said flatly.

"Wonderful," Nurcia said, sounding just as pretentiously insincere as her mother.

"We're all going?" Russ said.

"Unless you've changed your mind about needing a ticket?" Leyonella suggested.

"Not a chance," Russ said, grinning. "Humans love taking long, socially awkward trips. Me especially."

Nurcia giggled. She grabbed Russ's arm and held it against her chest. "See why I want to bring him along?" she said. "I predict you'll eventually love Russ with the same unconditional love you have for your daughter."

Now it was Russ's turn to look from Nurcia and Leyonella and back again. He was trying to decide why Nurcia's seemingly sweet words felt so much like a threat.

Leyonella sighed. She touched her throat, slowly removing a beautiful silver pendant from beneath her dress. The stone in the center glowed slightly. She held it between her thumb and forefinger. Then she tucked it back into her dress. Without another word, the older woman turned and swept back into the main room, the tail from her headscarf flowing elegantly behind her.

36

RUSS

NINA WASN'T AROUND WHEN RUSS Waypointed back to the motel room. He glanced at Clark's empty bed and Applebum's empty reading corner. He texted Nina: *Where are you?* She did not reply.

He stuffed his hands in his pockets and walked out of the motel room, pulling the door closed behind him. He crossed the parking lot and knocked on his grandfather's door. When no one answered, he walked out to the pool deck and sat on the lounge chair, deep in thought.

If Applebum had been there, Russ knew just what he would say: heroes were supposed to draw people to them and collect allies. Then as a united force, they overcome all obstacles and win the day. Russ was taking a slightly different approach, provoking powerful people, losing friends, and getting exiled from various municipal organizations. He estimated that in his lifetime he'd been fired close to twenty times—including jobs that he'd simply walked away from. Screwing up with Lanie and Linnie hurt worse than usual, though. He wasn't blind to Nina's efforts to usher him into a greater sense of care for himself and his responsibilities. He also knew that if he took the time to consider the consequences of his decisions before making them, he'd be putting himself less at risk *and* might have more money than just the change in his pockets.

Russ removed the algae scraper from where it hung from hooks on the fence. Then, in the fading light, with a soft mist that was not quite rain blowing against his face, he cleaned the pool. He was trying to figure out how to turn on the dormant pool pump when Clark slipped out of room 22 carrying a medium-sized white sack in his hands. Clark was doing a small jig and singing, his old, cracked voice carrying through the mist, "Fifteen men on the dead man's chest—Yo-ho-ho, and a bottle of rum."

Russ leaned forward, resting his elbows on the top of the pool fence. "What've you got there, Grandpop?"

Clark jumped slightly, surprised. "Russ, my boy!" he called out jovially. "Good news. That's what I've got." The old man was racked by a fit of coughing, but he still managed to hold the white sack above his head, triumphantly. He trotted over to the fence. "For five months I have been looking and looking and . . . look at this!"

From out of the sack, Clark drew the Obinz stone. Finding that same stone in his grandmother's bookstore had launched Russ on this adventure so many months ago. He had mixed feelings about seeing it again.

"I finally had enough credits to buy the information I needed to find it. An outlaw gang were using it to power their fleet of electric motorcycles on Fortune Prime. Hopefully they won't have far to drive tomorrow morning," Clark snickered, "because their bikes aren't going to be charged."

"You said it wasn't safe for you to leave the motel room. Ever since you came back you've said that, and you're running around on Fortune Prime."

"Generally, it's not safe, but for this—"

"Why did you want it back so badly?" Russ interrupted. His grandpop opened his mouth to answer and Russ waved him off. "You know what? You're not going to tell me the truth." Russ didn't want to yell at his old, sick grandpop, but he felt the words rolling out of him. "We could have used that money for so many things. We could have bought the life insurance we were supposed to buy. We could have hired a smuggler to take us to Applebum instead of having to fake my way onto a cruise ship populated by snobs and murderers." Russ studied his grandfather's face to see if the old man could even understand the consequences of his recklessness. "Applebum has been gone for days. I can't stop thinking about him stashed in some research room, scared, totally alone—"

"The robot can't feel feelings," Clark said.

"I think he can." Russ tapped his grandfather's forehead with two fingers. "You know who definitely can? Derch's mom. And you spent her son's life insurance . . . on a rock!"

"Not just any rock," Clark promised.

"I think you used to be better than this," Russ insisted. "I think the Clark I knew when I was a kid would not be leaving Norma in the arms of somebody else while he visits strip clubs and chases after who knows what. And . . . and . . . you're bleeding," Russ realized. His eyes snapped to a large gash across Clark's right hip. Russ vaulted over the pool fence and led his grandfather back inside room 22. The Waypoint was still crackling from Clark's recent jump.

Russ went to the bathroom to collect the disinfectant they'd used to treat Clark's last injury. The old man lay on the bed studying the Obinz stone while Russ poured peroxide over the wound and then dabbed at it with gauze.

"How did this happen?"

"It doesn't matter," Clark said, coughing. "It won't be important soon. With the Obinz stone back, I have everything I need to milk another twenty or thirty years out of this old body." Clark coughed again.

Russ placed his palm on his grandfather's chest, feeling him take ragged breaths. "It doesn't sound like you have twenty or thirty more minutes."

"I had to get the stone, Russ. None of the rest of that matters now that I have it. I'll be out of your hair soon. Please bring me more blankets. I'm getting a chill."

Russ took the comforter from the second bed and layered it on top of his grandpop. He placed the back of his hand across his grandfather's forehead. "You don't have a fever and the wound is patched."

Clark rolled onto his back to look Russ in the eyes. "It's not the cut. That's just a scratch. The other thing is coming back," Clark said.

"What other thing?"

"Death. The grim reaper wants another shot at me." Clark coughed into his fist. "I think it's my lungs this time. After you die once, you get better at seeing it approach. I promise that I'll be out of your life soon."

"I don't want you out of my life," Russ said patiently. He combed Clark's thick hair away from his face. "You're my grandpop, and I love you. You're the closest thing I had to a dad, even before mine took off. But you've got to stop taking advantage of people. And you're going to have to fight off death for at least another week because I'm going on a cruise tomorrow."

"Now look who is prioritizing themselves." Clark was racked with coughing. Russ thought he detected a few extra coughs thrown in for emphasis.

Russ stood up and looked down at his wounded grandfather. The man had been dancing a jig in the parking lot not fifteen minutes prior. That was the problem with selfish people. You couldn't always tell the difference between when they wanted your help and when they actually needed it. "I found Applebum. I'm taking the cruise to Beta-9 first thing tomorrow to get him. Since I'm broke, it's the only way."

Clark shook his head and murmured, “You won’t have to worry about me any longer. Old Clark finally has what he needs.” When Russ didn’t respond, his grandpop closed his eyes.

Russ stayed by his side until Clark settled into sleep.

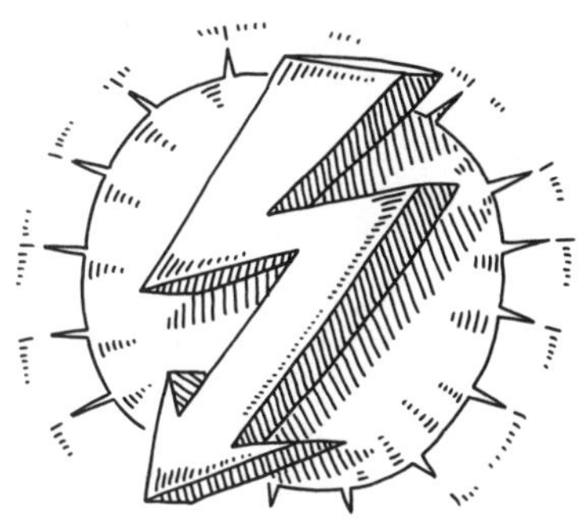

37
NINA

"THIS STYLE DOESN'T REALLY WORK with my body type," Nina said, shifting around in an effort to keep her pants cinched up around her collarbone.

"Yeah, this is terrible," Russ agreed. Nurcia had left him a package at the Alphane S Transportation Hub. He had eventually emerged from the restroom in a pair of silky, dazzling overalls and a diaphanous shirt. At first, he'd also put on the included fedora, replete with an exotic feather in the band but, to Nina's relief, shortly after getting dressed, he'd taken off the hat and tossed it off the end of the high docking station. They'd leaned forward to watch it flutter thousands of feet downward and out of sight.

Nina had made her own outfit. She'd stitched it together from fabric purchased from the Walmart in Banville, inspired by a series of pictures Kendren had sent to her transponder.

They were not the only ones dressed extravagantly on the docking station. As they waited for their ride to the tournament, the crowd around them had slowly thickened and now numbered close to five hundred.

In the distance, the giant ship that would take them to Beta-9 drew ever closer. Nina studied the words on the side: Providence Travel Solutions Super Cruiser 9JAX9 Marcy Hedron. She was excited, despite herself. The ship was blasting dance music, the beat growing louder as the cruise liner slowly matriculated through the clear skies of Planet Alphane.

Kendren waited and waved at them both from the other side of the loading ramp. He was wearing a number fifty-eight Huvvel Vaquals jersey and immaculately tailored pants that tapered to a stop just above his ankles. Russ didn't say much to Nina as they waited shoulder to shoulder in the crowded line. Far ahead, the captain scanned their tickets and let them onboard one at a time.

While they waited, jugglers emerged from the cruise liner tossing burning stunsticks. A woman in a collared shirt and a short black skirt offered Nina a free drink from a salver. People backed into Nina and bumped her from behind, some mumbling apologies, others ignoring her completely as they argued about who was the greatest (living!) Bootball player of all time.

The crowd noise came to an abrupt stop as an SAS unit appeared behind Kendren.

Nina had never seen anything like it. Judging from the hush of the crowd, they hadn't either. Its head was rotund, with a black visor hiding its eyes. Large metal cylinders protruded from its back like cyberpunked angel wings. Its arms were made of thick braided chrome, giving it the semblance of a weightlifter. Blazoned on its chest were the words Tech 13—Prototype.

The SAS waded into the crowd, temporarily halting boarding. Aliens scrambled to clear its path as it marched confidently toward where Nina and Russ stood in line. When it reached them, to Nina's surprise, it stopped. Waves of cold wafted from its beefy forearms.

"Are you Russ Wesley, honored guest of the Fragnar family?" the giant robot asked.

"Uhh . . . no," Russ said. "I am Johnny, uhh—"

"Identity confirmed. Please come with me." The Tech 13 wrapped its strong fingers around Russ's wrist and pulled him toward the ship.

"Meet you inside?" Russ called back to Nina, scrambling to keep pace with the huge machine.

"Just the one bed?" Nina asked as Kendren showed her the suite. There was certainly room for more than one bed. The suite was at least a thousand square feet, with floor-to-ceiling picture windows looking out over the thinning atmosphere of Planet Alphane.

"It's what they gave us," Kendren said, shrugging. He stripped off his jersey and sniffed it before dropping it over the back of a chair. He flopped shirtless on the bed, poking at his transponder. His stomach muscles rippled with the slightest change of position. They were so solid it almost seemed to Nina that they should impede his movement, like someone had grafted a steel plate to his midsection.

"I'm going exploring," Nina decided. "Do you want to come along?"

Kendren shook his head. "I'm tired. I've been tanning and lifting weights endlessly, just to prepare for being on camera tomorrow. The whole idea of it has me sort of worn out. Gonna apply a fresh layer of polish to my teeth and then rest a while. If I'm asleep when you get back, wake me up." Kendren rose from the bed and shimmied out of his pants. Nina hurried for the door before she could catch a glimpse of his perfect glutes.

Partygoers zigged and zagged as she climbed the stairs toward the back side of the massive cruise ship. The dance music continued to thump, and Nina felt herself tapping her thumb against her thigh to the beat. She checked her transponder but found no text from Russ.

When he said, "Meet you inside," guess he meant over dinner? Nina thought with dissatisfaction. *Or maybe he's too busy being the honored guest of the Fragnar family?*

Russ didn't seem too busy. At least not when Nina spotted him on the pool deck with a stunning, bikinied Divian by his side. The Divian was so beautiful that Nina had a hard time looking at her, as if her exotic, yet perfect, facial symmetry was too much for even Nina's powerful brain to comprehend.

She realized that she wasn't the only one watching the handsome couple. Her eyes fell on another Divian on the far side of the Lido Deck. The older woman's elegant gown and jewelry were so fine it made Nina tug self-consciously at her own Walmart haute couture. It was then she noticed a man in the back, tucked away near the portable trash compactors. He was a slender Lixil with greasy hair, and he seemed fixated on the older woman. Nina frowned. The older woman was clearly wealthy, someone of consequence. Nina wondered if the rough-looking Lixil was hired to protect her, or something else entirely.

Russ was oblivious to the various eyes watching him, focused instead on an illusionist performing from a raised platform beside the pool. The illusionist swallowed a smaller audience member, only to have the tiny alien reappear standing atop the man's belt buckle. The small alien yelled, "Park Union Brawlers for life!" in a squeaky voice, his teeth glittering gold. A man in the crowd responded, "Huvvel Vaquals Va-Va-Victory!"

A chill ran through Nina's body when she spotted one more person watching Russ and Nurcia. Aldos Verch lay on a pool lounger in only his swim trunks, his fingers interlocked behind his head. His enormous beard lay untended atop his matching gray-and-black chest hair. He watched Russ and Nurcia with murder in his eyes, as if he was ready to spring up at any moment and tear the couple apart—and then smash Nina into small pieces as well, just to make sure the mess was completely cleaned up.

38
RUSS

RUSS LOVED ILLUSIONISTS. He circled slowly around the raised stage, trying to see how the illusionist could swallow the tiny alien without hurting him.

The moment the show ended, the Tech 13 SAS escorted them back to the master suite. Many in the crowd reached out and touched its thick, cold steel forearms. The SAS marched through their outstretched hands, clearing a wide path for Russ and Nurcia.

The suite had four separate rooms. The main foyer was twice the size of Norma's home in Evanstown, but Leyonella Fragnar filled every inch. She stood stick-straight and never smiled, judging Russ with her eyes as he sat politely on the far end of a long couch. Nurcia hadn't bothered to change out of her bikini. She stretched across Russ, legs draped over his lap. He tried, unsuccessfully, to find a place to rest his hands where they wouldn't be touching some part of her body.

"Is your mom going to be here the whole time?" Russ whispered to Nurcia.

"She's staying with us, silly. Don't worry, she goes to sleep early." The lotion on Nurcia's legs smelled like the universe's most beautiful flower had a baby with the universe's tastiest fruit. Her head was no more than ten inches from his and Russ stared for a moment into her neon eyes. She stared back, boldly. He carefully removed her legs, rose to his feet, and faced Leyonella.

"Do you have a favorite team in the tournament?" he asked her.

"I haven't the faintest idea what you're talking about," Leyonella said.

"He's trying to bond with you, Mother," Nurcia said languidly. "He doesn't know that you naturally dislike every species that doesn't have purple skin."

"All species are wonderful," Leyonella said, half-heartedly. "But Divians are responsible for civilization in its current, productive, effective form."

"Two teams are playing in the game tomorrow. I was wondering if you had a favorite," Russ tried again.

"Oh!" Leyonella said, as if the idea amused her. "Sporting events exist to give the uneducated masses something simple to care about. They are a vehicle of social control mixed with useful brand marketing. I'm traveling to Beta-9 for business. There's a project at our research and development center that I need to check on." Her eyes traveled to the SAS unit standing sentry in the corner. "I also didn't want to miss the chance to spend time with my darling daughter."

"What's so important that you have to travel to Beta-9 with us?" Nurcia asked. As with everything she said to her mother, her tone was 50 percent judgment, 50 percent challenge.

"It's just an errand," Leyonella said. "Nothing either of you should give a second thought to."

Nurcia rose from the couch and draped her arms around Russ's neck. She leaned close to his ear and whispered, "She's headed there to kill your robot, I think."

"What are you talking about?" Russ asked. Her words made his heart race, but he concentrated on keeping his expression neutral.

Nurcia shrugged. "I know powerful people. And when you're invisible, you get to go a lot of places and hear a lot of things. Is it common for your kind to share a bed but not mate, like you did with the fleshy curly-haired Earthling? What was the purpose of that ritual?"

"Tell me what you've learned about Applebum," Russ urged her.

Nurcia shook her head slyly. Still resting her arms on his shoulders, her fingers danced across his chest. She raised her voice, her tone filled with mock outrage. "Not with my mom in the room, Russ! Let's wait until we're alone."

Russ blushed. Leyonella managed to look disappointed, disgusted, and offended all at once.

The cruise liner's large banquet room was filled with the sounds of mandibles smacking together and utensils clacking against expensive plates and more than slightly drunk guests laughing and arguing.

It was just Russ, Nurcia, and Leyonella at a small, private table in the direct center of the room. They'd left the SAS unit powered down in the suite. Russ kept glancing over at Nina who ate alone a few tables to their left. She wasn't physically alone. Aliens of all shapes and sizes sat around her, but Nina kept to herself. When Kendren never showed for dinner, Russ texted her an invite to join the Fragnar table, but she politely declined.

A third of the way through the entrée, Leyonella glanced toward the clock on the wall and stood up. She quickly dabbed her mouth with her napkin. Without saying a word, she swept toward the exit to the ballroom. Russ turned to Nurcia expectantly.

"Why do you think she's going to hurt Applebum?" Russ asked Nurcia. "What do you know?"

"My mom is idealistic to the point of idiocy. That's what I know," Nurcia said. She stood up and watched her mother until the older woman disappeared to the other side of the door. "I haven't put it all together yet, but as far as I can tell, an asset of tremendous value—Steven Applebum—has fallen into her lap and the only thing she can think to do is destroy it." Nurcia started toward the exit.

"Tell me what else you've learned." Russ rose from the table.

Nurcia didn't speak. She took a few steps toward the door. When she turned to look back at Russ, she had a grim expression on her face.

"Nurcia!" Russ demanded. He felt like he was trying to coax critical information from a toddler. Out of the corner of his eye he caught Nina watching them.

Nurcia shook her head and followed her mom's path across the room.

As Russ hurriedly wiped his palms on a napkin a meaty hand reached out and landed on his shoulder. Aldos Verch appeared beside Russ.

"Hello, lover boy," Verch rumbled. "Let's you and me take a walk."

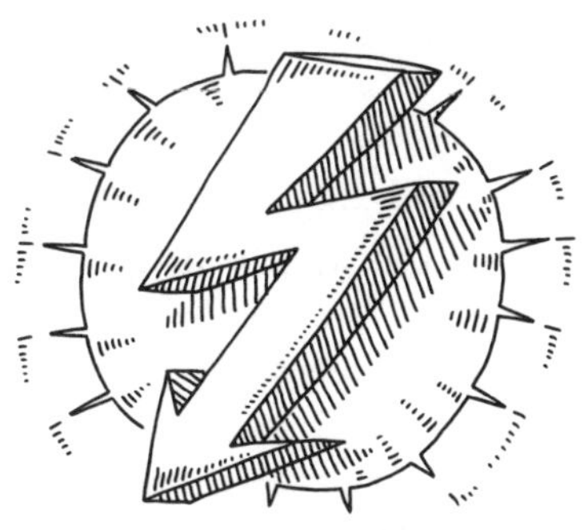

39
NINA

NINA WAS ANNOYED THROUGH MUCH of dinner. The food itself was fine, some sort of shellfish, cooked in butter and salt. Anything tasted good with enough butter and salt. What annoyed Nina was the way Nurcia couldn't go twenty seconds without draping her purple paws all over Russ's arms, shoulders, and neck.

She was relieved when Russ and Nurcia began to fight and Nurcia rose to follow her mother out of the banquet room. Nina had taken two steps to join Russ at his table when Aldos Verch materialized from the crowd. After a brief exchange, Verch grabbed Russ's arm and dragged him away from the table. The two men walked haltingly toward the exit. Nina followed at a generous distance.

Verch didn't spot her as he hauled Russ down the main viewing corridor. The cruise ship was fully sealed against the vacuous forces of space, but the entire deck and most of the left and right main corridors were encased by transparent walls, giving the sensation of standing unprotected against the vast universe. Stars sparkled down on Nina so brightly she felt hiding would be nearly impossible. Worse yet, she could be no help against Verch. If he had his shield up, he was an impenetrable fighting machine.

Verch dragged Russ down the portside corridor, then used a key card to access a door labeled Employees Only. He pulled Russ inside. Nina reached the door seconds before it slammed shut but waited, holding it open a fraction and listening. She took a deep breath and quietly snuck through. An ominously lit staircase led down into the hull. She descended, listening for any trace of the two men. The staircase was silent except for what sounded like the persistent droning hum of the ocean. Her hands felt along the narrow walls until the staircase opened up into a huge cargo hold. Giant cages of thick metal and dense polymer lined the deck of the hold. Most of them were full, and Nina recognized all sorts of dangerous animals from her work with the Intergalactic Exterminators. One cage held a giant blob-like Buuffaaffaa. In another a Grendo-Fend pranced and preened, too proud to acknowledge its small confines. A third cage held a Pliasis, its feline ears perked and rotating toward every sound.

The hum she'd heard from the top of the stairs wasn't the ocean. It was the collective caterwauling of a dozen dangerous animals. "Murder zoo," Nina mumbled.

Voices raised in argument. Nina moved quickly toward them. Verch had Russ backed against a giant hydraulic crane with teeth large enough to move even the biggest of the cages.

"What's the point of this?" Russ asked. He was wiggling his shoulders, trying to squirm free of Verch's powerful grip. "Why kill a bunch of below-the-line CERTs? How are we going to do any harm to you rich fuckers?"

"It's not personal," Verch promised. "It's called a 0-4 Wipe. You remove something by killing everyone who ever came in contact with it. It erases the object, not just from existence, but also from history. It's barbaric and costly, but I'm more than halfway done."

"You're trying to erase Applebum? Why? Aren't you going to mass-produce him? Make him everywhere?"

Verch pointed at Russ's face as if he had just offered a good idea. "You'd think so. Leyonella has other plans."

"So how am I going to die?" Russ asked.

"From what I've seen and read, you're reckless. I thought about just waiting for you to die on your own, but then I saw you in the banquet hall—" Verch stopped speaking. He seemed on the verge of admitting something. Instead, he said, ". . . and I realized you'd make a good dinner. Earthling sneaks into the hold to see all the dangerous creatures down there. He gets too close to a cage and one of them just"—Verch put his hand on the bar of the nearest cage—"pops his head off."

Russ's eyes scanned the room. Nina could see he was looking for some way out of his situation. His eyes fell on Nina, partially hidden behind her cage, and relief flooded his face.

"I've got you, Russ," she murmured. "Hopefully, somehow."

Russ nodded back to the stairs. Nina thought he was telling her to run, but when she turned, she spotted what he'd wanted her to see. On a ledge overlooking the entire hull, a gun was mounted in a hard polymer shell. Its barrel was more than six feet long. Across the shell were the words "Fusion V-Series 900a, Lullaby. Will auto-unlock and arm when ship is in emergency status only."

Nina measured the size of the weapon with uncertainty. *I can't reach it; I can't lift it; I'm not sure it will penetrate the shield; the ship's not in emergency status.* Her mind raced through all the problems with the plan. *There's got to be another way . . .*

Russ's voice drew her eyes back to him. "Why are you making the deaths look like accidents?" he demanded. "Who gives a shit about us enough to care when and how we die?"

Verch shrugged in response. "It's the book on 0-4 wipes. The doctrine of plausible deniability."

"Waymore seems like an awesome place to work."

"That's sarcasm, right? It must be a big part of your culture?" Verch chuckled.

"We never use sarcasm. We only care about sincerity," Russ said. "And rainbows."

Verch roared with laughter. "It's been a long time since I met someone who wasn't afraid of me. You've got a lot of courage. I'm genuinely sorry about this."

"About what?" Russ said, seconds before Verch punched him hard in the face. It knocked Russ to the ground, and he rolled back against the bars of the cage. A ferocious ophidian had been lounging inside. It popped up on two legs. The spikes along its spine went erect and its long tongue slithered forward, dragging over the top of Russ's head.

Nina had to hold her own mouth shut to keep from screaming. She glanced back at the long-barreled rifle again, then between the bars of the nearest cage. Inside, the Pliasis darted its dark, unblinking eyes between her and where Verch stepped forward to plant his boot squarely on Russ's chest.

Still prone, Russ ignored the threatening lick of the Ophidian. Nina saw him toss an entire roll of pain pills in his mouth, still in their foil wrapper. He chewed them urgently, but he didn't try to get back to his feet. "You didn't try to hide Jaq'li's death," Russ said, his mouth chalky with pill dust. "You stashed her on a ship owned by your own company—"

Russ is interrogating him, Nina realized. It was the oddest interrogation she'd ever seen, with the interrogator lying bleeding at the feet of the giant, indestructible interrogatee.

"A simple tactical error," Verch said.

"You wanted to get Nurcia involved," Russ said. "You knew she'd investigate."

Verch shook his head no.

"All the blood drains out of your face whenever she's around," Russ continued.

Verch grabbed Russ by the collar and lifted him back to his feet. He swung Russ in a half circle so Russ's back was once more against the bars of a cage. Verch's fist flew forward, and the large room echoed with a sound like a tree branch snapping. Russ grunted.

This time Nina did scream, but the sound was lost in the reaction of the caged animals. They hooted, hissed, screeched, thumped and rattled; their bodies tensed to reflect the violence happening in the center of the hull.

Verch was holding the top of Russ's glittering overalls, and blood was running freely down Russ's nose and onto the shoulder strap of his diaphanous tank top. The ophidian jammed its nose through the bars, desperate for a sniff of Russ's blood. When it couldn't get any closer, it bobbed its head in quick zigs and zags.

"You're in love with her," Russ finished. "I guess everybody expresses love in their own way."

"You're being sarcastic again?"

"No. Definitely not," Russ said.

"I can't tell if that was also sarcastic," Verch grumbled before punching Russ in the face again. Russ's head snapped back and hit the bars.

Nina crept to the next cage where the powerful Pliasis paced back and forth. It was mammalian, with brindle-colored fur covering close to six hundred pounds of coiled muscle, pointed teeth, and sharp claws. Nina put her hands on the door release, saying a silent prayer that she wouldn't have to pull it. The Pliasis stared at her, its eyes focused intently on her hands gripping the lever.

"You've spent time with Nurcia," she heard Verch say. "You've felt it. The intoxication. I saw you two on the pool deck. Why don't you drop the sarcasm and admit that Nurcia has cast her spell on you too?"

Nina held the door release, but it was almost completely forgotten in her hand.

Both she and Verch seemed to be waiting for Russ's response with the same elevated intensity.

For a moment, Russ didn't have one. He just stared back at Verch, blood dripping from his nose. Then he shook his head, slowly. "No."

"You're lucky," Verch grumbled. "I can't stop thinking about her." He put his hand on Russ's neck and began to squeeze. Russ brought both fists down against Verch's forearms, but the giant didn't even register the hit. Nina looked into the ferocious eyes of the Pliasis, said a short prayer, and pulled the lever. The cage began to open, one chain link at a time. The Pliasis bellowed and Nina ran in the other direction.

Then a scream filled the air. Someone on the far side of the hull was yelling, "No! Stop! Let me go!"

On the far side of the room, there was a popping sound followed by a shrill scream. Seconds later, an enormous alarm blasted across time and space. It blared from every speaker, a discordant echo of the high-energy dance music that had been playing all afternoon. The piercing alarm vibrated through the walls, shooting through the cargo hold with terrible urgency. The distant voices were drowned out by the noise and the creatures' howling response.

Verch released his grip on Russ's neck. His eyes searched the hull, barely registering the Pliasis's cage slowly opening. Verch cocked his head, his eyes bugged. "Nurcia!" he cried out. "Leyonella!" He dropped Russ in a heap and raced off in the direction of the voices.

Nina sprinted just as fast back to the Pliasis cage. She leaped through the air, an ungraceful, desperate lunge, and got her hands on the lever, letting her falling body weight yank it back closed. The cage slammed shut and the Pliasis bellowed again, this time in rage.

The plastic case on the V-Series Lullaby popped open.

A robotic voice said, "Warning: portside cargo bay airlock partially compromised. Biological entities at risk." A second later the horn blared again. "Warning: portside airlock fully compromised. Biological entity lost."

Nina ignored the rifle and raced to Russ's side. He was groggy from being punched twice. She helped him to his feet. "Took you long enough to rescue me . . ." Russ said.

"I'm still figuring out this hero shit," Nina told him.

The alarm blared again. The speakers announced, "Deploying quarantine shields until system pressure is restored. Please stay clear of section nineteen."

They heard a deep clanging of walls shifting and moving in the dark.

"Portside integrity restored," the robotic voice said a moment later. "Please enjoy the rest of your cruise."

"Can we get out of here?" Nina said.

"Yeah."

She half carried, half dragged Russ up the stairs and out onto the Lido Deck. When they reached the top, she looked along the deck for a place to hide, somewhere out of the main corridor. Something else caught her eye—just on the other side of the translucent barrier that separated the main corridor from the rest of the swirling star system. Peering out into the star-speckled light, she could see a small object tumbling toward the ship. It was a glittering chain about the size of a necklace. A stone at the apex emitted a faint, inconsistent light. At first it seemed to be transmitting morse code. It glowed on, then off, then on, then off, permanently.

The chain reached the ship and made contact with the barrier, then ricocheted back in the other direction. It glittered for a moment, reflecting the lights of the Lido Deck, then began a long journey in the other direction. Soon it had traveled far enough to be swallowed up by darkness and distance.

40

NINA & RUSS

RUSS AND NINA STARED AT each other across Kendren's snoring body. Kendren had not woken up when they'd snuck quietly into the room, so they'd simply taken their normal sides of the bed and let the big man sleep in the middle.

Before getting under the covers, Russ had watched Nina carefully remove Kendren's whitening strips, pulling them from his large mouth to reveal long strands of spittle and sparkling white teeth.

Russ's eyes went to the door, then back to Nina. She was tapping at the face of her transponder.

Nina: *who screamed? verch seemed to think it was one of the divians*

Russ: *Only one way to find out. I'm going to rejoin Nurcia when we reach Beta-9 tomorrow morning.*

Nina: :*(*is that safe*

Russ: *It's the best chance to get answers. And find Applebum.*

Nina studied the message, and Russ could see she was unhappy.

She glanced at him across Kendren's broad chest. She was propped up on one elbow, her beautiful face the only thing clearly visible in the light of the transponders. She typed.

Nina: *can you please be careful. maybe take fewer risks? losing you and applebum would be too much. it's too much just thinking about it*

Russ was in the middle of typing a response when another message from Nina appeared. It simply said: *oh, fuck it*

He glanced up in confusion, and Nina was there. She had quietly circled around the bed and was standing beside him. He sat up, looking at her. And then she kissed him.

It was the very last thing he expected to happen, and it felt a bit like he was being punched in the heart by a lightning bolt. Her body was suddenly pressed against his, while his hands instinctively rested on her hips. Her lips were both soft and supple yet somehow also coursing with electricity.

It was not the first time he'd been kissed unexpectantly. The first time was way back in sixth grade on the playground when Christina Lin boldly chose dare in a truth or dare game. "I've got a good dare for Christina," his classmate Marc had said, looking at Russ slyly. It was one of his oldest memories, as if Christina's lips had catalyzed his temporal lobes directly into existence. The second time, his best friend's older sister Mia had grabbed him while they both stared at the engine of her half-restored 1978 T-Top Firebird; in between kisses, she'd kept whispering, "Don't tell Bud. Don't you ever tell him." Almost a decade later, he'd been caught off guard by a Brazilian girl, Paola, their bodies drenched with water, as he loosened the last lug nut on her flattened tire during a hurricane evacuation on the Florida panhandle. He'd even been kissed by Mrs. Cherry Lucas when she hired him to teach her a few chords on the guitar. He'd showed up on a Wednesday to find her crying in the kitchen, a half-eaten plate of pasta smashed on the floor, Mr. Lucas speeding away in his raised Ford truck. Cherry's mouth had surged toward his like the gaping maw of a steelhead trout.

Nina's kiss dislodged all those memories, happy and unhappy—sending them spinning outward into quiet irrelevance.

A moment later, she disengaged and moved back to the other side of Kendren. In the low light, it was difficult to tell what happened next, but it appeared she lay her head down on the bed and went to sleep. Russ considered circling around to her side of the bed and kissing her again. He watched her in the darkness for any sign of movement. Kendren's large chest rose and fell between them, and Nina's eyes remained closed. Russ sighed. He rolled onto his back and stared up at the ceiling.

He texted Applebum: *You there buddy? It's getting pretty confusing around here. I could use your wisdom.*

He stared at the screen of his transponder for a full five minutes, feeling his heart gradually decelerate to its normal rhythm. There was no response.

When Nina woke up the next morning, they had reached Beta-9. Russ was gone from the far side of the bed.

The garish golden cruise ship with its ever-present thumping bass was gliding into a docking station on the biosphere. Nina watched from the porthole, still thinking about kissing Russ. An unexpected sense of relief ran through her but she couldn't explain it, much less justify the sensation. Russ was still reckless, still apt to die—like he nearly had a handful of minutes before she kissed him. She idly wondered if she could convince him to go somewhere with her, far away from all of this.

Outside, confetti rained down on the passengers who were already beginning to line up outside to disembark. As the cruise liner engaged with Beta-9's docking stabilizers, Nina kneeled on the bed, shaking Kendren gently.

Kendren sat up, looking out the porthole through groggy eyes. "Is it morning? Why didn't you wake me when you got in?" he said, annoyed.

She told Kendren about Verch's attempt to murder Russ, the scream, and the odd floating chain they'd seen afterward.

"What do you want to do?" he asked. "I can't skip the game; my agent would kill me. But—but—if you need to stay here."

Nina looked out the porthole again. "I'll come along. The answers to this mystery are out there, not in here. But we better hurry. The line to get off the ship is already a mile long."

By the time they reached the top deck, the crowd waiting to exit was in the thousands. Despite the existence of four fifty-foot-wide ramps, the crowd was jostling back and forth, many already drunk despite the early hour. Progress was slow.

Once they had finally disembarked, a wheeled vending machine rolled up to the edge of the ramp and blocked both their paths. It spoke: "Are you feeling hot? Your body temperature is 104 degrees. A little high for a . . . RreRriaNnian. Try Maxibrew to cool down." After it finished its pitch, the vending machine didn't move. Nina tried to step left but the billboard scooted to the left to remain directly in front of her. An arrow flashed where she was supposed to tap her transponder to transfer enough credits to buy the beverage.

Nina wound up and kicked the machine as hard as she could. It flopped to the ground but immediately tried to reset, reticulating arms disengaging from each side and planting into the ground to raise it back upright. She kicked it again before that could happen. Kendren joined in and they stomped it until it stopped moving or making noise.

"Now I do feel like some Maxibrew," Kendren said, wiping sweat from his forehead as they both moved down the street. Pennants of various Bootball teams hung from streetlights. Behind them, a marching band tromped by, banging away at alien instruments. "Thank you. I needed to stomp on something," Kendren admitted. "That was cathartic."

"It's why I let you sleep," Nina said. "Everyone can tell that something is really bothering you."

"Your life was in danger. You should have woken me." He wrapped his arm around her waist as the two of them circled a Sikkie-Bruzz in the gutter, sleeping, passed out, or dead. The stadium loomed in the distance, a five-hundred-foot-tall mishmash of concrete, steel, music, and lights. As they got close, they were funneled inside an entrance tunnel. A digital banner read "Welcome, CERTified heroes!"

Her mind drifted back to all the things that had happened the night before. "Why was the ship's hull stuffed full of dangerous creatures?" she asked.

"You've never seen a Bootball game?" Kendren said. "Those creatures are part of it. It's illegal to transport that class of intergalactic threat through a Waypoint. It violates all sorts of UAIB sanctions. Being onboard with those savages just below deck is one of the unspoken thrills of this whole experience."

A Plutorach walked alongside Nina trying to sell her a discount shirt for Team TenRen, the colors faded and cheap looking. "They'll make the tournament next year!" he insisted.

They found their seats on the lower levels, among the stylishly dressed bourgeois. "I'm being honored," Kendren said apologetically, as if he regretted being among the wine and cheese crowd. Nina looked over her shoulder at the upper levels where a rougher crowd was congregating. On the retail platform between sections, a large inflatable Vaqual squatted just above the mezzanine. It was two stories high, its fat arms held in place by giant steel ropes.

She texted Russ: *can you see the inflatable vaqual from your seats?*

Russ: *I'm in the owner's box. I can see everything.*

Nina: *meet under the vaqual two minutes before halftime*

A horn blew across several thousand watts of digital sound, drawing Nina's eyes back to the field. The crowd rose to their feet in a thunderous cheer, and the stadium itself trembled. Two different teams spilled out of the tunnels directly in front of her, charging dramatically through thick smoke.

Kendren grabbed her hand again. He'd been touching her, nearly nonstop, since they'd left their suite. "Thanks for inviting me," she told him.

The big guy blushed. "You are having fun?"

"Absolutely."

Nina took a moment to examine the large man beside her. She had always taken his mild flirting as coy, bordering on arrogant. But he hadn't bothered to stare when she'd been naked onboard the Kwiky Pest & Nuisance ship, and he'd slept through most of their romantic cruise, leaving her to eat and fight alone while Nurcia rubbed against Russ like a cat marking its territory. She thought about the profoundly sad expression Kendren had had on his face when she'd snooped on him sitting alone on the dock in the VTR. At the time, she'd just attributed it to exhaustion from pushing himself so hard to appear perfect in the face of all the media attention. She theorized she had been reading him incorrectly all along. "What would you have done if last night had gone differently?" Nina asked, curious. "If I had come back to the room alone and crawled into bed with you?"

Kendren grinned. "If you knew how strong the current of hormones are that run through RreRriaNnian blood, you wouldn't have to ask that."

"I did ask it though," Nina said, her eyes drifting to an advertisement flashing on the jumbotron, "and you didn't really answer."

She glanced back at Kendren in time to see a look of false outrage pass over his face, then drop away. He leaned in close enough to whisper in her ear. She could barely hear his words over the din of the crowd.

"Something is wrong with me."

41
RUSS

RUSS WAS HANGING HIS ARMS over the edge of the wall separating their chairs from the field far below. Aliens raced across the turf jostling for control of a ball. A Bryn-Tyr in blue threw a long pass to a Southern Blurn in blue and half the crowd went wild.

Sitting beside him, Nurcia adjusted the jersey she was wearing. She'd cut the neck into a V shape to make room for the gray sling she'd tied across her chest. "You didn't come to my room last night even though my mother was sleeping, and I left the door ajar."

"Maybe I was just being gentlemanly?" Russ suggested.

Russ saw an emotion play across her face, but her features were so exotic that he couldn't read it. He studied her face for further clues. While he did, she slipped her hand into the sling around her neck and briefly faded from view.

He was taken aback. Was this just a childish response to things not going the way she wanted, or was she gone? He reached out, his fingers wrapping around her arm. She was still sitting in the same spot.

She reappeared again. "Two Chenuls!" she shouted at the attendant who was standing nervously over by the door. The attendant immediately handed her two champagne flutes. She shoved one into Russ's hand. The liquid inside bubbled a brown green, spilling over onto his wrist.

Russ watched the game for a moment, stealing an occasional glance at Leyonella. Whatever had happened last night, both women were waiting for him in the hotel room when he'd snuck back in that morning. Now, the older Divian leaned forward in her seat, her eyes following the action on the field.

Far below, a slender TEN-awtch knifed between two lumbering defenders. In a feat of incredible dexterity, he stepped high on the wall and smacked the ball onto the elevated shelf. He slid down the wall, but the ball remained. The crowd seemed to be holding its breath. A bell rang over the loudspeaker and everyone cheered.

"This is pretty cool," Russ said, trying to keep the vibe positive. He glanced at Leyonella again. She was too focused on the game to notice his attention. Her transformer glittered in her ear. Over her shoulder, a digital wheel appeared on the jumbotron hanging high above the field. It was split into six pie shapes, each bearing the silhouette of a large animal in profile. The wheel began to spin. Russ heard various clusters of people chanting "Vaqual," "Dreadwalker," and "Pliasis." The wheel settled on one of the pie slices. The picture inside enlarged and filled with color, and the crowd rose to its feet, all eyes fixated on the field. The players continued to jockey for the ball, trading possession.

Far below, one of six portcullises opened in the wall of the stadium. A savage Tharcus bound out, its claws flashing in the bright stadium lights. It leaped toward the slender TEN-awtch who was once more sprinting toward the opponent's goal.

His teammates dove ineffectively toward the legs of the Tharcus. The TEN-awtch bobbed and weaved, but the giant primate lunged forward and hooked its huge paws around his shoulder. It tore the man's arm off, taking the ball with it. Half the crowd groaned audibly. The Tharcus sniffed the ball and began to eat it. *It must be covered in Spindex*, Russ realized.

Both teams retreated to their respective bullpen as the TEN-awtch player's team was penalized three points. The jumbotron hanging above the field replayed his arm being torn off in slow motion, blood and bone shards splattering the camera. The replay gave way to a commercial for Limian Life Insurance as a wrangler subdued the Tharcus and a plastic-clad hazmat team came out to bundle up the TEN-awtch and carry him to the on-site CRC machines.

During the break in the action, Leyonella stood up from her seat. Her eyes lingered on the game as if she regretted having to miss the ending. She tucked her head scarf into place, looked at Nurcia, then left the luxury box.

Russ stared at the man's arm, which still lay palm up on the grass. "I've got to use the facilities. Be right back," he told Nurcia.

She shrugged. She was pouring herself another glass of Chenul.

Russ followed Leyonella at a distance. The older woman moved past the bathrooms and down a steep staircase. When her course took them past the inflatable Vaqual, he lingered there a moment, hoping Nina would show up. She didn't. Forty feet down the concourse, Leyonella was getting far enough away that it was difficult to track her in the crowd. Russ left the inflatable Vaqual to keep pace. Leyonella disappeared into the crowd but reappeared a moment later. He broke into a light run to close the gap.

Out of the corner of his eye he could see the game clock ticking down on the jumbotron. A moment later, the screen displayed Nina and Kendren sitting in their stadium seats. They were deep in conversation until they noticed that the entire stadium was watching them. Russ had to laugh as fifty-foot-tall versions of Nina and Kendren smiled and waved enthusiastically. Beneath Kendren, words flashed:

CERTIFIED HERO: KENDREN OCKANIAN!

A voice came over the loudspeaker reading quickly from what sounded like a prearranged script. "Kendren found fame saving another exterminator crew from a dangerous outbreak. Since then, he has been a motivational speaker and a star on the hit dating show *Genetic Mixxx*, however, sorry ladies, he attends today's contest with his new girlfriend Earthling Nina Unknown."

A jaunty song played over the speakers, and Kendren's name on the jumbotron morphed into the words **SEXY TIME!**

"Kiss! Kiss! Kiss!" the crowd chanted, and Kendren's cheeks flushed bright red. He leaned over and whispered something in Nina's ear. Then he pulled her to her feet, they embraced, then kissed deeply.

It was Russ's turn for his cheeks to color. For the second time that week, he couldn't seem to keep his fists from clenching and unclenching. To make matters worse, Leyonella had turned right behind a concourse café and disappeared from sight.

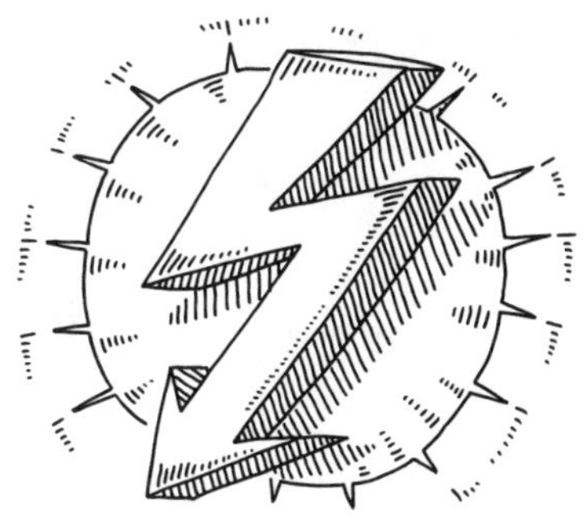

42

NINA

WHEN THE TEN-AWTCH LOST his arm, Nina put up her hands, partially to hide her eyes, partially to avoid the blood splatter. The crowd around her cheered lustily. “Holy crap!” Nina said, shocked. “This game is terrible.”

“They’ll reprint the arm in the CRC,” Kendren reminded her.

“The body can only take so much damage before the CRC machine stops working.”

“That’s what makes it exciting,” Kendren said. “Injuries force a lot of players into retirement when they’re still very young.”

A commercial began to play on the jumbotron. “I’ve got to go soon,” she told him.

“Not until after the feature,” Kendren pleaded. “Remember, I’m going to be in the spotlight for just a few moments. It’s part of the reason I invited you.”

The moment the words left his mouth, it was clear that Kendren knew he’d overspoken.

He reached up to cover his face but then let his arms settle gently back down at his side.

Nina took his huge hand in hers. "Why don't you tell me what you meant, about something being wrong?"

"Don't worry about that—"

"Kendren. You haven't been the same person since the rescue on the *Flashaway*. Or, at least, since you took credit for saving the crew. You've been stressed, unhappy, constantly on the brink of exhaustion. I should have recognized it sooner because that pretty much describes me for the past year. I let negative feelings live inside me for so long that even when my problems were solved, I still couldn't get them all the way out. Tell me what's bothering you, and I promise I'll do anything I can to help."

"You're already helping by being here with me," Kendren said. "But"—Kendren blew the air out of his cheek—"you're also part of the problem."

"How do you mean?"

"It's just . . ." Kendren was quiet, staring at the field. Then the words started rushing out of him: "I see your beauty—your wide smile, your strong calf muscles, the way nature has blessed you with bountiful tools for childbearing—"

"Gosh," Nina said, blushing.

"—and I know how I'm supposed to feel. I'm supposed to want to rip off your clothes and lay my body on top of your body. But I just . . . don't. I don't feel anything at all. It's been that way my whole life. When I hit second puberty and all my friends started talking about sex with our female classmates, I pretended to want the same. But I didn't feel any of what they were describing. It wasn't a big deal when I was a working stiff, but fame has made it worse somehow. The dating shows, the news profiles, the paparazzi. Being honored at Bootball tournaments. I feel like I'm letting people down by not wanting to spread my seed everywhere."

"It's okay to not want to be romantic. It's only fun if it's fun." Nina put her left hand on Kendren's shoulder affectionately. "It's okay to be any way you want to be."

"Not in my culture. Not on my home planet. Males are a certain way. Females are a certain way. The powerful and the beautiful get together, have sex, splendid babies are produced, and our species grows stronger. It's the way of things and it's very simple, very natural."

"It's never simple," Nina said. "We used to pretend it was on Earth, and it was also toughest on our famous people. When I was growing up, every single actor pretended not to be gay—"

"I'm not gay!" Kendren insisted. "I don't feel anything toward males either. I wish I did. At least that would make some sense. I don't feel sexual urges toward anyone."

"I think that's okay. The only way to do it wrong is to not be true to yourself." Nina rubbed her temple. "I'm being hypocritical. I feel a lot of sexual urges and actively work against ever doing anything about them—which is another way of not being true to myself."

"I don't want to have sex with you," Kendren said, awkwardly.

"That's not what I meant." Nina blushed. She squeezed his shoulder again, gently.

"Why don't we both try to be more honest? With ourselves, each other"—Nina gestured to the crowd—"with the universe." She was suddenly glad she'd taken the chance and kissed Russ eight hours before. "You just told me your secret and nothing bad happened. How would the RreRriaNnian culture react if semifamous Kendren Ockanian explained his situation to everybody in the same way he just explained it to me?"

"I never, ever want to find out. I'm a coward, Nina. I ran from the Triwin while you stayed and fought. I'll keep running from this too."

"In the end, not facing your true feelings is a lot harder," Nina cautioned. She didn't want to be too insistent. She knew next to nothing about Kendren's culture and understood that he had to make the decision for himself. "However you want to be, I'll support it." The commercials ended and she looked at the game timer on the jumbotron. There were two and a half minutes until halftime. "But right now, I've really got to—" she was interrupted by Kendren's hand on her hand. He nodded toward the jumbotron. The timer was gone, replaced by Nina, seventy feet tall and looking a little bit embarrassed. Kendren spotted the camera that was pointed at them and waved. She did her best to follow suit.

The announcer began a prerecorded message about Kendren, which ended with, ". . . his new girlfriend, Earthling Nina Unknown"

"Girlfriend?" Nina repeated, surprised. "My last name's Hosseinzadeh." Beneath them both, words appeared:

CERTified Hero: Sexy Time!

The crowd began to chant, "Kiss! Kiss! Kiss!"

Kendren waved to the crowd once more, then he turned to her and mouthed the words, "Kiss me." He was smiling, but his eyes blazed with intense energy.

The camera and the attention of the enormous crowd seemed to be drilling into him, compelling him to his feet.

"Uhh," Nina said.

He stood and drew her up beside him. "If you really want to support me, let me kiss you. Please."

She let him kiss her.

For that single moment, she was in the pages of one of her favorite romance novels, *The Loner's Guarded Heart*. Held tightly in Kendren's arms, she could smell his flower-scented cologne mixed with the natural aroma of his skin. It felt like she was being held by springtime and sea-salt spray and a giant, very sexy man. She was reminded that she wasn't like Kendren and did feel sexual arousal. She bent her left leg at the knee, and the crowd erupted in its loudest cheer yet.

And then the game resumed, and they were once again just two random people in a packed stadium. Nina broke the embrace with Kendren and glanced toward the inflatable Vaqual on the mezzanine. Russ was nowhere to be found.

43
RUSS

RUSS WALKED ALONE DOWN THE long exit ramp outside the stadium. Leyonella had disappeared behind the café, and this was the only route she could have taken. The ramp was nearly empty as most of the fans were glued to their seats watching the conclusion of the first half. He could hear the ticking of the Adversarial Wheel, then the crowd roaring with excitement as another portcullis rose and some manner of dangerous creature was loosed.

Russ liked Bootball, but he couldn't care less how the game ended. He kept seeing Nina latching her mouth onto Kendren's. *There is only one decent, trustable person in the entire universe, and his name is Steven Applebum,* Russ told himself. *It's past time I rescued him.*

At the bottom of the ramp a series of self-driving cabs waited, their electric engines buzzing. Other cabs were pulling away from the curb. He looked through their windows to see if any of them held Leyonella.

Russ tapped on the entrance door of the closest cab and the message said: "Anywhere on Beta-9, 300 credits."

"Fuck," Russ grumbled. He opened his transponder banking app, but no money had mysteriously appeared. Leaving the cab behind, he began the five-mile walk to the Waymore Industries Research and Design Lab.

About half a mile down the road, another self-driving cab veered off the main road and pulled up beside him. The cab was empty, but the door was open, the sign reading "Credits paid." Russ looked inside, warily. "Waymore R&D?" he told the vacant driver's seat and a light on the dash turned green. The moment Russ chose one of the seats, the cab scooted forward on rear-wheel drive.

"How many times did I warn you not to get involved in all this?" Nurcia's voice said from the seat beside him.

Russ jumped in surprise, smacking the back of his hand against the hard clear polymer roof.

Nurcia giggled. "Twice? At least?"

"Have you ever had somebody you really care about who needed your help?" he asked her.

"My mother is one of the most powerful people in the United Alliance of Intelligent Beings. There's literally no one in my life who wouldn't benefit from my help in some way." Nurcia suddenly materialized beside him. "But I assume you're referring specifically to SAS unit model number 233771.4512.7.9ii1?"

"We call him Applebum," Russ said.

"I know," Nurcia said. "I've spent a lot of time lately learning about Steven Applebum. What I can't figure out is how you got involved."

"He saved me a while back. I'm trying to return the favor. And I like him. People let you down a lot of the time. More often than they don't." Russ grimaced. "I can't let your mother harm him. Applebum is the best human I know."

Nurcia opened her mouth, likely to challenge that classification, but then she closed it again. She leaned against Russ and put her hands on his bicep.

A moment later she relaxed her head so it rested against his. "We'll have to get him back then."

The intimacy was surprising, but her touch actually helped him relax. The worst of the sting of Nina and Kendren's kiss seemed to evaporate, as if Nurcia's carefully manicured fingers on his arm were tip-tapping it right out of existence. "You didn't come to my room last night. And then you abandoned me at the game. Did you think sneaking away was going to make me less interested in you?" she asked, laughter in her voice. "Your seduction technique has been nearly irresistible."

Russ could feel the small cat wiggling in the sling against his elbow.

"Most Divians don't like sex," Nurcia continued. "It's all but disappeared from our cinema and our art. Over the last two hundred years we just compartmentalized it right out of existence. We pretend to avoid sex because of unbalanced power dynamics, because of hygiene, because it's 'perverse'—whatever excuse we can think of—but the truth is we're a bunch of confused prudes too wrapped up in our own heads to let ourselves be vulnerable." Her fingers danced up to his shoulder, then his neck. "The less refined cultures think we're crazy—and we probably are. Your friend Kendren is lucky to be RreRriaNnian. They have so many babies. Those folks really know how to screw."

"Fantastic," Russ said.

"I've been learning about more than just Applebum. I also studied our compatibility. Divians and Earthlings have enough common biology to have sex, but unassisted cross-species fertilization is very, very rare."

"I think I understand what you're getting at," Russ said.

"And our species only share one sexually transmitted disease. What is gonorrhea, by the way?"

"You don't want it."

"Do you have it?"

"I don't believe I do."

"Perfect," Nurcia said, her voice full of music.

Russ smiled despite himself. She grabbed his hand and brought it across her body until it was resting on her left knee.

The cab pulled to a stop in the large empty parking lot of the Waymore Industries Research and Development Lab. To their left an enormous white building blocked out the horizon. Nurcia swiveled in her seat so she was facing him, and Russ welcomed the distraction of her sparkling neon eyes. For the second time in less than twenty-four hours, a beautiful woman kissed him, only this one didn't go to sleep directly after. Her jersey was cut into a deep V-neck, but he was still surprised at how easily it slipped from her shoulders.

The sling came off after the jersey, thudding heavily on the floor of the cab thanks to the added weight of the knives sewn inside. The cat wiggled free from its carrier and bound to the top of the cab behind the rear seat headrests. It hissed at Russ.

Nurcia was lying topless across the backseat kissing Russ passionately. He broke the kiss to shoot a nervous look at the cat, and it hissed again. Nurcia tilted his head back toward hers for another kiss while Russ struggled to free himself from his own shirt.

When they broke the second, much longer kiss, Russ looked outside. The cab was nearly all windows and he could see the empty parking lot and other cabs racing by on the road just beyond. Nurcia was sliding out of her skirt.

"What are the rules?" Russ asked.

Nurcia kissed him again. Her lips tasted like sugar. "Huh?" she asked.

"About doing this in public? What are the rules on this planet?"

"I just told you—" she kissed him again. "Divians are prudes. They don't even want to read about sex, much less watch it. This whole biosphere is Divian property. If we're caught, I'll be fired. You'll be killed, maybe. Depends on who's caught us, I guess." Her mouth moved down his neck and he realized she was mostly naked. "Mind-wiped at least," she added. He realized he was mostly naked too.

Russ looked out the windows again. Despite what he'd just seen at the Bootball game, his mind kept drifting back to Nina and he was feeling a decent amount of guilt.

Nurcia studied his expression. It must have given away his uncertainty. "You're not careful about anything except this?" she asked, laughing. Then she pouted. "Your recklessness is usually so hot. Don't get caught up in your own head, keep following your instincts." She studied his face again and then moved out from underneath him, humping into a sitting position. "Maybe this will help?" Nurcia put his left hand on her breast. She took his right hand in hers and interlocked their fingers. She moved their hands together to the seat headrest. The Coffin Cat was still perched up there. It bit down on Russ and Nina's fingers before he had time to yank them free from its tiny, saliva filled mouth.

Nurcia disappeared, and he did too. He tried to shake his hand free from the creature's mouth, but it had an incisor buried deep in his pointer finger.

He looked at the empty bench seat beside him. Nurcia was there, but not there. He could still feel her breast in his left hand and her mouth as it traveled back to his neck. He could also still feel the guilt, but with each kiss on his neck and chest it seemed to matter less and less.

Fifteen minutes later, Nurcia was once more holding his bicep as they quickly pulled on their clothes and exited the cab.

"Don't take the cruise liner back home," Nurcia told him. "I have my own private craft nearby. I'd like you to come back with me in that."

Russ held the large glass door open, letting Nurcia enter the building before him. He rubbed at his finger, still bleeding from the cat's bite. "Yeah, maybe," he said, nodding.

The lobby of the Waymore Research and Development Lab was empty except for a long security counter. A quadruplet of guards huddled around a small screen. Russ could hear the Bootball game emitting from tinny speakers. The announcers' voices squawked with excitement.

"How do we get past the guards?" he asked Nurcia.

"Are you joking?" she said.

One of the guards looked up at the sound of their voices, a hand drifting to his weapon, but it wasn't in his holster. Russ could see he had left it lying across an unoccupied stool at the end of the security counter. The guard seemed to recognize Nurcia and quickly smacked the shoulder of the guy next to him. Soon, the game was snapped off and all four men stood at attention behind the long counter. "Evening, Ms. Fragnar," one said, sheepishly.

"Va-va-Vaquals Victory," Nurcia told them.

"Darn right," the boldest of the four replied.

Like much of the planet, everything in the lobby was inorganic. The wall of ivy that spread behind the security desk was thin polymer. Russ touched an outcropping of compressed foam rocks that sprang up in a sculpture near a host of elevators. He leaned against the wall on his right and discovered it was made entirely of reinforced plastic. It was, in fact, a floor-to-ceiling fish tank. The water was crystal clear, and the tank was almost as unoccupied and lifeless as the lobby, but something large and gray moved behind the first pane. Russ walked toward it, showing Nurcia his back so she couldn't see him text: *I'm here. Be ready to go.*

A simple line of text appeared in response: *Russ?*

In the lobby. Be ready. Don't trust anyone except me.

On the other side of the transparent, acrylic wall, an adolescent Zypper, no more than five feet long, swam up to look at him. The back end of its body and tailfins moved in a smooth rhythm, keeping it eye level.

"I think I met your dad a few weeks ago," he told it.

The Zypper opened its mouth, showing rows of sharp teeth. It seemed to be smiling at him in the same way Aldos Verch had the night before. Russ put his open palm over the plastic, and the Zypper lunged, smashing its nose against the tank.

The hollow underwater *thump* reminded him of the silver chain bouncing off the wall of the Lido Deck the night before. The noise also drew the gaze of Nurcia and all four guards. "I'm going to show my friend the complex," Nurcia told them. "We'd like a little privacy, so please stop any patrols until we get back topside. Just keep enjoying the game."

"Yes, ma'am," The bold guard spoke up again, remembering something. "Your mother is already inside."

"I know."

"The FOXNAR team left you a device prototype on the third floor. They said you'd requested it?"

"I was hoping that was the case," Nurcia said.

Russ and Nurcia boarded one of the elevators. It was a steel-colored box with no buttons. The doors fit together so precisely that Russ felt a quick rush of claustrophobia he hadn't been aware he had. Nurcia waved a key card at a pale, smooth square near the door and the elevator slid downward.

A message appeared on his wrist: *PEOPLE ARE RIGHT OUTSIDE MY DOOR*

"Want to see something cool?" Nurcia asked.

Russ shook his head. "Let's just get to Applebum."

The elevator rushed deeper into the complex. Russ combed his fingers through his hair and adjusted the goofy diaphanous shirt Nurcia had given him.

Nurcia waved her key card in front of the door again, and a moment later the elevator eased to a stop. A voice said, "Subterranean level three."

"Is he here?"

"He's probably on four," Nurcia said apologetically.

"Take us down one more floor," Russ told her.

"Wait, silly, look."

The doors slid open. Russ followed Nurcia to the end of a long corridor that abutted to an extended viewing window. He found himself looking out over a ten-thousand-square-foot warehouse. Down below were row after row of robots, a terra-cotta army's worth of SAS. They didn't have any badging or identification painted on their chests, but Russ could tell they were Tech 13 units.

They had the dark, burnished pewter color he had come to associate with Fromantium. He pressed his hands against the glass and found it unnaturally cold.

Nurcia had moved into a small lab off to the left. She emerged again with a metal cylinder in her hand. She pressed her body against his back. Once again he could feel the Coffin Cat squirming—probably hungry for more of his flesh. Its claws dug at the base of his spine. "Waymore's private robot army," Nurcia purred, gazing over his shoulder at the robots lined up below. "Too bad they're made of shit-metal."

Russ pushed himself in a semicircle. He was nose to nose with Nurcia. Her neon eyes glowed back at his. Her purple hair cascaded forward, trickling across his cheeks and chin and sticking to his week-old beard stubble. She kissed him and waved the metal cylinder in front of his eyes. When she tapped her finger against the end, a three-inch, white-hot flame burst forward. Russ felt the intense heat on his cheeks.

"For Verch's shield belt," she said. "It'll burn through anything short of Fromantium. Of course, Verch doesn't seem to be here, does he? I think we're completely alone." Nurcia lowered the cylinder and moved her mouth toward his again.

Russ raised his hand, blocking her lips with a pair of fingers. "Your mom is here somewhere. Let's get to floor four," he said gently.

Nurcia pried aside his fingers and stuck her lips on his lips. She ran her free hand over his body.

He returned the favor, running his hands along her hips. His fingers moved down the sling, feeling the edges of the rows of knives she had stashed there. They traveled to her back, riding along her spine until he reached the top of her pockets and the round curve of her ass. Then he pushed her away.

"What are you doing?" she said.

Russ showed her the elevator card key, which he'd just extracted from her pocket. "No more games. No more delays. I'm going to get Applebum. You can help me, or not."

Russ left Nurcia in front of the huge window and moved back to the elevator. Moments before he got there, the elevator doors opened. Leyonella Fragnar waited on the other side. She was just as surprised to see him as he was to see her.

Russ was unintentionally blocking her exit from the elevator.

"Excuse me," she said, more a demand than a pleasantry.

Russ was about to stand aside to let her pass, but he caught a glimpse of her necklace. It was a beautiful silver pendant with a stone at the center that glowed slightly. Russ had seen the necklace twice before. Once on Leyonella's neck on Gorrillian Green and a second time just the previous night floating untethered through space. *Biological entity lost*, Russ thought.

He punched the elegant, regal Leyonella in the stomach. The older woman let out a cry of pain and buckled forward. Russ ducked low, using leverage to drive his shoulder into her chest and force them both backward into the elevator.

Their momentum carried Leyonella to the far wall and she struck her head hard against it. Russ let her body slump to the floor. He slapped the key card against the control panel and the elevator doors began to close. At the end of the hall, Nurcia slid her hand into her sling. A moment later she blinked out of existence.

The last thing he could make out was her expression of pure fury.

The elevator doors sealed shut, a half second after he heard a distinct cough just on the other side. He waved his arms frantically in the empty elevator, making sure Nurcia hadn't cleared the opening.

Satisfied, Russ leaned down and grabbed a handful of Leyonella's hair. It felt soft and well managed, and for a moment he worried he might have just sucker punched an old woman. But when he popped the transformer from her ear, her hair became greasy and receded. In fact, her whole body morphed from elegant matriarch into a grubby, working-class Lixil. It was the man Russ had seen through the window of Nurcia's studio apartment on Gorrillian Green. The one who had been wearing the same hard-light transformer Russ currently held in his hand. He pushed the Lixil to the side of the elevator, hiding its slim body as much as possible in the small space.

Russ was still processing what had just happened when the elevator arrived on the fourth floor and the doors opened. Standing less than ten feet away was the murderer Aldos Verch. Verch had his back to the elevator, but Russ could still tell that the giant held the remains of Steven Applebum against his chest, his long beard pointing toward the shining shield belt around his waist, his fiery blade hanging from his back.

44
RUSS

VERCH SWIVELED AROUND, REACTING TO the sound of the elevator doors. He lowered Applebum, instinctively freeing his hands to reach for his blade. Russ had managed to get the hard-light transformer attached to his ear just in time. He appraised Verch, who was blocking his exit to the elevator.

"Excuse me!" Russ/Leyonella demanded.

Verch's cheeks colored. "What is it? Have you changed your mind about something . . ." more quietly, Verch added ". . . again?"

Russ stood as stiff-straight as he could, trying to mimic Leyonella's posture. He projected his voice: "I have no idea what you're talking about." He removed the pendant that hung on his neck, holding the stone between his thumb and forefinger. He'd seen Leyonella do the same.

Verch shrugged. Russ could tell he was annoyed but trying not to show it. "You had me travel here to destroy the asset," he said, nodding to Applebum. "And then you show up and tell me just the opposite.

I'm to bring the asset to your daughter's private ship and store it for transportation to Ren'Div. What would you like me to do now?"

"That is still the plan," Russ bellowed. "But you must bring one of the Fromantium units as well. We need it to repair the unit's body."

Verch took a step toward him and grabbed his arm. Russ jumped, surprised by the giant's boldness. "Sorry," Verch grumbled. "Standard procedure to check for transformers."

"I am who I say I am," Russ/Leyonella insisted.

Verch nodded. He propped Applebum against the corridor wall and headed toward the warehouse entrance where the SAS units waited. Russ watched, willing him to clear the door and give Russ time to drag Applebum back into the elevator. Verch was halfway there when they both heard the *cough*.

"Nurcia killed her mom," Russ called out.

Verch swiveled back to face him, a look of confusion on his grizzled face.

Russ popped the transformer out of his ear, standing in the elevator as Russ Wesley.

"Russ!" Applebum cried out. "I'm so happy to see you."

"Hey!" Russ greeted his friend. "I came and got you. Sorry it took me so long."

At the other end of the hallway, Verch didn't ask questions or hesitate in any way. He drew the blade from his back and it blazed with fire. He raced back toward Russ.

"He's coming!" Applebum observed. "Can you get us out of here?"

"Nurcia killed her mother," Russ called out to Verch again.

From somewhere Nurcia's voice filled the corridor. "My mother is alive and well at the Bootball game," she promised. "This Earthling is here to steal the asset. Don't let him fool you."

Verch kept coming.

"You recognized Leyonella's cry for help in the cargo hold last night. Just before Nurcia pushed her out the airlock," Russ said. He had both hands on Applebum and had begun to drag him back toward the elevator. It likely didn't help his argument that he was, in fact, actively trying to steal the asset.

Yet . . . Verch slowed down. He kept advancing, his heavy boots ringing out on the steel floor; but he was deep in thought.

"He's still coming, Russ," Applebum said. "Perhaps you could drag faster—"

"My mother will not be pleased if you let the robot out of your sight!" Nurcia yelled.

Verch was nearly upon them. Russ dropped Applebum and dodged back into the elevator. He saw Applebum squeeze his eyes shut as Verch loped past. The giant charged Russ, leading with the point of his sword.

Russ scooped the Lixil from out of the corner of the elevator, hefting him up by his armpits. "This guy was wearing Leyonella as a disguise. He was just here, talking to you, changing the plan. And where did he tell you to take Applebum?"

Verch came to a complete stop just a few feet from Russ. It felt a little bit like Russ had been tied to a train track and the conductor had gotten the brakes engaged just before it reached him.

"He told me to take the asset to Nurcia's private ship," Verch growled. He relaxed his grip on the sword and it cooled to a simmer. Verch stared at the unconscious Lixil in Russ's arms. Verch's chest was still heaving, either from rage or exertion. "Bunda K'Otaryn. I know him. A criminal. A member of the Crimson Coalition. And a known associate of Nurcia's." Verch grunted again and a look of pain crossed his face. He clenched his eyes shut for a moment. "Leyonella's dead?" he said.

"I'm afraid so. I saw her necklace. Outside the cruise liner. Just after the alarm went off."

They heard the cough again, much closer this time. Verch turned his back to Russ as he pulled a metal cylinder from his pocket. He tapped the end and a spectrum of light emitted from the other side. He held the cylinder high, scanning the room with its rainbow projection. When the light fell upon Nurcia, it bent around her. She was leaning against the wall on their left, her body visible in an amalgam of bright colors. Russ watched her raise her hand to her face. He couldn't see her expression, but he imagined it was one of mild alarm.

"FOXNAR made that for you?" Nurcia's voice called.

"At my request."

"They do good work. I'll show you what they made me," Nurcia said. Russ saw the light bend around the small cylinder she held in her own hand. She crossed the room toward Verch, her own FOXNAR cylinder blazing.

"Leyonella loved you!" Verch spat.

Nurcia had crossed half the distance between them. Her shimmering rainbow form stopped mid-step. "Is that why she exiled me to the Darkzone? Is that why she never let me be involved in a single important decision? For love?"

"Your mother—"

"My mother loved Waymore Industries," Nurcia interrupted, "more than both of us combined. And now it's at risk because you morons failed to properly vet Fromantium." Nurcia's shimmering silhouette shook its head. She pointed a finger at Applebum. "But we have the opportunity to keep the business upright and solvent. We have a sentient robot capable of advanced, self-directed learning. One showing signs of developing a true organic spirit—"

"Thank you," Applebum said.

"—and do you know what she wanted to do with it? She was coming here to destroy it. To erase it from existence. She thought the technology was too dangerous."

"Your mother was the wisest person I've ever met," Verch said. "If she said the robot was too dangerous, then it was. Especially to mass-produce!"

"Wrong," Nurcia said flatly. "You're wrong and my mother was wrong because you both only know half the story." She stood upright, shimmering into view. "Eighteen months ago, a Providence contractor scouting new routes through the Darkzone stumbled onto a Kyrillian settlement. It was unlicensed and undocumented, but that's hardly unusual—they were from a fringe religious sect that worships absolute freedom. This particular settlement hadn't found the new home they were looking for. Attackers butchered them in their beds. The sole survivor, a six-year-old fledgling, told a story of large humanoids that made ticking sounds like an insect and had bones growing from their shoulders and back. Bones they wielded like dangerous blades. Liafen."

Verch scowled. "I'm the head of security at Waymore Industries. If that had happened, I would have known about it."

"I've spent the last year and a half doing more than you ever could," Nurcia promised. "Providence's CO sent me on a mission to bury the story, but I realized that attack was the secret to saving the entire company. Unprovoked violence against nonmilitary UAIB targets is the excuse we need. The UAIB council has already voted to allow our SAS units to work immigration. People fear aliens. Planetary defense is the next logical step. We would sell thousands—maybe millions." She nodded toward Applebum. "He's the final piece. It won't matter what the Liafen are planning. He can protect the UAIB. Think about it. The entire border patrolled by intelligent, nearly invincible SAS forming a vanguard against a dangerous alien threat. And no organic lives are compromised in the process."

"And Waymore Industries becomes impossibly rich," Russ pointed out.

"And Waymore Industries remains solvent," Nurcia corrected. "We reach the market position we should have had with our so-called super metal." She addressed Applebum, "What do you say, Mr. Applebum? Will you work with us to protect every decent living thing in the universe?"

"I will need some time to verify and process this information," Applebum said.

"It doesn't matter what he decides," Verch growled. "The UAIB governing bodies will not allow self-perpetuating artificial intelligence any more than Leyonella would have."

"Anybody who's read even one science fiction story knows how bad an idea that is," Russ added.

"That's hurtful," Applebum said. "But true."

Verch dismissed Nurcia's idea with a wave of his hand. "One Kyrillian settlement being massacred—no matter who did it—isn't going to be enough to reverse the council's long-held beliefs about SAS units taking more jobs, or self-perpetuating AI—"

"Evolution is constant," Nurcia said, slyly. "Politics are no exception. Unexpected things happen, minds get changed. An idea that seems impossible today may seem possible just a few short cycles from now."

Ominous, Russ thought.

Nurcia grinned. "It was the most satisfying thing I ever did, pushing my mother out the airlock last night. Do you know what she said as I did it? She said"—Nurcia scrunched up her nose, mimicking Leyonella's regal voice—"it seems you're finally ready to take over at Waymore."

Verch snarled. "If being capable of murder is all it takes, I'll do the job." He leaped toward Nurcia, grunting as he swung his heated blade with enough force to separate her head from her shoulders. She ducked the swing, and the blade buried in the wall. Before he had fully yanked it free, Nurcia was already inside his defenses. She phased out of view and melted the shield around his right shoulder with her FOXNAR cylinder.

Feeling the heat, Verch danced backward, huffing for breath. He managed to wiggle the blade free just as Nina plunged a knife into his shoulder.

He shrugged off the pain and dove at her again, swinging his blade without mercy.

"I'm the good guy, Russ!" Nurcia called out to him. "This has to be done."

Verch clipped Nurcia's left hip, sending her rainbow image spinning. The spectrum of light around her flexed concave and convex.

Russ lifted Applebum to his chest and crab-walked backward into the elevator. He pressed the keycard against the wall. The combatants disappeared from sight as the doors sealed shut and the elevator headed back to the surface.

Russ was half carrying Applebum, half dragging him by his right arm. "Are you okay?" Russ asked.

"I am very happy to see you," Applebum said. "Thank you for coming."

Despite the words, Russ didn't sense happiness from his old friend. "Did Waymore harm you in some way? Beyond removing your arm and both your legs?"

The SAS was silent. Russ looked into Applebum's optics and saw a fragile innocence there. It reminded him how young Applebum actually was.

The robot had gained true sentience barely five and a half months before. In that amount of time, he'd made himself into a repository of vast knowledge, but knowledge wasn't the same as experience. Information wasn't the same as wisdom. Russ understood that for all intents and purposes, Applebum was a teenager. A very well-informed teenager, but a teenager just the same.

The elevator doors opened again. On the far wall, the Zypper swam at eye level, watching them as they exited. The four guards were still behind the security counter, their eyes locked on the small screen broadcasting the Bootball game.

Applebum said, "I have read a lot of books. Generally, the hero doesn't flee from the climactic battle."

Russ sighed. "I can't go back down there. Everyone keeps telling me to stop being recklessly heroic and start making better decisions. Getting you to safety is the most important thing."

"Someone told you to stop being a hero?" Applebum asked. "Who would do that?"

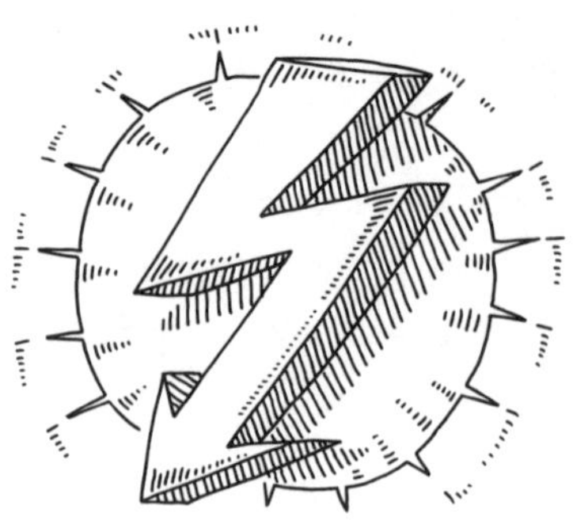

45
NINA

IT HAD TAKEN NINA A long time to walk to the Waymore Research and Development Lab. She cursed her own empty bank account as cabs raced back and forth past her on the street. When she did open the large glass doors, the four guards behind the counter fully ignored her. In fact, as far as she could tell, they hadn't yet seen Russ crouched by the elevator, whispering to Applebum.

Nina crossed the lobby with confidence, approaching the guards. She tapped her fingers on the desk until one of them looked up. "I've got a pickup scheduled," she told them. "I'm with Dolgen's Refuse and, uhh, Corporate Waste Disposal." She made a show of tapping at her transponder. "Looks like I'm supposed to pick up a nonfunctional, one-armed SAS?"

"You're not dressed like Trash Remediation. You look like a tourist," the first guard said.

"About time you got here, Ms. Orangebutton," Leyonella Fragnar said. "I had to lug this thing upstairs all by myself."

Nina did a double take. Leyonella was standing just where Russ had been moments ago. The guards snapped immediately to attention.

"Sorry, Mrs. Fragnar," one of them said.

"Be better," Leyonella told him.

Nina hurried away from the desk to where Applebum waited by the elevators. She tried to lift Applebum by his shoulders. He was only half there, but he was too heavy for her to move on her own.

The guard's transponder glowed briefly. He tapped the screen and Nurcia's voice boomed from its speaker. She was huffing as she spoke, "The man I entered the lobby with may be . . . trying to leave . . . do not let him . . ."

"She's right. If you see him, stop him," Leyonella assured the guard.

Leyonella came over to help with Applebum, giving Nina a quick wink. Nina lifted Applebum from the shoulders, while Leyonella grasped his torso. Leyonella arched her eyebrows and nodded toward the door.

"The man is attempting to leave with an important asset; it is proprietary Waymore technology," Nurcia said. "Restrain him without lethal force. Also, do not harm the asset. I . . . am sending . . . help . . . now."

The fourth guard left the counter and blocked their path to the door. He casually removed a stunstick from his belt and tapped it, unpowered, against his open palm.

"Excuse me!" Leyonella demanded in her most regal voice.

"Just got to verify that you're who you say you are, ma'am."

Nurcia's voice came over the transponder a final time, "He . . . may . . . be . . . disguised . . . as my mother." Nurcia was gasping for breath between each word. Nina thought she heard the clang of a blade striking a metal wall in the background.

Another guard circled around to stand directly behind Leyonella and Nina. "Take off the transformer," the guard ordered Leyonella.

She did, instantly becoming Russ Wesley. "Hey, Nina," Russ said. "Get behind me."

The first guard tapped at his transponder. He spoke into the screen, trying, without success, to keep the uncertainty out of his voice. "Just to confirm . . . we're not supposed to kill who?" he asked.

Nurcia did not respond.

"I heard her say to use lethal force," the second guard said.

"I'm not killing anyone. I got into this business to help people," the third guard said.

The one with the stunstick hadn't spoken yet. He was a grizzled old Southern Blurn with a patch of faded scales around his mouth somewhat in the shape of a goatee. "She said to restrain the male and the robot," he grumbled. "We can kill the woman."

"How?" the second guard asked curiously.

"Just the regular way, I guess," he said, holstering his stunstick and drawing his gun. He pointed it at Nina.

On the far side of the lobby, the elevator doors opened and an SAS unit marched out. The robot moved toward them swiftly, its skin emitting waves of cold. The first three guards scuttled back to the far side of the security counter. The Southern Blurn stood with his gun drawn but pointed downward. He seemed suddenly redundant in the shadow of the powerful SAS.

The robot marched toward where Russ and Nina held Applebum. Russ dropped his end of Applebum and hurried toward the security counter. The Tech 13 pivoted in pursuit, driving its heavy clubbed feet so hard against the ground Nina thought the floor might fracture. The Tech 13 reached Russ at the same time Russ reached the security counter.

It extended its powerful robot arms toward him at the same time he reached his regular human arms over the counter and swiped a pistol that was sitting idle on one of the stools. "She said no lethal force!" Russ told the robot. Without turning around, he pointed the pistol over his head and fired. The bullet missed the SAS unit, flying harmlessly into the wall on the south side of the lobby.

Nina had never seen Russ miss a shot before. "Turn around! It's going to kill you," she shouted. The robot grabbed the back of his neck and lifted him in the air.

Over Nina's left shoulder, water sprayed out of the bullet hole in the wall like it was firing from the end of a kinked hose. Nina realized the entire wall was a fish tank. There was a cracking sound and a long jagged line formed in the acrylic structure. The line branched north, east, and west. Then the tank came down in an enormous crash, twenty-five thousand gallons, flushing south.

The fourth guard was swept off his feet, pushed forward by the rushing water. Nina watched the tank's only occupant, a five-foot long Zypper, come tumbling out. Together they slid across the floor, a crashing wave of crystal clear water, tumbling guard, and fish. The wave hit the SAS unit just as it squeezed Russ's neck. Its legs and torso began to hiss, and steam climbed toward the ceiling. Bubbles burst along its skin. When the bubbles popped, there was less of the SAS then there had been before. A fraction of a second later its legs completely dissolved, toppling its owner into the still onrushing water. The robot turned milky chrome, its body trickling into the current. As the core of its structure dissolved, handfuls of components popped free and tumbled like dice across the wet floor.

Russ landed hard, not ten feet from where Nina still held her half of Applebum, her back pressed against the rock sculpture. The flow of water was slowing as it spread across the huge lobby. Nina flinched as it reached her, crashing into her knees and ankles and spraying onto her forearms which she held crossed to protect her face. She expected the water to be acidic, but it seemed to be . . . salty.

She dropped Applebum and grabbed the stunstick from where it had washed up against the security counter. The fourth guard was climbing back to his feet. Nina clubbed him unconscious, then carefully rolled him over onto his back so he wouldn't drown.

46

RUSS

THERE WAS NO UNSUSPICIOUS WAY to move Applebum. Even with three of his four limbs missing, Russ and Nina had to share the weight, Russ now carrying his shoulders and Nina holding his torso. They had wrapped him in a Gnu Gnaru Gnarlers banner and were making the long walk back to the cruise liner. Self-driving cabs whizzed by on the street, packed with revelers hoping to beat the throng of biologics who were pouring out of the stadium. They blended into the large crowd as best they could.

From behind the Waymore Research and Design Lab, a sleek private ship rose into the air. It was jet black with nearly silent twin thrusters firing from the rear. Russ watched it reach cruising altitude, then blast through the artificial atmosphere and out into space.

Russ and Nina stared at each other. "Nurcia's private ship," Russ said. "She sent it here to smuggle Applebum off-world."

"So why is she leaving without him?" Nina asked.

"I'm not sure," Russ admitted.

Many of the crowd had stopped to watch it as well. “How come the rich assholes always get to go home the fast way?” a Bryn-Tyr grumbled, the smell of Maxibrew emanating from his shirt.

By the time they reached the cruise ship, Tech13 SAS units were stationed on either side of the long onboarding ramps.

Without a word, Russ and Nina maneuvered the banner-wrapped robot behind an unused ticket kiosk.

“Why are we stopping?” Applebum asked from beneath the cloth.

“The ship is under guard,” Russ whispered. “We’re not getting on—not without saltwater.” Russ peered around the kiosk and looked down the length of the entire ship. His eyes drifted to the name: *Providence Travel Solutions Super Cruiser 9JAX9 Marcy Hedron*. “Marcy Hedron,” he said under his breath. He turned back to Nina. “We’re not getting on the ship at all,” he realized.

“You brought a portable Waypoint?”

Russ nodded. “And security took it away at the entrance to the stadium. So, it’s gone.”

“There’s an alternative entrance—the portside air lock in the cargo bay. Once the Bootball creatures are safely returned to their cages, we might be able to sneak onboard with them—” Nina said.

“We don’t want to be onboard,” Russ said. “Remember the Thufflin Box I found on the floor at Waymore HQ? It had information on a cruise liner, the *Marcy Hedron*.” Russ pointed to the huge ship. “That cruise liner.”

“What kind of information?”

“Travel schedules, security details, blueprints, crew rotations,” Russ said. “Nurcia’s last words to me in the design lab were,” Russ thought for a moment, “Unexpected things happen. Minds get changed. An idea that seems impossible today may seem possible tomorrow.”

"I don't get it."

"She wants to sell a military workforce of SAS units. What better way to change minds than hiring somebody to massacre a bunch of UAIB citizens?"

"Nurcia seemed driven, but not psychotic."

"She killed her own mom," Russ pointed out. "And she had a Thufflin Box with every critical detail about that ship. And she tried to talk me out of taking it home. Something is going to happen to it. Something that will convince the UAIB to buy Waymore's shitty robots to protect the Alliance." Russ adjusted the banner that was slipping from Applebum's broad shoulders. "You owe me seventy-five cents."

Nina's expression was grave. "You think she's going to destroy the cruise liner? In order to sell robots? I don't know. Could someone be capable of that?"

"I'm not going to underestimate her again," Russ said. "Call Kendren. Tell him to meet us here as soon as he can," Russ tapped at his transponder. He tried Lanie's number, but it went immediately to voice mail. Linnie's did the same. So did Trell's. He tried the direct number for the *Nightfire*.

"This is Intergalactic Waste Management, LLC, Odette speaking."

"Odette, this is Russ Wesley. We're in a bit of trouble and need to be picked up on Beta-9."

After a pause, Odette said, "The *Nightfire* is a state-of-the-art Refuse Disposal craft. Traveling to Beta-9 for any reason would violate our charter and Waymore travel restrictions, thereby endangering our contract and our livelihood. Not to mention putting unnecessary strain on the ship's resources. Also, you've been fired."

Russ took a deep breath, trying to figure out how to phrase his request as a question. An incoming call from Trell appeared on his transponder so he hung up on Odette. "Your girlfriend is really great," he told Trell.

"Why do you think you're lying?" Trell asked.

"We need a pickup from Beta-9. We've got a package we have to get off planet discreetly and our planned transportation has been compromised."

"Your package, it's not a—"

"—not a Liafeen," Russ assured him. "I know you count on your job to provide for your family. I promise I wouldn't be asking if the stakes weren't so high."

"How high are we talking about?"

"Potentially thousands of lives. Even more if we can't get our package off planet safely."

Trell sighed. "I can tell you mean that. This will almost definitely get me fired, but I guess fair is fair. We're close. I'll be there in the *Lumina* in less than an hour. Send your exact coordinates."

"Bring a portable Waypoint. That part is very important."

As the *Lumina* docked, Russ watched Nina and Kendren, huddled together and talking in hushed whispers. He tried not to be jealous. He tried not to be impressed either when Kendren lifted Applebum's heavy body without any difficulty and the four of them packed into the small ship.

On the far side of the enormous docking station, the *Marcy Hedron* was raising her long ramps and sealing her hull for intergalactic travel.

The ship's speakers were so loud Russ could hear the announcer: "We at Providence Travel Solutions sincerely hope you've enjoyed your trip, including the Vaquals' narrow loss to the Park Union Brawlers. We are just a few hours away from the final portion of our journey, a thrilling adventure into the lawless Darkzone. Buckle in and get ready to be walking on the razor's edge."

Trell piloted the *Lumina* away from the dock, and Russ tried calling Lanie again. Her face appeared on the screen, her expression clouded.

"You're like a viral infection of insubordination," she said, unhappily. "How did you talk my junk pilot into stealing my ship and taking it into restricted air space?"

As quickly as he could, Russ explained about the Thufflin Box; how he'd found the metal box on the floor of Leyonella's office but now knew it had fallen from Nurcia's pocket right after their fight among the Mortumzees. "It held all the information someone would need to ambush the *Marcy Hedron*," Russ told her. He remembered something else Algadon had told him about the contents. "It contained the location and security code of every emergency Waypoint onboard. If someone sabotaged or removed those Waypoints, the people on that ship would be sitting ducks."

"That's a hell of an assumption," Lanie said.

Russ repeated Nurcia's cryptic warning, "'An idea that seems impossible today may seem more possible tomorrow.'"

"Those were her exact words?" Lanie asked.

"Yeah. I'm thinking you should move the *Nightfire* within range of the *Marcy Hedron*, just in case something happens to it—"

"We should move away from the *Marcy Hedron*," Lanie said quietly. "We're a municipal craft. We have no combat capabilities. This is a problem for Transport Security, not Refuse Disposal. Plus, the *Marcy Hedron* reached Beta-9 safely. What makes you think it won't make it home safely?"

"If I'm wrong—no harm. If I'm right—"

"If you're wrong, there's plenty of harm. We're leveraged, Russ. If we lose this contract, Linnie and I are homeless. Our credit is destroyed. We've built something we're proud of, and you're asking us to put it all at risk because of what is, at best, circumstantial evidence. Sometimes it's smart to play it a little bit safe."

"I've heard that," Russ nodded. "And I understand. Could you pass on the information to SavUQuik? And all the other security teams? Just make sure they're ready for anything unusual?"

"Yes." Russ could see through the screen of her transponder that she was already typing away at the *Nightfire*'s HUD. "Please tell Trell he's fired," she said as she typed.

"Copy that," Trell said.

"Stay as close to the *Marcy Hedron* as you can," Russ told Trell as Lanie ended the connection. Then he added, "Sorry about your job."

Trell engaged the thrusters and nestled the *Lumina* along the curved hull of the cruise liner. They were so close Russ could see parasitic barnacles that had attached to the hull suffocate and die as they passed through the artificial atmosphere and entered the vacuum of space.

The arthropods released from the hull and hung suspended in zero gravity while the ship motored slowly forward.

"It's all right," Trell said. "I'll sure miss Odette though. Think she'd be interested in an unemployed dude who can't afford to care for the child he already has with another woman?"

"Yeah," Russ said. "Of course."

Trell exhaled, frowning. "It was my harebrained scheme that got you fired, so I guess we're even."

"Russ? You got fired? Again?" Nina asked, also frowning.

"I didn't tell you about that?" he asked.

"Playing it safe has many rewards," Kendren said, puffing out his chest slightly. "You stay alive, stay employed; you get the girl. Sometimes you even get famous."

Trell pointed at Kendren. "He thinks he's telling the truth. And he may be. I'd still have Odette. And a paycheck. It's not the worst idea to try and be more cowardly in the future."

Trell kept the *Lumina* nestled next to the portside stern. Kendren went back to whispering with Nina, so Russ moved to the back of the ship to check on Applebum. Applebum was stuck in the corner right where Kendren had put him. He looked wholly pathetic without most of his limbs, especially with the sad expression that seemed permanently affixed to his face.

"They really did a number on you, buddy. Can I help somehow?"

Applebum raised his one arm, but he'd been using it to stay upright so he immediately started to slide sideways down the wall. Russ caught him and righted his body, balancing his torso to better stay upright.

"An SAS unit tore off my limbs when it captured me in Jaq'li's apartment. A Tech 13. They are dumb as rocks but powerfully strong." Applebum stretched his one arm, glancing down at it. "I wish I could say the problem was physical, but it's not. I've been in the process of creating an emotional repository, which I believe has now been compromised. I accidently used a new application on Nina's transponder to discover the internet and—"

"You did what?" Russ scolded him. He realized he was shouting. "We talked about this. So many times . . ."

"Everything I read in your books indicated that mankind was good, that your people were worth saving. You once convinced me that a hero believed in the potential of all people. That he would take great risks to bring out the best in those around him; he would reinforce the positive qualities of his allies and set an example of compassion and moral strength for his enemies. Heroes in books often do the same. But the internet—the internet told a much different story . . ."

"All you have to do is not use it!" Russ said.

"I used it," Applebum said somberly. "Why is it predicated on such different values? Aggression, wealth, anger, dominance, division, vanity. And the sex? Human sex is abhorrent."

"It's not all abhorrent, I promise," Russ said. "It's just like anything else. It kind of depends on who your partner is." Russ felt a pang of guilt for having sex with Nurcia. He glanced at Nina, who was still whispering to Kendren. "The minute we get home, I'll get you a nice book to read."

"I don't feel like reading," Applebum said miserably. "Unless you happen to have my copy of *Catcher in the Rye*."

"I'll find it. I promise."

An hour into the journey, they passed the space buoys indicating the end of UAIB governance. Russ was practicing with the stunstick Nina had stolen from the guard, swinging it carefully in the cramped ship to see if he could get used to its weight and balance. He felt the old impulse to leave and try to find a place where there wasn't a big emotional mess to sort through. Where people didn't know him. But even that fantasy didn't make him feel any better because he knew he'd be inevitably drawn back. Russ watched Nina where she sat with her arms crossed and one of her feet resting on the edge of the control console.

He powered down the stunstick and looked out the starscreen toward the hundreds of people who had gathered along the Lido Deck of the *Marcy Hedron*. They held hands, kissed, and drank flasks of Chenul, all the while staring with anticipation into the dangerous, lawless world of the Darkzone.

"If they're doing their job right, Intergalactic Waste Management is just ahead of us, sweeping through the space debris," Trell told Nina at the front of the small ship. "It will be harder without the *Lumina*, but we'll get her back as quickly as we can. And hope Lanie and Linnie don't press charges."

"They're not doing their job right," Russ said, pointing. Not a thousand yards from the cruise liner, the remains of another ship did slow somersaults through the void. It was torn to pieces, the aft and the stern floating together but bifurcated by a jagged tear through the center of the ship.

Nina moved to the starscreen. “What is that thing?” she asked.

“Space debris. Lanie and Linnie are supposed to get it cleared—leaving only a little for dramatic effect. They plan these routes extremely carefully. Maybe I distracted them with the call, but I’m still surprised they’d be so careless that—” Russ’s voice trailed off.

The derelict ship had turned another full somersault and its brand was suddenly visible. Stenciled in bold letters across its bow in red crimson font was the word *SavUQuik*.

47

RUSS

"EVERYBODY BUT ME AND TRELL need to jump the Waypoint home, right now," Russ said as he pulled on his compression gear and tightened the cinching levers on his gravity boots. Once he had his sleeves, vest, and legs secured, he began to assemble the portable Waypoint. "Can we talk to the *Marcy Hedron*? Warn them that they're in danger and their security detail is already crippled?" Russ asked Trell.

"I'll try to find their communication frequency," Trell said, rolling a knob on the *Lumina*'s small dashboard. "Large cruise liners like this usually rent private frequencies, but we might get lucky."

A gentle chime played over the Lumina's speakers, and Trell stopped fiddling with the knobs. "I think I tapped into the broadcast frequency instead," Trell realized. He turned the knob slightly, but the chime was playing on the next channel as well. "It's an emergency broadcast," Trell realized. "Playing on all open channels."

The chime ended and a soothing voice said, "At this time, Providence Travel Solutions requests that you return to your cabin. This is only a precautionary measure and there is no need to panic. Anyone found to be not actively moving to fulfill this request will be subject to sanctions including a one-thousand-credit fine. If you have a disability that prevents you from moving quickly, Providence Travel Solutions crew are available to assist you."

Russ heard Nina gasp, and he followed her gaze to the right of the starscreen. A ship had appeared out of the darkness, its wings dazzling with electricity. As he watched, the wings peeled off and rolled untethered through space, still blazing. A pulse of dark energy enveloped the remaining fuselage. The central shaft flexed as cracks appeared across its length. Then the whole ship split into space debris. Russ caught a last glimpse at the badging on the side, a red shield with the words *Asset Protection Plus*.

Behind the destroyed security craft, a second ship descended, enormous and glowing like an ancient god. It glided through the wreckage, shadows from the severed wings dancing along its face. It was gigantic, at least half the size of the lumbering cruise liner, but sculpted from the sleek metal of a combat ship. The new arrival was of an alien design like nothing Russ had ever seen, a series of spherical triangles, stacked in serpentine scales. They tapered downward in size toward the front of the ship, ending with a gaping mouth that belied the symmetry of the rest of the craft. The plates spun slowly as the ship slithered toward the *Marcy Hedron*. It moved despite no sign of thrust or backblast, and its speed made the cruise liner seem stationary. Dark-yellow energy gathered around fang-like prongs jutting from the opening of the mouth.

Despite the broadcast warning, a handful of people had remained on the Lido Deck, watching the ship arrive. As the energy gathered and strengthened, it must have been like staring straight into a lightning storm.

A gentle chime sounded, "Providence Travel Solutions has instituted a mandatory lockdown. Please return to your room and await further instructions. We are entering full emergency status. For more information, consult the rules and guidelines brochure found in the bedside table of all sleeping compartments."

Russ deployed the docking bridge, waiting as a layer of membrane formed between him and the exit hatch. He secured the rebreather in place, then turned to see Trell, Nina, Applebum, and Kendren all staring at him. "If you're going to jump the Waypoint, now is the time. I need to take it with me."

Kendren got to his feet. Russ powered on the Waypoint, and Kendren readied to jump through. Nobody else moved to take his offer.

Russ handed Kendren Ensine's hard-light transformer. "Could you take this to a Corporal Rufus Ensine on Earth? In case we don't make it back?"

Kendren nodded. "He was my CERT trainer. I can find him."

"In case we . . ." Nina considered Russ's words. "You're boarding the *Marcy Hedron*?" she asked as Kendren disappeared to safety.

"When everybody else is literally dying to get off?" Trell added.

"Unless somebody else can think of a way to get the Waypoint onboard," Russ said. He looked at their concerned faces.

"I thought the ship would be attacked by pirates. Not that." Trell pointed to the alien warship on the far side of the cruise liner. "I think we need to get the fuck out of here." Balls of electricity continued to gather around its fanged front end before launching forward to pummel the *Marcy Hedron*'s weakening defense system.

"I know this is the kind of thing you want me to stop doing," Russ told Nina. "I will. I promise. I'll get a regular job and play it safe." He raised the exit hatch, peering through the membrane to watch the docking bridge inflate. "Starting first thing tomorrow."

"Yes! Go Russ!" Applebum cheered. "Save the day!"

"Get Applebum through the Waypoint," Russ said.

"I brought two. Because you mentioned how important they were," Trell said. He tossed Russ a second Waypoint kit.

Russ stuffed it into the holster on his back.

Nina opened her mouth to say something, but Russ couldn't hear her over the schloop of the membrane as he attached the tether and pushed himself up and out of the exit hatch. He let his momentum carry him through space until he reached the *Marcy Hedron*'s portside mezzanine airlock. He put his hands on the external release mechanism and tried to crank it open but it barely budged. A Divian woman in a cocktail dress ran by on the other side. Her eyes widened when she saw Russ. She didn't stop to help.

Far above, the alien ship closed the gap between itself and the cruise liner. It fired more energy pulses at the translucent siding of the Lido Deck. With each impact, the ship shook and Russ's tether flexed and bounced, sending him sliding sideways like a kite in a storm. He locked his feet against the side of the ship with the gravity boots. The shaking from the impact of each blast moved up his legs into his chest.

In between the impact of the blasts, the tether tightened. He saw Nina wearing full compression gear on the bridge below, anchoring the tether with both hands. He released the gravity hold, and she swung him back into position, then began to climb, hand over hand up the tether.

Without saying a word, she grabbed the release lever. Together, they yanked hard just as another blast struck the ship. The entire portside airlock came loose, almost taking them with it as it went spinning into space.

The ship's emergency systems dropped a wall of membrane to replace the missing airlock. Russ grabbed Nina under her arms and hoisted her through. He unhooked the tether, then clawed through the membrane himself. Once he passed into the controlled atmosphere, he was hit by a wall of sound. "Portside airlock fully compromised. Biologic entities at risk. Portside viewing wall compromised. Full collapse imminent. Portside upper deck compromised. Possible hostile entities onboard. Starboard side generators reaching critical output levels."

Russ quickly constructed and powered on the portable Waypoint. A Kyrillian porter was shivering behind an overturned table. He climbed cautiously to his feet. Russ made eye contact and nodded, and the porter ran to his side. "Where's everyone?" Russ asked the Kyrillian.

"I don't know. Emergency protocol says the p-p-passengers should bunk in their rooms, while the staff goes to the dining hall for further orders. But the Waypoints—"

The porter didn't need to finish his sentence for Russ to know the emergency Waypoints hadn't been where they were supposed to be.

"Raise your arms."

The porter raised his arms, and Russ dropped the Waypoint over his head. When it clattered to the ground, the man was gone.

A scream filled the air, loud enough to be heard over the repeated structural warnings. There was a thump, and the body of the Divian in the cocktail dress bounced hard against the ground, not fifty feet from them.

A stark-white chain retracted from the Divian's perforated body. It was attached to the back of a Liafeen twice the size of Charlie. It was over six feet tall, but the twin chains of bone periscoping from its back made it seem even taller. The bones were slowly retracting from the corpse at its feet, and they dripped with gore.

The flesh on its face was long gone. All that remained were jet-black eyes peering forth from the deep sockets of its exoskeleton. Bony splinters lined the area above its eyes, like the tentacles of a sea anemone. The alien wore a simple blue military jumper with yellow bands around the bicep and forearm of both arms. Russ couldn't see beneath the jumper, but he imagined whatever thin veneer of flesh it had been born with was long since sloughed off.

"Fuck," Nina said.

A TEN-awtch went screaming past, catching the Liafeen's attention. Russ and Nina sprinted the other way, in the direction of the dining hall.

When they reached it, they found the giant entrance doors had been knocked askew by the repeated blasts from the Liafen ship.

Nina was huffing from the sprint. "Did you notice its uniform?"

"I was too busy being scared to death," Russ admitted.

"It was frayed on the shoulders. One of the buttons was missing."

Russ didn't care about its missing button. He buried his fingers in the crack in the door frame and yanked it open enough for them to squeeze through.

A crowd of about three hundred waited on the other side. They were in various states of distress, some barely able to stand, others huddled in groups, still others trying to arm themselves with broken chair legs and metallic table dressings. Many desperate eyes looked up at Russ fearfully. He powered down the stunstick, but it didn't calm them. When Nina followed with a glowing Waypoint in her hand, the crowd surged forward.

Most of the people inside were wearing Providence Travel Solutions work uniforms, but a handful of passengers were there as well. They all began to jostle for position. An older woman fell and was trampled. Russ powered the stunstick back on. He stood in front of the Waypoint, the baton crackling with electricity in his hands.

"This will take you safely to the Alphane S Hub. Line up. One at a time. The trampled lady goes first, or no one goes at all."

"Are you serious?" someone asked.

"If you're not sure, come find out," Russ said. "Nobody cuts the line."

Two Kyrillian from the wait staff and a Divian in a three-piece suit helped the trampled woman to her feet. They half carried and half dragged her toward the Waypoint. Nina put it on the ground and they dropped her through. Then the Divian followed her. Russ nodded to the Kyrillian, and they jumped through after. People in the loosely configured line continued to disappear to safety, one after another.

The ship shook again, but the line held, and more of the staff of the *Marcy Hedron* jumped through the glowing galactic gate. "We've got emergency Waypoints," one said just before he jumped. "They were supposed to be stored here at the gathering spot. They weren't."

"There's one here now," Russ said, grabbing the man by the shoulder and hurrying him along.

Nina pointed to a female Divian who wore the suit of a ship's captain. "Get on the loudspeaker and let everyone know there's a working Waypoint in the dining area," she demanded.

The captain left her place in line and slipped warily out the gap in the door. *Nice to meet another hero*, Russ thought as he watched her go. Behind where she had stood, a familiar, hulking form sat at one of the tables.

He was slouched in his chair and had the heels of his feet planted on two ornate place settings. Blood was dried on his forehead and shoulder. His clothes were badly damaged and one of his boots was missing.

He took a long drag from an electronic cigarette, then stood from the table and approached the Waypoint. Even in his bedraggled condition, the crowd parted to let him pass.

"Hey Verch," Russ said.

Verch activated his shield belt. It was only about 60 percent functioning, with big holes in the left shoulder, right thigh, and back. "You know why all this is happening, don't you?" he asked Russ.

"I believe I do. Nurcia arranged it. To convince the UAIB that they need SAS more than they think. How long has she been putting this together?"

Verch shrugged, his broad shoulders moving up and down. "I haven't been watching her like I should. She must have been in contact with this mercenary gang of Liafen."

"Seems like an invading force to me," Russ said. "Why do you think they're just mercs?"

"Because of their uniforms," Nina chimed in. "They're threadbare. This isn't a real army. They're either deserters turned mercenaries or they're wearing second-rate disguises."

"And the ship's not Liafen technology. No way they could manufacture something like that." Verch grumbled. "Nurcia knows the only way to change UAIB policy is to spill the blood of innocent citizens. She set all this up. She must have been working on it at least since she began her investigation of the Kyrillian settlement. This is her show and she's left us front row seats. Hell, we're on the stage."

The ship shook dramatically, as if to punctuate his words. A terrified Toer in a maintenance uniform slipped through the crack in the door. His skin turned bright green with happiness when he spotted the Waypoint.

"Get moving!" Nina shouted at the line. The people at the front hustled to the Waypoint, moving nervously around Verch to dive through. "C'mon. He won't hurt you," Nina said, pulling a Quen-total toward escape.

Verch smacked himself on the forehead. "I found the Thufflin Cube with all the information on the Marcy Hedron and still didn't put it together in time. I could have saved Leyonella." He looked back at Russ. "I got too distracted by the robot."

Verch rubbed at the blood on his shoulder. Russ could see the wound was so deep it was still actively bleeding. "Fucked up thing is, I still love her. Love's strange; isn't it?"

Russ watched Nina hurry to the line and help an older Gnurian who'd been knocked off her feet by the last energy blast. The poor woman was frail and her tight, sparkling cocktail dress limited her range of motion. The headscarf she wore hung half-unwrapped down the center of her back. Nina helped her forward, stabilizing her.

Verch stepped to the edge of the Waypoint, putting his meaty hand on the chest of the TEN-awtch who was about to jump through. "I'm cutting. Try and stop me and I'll take your head off."

"You can cut," the TEN-awtch said, fear in his voice.

Russ wasn't sure the giant's huge shoulders would even fit through the portable Waypoint. Verch drew his blade and Russ stepped back involuntarily. Verch flipped the blade so he was holding the end and offered Russ the hilt. When Russ took it, Verch shrugged out of the shield belt and handed that to Russ as well. "God be with you, trash-man," he said. Then he disappeared into the swirling quantic pattern.

Nina helped the woman jump through right after the TEN-awtch.

After that, the line moved quickly, in semi-ordered fashion—but it still seemed to take forever. Russ was counting the remaining people when something heavy thumped against the ornate wooden door behind him. He turned to see a gory red-and-white tip of bone peeking through the wood before it retracted again.

Nina saw it too, her eyes drifting quickly toward the Waypoint as another Providence employee jumped through. "I suppose it would be a waste of time to try and get you to leave now?" she asked Russ.

"I'll meet you on Alphane," Russ promised her. He activated the belt and watched with satisfaction as a semicomplete, semitransparent shield formed around his body, cinching itself against his skin. He raised the blade away from his body, gripping the hilt, smiling with satisfaction as it burned with glorious flame. Then he stepped through the opening in the door. As he did it, he wondered if this would be the time he finally pushed his luck a little too far.

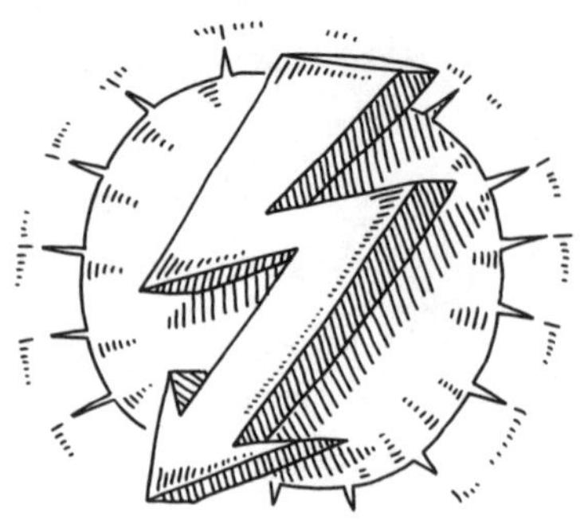

48

NINA

NINA HELPED DOZENS MORE PROVIDENCE employees jump through the Waypoint. By her estimation there were about forty left. After Russ disappeared through the door, the bone blades stopped thumping, but the lack of noise coming from the other side of the door was just as terrifying. Her stomach twisted with anxiety.

The loud blaring of the ship's emergency broadcasts stopped for a moment. A woman's voice came over the loudspeaker: "This is Klarnoa Penson, acting captain of the 9Jax9 *Marcy Hedron*. I'm at the controls. The ship is badly damaged, and we have been boarded by dangerous hostiles. I'm not going to lie to you: the readings aren't good. If something doesn't change, the *Marcy Hedron* will succumb to her injuries in less than twenty minutes. There is at least one working Waypoint in the dining hall. All passengers and staff are encouraged to make their way there while being cautious of attracting alien attention. I will remain at the controls and shift the emergency resources manually to help the ship hold together as long as possible."

In that moment, Nina understood that the Waypoint couldn't leave the dining hall. She either needed to jump through or somehow get Russ back inside. A Gnurian waitress left the line and stood beside her. The woman was short and stocky and had the same determined set in her jaw that Nina had always admired about Jaq'li.

"You can jump through," the woman said. "We owe you that much for saving us. I'll stay here and make sure the line remains orderly."

"Thank you," Nina told her. She looked longingly at the Waypoint. *A survivor takes that advice*, she thought. *A hero doesn't.* She headed out through the gap in the door.

The burned body of a smaller Liafeen was prone on the ground outside, its bone blades broken and lying like a string of Christmas lights next to its blackened torso. Glancing down the long corridor, Nina could see Russ facing one more. The alien was moving backward in the face of Russ's frenetic attack. Russ swung the flaming blade in sweeping arcs, but he was already bleeding from fresh wounds from his unprotected left shoulder, and his motions were imprecise, discombobulated.

She reached the combat just as the two spilled out onto the Lido Deck. A pulse from the alien ship struck the wall and Russ hazarded a quick glance—probably wondering if the fragmenting barrier would hold. In the twitch of an eye, the Liafeen's blade dragged across his unprotected thigh, leaving another deep gash. The alien clicked and purred in vicious triumph.

This Liafeen did not have bone chains growing from its back. It wielded bone blades that jutted out a foot and a half from its wrists. It stepped back out of Russ's range and began to rub its wrist blades together.

The grinding bones elicited no sound, but Nina saw a pained expression on its face and understood immediately. It was creating noise in a pitch humans couldn't register.

It was calling for help.

Russ held the wound on his shoulder while his own blood squeezed through his fingers and rolled down his arm.

"He's calling more Liafen. We've got to draw him away from the dining hall," Nina told Russ. "After that announcement, everyone still alive on this ship will be on their way here." Nina looked across the Lido Deck to a familiar door with the words Employees Only badged on the front. "This way," she urged Russ.

The Liafeen stared at them, hissing and clicking. It continued to rub its arm bones together. Russ kept the flaming blade held high as he and Nina backpedaled toward the door. Two more Liafen were arriving from the aft. One was enormous, the tall murderer they'd seen tear apart the Divian in the cocktail dress.

The ship shook and Russ and Nina ran. Verch's sword severed the lock on the door, and they hustled down the stairs into the huge cargo bay. They had only made ten steps down when the tall Liafeen came smashing through the door frame behind them. The bone chains jutting from its back dug into the narrow staircase walls, and it used them to fling its own body forward like a slingshot.

They reached the hull, and Nina was greeted by the sight of dozens of dangerous creatures pacing back and forth in their restrictive cages. They were honking, growling, and howling, already agitated by the shaking of the ship and the blaring of the alarms. The presence of the Liafeen—the bones from its back whirling overhead—had an amplifying effect. The closest cage held the Tharcus. The enormous primate had been pacing restlessly, but as the Liafeen grew closer, it pounded on its chest and howled a mighty challenge. Nina yanked the release lever on the cage door and the Tharcus bound through.

It met the Liafeen mid-leap, colliding with a mighty crash. Russ and Nina continued through the cargo hold. Nina opened the cage of the Grendo-Fend, and the bird immediately took flight. It circled the ceiling on mighty wings before dive-bombing directly into the chest of a Liafeen who had just reached the bottom of the stairs. Russ freed the

Buuffaaffaa and the Beuala and the Mousrut. The Buuffaaffaa and the Beuala immediately turned on each other in a flurry of flailing limbs, powerful grip meeting jackhammer punch. The Mousrut pivoted to face Russ and Nina, its razor-filled jaws opening wide enough to swallow them both whole.

"Fuck," Russ said, yanking open another cage before either of them had the time to see what was inside. A King-Polumba-Lux came storming out, twisting its long neck to snap its scale-covered snout forward against the Mousrut's open jaw.

Russ slipped into the King-Polumba-Lux's cage and pulled Nina inside with him. All around them bloody battles raged. Nina watched a handful of Liafen emerge from the stairs.

Right on the other side of the bars, the Mousrut buried its hooked claws into the neck of the King-Polumba-Lux, and the scale-covered Lux went limp. The Mousrut stared into the cage with bloodshot red eyes. Not losing eye contact, it wrenched chunks of meat from the King-Polumba-Lux and shoveled them into its mouth.

Nina looked down to realize Russ was cinching the shield belt around her waist.

"What are you doing?" she asked. "I won't let you sacrifice yourself for me."

"I ain't doing that," Russ promised. He pointed to a ledge at the top of the hull, just to the left of the stairs. The V-Series Lullaby hung there encased in its plastic shell, its giant barrel looking like something out of a Japanese video game. "Do you think the ship is in emergency status?" Russ asked just as another giant pulse struck. The ship quaked. The sirens blared. Dangerous creatures and savage aliens tore each other apart all around them.

"Yeah," Nina said.

Russ handed Nina Verch's fiery blade. "I can do some damage with that thing. Give me a distraction so I can get up there. Starting with that evil bastard." He nodded at the Mousrut.

"You want me to fight that?" Nina asked, terrified.

"You can take him," Russ urged her.

Nina's heart was beating so hard in her chest she swore it would bust right through that protective barrier of the shield belt. The Mousrut tracked her as she opened the cage. Its eyes were large and unnaturally close together, the eyes of a species that was always hunting, always moving forward, and not worrying a single bit about being hunted. Her shield glowed around her, but she was hyperconscious of the holes on the shoulder, thigh and back. She led with her right hand, keeping the Mousrut away from the gaps in the shield.

Nina held the blade between herself and the Mousrut. Behind her, she sensed as much as saw Russ slide out of the cage and cross the distance back to the staircase. The Mousrut took a few quick steps in pursuit, but Nina rushed toward it, cutting off its angle to Russ. Its demonic eyes returned their focus to her, but it didn't engage. Its feathery chest rose and fell. Nina had the impression it was silently laughing. It circled left and raised its hooked claws, coiling its thin arms back like twin cobras. Then it struck. Both arms flung forward with feral velocity. It moved too quickly for Nina to react, but the first strike bounced harmlessly off the shield. She raised her left arm to block the second. Then the third. The Mousrut's eyes narrowed in frustration. "Badass," Nina muttered. The blade was so heavy in her hand that she couldn't swing it as much as just poke it in the creature's direction. She dodged toward it, lunging the blade forward. The lithe beast dodged easily and swung a claw at her neck, its attack bouncing ineffectively off the shield.

They were at a standstill.

Nina glanced at Russ, who was pulling himself up onto the platform and detaching the huge rifle from its plastic shell. She took another furtive look at the rest of the hull. The largest Liafeen had gotten himself in position behind the Tharcus and was slowly choking the creature to the ground. The Tharcus swung its muscular arms, trying to get a grip on the equally muscular Liafeen, but it couldn't get any oxygen into whatever it had for lungs. Its flailing became slower, less frenetic, then it fell to one knee. The Liafeen rose on up behind the fallen creature, its bone blades snapping against each other, *snap, snap, snap.* It buried one of the blades into the backside of the Tharcus, then cried triumphantly, a powerful trilling wail.

49

RUSS

RUSS LOWERED THE ENORMOUS RIFLE from the wall. He quickly engaged the bipods on either side of the barrel and propped the gun on the edge of the ledge. He was in perfect sniper position. The gun was at least as long as he was tall. Russ checked the barrel for ammunition, keeping one eye down on the floor of the hull where Nina sparred with the Mousrut.

The only ammunition he could see was a series of pointed darts feeding into the barrel on a belt. He ticked up the scope, trained the sight on a Liafeen across the room, and fired. The alien had been wrestling with the Grendo-Fend, twisting the bird's wings while it snapped back at him with its sharp beak. Russ saw the Liafeen twitch when the dart hit him. He didn't fall, but his movements slowed. The Grendo-Fend pressed the advantage, flapping its wings in the Liafeen's face and digging its legs into the alien's stomach in a series of brutal rabbit kicks.

Just to the left, the large Liafeen was driving its bone blades into the Tharcus without mercy. It howled a battle call, and four other Liafen disengaged from the creatures they were fighting and moved to his flank. Together they moved to the Grendo-Fend and punctured it through the lungs. The beast tried to swivel to meet their advance, but they were approaching from too many sides. Together they moved on the next nearest creature. Their motions were swift, coordinated, and lethal.

Russ swiveled the barrel and put two darts into the back of the Mousrut. He watched as its movements slowed, almost to a crawl. Nina drove the flaming blade into its chest. He heard her howl in her own bestial triumph as the Mousrut curled into a ball on the floor and stopped moving entirely.

On the other side of the hull, the dangerous creatures were falling one after another to the Liafen's coordinated attacks. A two-ton Buuffaaffaa was pinned between four stacked cages. It leaped toward the Liafen with its single gumboot leg, trying to smash them flat against the floor of the cargo hold. The Liafen struck against the Buuffaaffaa in coordinated fury, but its porous skin absorbed their blades, letting them enter and exit without meaningful effect.

Russ took careful aim and buried a dart into the back of the Liafeen on the right of the Buuffaaffaa. He rotated the barrel and fired a dart into the forehead of the Liafeen on its left. The Liafeen tore the dart from its body, looked at it, annoyed, and its eyes turned to see Russ high above. He shot a second dart into its neck.

Five more Liafen came storming down the stairs, running right past where Russ perched on the ledge without noticing him.

Russ checked the feed belt. He had roughly ten darts left. "Trell. Can you hear me?" Russ whispered through the comms. "Trell, do you copy?"

When the Klung didn't answer, he tried Lanie. Then Linnie. Desperate, he spoke into Linnie's voice recorder: "We're in the hull. Trapped on the wrong side of the exit. We'll be dead in three minutes without a rescue. Portside hull. Three minutes"—Russ looked at the battle below where the Liafen were slamming their bone blades into the Buuffaaffaa five or six at a time—"maybe less."

One of the Liafeen he'd shot was on its knees, shaking its head like it was having trouble staying awake. The other seemed unbothered by the two darts Russ had buried into its exoskeleton. The Buuffaaffaa, meanwhile, was losing viscosity; the right side of its blob-like body had gone lax, and trickles of brown liquid were seeping out from where the Liafen blades had struck.

Russ looked at the thick metal plating on the inside of the hull and remembered the portside cargo airlock from the night Leyonella had died. He texted Nina: *One card left to play. Get your rebreather on. We're the only ones in this cargo bay who can survive in space. That's our exit.*

He took aim at the smallest Liafeen, hoping the darts would have more effect on those with less body mass. He hit one in the thigh, another in the neck, one through the eyeball, one (disappointingly) in the shoulder, and the last, just for fun, in the crotch where it may or may not have held its reproductive organs. The gun clicked empty as the end of the ammunition belt disappeared into the large barrel. Russ could see several of the Liafen slowing down. One sat on a crate and put a gory white hand to its temple. Another glanced up at where he lay on the ledge.

Russ jumped from the ledge and raced back down the stairs.

Beyond Nina, the Buuffaaffaa lay in the center of the cargo hold, as empty as a popped water balloon. He raced past her. "Don't follow me; get in the cage!" he yelled as he sprinted blindly toward the direction where he remembered hearing Leyonella's scream.

The big Liafeen gave chase, wrapping its bone chain around Nina's neck and drawing her backward off her feet. Nina screamed in surprise.

Russ paused a moment, nearly sprinting back to Nina, but he knew his best chance was the airlock. He yelled at the Liafen. "Over here, motherfuckers!" He almost smiled when five of the six ran past Nina, their bony legs driving in his direction. The one that stayed behind was starting to sit down on the floor. It looked like his head was spinning.

Russ found the airlock tucked in the corner next to a service exit ramp. He put his hands on the wheel lock and began to pry it open. Almost too late, he remembered his rebreather and lowered it over his face.

The first Liafeen made the corner, advancing on his position. Russ waited as long as he could then disengaged the airlock. There was a great popping sound and a whooshing of air, similar to lighting a BBQ when you've left the gas on too long. The Liafeen stumbled a few steps toward the opening.

Russ waited to be hit by gale-force winds sucking them all into space, but the air was mostly still. A membrane deployed from the wall, sealing the gap and restoring pressure to the cargo bay. The Liafeen that had fallen in the initial whoosh of air got to its feet, flexed his arms and shoulders to check for damage, then turned and faced Russ.

"Damnit, science," Russ cursed. He turned and leaped for the membrane. It caught him, as it was designed to do, but he managed to wiggle the front half of his body through. Not fifty yards in the distance he could see Trell hovering nearby in the Lumina. He could just make out an expression of deep worry on Trell's face.

Then he felt a chain of bone wrap around his ankle, and he was dragged back through the membrane and deposited on the cold graphene floor of the *Marcy Hedron.*

The five remaining Liafen were there now. They surrounded him in a semicircle, hollowing.

He hoped Nina was long gone. She wouldn't have to see him die. He blind texted:

Run. Please RUN! Use Lido deck airlock!

The big Liafeen howled again, "... krriiiinnniii ..." then it struck; its bone chains snapped forward and sliced another deep gash across Russ's forearm. He felt another wound open on his calf and his chest. The big one was either too fast to track or other Liafen were attacking from his left and his right.

Russ felt something inside himself break. A flood of emotions poured onto his shoulders. His skin became deeply sensitive, such that he could almost feel the molecules moving through the air. Goose-bumps rose all along his arms and his breath caught in his throat.

in love with you

The Liafeen struck again, battering his shoulder and tearing his compression suit. Another stabbed its bone blades into his ribs. A third drilled a bone dagger into his right thigh. He was stabbed again. And again. Each blow was a new explosion of pain. The big guy snapped his chains above his head, clapping to the coordinated rhythm of the attacks.

Nina appeared behind the clapping Liafeen. Before Russ could shout her away, she buried the giant's fiery blade into the largest Liafeen's neck. It found purchase, but it pulled out of Nina's hand and skittered across the ground next to Russ as the Liafeen dropped dead on the floor.

Russ hurtled himself toward the nearest Liafeen, wrapping both his arms around the creature's legs. He scrambled for, and managed to raise, the blade, straddling the fallen creature. The alien was disoriented and the wriggling anemones it had for eyelids writhed in pain at the bright light of the blade's flame.

Then a light ten times brighter was flashing through the membrane. It traveled north and south, leaving a splash of permanent color in its wake. The light painted its way up Russ's chest. He was bleeding from five or six serious injuries and the laser made his blood glow an eerie green. Looking down, he saw the Liafeen beneath him had no iris, and the deep black of its pupil flexed in and out under the assault of the dense laser. The creature lashed its bone blades forward, not to impale Russ, but to cover its eyes.

Russ tumbled away from the creature. Nina helped him climb to his feet, and they trudged toward the empty cage of the King-Polumba-Lux. He couldn't tell if the Liafen would give chase or if they were too disoriented by the blinding light, but the hollow feeling in both his legs told him he couldn't go any faster anyway. Nina helped keep him upright. She was fumbling to get the shield belt off her waist and around his.

The injuries felt like parts of his body were actually missing, carved out of existence. He moved what was left of himself with dogged determination, patting his chest where he usually hung his pain pills. He mumbled, "Keep the belt on!"

There was a tremendous grinding sound, and a deluge of sparks rained down from the high walls and ceiling. Russ looked toward the top of the hull, shielding his eyes as sparks filled every inch of the cargo hold and Big Sister cut a fifty-foot seam straight down the belly of the *Marcy Hedron*. The giant blade followed the perfect laser line Trell had drawn, tearing and grinding the metal into slag, whirling with magnificent, industrial might.

With Nina's help, Russ stumbled to the cage, but it was already drifting toward the giant perforation in the side of the ship. Nina ducked into the cage, trying to pull him in after her, but all Russ could do was lock his gravity boots against the outside bars as the *Marcy Hedron* belched the contents of her belly—chittering, howling Liafen, animal carcasses, cages, Russ and Nina—out into the vastness of space.

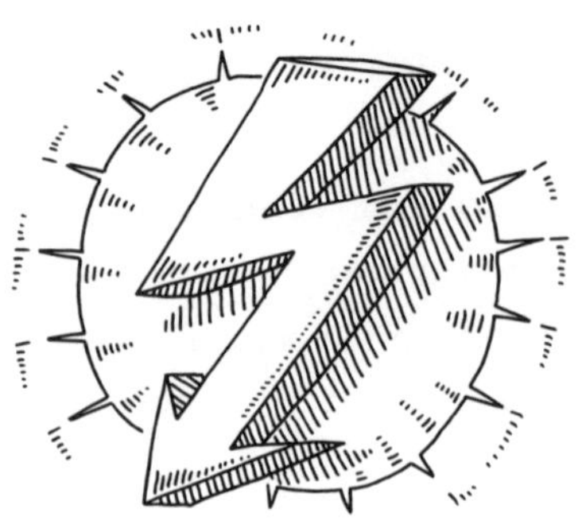

50

NINA

RUSS WAS UNCONSCIOUS WHEN THE giant claw on the top of the *Nightfire* closed around their cage and drew them into Lanie and Linnie's cargo hold. Nina watched him, very worried. His skin was freezing where his compression gear had been torn by the Liafeen's blades, and his blood had crystalized in the coldness of space.

Lanie and Linnie had him out of his boots, hustling him into the Medbay before Nina could even extricate herself from the cage.

She could see through the starscreen that Odette was moving the *Nightfire* as fast as possible away from the *Marcy Hedron*. The giant buzzsaw ripping a hole in her hull had been the death blow. Her entire bottom half crumpled as the top half split apart. The corpse of the ship tumbled deeper into the Darkzone, a last cinematic piece of trash for Providence's grand circus.

The Liafen craft hung in the air for a moment as if posing for a picture, then turned back to wherever it had come, leaving both the *Nightfire* and the Lumina completely unmolested.

When she reached the Medbay, Russ was lying on his back. The only part of him moving was his mouth, chewing on pain pills like they were peanut M&M's. He was still bleeding from wounds on his shoulder and thigh.

Lanie and Linnie were both hovering around him. Lanie held his left leg, testing out an unnatural wobble in his knee. Linnie was trying, unsuccessfully, to comb his hair.

"Did he leave the CRC early?" she asked them.

"It ran out of repair paste," Linnie said in disbelief. "We didn't have a lot. Trash remediation is peaceful work . . . usually. We're going to have to grab more the next time we're at a supply depot."

"Not that we will be able to afford it, necessarily," Lanie said.

"We're also worried about his percentages," Linnie said. "He took a *lot* of damage."

"You saved our lives."

"That's what friends do." Linnie went back to combing Russ's hair. "But I am starting to see the wisdom in Bah'ren suspending you," she told him quietly. "You have a tendency to get everyone around you fired. Even your bosses."

". . . are you fired too?" Russ asked, his voice barely more than a moan.

"We haven't heard anything yet, but that's probably because Providence Travel Solutions has bigger things to worry about. Even if they don't terminate our contract, I suspect rides through the 'treacherous' Darkzone will be on hold for the foreseeable future."

Russ didn't respond. He looked exhausted, and defeated, and not just because of his injuries. Linnie's words were gentle, even playful, but Russ wasn't in the mood to be teased.

Nina offered her hand and lifted him gently into a sitting position. He seemed unwilling to meet her gaze. "Do you mind if I take him home?" she asked the twin Kruxfasian. "It's been kind of a long week for both of us."

"Tell me again what you thought would happen?" Nina asked as they materialized in room 22 of the Riverview Motel. It was no small task supporting Russ while also dragging Applebum. They'd made a sled out of the Gnarlers banner. After she helped Russ hobble to the bed, she used the sled to drag Applebum over to his reading corner. She grabbed his copy of *The Dain Curse* and put it into his hand, but he didn't read it. She was worried about how quiet he was being.

Russ sighed and said, "I thought the vacuum of space would drag everything outside. Like in every *Alien* movie. And *2001: A Space Odyssey*. And *Avengers: Infinity War*."

"We've been working in space for half a year. Has anything like that ever happened?"

"There's always a membrane between an open airlock and the pressurized cabins," Russ pointed out.

Nina almost commented on how it was a risky strategy to bet his life on Hollywood film science, but he was so morose she bit her tongue.

"I think being around you turns me into a complete, babbling idiot," Russ said somberly.

"Being around me?"

"I almost died again. And for the first time I felt scared. Scared of death. Scared of you having to watch me die. Scared of *you* dying . . ." Russ looked at Nina. "Worse yet, we only saved a fraction of the passengers and crew. How many died?"

"A lot less than would have otherwise," Nina said, softly. "Maybe thousands less. We don't know how many made it to the dining hall before the Hedron fell apart. How many got there safely while we kept the Liafen occupied in the hull. While you ran through the ship fighting singlehandedly against the forces of darkness. Aside from my modest assistance."

Russ's face brightened slightly. "You were very helpful."

"Shut up. I was trying, but also scared to death. Ferocious creatures made of bone. An alien ambush. That was more hectic than dropping gas on invasive insects. Or even battling Triwin." She sat by his side and pulled his hand into her lap, their shoulders touching. She laced her fingers with his.

"You did a lot more than Kendren. Think he'll take credit again?" Russ asked.

"Kendren's probably had enough of fame," Nina said. She pushed her cheek against Russ's mop of brown-blond hair. They were sitting so close as to be almost intertwined. She let herself feel the rise and fall of his chest against her arm. Only then did the anxiety that was still coiled inside her stomach begin to slip away. "You're not a babbling idiot. You saved the day. Again. I shouldn't have tried to change you. You are who you are."

Thought lines formed on Russ's face.

Applebum finally spoke. "Is someone in the shower?"

Nina realized he was right. She'd been so relieved to be home with the team mostly intact that she hadn't noticed the water running. "This better not be Clark," she said as she extracted herself from Russ and swung the bathroom door open.

It wasn't Clark. Rufus Ensine had dragged the desk chair into the shower and he was sitting on it, letting the water rain down on his slumped shoulders. His fish scales sparkled like albacore.

"Rufus?" Nina asked. "Why are you in our shower? Why are you in your natural form? Did Kendren not bring back your hard-light transformer?"

"No. I got it." Ensine blew air from his cheeks. "It didn't work," he said.

"The transformer isn't working?"

"The transformer is working fine."

Nina waved her hands through the air. Ensine was sad to the point of inconsolable. "What didn't work?"

"Clark's Liafen CRC machine. I mean, it worked, but just like any other CRC machine. We loaded the repair paste. We figured out how to set the machine. Clark climbed in, and . . . nothing special happened." Ensine slumped back in the chair so the shower water rained down on his chest.

"I'm so sorry," Nina told him. "It was kind of a fairy tale from the start." Nina reached around Ensine's slumped form and turned off the shower. "So, what happened to Clark? Is he still sick? Where is he?"

Ensine raised his head to meet Nina's eyes. He was covered in water so she couldn't tell for certain, but it appeared that he might be crying. "All the work he put into acquiring the device and he couldn't accept that it wasn't going to fix him. He tried again and again. His body started rejecting the paste almost immediately. It accelerated the cellular degradation process."

Nina shook her head. "What?"

From the other room she heard Russ mumble, "What? Where's my grandpop?"

"I let him go home," Ensine said, "one last time."

51

RUSS

RUSS FELT HOLLOW, AND NOT just from his injuries. Worrying about the people on the *Marcy Hedron*, taking care of Applebum, watching over his grandpop, worrying that Nina would have to watch him die, worrying that Nina would die, failing to save Charlie, fighting that really scary-looking Mousrut and that huge Liafeen, misunderstanding the physics of space . . . it was a big adjustment for a guy who spent his first twenty-seven years avoiding every type of responsibility. *Once you started caring about people, life got exponentially harder. Probably 50 percent harder per significant person,* Russ thought, trying to settle on the equation. Loving Norma, Clark, Nina, and Applebum put him at an increased difficulty curve of, at least, two hundred percent. *Add another 15 percent each for folks like Bah'ren, Starland, Atara, Trell, Ensine, Lanie, and Linnie.* It was really tiring. And his body was definitely not working right without more time in the CRC.

Norma's front door was unlocked and the house lights were off. They moved inside, following the sound of soft voices to the backyard.

Norma was there, swinging gently in the hammock. Sitting beside her was Rufus Ensine. The moonlight reflected off the transformer in his ear. Norma held Ensine's hand, and they whispered softly to each other. It was odd in that they had just left Ensine behind, sitting in the motel room shower.

The river was mostly still and the night was quiet enough that the words just reached Russ's ears.

"You seem different tonight," Norma was saying.

"Worse or better?" Ensine asked.

"Neither, but more familiar. Like—I don't know how to describe it."

"No need to try," Ensine said, coughing. "Let's just sit here a moment longer. I can't tell you how much I've missed this."

Norma giggled. "We spent most of the last month in this hammock. We're in this thing so much I'm afraid the ropes are fraying under our old butts."

"Okay. That's okay," Ensine said. He looked up at the sky while Norma ran her hand through his thinning white hair. "That whole big universe up there—isn't it ironic that the best place to be is right here beside you?"

"Oh geez," Norma said laughing. "You are being sentimental tonight."

He rested his head on her shoulder and snaked his arm around her waist, holding her close.

Norma yawned. "Do you want some coffee? I think the pot is finished brewing."

"Can we stay here just a moment longer?" Ensine asked, coughing.

"Gosh. You really are sick. I don't mind if I catch it." She kissed him gently. "We've got plenty of time to enjoy this. And the caffeine will help us stay awake. I'll get a cup for us both."

While she extricated herself from the hammock, Nina and Russ faded back into the darkness beside the rickety carport. Nina stayed there, but Russ hobbled forward to speak with the man in the hammock, staying near the trees so he couldn't be seen through the kitchen window.

"Hey Grandpop," he said. "Nice of Ensine to loan you his transformer."

"Hello Russ," Clark said. "It might just be the best thing anyone's ever done for me. Far more than I deserve." He was hit with a fit of coughing. Russ wiped blood from his grandfather's cheek, gently, with the back of his hand.

"Should we go?" he asked his grandfather. "Or can you make it a little bit longer?"

With some effort, Clark looked back toward the kitchen window where Norma poured coffee into two mugs. "We better go," the old man said, sadly. "I think it's finally time."

Clark's second funeral was a much less elaborate affair than his first. Russ, Nina, and Ensine snuck into the Evanstown graveyard one night, dug out his empty casket, and lowered his body into it. Russ could feel every one of his injuries, but he insisted on doing all the digging.

He said a few words over the darkened coffin. The happiest days of Russ's childhood were spent "way out east" in Wyoming, marveling over one of Clark's new discoveries or talking about the old man's traveling adventures while Norma served them delicious plates of tacos. He tried to eulogize those happy moments, but he stumbled to an awkward conclusion despite the unthreatening and intimate audience of two.

"He had an infectious spirit," Ensine said, adding to the eulogy. "He tended to draw you into his life and make it more colorful. He wasn't a good man—not exactly—but he was a better man than he appeared to be." Ensine cradled Clark's Obinz stone between his hands.

Russ thought he was going to put it in the coffin with him. It would have been a fitting gesture. In the last year of his life, Clark had cared about the stone more than his own family. But even after they'd lowered the coffin back into the ground, Ensine was still holding the stone.

"What did you mean by that?" Nina asked. She was crying, despite herself. Russ shuffled over to stand next to her. He held her hand.

"Do you know what this is?" Ensine asked them both. He handed the stone to Russ.

"An unrefined power source? Right? Weren't bikers using it to power their rigs?"

"It can be that. But this one was heavily modified. I didn't notice when I sold it the first time, but—I think it's hard-coded with coordinates. See these yellow lines?" Ensine gestured to where yellow lines had been fused into either side of the fist-sized stone.

This was the first Obinz stone Russ had ever seen, and the only one in an unrefined, raw state.

"They don't all have those yellow lines," Nina realized.

"This is a very unique stone," Ensine admitted. "I think this is some type of intergalactic map. It will power a Waypoint, and it will also force the Waypoint to take you to a specific, predetermined destination. I wish I knew how he did it. I could have a side business."

"Where? Where does this one go?"

"I have no idea," Ensine said, cagily. "I thought you two should be the ones to find out."

52

NINA & RUSS

RUSS AND NINA PUT TOGETHER the Waypoint. Russ had bungee-corded Applebum to a wheeled dolly for easy transportation. The SAS unit was propped in his reading corner, using his only limb to flip through the pages of *Catcher in the Rye*.

"I'm getting nostalgic," Russ told Nina. "This is how it all started. My first intergalactic jump was with this stone." Russ patted the stone in his pocket. He turned to Applebum. "Have you decided what you're going to do yet, buddy?"

"About lending my brain to Waymore Industries to help stop the Liafen invasion? I still haven't made a decision. Waymore intends to build a fleet of robots that can think and act and read, just like I can," Applebum explained to Nina. "The idea is reckless and lacks foresight. But it is also thrilling. Would I be their mother? Father? Or their god?"

"Whatever Waymore wants, we want the opposite," Nina said. "We have good reason to believe that wasn't an actual invasion. More like a well-funded, well-organized mass murder."

"I've got to get my mobility back and then I would like to live with the Pios while I research likely consequences and outcomes," Applebum said. "Do you know the Pios? I met one when I traveled to Jaq'li's apartment. They are tremendously polite and accommodating . . . they seem to be everything I thought humans were."

Russ smiled to himself. He had been asking if Applebum wanted to come with them through the Waypoint jump. He could tell the robot had a lot on his powerful mind. "I don't want to lose you," Russ said honestly. "For what it's worth, we're better than our internet. It doesn't represent the whole culture. It's just a place where some people get lost and adopt negative values. Like a drug den, or a huge college fraternity, or politics."

"Some people?"

"Lots and lots of people," Russ admitted. "Almost everyone under thirty-five. Speaking in the shorter term, have you decided whether you want to come with us to see where the Obinz stone leads?"

"Oh. Yes. Of course I do. Fire it up."

Russ found himself on a familiar planet, standing in the frame of a familiar Waypoint, its metal hardened by rust. All the familiar landmarks were there, the thin green brush with its blue and orange blossoms, the thick outcroppings of rock. Last time he'd been here was his very first trip into space. He'd nearly been pecked to death by a flock of ratbirds, then nearly skewered by a Vaqual, then nearly suffocated by the thin oxygen in the atmosphere.

One of those same ratbirds was perched on an alien tree, its branch growing in a lazy spiral. The bird eyed Russ, Nina, and Applebum warily. "Don't feed it anything," Russ cautioned Nina.

Nina was glancing around the long tabletop vista where they found themselves. During Russ's last visit, it had been nighttime, and with no moon in the sky, he hadn't been able to see more than a foot in front of him. This time, the planet was bright and alive with color and the views stretched for miles. Lush plant life speckled the distant valley below. There were no visible structures, no terraforming. Aside from the faded antique Waypoint, there were no signs of any meddling by so-called advanced lifeforms.

Nina took a few steps to their right, amazed at green and yellow chaparral plants that sprang up from the mountainside.

"What's happening? What does it look like?" Applebum asked. Russ spun the dolly in a half circle and wheeled Applebum up the side of another peak so he could appreciate the view. On the way up the gentle incline, the wheels of the dolly grated against something. Russ bent down and brushed aside thin white sand to reveal the top of a six-by-seven-foot metal box. It chugged with power, humming like a portable generator.

"Dang," Russ said, frowning. "I thought this place was completely undeveloped. What is this?"

Applebum planted his only arm and swiveled the dolly so he could see it better. "That is a biogenerator," he said. "They're common in colonial communities, used for regulating oxygen and temperature to fit the colonists' needs. They're usually much larger, designed to power fifty or sixty homes. I doubt this one could power more than a thousand square feet or so."

Russ circled the biogenerator, his toes losing purchase in the soft white mountain soil. On the left side of the box, a copper-colored tube bent into the dirt. "There's a pipe leading right into the ground. Hang on a second," he told Applebum. "Nina, come here!" he called to Nina, who was inspecting a plump fruit hanging from the spiraled tree.

Too excited to wait for her, he circled around the curve of the mountain peak. It rose up from the west side of the vista, climbing another hundred feet into the sky but was only about fifty feet wide in circumference. On the far side of the peak, facing a thousand-foot drop into the lush valley, Russ found windows carved into the side of the mountain. The windows were at least fifteen feet tall themselves, covered by the fine white dust constantly underfoot. Russ used his forearm to wipe away the dust and peer through the window. Inside he could see a large darkened room carved straight out of the center of the mountain. He edged along the cliffside.

"Russ—" Nina started to say.

"I'm being careful," he told her. "I also found a door."

On the far side of the tall windows, a human-sized door was built into the rock. Russ studied the combination lock on the door lever for a moment. Four of the numbers had been recently wiped free of dust: zero, four, six, and eight. On a hunch, he punched in his grandma Norma's birthday, 06/48. The door beeped and swung open. Russ stepped inside.

The door swung shut on its own followed by a hissing sound as the room pressurized. Russ took off his rebreather and sucked deeply at the clean, cool air. The room had a kitchen, a couch facing the windows, a king-sized bed, and a small alcove to the side with a large shower and a porcelain toilet.

Sensing his movement, lights came on throughout the room. One entire wall was filled with books, mostly Louis L'Amour westerns and Harlequin romance novels. Another wall was covered in framed pictures. His studied each of them: Norma and Clark at the beach in San Diego. Norma and Clark posing next to an antique British sports car. Norma and Clark fishing with Russ's mom. Norma and Clark wearing orange in the bleachers of Mile High Stadium.

And the pictures went on and on. Russ was relieved to find one of himself, his junior year football picture. His younger self kneeled in the grass at Mission Bay High School, helmet under his arm, trying to look mean.

Russ's missing Whitefeather rifle was propped against the wall at the end of the hallway. "There you are, my precious," Russ said.

He was still carrying the Whitefeather as he approached the Liafen CRC machine, which occupied an entire corner of the main room. It was alien craftsmanship, faintly similar in architecture to the Liafen combat ship. Russ touched the machine and it powered on. A ragged box of repair paste lay open on the floor beside it, the bags covered in unrecognizable alien kanji. Russ's eyes were drawn to the tabletop in the kitchen area where the skeleton of a three-eyed cat was posed, a single claw swiping in his direction.

A shadow crossed the dust-covered window outside, and Russ put down the rifle and moved back to the door, opening it to let Nina inside. "Welcome to Clark and Norma's love shack," he told her.

They had propped Applebum next to the couch near a video projector. Nina was petting the cat skeleton, a series of romance novels spread out on the table in front of her. "A lot of these are from the Mysterious Universe bookstore," she said. "I think this one is actually mine."

Russ continued to move throughout the room. "Some of this stuff seems pretty valuable. We'll have to get forty-thousand credits worth to Drench's mom somehow."

"Of course," Nina said, smiling.

Russ opened the food storage locker and marveled at the rows and rows of compressed, condensed foodstuffs. "He was setting up a nest," Russ realized. "Once he got the CRC machine working and was assured he wouldn't be dying"—Russ's voice broke slightly, but he pushed through it—"he must have planned to bring Norma here. Why else have her books? And the pictures? And her clothes . . ." they had found a dozen of Norma's dresses hanging in the closet. "That's why he was living it up. He was going to spend the rest of his life here with her and enough repair tech to keep them both going. I bet he didn't tell Ensine about that part of the plan."

"He loved Norma until the very end," Nina said. "So much that he was protecting her heart until he knew for certain they could be together long term." She shook her head. "Dang it, that's romantic. And pretty sad, I guess."

Russ went over to the bookshelves. "Applebum, what would you like to read? Looks like we've got L'Amour, McMurtry, Michener, McCarthy . . ."

"I haven't felt like reading anything except *Catcher in the Rye*," Applebum said.

"No problem," Russ said gently. Then he took off his shirt. And his pants. He punched a few buttons on the Liafen CRC. The tray opened out of the mouth of the device and slid to the floor.

Nina stopped petting the skeleton and stood next to him. "I can figure it out," she said. "But are you sure you want to get in this thing?"

"Ensine said it worked like any other CRC machine. And I'm running out of pain pills."

The CRC machine hummed mightily as it worked on repairing Russ. Nina watched the display screen, but she couldn't make heads or tails of the symbols as it counted down from something to something. Her transponder lit up with a call. She answered, reluctantly.

The room was filled with the sounds of babies gurgling, cooing, and crying. "Nina, it's Bah'ren."

"What's up?"

"The insurance check came through. We're a few cycles away from being back in business. Will you come and work with us again? With full pay? We owe you for what you did on the *Aldersochi*. You can bring Russ too—I guess."

"Yeah," Nina said. "It will be nice to get a paycheck. Someday. Just let us know when and where to show up."

"It's not so easy," Bah'ren said. "We might need you both to get reCERTified."

"What do you mean?"

"Liafen have been spotted all along the border of the Darkzone. After what happened with the *Marcy Hedron*, the UAIB has shut down all the rim-world Dexadrive lanes and any Waypoint more than ten star clusters outside of Ren'Div. But folks still need to get supplies to the outer colonies. Businesses still need their convoys to reach the Darkzone to dump all their hazardous waste. Transportation is getting more and more difficult. And more and more lucrative. I was thinking of putting the insurance money toward a new IP. Maybe *Honest Comet Transport, LLC*? Or, *We Will Get You There*? I'm still workshopping the name."

"You want to switch industries?" Nina asked, surprised.

"We may have to. Our insurance premiums are through the roof. And with pest control, we've been living on the edge of solvency since the very start."

"Could you hang up, please?" Starland said, her voice farther from the microphone. "It's not time for business. The babies are nowhere close to ready for their baptism, and it starts in two hours."

"Wait!" Nina said. "I've been meaning to ask . . . do you two believe in God?"

"Believe? What do you mean?"

"Uhhh . . . just like it sounds," Nina said.

"The Great God Ren is a living deity. A supermassive black hole in the act of constant creation and devastation. Only the truly ill-informed doubt her existence."

"The Great God Ren," Nina said. "Bah'ren."

"It means blessed by God."

"And Kend-ren."

"It means child of God. The capital planet of the entire UAIB is called Ren'Div."

"God's everywhere," Nina said.

"Actually, she's in the Camrio Quadrant."

Over Nina's left shoulder, the CRC machine stopped shaking and the lights began to shift color. "I've got to go," she told Bah'ren. "Enjoy the baptism!" She put the transponder to her mouth quickly. "I think *Intergalactic Transit Solutions*."

Nina hung up and grabbed a blanket from the edge of the bed. She hustled to Applebum, unfolded the blanket and draped it over him.

"What are you doing?" he asked.

"Just read under the blanket. Or listen to loud music, preferably," Nina said quickly. She could see the tray was slowly sliding out of the CRC machine with a naked Russ on it.

Nina crossed the room. As she did, she removed her compression gear, her shirt, her pants, her left sock and her right, her bra, and her granny panties. By the time the tray had fully exited the main portion of the machine, she was standing in front of Russ, stark naked.

Russ swallowed. "Do you need the CRC machine too? I don't see any injuries."

Nina shook her head. She closed the gap between them and put her hand on his arm.

Russ didn't reach out to her or respond in any way. He said, "Is this affection? Why did you kiss me one day and then Kendren the very next day?"

Nina blushed. She crossed her arms over her bare chest, surprised by the anger in his tone.

"Do you remember doing that? We could always ask the thousands of spectators who witnessed it if you've forgotten the details," he said. "Nina Unknown, the announcer called you. Kendren doesn't even know your last name!" Russ locked his fingers behind his head. His nakedness somehow made him seem even more vulnerable than the hurt in his voice.

Nina leaned an elbow on the repair tray. She reached out again and touched Russ's cheek. He didn't draw back but his jaw tightened.

"Kendren doesn't know my last name because he's not interested in me," Nina said. "I'm a prop for him. Like the muscles and the tan. He's pretty lost. I could you tell more. I promised Kendren I wouldn't, but I think I owe you the explanation more than I owe him his privacy."

Russ looked a little pale. "There's something I should probably tell you too . . ." he began.

Nina leaned forward and kissed him on the elbow. Then she kissed him on the bicep. Then the shoulder. She lifted herself up onto the repair tray, leaned against his arm and kissed him on the neck.

"Are we sure this is a good idea?" he said.

"Your penis seems to think so."

"Ignore him," Russ said. "He doesn't understand how complicated and confusing and, frankly, emotionally exhausting loving someone can be."

"Love?" Nina said. She glanced down at her last message to him on the transponder. *in love with you.* Neither of them had texted each other, or mentioned the message, until this moment. She let his words circle around in her brain.

Russ finally looked her in the eyes. He put his hands on either side of her face so he could do it. "There's something you've got to understand about Russ." He told her. "He doesn't like responsibility. He doesn't trust himself to handle it correctly. He makes stupid decisions. Loving him—" Russ let his shoulders sink, defeated. "Loving me is probably a terrible mistake. But, I'm totally in love with you. Have been for a while."

Nina sat down, her back against the tray. "I love you too," she said, softly. "I tried to tell you when the *Aldersochi* was crashing but I just . . . chickened out. I think I have since the hallway—that day the bookstore reopened. I only managed to get it out on the *Marcy Hedron* because I thought you were about to die."

"I'm always about to die."

Just like when she'd survived the crash, she felt the weight she carried lift from her shoulders. She wondered what had lifted it and for how long? Was it the hormones, the adrenaline, Russ's words, or her being honest about her feelings, finally? She rolled back onto her knees and kissed him again. "Can we have sex? Please? If I don't have sex soon, I think my body is going to spontaneously combust. Afterward, we can clean the dust off those picture windows and watch the sun set?"

Russ paused a moment to consider the offer. "I agree to those terms," he told her.

Nina was unable to keep a broad smile from stretching across her face. She straddled him, pressing the length of her naked body against his, and kissed him deeply.

EPILOGUE

STEVEN APPLEBUM

STEVEN APPLEBUM TRIED WATCHING YOUSTAR on Nina's hastily discarded transponder with the volume cranked up. All the top videos were people reacting to news reports about the attack on the *Marcy Hedron*. He recognized Nurcia Fragnar on one of the screencaps. Would she mention him? Identifying his unavoidable emotion as "curious," he played the video. The YouStarer was in a crowded room, jostling with civilians and reporters to get an unobstructed video of the dais. Nurcia stood at the center, speaking from behind a podium. A digital banner behind her read, "In Loving Memory of Heroic Captain Klarnoa Penson and All Those Lost on the *Marcy Hedron*." Aldos Verch stood at attention beneath the banner with his arms crossed over his chest, his hair cut, and his beard shaved. ". . . we must not let their sacrifice be in vain," Nurcia was saying, "whether that be rooting out the treasonous among us or modifying our charter to allow benevolent corporations to take sensible evolutionary steps forward, solely in the interest of intergalactic defense."

A Divian in a smartly cut suit next to the YouStar reporter raised her hand and asked, "Is there any evidence of treason?"

Nurcia continued, "We are not able to comment on that at this time, but Providence Travel Solutions and our parent company, Waymore Industries, have launched an extensive investigation. We've already recovered the pilot's log from SavUQuik, one of the security teams tragically lost trying to protect the *Marcy Hedron* against the Liafen invaders. The log indicates Liafen sympathizers may have been working among the ranks of our very own municipal teams. A Klung named, Trellinanium ViV Klurppewpuu is wanted for questioning as well as two Kruxfasians, Lanie and Linnie Linderholmen. We promise to leave no stone unturned . . ."

Applebum shut off the video, filing his response under "disgusted." Why did any species allow the worst among them to utilize communication standards like YouStar, and the internet, to gain and sustain attention? Especially when they were just going to use that attention to misrepresent information? To the educated viewer—and Applebum was about as educated as possible—levels of attention didn't actually equate with veracity, value, or quality. In fact, they were usually inversely proportional.

Irritated, he groped around for his copy of *Catcher in the Rye.* Unable to find it, he took off the blanket to widen his search. His eyes drifted to where Russ and Nina were interlocked on the CRC machine repair tray.

Steven Applebum had read a lot of books, including books about the mating habits of wolves, penguin, the peregrine falcon, and saltwater crocodiles. He had watched roughly one thousand Pornhub videos before giving up on his hope of finding a single one that communicated anything he felt qualified as "love" or even "intimacy." Watching Nina and Russ—what was the right verb here—romp, play, wrestle, mate—whatever it was, it was like nothing he'd ever experienced before, and it restored something in his emotional matrix.

Russ put his hands and mouth everywhere on Nina's breasts and face. He seemed to be savoring every inch of her. She glowed in response, her soft skin darkening under his insistent touch. Then they rolled together off the tray, laughing. Applebum watched them grapple in careless bliss. They were trying to reach the bed but seemed unwilling to allow an inch to come between their bodies, which made transportation difficult. They finally made it, tumbling out of Applebum's line of sight, but their nervous, blissful laughter carried across the room.

As the sound of their laughter drifted over him, Applebum reopened his emotional database in order to create a new location. He labeled it "joy." The location was empty, but he now had a much better idea of what belonged there. He spun the wheels of the dolly in a short circle. A light rain had just started to drizzle on the windows, washing them of the white dust. The whole boreal valley was visible far below.

Humans might not be as polite as Pios or as consistent as Gnurians or as intelligent as Kruxfasians. But if you found the right ones and watched them carefully enough, they weren't all that bad. They got in their own way, a lot, but they also had a capacity for heroism, sacrifice, love, and happiness that made you feel everything was right in the universe—even if it was just for a single, joyful moment.

Applebum picked up Nina's transponder and deleted both the YouStar and the www applications. Then his eyes drifted to Clark's bookshelf, scanning the titles for something new to read.

APPENDIX

Alphane S Transportation Hub: A densely populated planet which boasts one of seven centralized UAIB Waypoint hubs. Waypoints are manned by spaceclerks who log the bio-signature of every traveler.

Astrogrom: A unique phylum classification of biological organism capable of living and traveling through space. Ridiculed, and ultimately persecuted for his discovery in Divian year 05,11.11, scientist AL Munkpin presented his finding on Astrogroms at the Kruxfasian Konference for Scientific Advancement with the simple preface, "Nearly nothing can live in a total vacuum. *Nearly* nothing."

Beuala—*Who Snaps the Necks of His Enemies*: A four-armed subspecies with a powerful grip. Some tribes of Beuala have petitioned the UAIB for inclusion in their charter but have thus far been unsuccessful. Naysayers often cite the Beuala's long history of violence and cannibalism, as well as many tribes' flat refusal to abandon their savage cultural ways.

BLEB (Below-the-Line Employment Bureau): A government program implemented to resolve disagreements and to field complaints from employees who work in certain high-fatality job classifications.

Buuffaaffaa—*Whose Enemy is Left Flattened*: A dangerous subspecies weighing between one and ten thousand pounds. Buuffaaffaa are generally blob-shaped with a larger base circumference, and they move by constricting their upper muscles down toward their lower muscles, which creates a propulsion motion similar to leaping.

CERTification Training (Centralized Empirical Repulsion Tactics): All government workers who wish to perform work deemed physically dangerous must clear a series of tactical training standards. CERT training proves the viability of the worker, but it can also act as a government visa. Species that are not part of the UAIB charter are allowed access to UAIB space if they acquire and maintain CERT-based authorization. A combination work visa and CERT training are almost always associated with below-the-line employment opportunities. The CERTification process traditionally includes significant unpaid on-the-job-training hours.

Chenul: Chenul was created by the multi-conglomerate LenCorp to target the higher socioeconomic classes that traditionally ignored LenCorp's most popular product, Maxibrew. Boasting the tagline, "Refined Wine for Society's Best," Chenul now commands a 70 percent market share among twenty-one- to thirty-four-year-olds in the far-above-the-line-executive purchasing tier. Its ultra-rare top shelf specialty label, "Saint-Oats-Bubbly" sells for as much as one thousand credits per fluid ounce.

CRC Machine (Carbon Repair Chrysalis): The universal standard in healing. The CRC machine can 3D print bio-repair filament from stem cells in order to repair or replace organic material, making it capable of curing nearly everything except death. A companion instrument, the CRC wand, has the functionality to scan for organic damage in the field and report the information back to a ship's onboard med ward.

Darkzone: The edge of the universe remains undiscovered. Past the official boundaries of the United Alliance of Intelligent Beings lies the Darkzone, a lawless expanse beyond the reach of UAIB governance or the influence of the Shared System of Civics. The Darkzone is a popular retreat for intergalactic criminals, otherwise-illegal corporate waste dumping, and religious zealots seeking absolute freedom to pursue their beliefs.

Dexadrive Lanes: A system of interstellar transport utilizing wavelike propulsion technology. Before the commercialization of Waypoints, Dexadrive lanes were the primary transportation protocol, and they still crisscross the majority of UAIB space. Starcraft traveling within the lanes while equipped with Dexadrive engines can achieve much-faster-than-light (MFTL) speeds.

DFA Network (Divian Frontline Actual): One of three Divian home world news and entertainment networks. The popularity and reach of Divian culture is often attributed to the intergalactic presence of such networks, as well as the highly polished and highly budgeted nature of their programming. Disclosure: both this glossary and Divian Frontline Actual are owned and operated by the same parent company, Rascoff/VonGrun Universal.

Divian: One of the seventy-three species of the UAIB. A humanoid species with purple skin and neon, multicolored eyes, Divians are the founding species of the UAIB and enjoy special privileges. While once considered a culture of equality and high ethics, the Divians' popularity has receded over the course of the last century. Their home world, Ren'Div, widely accepted as the center of the universe, is also known for its ranch-estate living and astronomical real estate prices.

DOM Shot (Dynamic Organ Maintenance): Sometimes called "CRC in a bottle," a DOM shot actually works on a much different principle, using negative compounds to attract intrusive organic waste and carry it quickly through the body's excretory system, giving rise to the common slang phrase, "Wanna shit? Getta DOM."

Dreadwalker—*Whose Grip is Mighty*: A six-legged amphibian with a strong exoskeleton and two powerful claws. Dreadwalkers are universally feared, notoriously easy to influence, and breed under almost any conditions. They have a history of being produced or conscripted into war, where they make dangerous, tireless drone-like fighters.

FOXNAR (Forward Operations for Xenobiological Navigation and Astrobiological Research): The specialty research and development program of Waymore Industries. FOXNAR often pursues the grandest ideas of Waymore's Board of Directors, regardless of their commercial application. Despite this, FOXNAR has been responsible for some of Waymore's greatest commercial success (*see:* **Fromantium**).

Fromantium: Waymore Industries' new metallic compound has limitless applications in nearly every industry. It is expected to revolutionize intergalactic space travel and allow homesteading on even the most uninhabitable planets. Extensive tests show the metal can survive heat up to 10,000 degrees, cold down to minus 10,000 degrees, and impact up to 10,000 megatons. Its wide-ranging applications and lack of known weaknesses is expected to make Waymore the most powerful company in the United Alliance of Intelligent Beings.

Gas 'em and Trash 'em Unlimited and Kwiky Pest & Nuisance: Two of a handful of Ecosystem Preservation squads. These municipal squadrons perform dangerous exterminator jobs in hopes of collecting government subsidies. Also known as "Orange Suits," for the orange jumpsuits Ecosystem Preservation squads wear while working.

Gnurian: One of the seventy-three species of the UAIB. Average Gnurian height ranges from five to seven feet for males and three to five feet for females. They have pale purple, light blue, or aquamarine skin. Hyper-shifting splotches of colorful melanoma move across their skin in unpredictable patterns. A matriarchal society, Gnurian females are reputed to be highly capable. Contrarily, their home world, Gnu Gnaru, is widely known to struggle with corruption and issues with basic infrastructure and maintenance.

Gorrillian Green: A small rural peninsula on the West Coast of Ren'Div, the capital of UAIB space. Gorrillian Green is the vacation spot of celebrities and high-powered business executives and features a collection of universe-best nightclubs and other social gathering spots.

Grandveega Fungae—*The Mold that Ate the World*: Though not actively aggressive, Grandveega Fungae reproduces bidirectionally and at an extremely fast pace. Also called the Peaceful Reaver, when displaced or handled incorrectly, it can destroy entire ecosystems. Early century Darkzone explores shared potentially fictional accounts of entire planets being squeezed apart by a single misplaced mold.

Grendo-Fend—*Who Moves with the Grace of the Wind*: One of the oldest known species, which hunts with an elongated, sturdy beak made of both cartilage and bone. The Grendo-Fend is capable of flight due to a fixed membrane that runs between its outstretched wings, down the entire length of its legs. Fossil fragments have been carbon-dated all the way back to the era of the XVAS civilization, where scientists believe the Grendo-Fend was originally a tree-dwelling biped.

HelderTech Aquatic Cooperative: One of the smaller municipal contractors, HelderTech has remained sustainable on two of its popular products: the disposable EFlyer and the Boost Rocket, a shallow-sea submersible. The aquatic cooperative formed when HelderTech absorbed rival municipal contractor SeaSeeC Universal.

Hhzzees—*Who Will Pick the Last of the Meat from the Bone*: Carnivorous cave dwelling pack insects capable of stripping a person down to the skeleton in under three seconds. The Hhzzees would be universally reviled for the danger they possess were it not for their biological ability to break down pollen and store it in their hives as a sweet nectar known as Fukk. The quest for Fukk has attracted more than one thrill-seeker who has regretted their decision in less than three seconds. A dish called Domesticated Fukk is available for purchase in high-quality restaurants throughout the King's Closet Nebula, but is said to pale in comparison to Fukk harvested in the wild.

IBED (Immigration and Border Enforcement Department): The UAIB "border patrol" division, unique among municipal programs in their almost exclusive employ of inorganic SAS units. IBED agents' central task is to keep non-UAIB species out of UAIB space. Part of this duty requires the use of the non-fatal "mind cleanse," an artificial aging of the illegal alien species' brains.

Jinxden—*Whom None Have Seen Up Close*: Also called "the cloud of cacti," the Jinxden are oversized airborne insects capable of tremendously fast starts and stops. They travel in packs of several hundred that can shift direction with synchronous precision. When threatened, the Jinxden discharge small projectiles roughly the size of a sewing needle.

Klung: One of the seventy-three species of the UAIB. The Klung have gray skin that ranges from faint to a hardened, near black. At puberty they undergo a grafting procedure that grinds faint lines into their skin. The lines themselves are carefully considered and are often representative of cultural, religious, or familial values. Sometimes considered soft because of their high capacity for empathy, Klung are also capable of great violence when they reach critical emotional capacity, flying into a rage colloquially known as “Konvulsion.” Klung are capable of eating organic food but prefer to consume energy directly from electrical or electronic sources.

Kruxfas: One of the seventy-three species of the UAIB. The Kruxfas have hooked legs, elongated heads, and onyx eyes. Widely regarded as a highly intelligent species, they are responsible for a number of technological breakthroughs, including the Waypoint and the CRC machine. The Kruxfas are also capable fighters. Because of the combination of brains and physical dexterity, the Kruxfas often go out of their way to advertise their own cultural passivity so as to not threaten the other species in the UAIB collective.

Kyrillian: One of the seventy-three species of the UAIB. No one can remember exactly where the rift started, but Kyrillian and Divians across the universe share a barely subdued distrust of one another. As a result of wide-ranging Divian political and economic power, Kyrillian have often been deprived of basic education and regulated to below-the-line employment and even crime. Kyrillian have the distinction of being removed from the UAIB charter a record three times for various acts of sedition.

Liafen—*The Destroyer of Worlds*: An imperialist race culturally and genetically predisposed to kill without mercy. Born with a thin veneer of flesh over a powerful, adaptable exoskeleton, risk-taking and combat eventually tears the flesh from the skeleton, differentiating adults from pre-pubescent youth. The UAIB is often at its most prosperous between periods of Liafen invasion, and the lurking threat of the monster out in the Darkzone has kept UAIB species civil toward one another while inspiring persistent research into defense-related technologies.

Lixil: One of the seventy-three species of the UAIB. Lixil are a slim species with thin hair and little muscle. That, combined with their pointed jaws, gives them a faintly murine appearance, affecting their capacity for work in entertainment, politics and their effectiveness in cross-species romance. Though unearned, the term, "never trust a Lixil" is used universally when an individual of any species is acting with devious intent.

Maxibrew: Though popularly derided as "pisswater," Maxibrew is nonetheless the best-selling alcoholic beverage in UAIB occupied space. This is partially due to its far-reaching supply chain and relatively low production cost.

MERC Board (Registered Municipal Employment Collective): UAIB municipal teams were originally employed directly by the UAIB themselves. However, after a public pension scandal, the UAIB dismantled their municipal workforce and now rely on CERTified independent contractors. The MERC board is the official posting location of all available municipal jobs.

Mortumzees—*Who Will Wait Patiently for Your End*: Also called "Death Angels," Mortumzees move in large packs. They sustain themselves by devouring the flesh of dead animals (*see:* **Necrovore**). Critical to maintaining healthy ecosystems, Mortumzees play a key role in disease control and nutrient recycling. They have the semi-unique ability to travel through the vacuum of space (*see:* **Astrogrom**).

Mousrut—*Relentless Hunter*: The Mousrut is feared as much for its hideous visage as its capacity for violence. Its body is covered by patchy fur, so stringy it closely resembles thinning hair, or sometimes wispy, half-plucked feathers. Fur patterns present in two-color patterns for males and tri-color for females. Both genders have pointed snouts and beady, bloodshot eyes so close they're nearly touching, beneath a protruding brow. The Mousrut are known to play with their prey before feasting, and kill primarily with hooked talons.

Mulgrew Melville Bootball Tournament: Mulgrew Melville was a beloved mentor of Zurn, an early century Divian intellectual and philosopher. Zurn accidently created the game of Bootball during a scholarly discourse on male violence. When asked on his deathbed about Bootball being his lasting legacy, Zurn reportedly answered, "Fuck you! [undefined] you and your [undefined]. Mulgrew! Father! Make a place for me! I come!"

MUPmap (Multi-User Protocol): A crowd-sourced map of the multiple galaxies, considered the standard intergalactic navigation tool. Planet data is collected by individual travelers and shared with all other subscribers. Most data is collected passively by the Map's systems, but users ascribe specific icons to inform other travelers of a location's unique qualities.

Neo-Brindle Pulse: Until it was deemed illegal because of the danger it posed to the Klung, LenCorp had an instant bestseller with its technology-dampening Neo-Brindle Pulse and its catchy slogan, "Outmatched? Out-purchased? Get an NBP onboard and even the odds." The pulse detonates at a specific location and then moves outward via wave propagation, loading any technological device it passes with enough voltage to reboot or short-circuit.

Necrovore: A necrovore is a sub-phylum classification for any organic that feeds specifically on dead flesh.

NoxFire Personal Defense Industries: NoxFire entered the firearms market at a disadvantage against its far more established competitors

Waymore Industries and RNO-Tech, but they were able to corner the niche market for stylish, well-designed weapons intended as much for status as self-defense. Despite a risk-taking, snazzy style, NoxFire technology has poor secondary market appeal because of shifting, fickle design trends and NoxFire's tendency to prioritize form over function.

Obinz Stone: A battery capable of tremendous power, universally used to power Waypoints. Obinz stones are mined from the ground in an unrefined state. Planets which are found to naturally produce Obinz stones quickly become flush with wealth, and all the complications therein.

Pero-ru—*Who Will Not Break*: Initially identified as ideal beast of burden because of its four muscular legs and powerful flank, attempts to domesticate the Pero-ru were abandoned when the omnivore proved to be both a capricious eater and breeder. Worse yet, the Pero-ru resisted all attempts to control its behavior, regardless of the skill level of the technician hired to domesticate it. Legendary animal behaviorist KL JL famously said of the creature, "the universe tried to change the Pero-ru, and the universe lost."

Pios: A distant genetic relative to a far more dangerous species (*see:* **Liafen**). Like the militaristic Liafen, the Pios boast a powerful, partial exoskeleton that emerges from beneath their skin, usually around the shoulder blades. Unlike the Liafen, the Pios are a civilized, peaceful species that go to great lengths to differentiate themselves from their virulent cousins—even to the point of allowing themselves to be victimized and their natural resources exploited.

Pliasis—*Nature's Champion*: The apex predator of the Boguma cluster, boasting thick skin, powerful claws, lightning quick reflexes, and a top recorded speed of sixty miles per hour. The Pliasis's enigmatic attraction to Obinz stones causes them to roam the universe, whether it be venturing through Waypoints or stowing away on ships.

Planet Ekho: With an economy almost entirely supported by the tourist industry, Planet Ekho's Southern Hemisphere features three of the top twenty restaurants in UAIB Space [according to an affiliated DFA poll]. The Northern Hemisphere features a number of waterside resorts popular with young people traveling unsupervised during extended government holidays. Planet Ekho has a single satellite, the barren, uninhabited Moon called Triameed.

Planet Fidrrarrbore: The pre-colonial homeland of the RreRriaNnian species, Fidrrarrbore was late to the clean energy shift that began in Divian year 17,02.06. Much of the planet's natural resources have been irreparably damaged, a process exasperated by the RreRriaNnian tendency to push through adversity rather than take steps to alleviate it.

Planet Fi9: An unsettled world known for its unusual climate phenomena and diverse aquatic biosphere. Fi9 has no seasons and much of the year boasts days of eighteen to twenty hours of sunlight.

Planet Nustrix: A planet in the Bellatronix cluster that must be monitored to manage reoccurring instances of Jinxden overpopulation.

Planet Qello: A fringe planet in the Proxima Imperatus cluster known for its lethal bacteria, fauna, flora, and fungi. While no apex predator rules the skies, on land the carnivorous, highly territorial, four-legged Ophidian sits at the top of the food chain. Unique tectonic plant placement results in sporadic, unpredictable tremors, often followed by volcanic eruptions and tsunami.

Planet Torntula: A planet with almost no atmosphere popular with novice geologists, geochemists, and corporate mining engineers. Torntula boasts less than ten thousand permanent residents, with an additional three thousand Waypointing planetside each day to facilitate its economic industries.

Planet Xodli: With no sapient species, or above-water landmass of any kind, little is known about Planet Xodli.

Plutorach: Widely despised, Plutorachs hail from the cold and unforgiving planet Pluto, the ninth planet in the 5431st solar system. Known for their stubborn, irascible attitudes, Plutorachs are the only peoples from that cluster to have achieved interstellar travel, though most species in the UAIB wish they hadn't.

Polumba-Lux—*Who Crushes its Enemies with the Strength of a Hundred Warriors*: Ranging in length from three feet (Polumba-Lux) to ten feet (Zip-Polumba-Lux) all the way to twenty-five feet tip to tail, (King-Polumba-Lux), the Polumba-Lux and its genetic variations are the apex predators of the jungle planet Buris-Nine-Five. Many a trophy hunter has lost their life venturing to bring back the scales of the King, though others, upon seeing its size, instead settle for the Zip, and afterward submit the trophy to an amplification process known as "inlightening™."

Providence Travel Solutions: Providence Travel Solutions began as an upstart competitor feisty enough to challenge the market share of the industry-leading Zone-Wide Travel Unlimited. Purchased by Waymore Industries in Divian year 24,02.01, PTS shifted their focus to opulent, Patrician cruise experiences. As of this writing, they account for 21 percent of the UAIB tourist dollars spent, while serving less than 3 percent of its population.

Quen-to-tal: One of the seventy-three species of the UAIB. Culturally, ToTalians seek pleasure in every aspect of life, which makes them accomplished artists but frustrating and flaky coworkers. After a series of official warnings and dramatic shifts in value, the UAIB segregated ToTalian currency from the universal credit system, limiting the ToTalians' ability to sell their home planet's natural resources and crippling their participation in the intergalactic marketplace.

RNO-Tech (Rascoff Necraemia Originals): One of several major UAIB weapon's manufacturers. RNO-tech rifles use a piston system driven by onboard combustion engines. Their operation requires the use of both traditional ammunition and fossil fuels, but the 8000 series is renowned for being able to inflict damage on par with high-end energy weapons, despite being far cheaper to produce.

Romcube Corporation: The Romcube brand rose to prominence overnight, offering quickstop access and a variety of common shopping needs at strategically placed locations throughout the universe. Sadly, Romcube's fall was just as quick, as their business plan was linked to the use of intergalactic Dexadrive lanes that fell out of favor nearly overnight with the development of Waypoint travel technology. The Romcube ownership has changed hands a number of times as various business entities attempt to turn a profit from Romcube's dwindling and obsolete infrastructure.

Romgulangs: One of the seventy-three species of the UAIB. Even in an age of vast diversity, Romgulangs are often considered "exotic." Their eyes and mouths are almost double the average size ratio when compared to the other characteristics of their faces. Some claim the increased eye sizes give them an open and trustable appearance, others suggest the opposite, that their eyes evolved to better find prey. The Romgulangs' four prehensile arms (two on the left, two on the right) give additional credibility to the latter.

RQ Score (Ready Quotient): The employment standard by which CERTification trainees are measured. Though all CERTified individuals are qualified to work, those who graduate with a higher RQ score often have the advantage of finding more desirable employment.

RreRriaNnian: One of the seventy-three species of the UAIB. ReRriaNnian are on average larger and have more significant body hair and muscle mass than any other humanoid race in the UAIB charter. Thanks to their size, dexterity, and machismo culture, many UAIB professional sports leagues are dominated by RreRriaNnian athletes.

SAS Unit (Syvon Al'Supres): A multi-use android named for its founder, Syvon Al'Supres, who introduced the Tech 1 model in Divian year 17,02.06. After the unexpected deaths of Al'Supres and his entire family, the SAS's patent became publicly available. Multiple corporations manufacture SAS units, but they share version numbers to track value and functionality. The latest iteration, the Tech 12 unit, was first issued in Divian year 21,21.11 by Waymore Enterprises.

SavUQuik: One of a handful of transportation security crews who patrol the Darkzone, employed by Providence Travel Solutions to protect their intergalactic cruise liners when they leave UAIB regulated space. SavUQuik was originally under the umbrella of SavMore, but personality conflicts among the board of directors caused the organization to split into two, creating both SavUQuik and SecureMore Hard-n-Fast-Shield-Guard.

Shared System of Civics: A collection of fundamental civic standards that all municipal employees must adhere to. Failure to follow the standard results in immediate deCERTification. They are as follows: (1) A municipal employee must protect the anonymity and reticence of the United Alliance of Intelligent Beings. (2) A municipal employee must do no permanent harm to any planet's natural ecological balance. (3) A municipal employee must not remove a planet's natural resources for their own benefit. (4) A municipal employee must not be the direct cause of death for a civilian belonging to any of the seventy-three CERTified UAIB population groups.

Sikkie-Bruzz: One of the seventy-three species of the UAIB. The avian Sikkie-Bruzz are covered in tropical feathers, including across their impressive wingspans (the average male wingspan is eight feet; the average female is six and a half). Hailing from Planet Alplum Bruzlum, an enormous planet with high heat and heavy moisture, the Bruzz eventually lost their ability to fly thanks to years of coexisting with flightless species on other UAIB planets, as well as a fondness for greasy, high-fat Gnurian cuisine that doesn't metabolize well with Bruzzian physiology.

Sol Pest Control: An Ecosystem Preservation corporation. Sol Pest Control is part of a special government program testing out the use of SAS units for government municipal work beyond immigration services.

Southern Blurn: One of the seventy-three species of the UAIB. Southern Blurns are rare aquatic mammals. Covered in scales where most mammals have skin, Southern Blurns can breathe air from their mouths and water from the gills on their necks. A Southern Blurn who wishes to live out of water must drink copious liquids in order to maintain necessary hydrogen levels. Southern Blurns hail from the entirely oceanic Southern Hemisphere of the planet Blurn. While the land-dwelling Northern Blurns are known for their rich culture of avant-garde art and music, the water-dwelling Southern Blurns tend to prioritize family and recreation.

Southland Demolitions and Refuse Removal: One of a handful of Infrastructure Maintenance crews who perform repair work for government subsidies. Also known as "Yellow Suits" for the yellow jumpsuits Infrastructure Maintenance squads wear while working. Southland Demolitions was famously part of the Great Robot Riot aboard the Alphane S Transportation Hub.

Spindex: A low-cost creature attractant, Spindex comes in a variety of styles and flavors, generally consisting of a combination of sex hormones and bone, viscus hoof, and horns. Spindex is a registered trademark of Fine Foods, LLC, an umbrella corporation most well-known for manufacturing sausage products for general consumption.

Star's Crescent Nebula: Colonized shortly after the Third Intergalactic War, the planets of Star's Crescent Nebula were terraformed to make way for a series of low-cost, limited-space, high-density housing units easily affordable for surviving soldiers eligible for veteran housing subsidies. The providences of Star's Crescent are often named for beautiful natural geography, such as Windy Meadow, Snow Cap Peak, and Stonebridge Lake, though the landscape of the planets themselves is considered universally uninspiring.

STR Light Machine Gun: Superior Threat Reduction Corps' line of kinetic, multi-fire, multi-barrel light machine guns.

SUKTIS (Systematic Utility Kernel Technology Integration Software): Much of UAIB technological advancement came at a time of great economic growth, and its core programming language, SUKTIS, was developed as open-source and without trademark. Updated firmware is controlled by the benevolent SUKTOO, a non-profit organization that periodically collects vast repositories of user data solely to improve user experience, offer additional paid services, and facilitate third party data-sharing.

TEN-awtch: One of the seventy-three species of the UAIB. Cold-blooded, savage warriors who are also known to be equally gregarious in social situations. TEN-awtch walk upright on two legs but have long torsos and scales on their heads and tops of their arms. Their ectothermic nature requires special sleeping and eating arrangements but makes them more suited for work on hostile planets with limited breathable air.

Tharcus—*Whose Skin is Without Weakness*: Savage subspecies primate from planet Oi0. Hostile living conditions have evolved the creature to have nearly impenetrable skin. The average female outweighs the average male by several hundred pounds and has an ornate mane of coarse hair. The males of the species, while smaller in stature, follow far less predictable behavioral patterns.

Thufflin Box: Proprietary security technology owned by Waymore Industries. Thufflin boxes are utilized to store and transport information that is too sensitive to be allowed on cloud-based platforms. The boxes themselves boast a secondary operating system detached from the information itself that is capable of erasing the information remotely and reporting back the physical location of the box, as well as performing several other security measures that Waymore is unwilling to openly discuss.

Toers: One of the seventy-three species of the UAIB. Toers are bipedal with smooth skin, limited skeletal support, and almost no muscle definition. Culturally unaccustomed to verbal communication, Toers "speak" by shifting their skin color. Because of their weak physicality, they are highly untrusting of other species.

TRennus: The warmest month on the planet of Ren'Div. The last few years have seen record-breaking heat waves reaching temperatures as high as eighty-six degrees on the Universal Standard Temperature Index (USTI).

Triwin—*The Consonant Swarm that Blots out the Sky*: Triwin are three-to-four-inch insects with sharp beaks. Triwin queens, the leaders of their drone-colonies, reproduce asexually and have litters in the thousands. Classified as hypermutating mega-birthers, Triwin are capable of gigantic leaps forward in evolution when exposed to certain catalysts.

UAIB (United Alliance of Intelligent Beings): A loose conglomerate of seventy-three sentient species. Elected senators from each recognized species vote on universal rule changes and other matters regarding the intergalactic charter. Additional functions include the collection of taxes and the monitoring and funding of municipal services. Municipal services include Law Enforcement, Infrastructure Maintenance, Transport Security, Refuse Disposal, Ecosystem Preservation, and Emergency Response.

UFu (Universal Fertilizing Prep Kit): A budget over-the-counter prep kit intended as the first stage in non-compatible interspecies fertilization (binary and nonbinary, only).

Vaqual—*Who Haunts Children's Dreams*: A terrifying subspecies that can reach up to twenty-seven feet in height. That, combined with their nightmarish appearance, has made them popular in both ancient folklore and modern UAIB entertainment. The extremely powerful Vaqual have a thick muscle mass and arm bones that end in pointed hooks. With a single, underdeveloped eye, they rely heavily on their sense of smell. Adolescent Vaqual suffer from a skin condition that covers their face and shoulders with puss-filled abscesses. The Vaqual's unique features, combined with its long-lasting popularity in cinema, result in its perennial number-one-seller status in BeaBetteru's collectible line of miniature plushies.

Waypoints: Relatively new teleportation technology. Waypoints allow users to move instantly from one location to the next and, as a consequence, have revolutionized much of intergalactic life. They range from portable, single-use units to permanent, ornate structures that focus just as much on form as they do function. Due to IBED's limitations in regulating Waypoint travel, the proliferation of Waypoint technology has also caused a significant uptick in theft, the transfer of black-market goods, and illegal immigration. Thus far, the UAIB governing body has been slow to pass effective legal deterrents to protect against the unintended consequences of this emergent technology.

Waymore Industries: Originally known as Glinken Muldur Industrials, Waymore changed its name to emphasize its focus on emergent "Waypoint" technologies at the turn of the last century. Being one of the first corporations to mass produce Waypoints led to significant year-over-year revenue, allowing Waymore to grow into the ranks of the "big five" UAIB industrial titans, where it has remained ever since.

Wendiwamu: One of the few class B subspecies known to utilize tools in the act of hunting. The Wendiwamu are "trap-door" primates that dig deep into the substrate, where they lie in wait for prey to pass by. Once within range, the Wendiwamu will strike victims with a "Wamo," a hammer shaped rock or portion of bone, then pull their unconscious prey back into their makeshift lair to feast.

Woos—*Who Cleans Up Your Mess*: The peaceful, ocean-bound Woos is a living filter. It feeds on both organic and inorganic waste, breaking it down through a chain of nine, three-inch diameter stomachs before expelling purified limonene.

YouStar: High subscription costs have left many in the UAIB unable to afford access to professional entertainment and news networks.

YouStar is an open-source communication platform in which average citizens can record and post videos for a variety of purposes.

Zanglorian: Not one of the seventy-three species of the UAIB. Instead, Zanglorians are a rare species of Tier nine dwellers who know the secrets of the UAIB yet are allowed to remember those secrets free from the threat of a mindwipe. Zanglorians can even work UAIB jobs with special work visas, though for a variety of social and political reasons they are often limited to below-the-line employment opportunities.

Zypper—*Whose Smile is the Last Thing You'll See*: Nocturnal hunters, the Zypper moves quickly through ocean waters. It is capable of immobilizing prey in a variety of ways, including a jackhammer-like snout punch, or via its sharp tusks that grow between four and twelve inches. The Zypper's smooth gray skin is considered a delicacy among Toers—often served during semiannual Topolia celebrations—leading to a concerning dip in the Zypper population and its eventual classification as a fully protected species.

ALSO BY ASH BISHOP

ACKNOWLEDGMENTS

I WANT TO THANK THE fans for waiting a bit longer for this sequel. Hopefully it was worth it. I also want to thank my parents, Ash and Sue Bishop, for their endless belief in me; my wife, Jen, for loving me unconditionally and staying by my side through thick and thin; and my daughter and son for being perfect, and also for letting me bounce ideas off them and tolerating the click-clack of the keyboard while they try to watch TV. This book would never have existed without my brilliant agent Caitlin Blasdell and my brilliant editor Elana Gibson. Thanks to the *Intergalactic* audiobook readers (and Audie Award® winners) Scott Brick and Suzanne Elise Freeman for bringing their art to my art and making it better. Thanks to my beta readers Eric Wheeler and Jordan H. Bartlett (check out her books; you won't regret it). Thanks always to Norma Bishop (may you rest in peace), Chuck Bishop, Jared, Alan (for inspiring Aldos Verch), Carrie, Emme, Faithe and Kinsely, June, Gene, and to Marissa Holzer. And many special thanks to others who touched my life these past few years in ways that can't be explained or properly reciprocated: Binney Caffrey, Jen Fleischer, and Paul Slocombe.

ABOUT THE AUTHOR

ASH BISHOP IS A LIFETIME READER who loves all genres, especially science fiction, mystery, and fantasy. He has been a high school English teacher and has worked in the video game industry and educational app development. He even used to fetch coffee for Quentin Tarantino during the production of the film *Jackie Brown*. Many years ago, he earned an MFA in Creative Writing from San Diego State University. He currently works in veteran services, assisting members of the military's transition into the civilian workforce, but spends his best days at home in Southern California with his wife and two wonderful children.